S0-BCS-497

Tidings

Tidings

Ernst Wiechert

Translated from the German by
Marie Heynemann and Margery B. Ledward

PLOUGH PUBLISHING HOUSE

Published by Plough Publishing House
Walden, New York
Robertsbridge, England
Elsmore, Australia
www.plough.com

Original title: *Missa sine nomine* by Ernst Wiechert, 1950
www.herbig.net

Cover image: Repin, Ilya (1844–1930) *Vsevolod Mikhailovich Garshin* (detail)
© Metropolitan Museum of Art. Image Source: Art Resource, NY

ISBN: 978-0-87486-635-3
20 19 18 17 16 15 14 1 2 3 4 5 6

A catalog record for this book is available from the British Library.
Library of Congress Cataloging-in-Publication Data

Wiechert, Ernst Emil, 1887-1950.
[Missa sine nomine. English]
Tidings / by Ernst Wiechert ; translated from the German by Marie Heynemann and Margery B. Ledward.
pages cm
ISBN 978-0-87486-635-3 (hardback)
I. Heynemann, Marie, translator. II. Ledward, Margery B., translator. III. Title.
PT2647.I25M513 2014
833'.912--dc23
2014017548

Printed in the USA

In jüngeren Tagen war ich des Morgens froh,
des Abends weint ich; jetzt, da ich älter bin,
beginn ich zweifend meinen Tag, doch
heilig und heiter ist mir sein Ende.

HOELDERLIN

When I was younger I was happy in the morning,
and I slept in the evening; now as I have grown older
I begin my day in doubt, but
holy and serene is its end for me.

1

SO THAT WAS HOW a man walked when death had touched him between the shoulders.

He walked as lightly as if he had wings, but below the ground something moved with him, and that which moved beneath his feet was not light and had no wings, but was dark and heavy like the juice of poppy seeds.

But what did he who walked into the night know of the juice of poppy seeds? He could stand at the side of the road leaning his back against one of the apple trees, as above him under the full May moon the early dew fell on the clustering pink flower buds. He could shut his eyes, and the picture of the red blossoms of poppies at the edge of a yellow wheat field might appear before his closed eyes and the picture of a child who stood there shyly touching the blossoms, as if they were enchanted.

It was all far away and unreal as in a dream – the poppies, the field, and the child's hand.

There were no children's hands anymore – nowhere and never again, and the red of the poppies changed into another red which flowed together out of stains fused into a crimson liquid which ran on till it skirted the edge of the field, of all the fields of this earth; yes, right on to the rim of this dark star which rushed noiselessly along through the May night on into other constellations. And it seemed as if the constellations fell back before the star with the bloody rim into the outlines of the Milky Way to give it free space and to open for it the icy infinity which awaited it behind the constellation of Hercules.

The man under the apple tree opened his eyes and made a wry mouth. Over him hung stars, the full moon, and the Milky Way. Nothing had gone out of its course, and nothing would ever go out of its course. A voice began to sing behind the fields, but it was only the voice of a drunkard, as most of the voices had been which he had heard this evening. It was not the voice which he had expected to hear, that lonely, shadowed, distant and once uttered tone which would be pronouncing the words of judgment over the trembling earth: "He who sheds the blood of man, his blood shall be shed also."

A word – a field – a child – sunk into oblivion. And never more and nowhere would they rise again.

The man sighed and stepped back into the bright road, out of the shadow of the apple tree. He shivered in his brown suit which looked like a uniform of some kind, and he hung the coat over his bent shoulders. The coat was striped blue and white, a gay coat, but children avoided it, and grown people turned their heads away as if they had not seen it.

An hour later the man sat on the parapet of a village fountain and watched the moonlit jet of water which flowed into the basin. His feet ached in the new shoes which the victors had given him. He took some dry bread out of the pocket of his coat and held it under the flowing water before he slowly ate it. Then he smoked one of the strong, foreign cigarettes that they had stuffed into his pockets and gazed at the dark gables behind which the moon was shining. There were still lights in many of the little windows.

"There they sit and wait for the future," he thought. "All these years they have waited for the future. First for one of glory, now for that of the Prodigal Son. People are always waiting for the future, condemned by this terrible conception of time. The animal does not know a tomorrow – nor does God. Eternity has no tomorrow.

But they are waiting. Just as I am waiting. Perhaps I am more patient than they are, perhaps I am only more wicked than they, colder and more deadened. I was dead, and so the children turn from me. Animals and children scent death."

He pressed out the cigarette on the rim of the fountain and got up. There was not far to go now. He could see the castle on the mountain behind the gables. It was lit up from top to bottom, and it occurred to him that Belshazzar's castle might have looked something like it. "Midnight already drew near . . ." So many verses which he had learned as a child came to mind. There was now no hand which wrote on a white wall. Only the airplanes wrote letters of fire.

From here on he knew every turn of the road. He had often been here. He had loved the barren, melancholy landscape, and it was from here that they had fetched him. What people call time had passed, but for him there was no time anymore. He had been taken out of the fiery furnace, and now he had grown rigid. But he was not cleansed. Perhaps he had been taken out of the red heat too soon, perhaps too late. Only love cleanses, not violence. And he did not love anymore.

He walked up to the bright windows, because they belonged to him. He had inherited them, that's what he had been told. But he did not know whether a heritage was still valid, since all heritage had been wasted – that of generations and that of many centuries. He only went there to find a roof perhaps, a piece of bread, a fountain with water. If he did not find it there, he would walk on or sit down on a doorstep until the night frost fell over him.

He stopped for a while to give his heart a rest and turned around. The village lay below him in the valley and the steep roofs were shining in the light of the moon. The road ran like a white ribbon into the dark hills. A dog barked in the distance, and it sounded like a voice crying in the wilderness. In just such villages as these were born the men who have exalted the name of the nation, he thought. In quiet, darkness, and namelessness. And also those others were born in such villages: the hangmen and the murderers, and nobody knows whether they have not in their blood a drop of that which flowed in the veins of those who wrote the great melodies or the wisdom of their centuries. Wheat and thistles grow in the same field.

A shooting star drew a silver trail from the zenith to the dark northern horizon. Yet he did not think of wishing for anything. But he raised his tired eyes to the sparkling canopy of heaven. He felt the magnitude, the purity and the inexpressible strangeness of space – space had neither regarded nor taken part in what had happened: in what had happened for years, by day and by night. Cries had not reached it, nor curses, nor prayers. Constellations had risen and had set. Everything that had happened had noiselessly rushed with the turning axis into that sparkling space on and on toward the distant constellation of Hercules.

Was it beautiful, what he saw? Did happiness flow down upon his brow from that eternity? He had forgotten beauty and happiness and probably also eternity, which was not eternity at all but only an immeasurable time.

A bird called in the high forest behind him and he was startled. He turned round and his right hand slipped into his pocket. Somebody seemed to be walking behind him, lightly and stealthily, as the dead will walk – the dead who no longer wear any shoes. He had not pulled them off, but others would have seen to that. Shoes had become valuable.

He sighed and began climbing again. His shoulders ached with the straps of the haversack which they had filled with food for him. But he knew that he was carrying more than bread and provisions. Everybody had to carry an immense burden once his hair turned gray. Time, memory, the child he once had been. The living and the dead. They had learned how heavy the dead were to carry. Nothing had been added to their substance, and yet they were as heavy as if they were made of stone.

Chapter 1

"Settle yourself down up there, I'll carry you all right, I'm not afraid," he said gently. He had often talked to himself in these last years, because he had not spoken to anybody else. He did not want to become dumb.

He stopped and bowed his shoulders, as if he wished to make it easier for the other. But he did not feel anything. Nor had he felt anything when he had been carrying stones. He had dismissed his heart. And you can only feel the dead on your heart, not on your shoulders.

He climbed now without stopping until he stood before the archway of stone which opened into the yard. The great building with the steep roof glittered in front of him up into the starlit vault, and noise, singing and the music of loudspeakers came from all the windows. But he paid no heed to it. He looked up at the coat of arms above the gate and tried to distinguish in the light of the moon the blue field with the golden lilies carved into the stone. It was no longer there. Probably they had thrown stones at it or shot at it with pistols. Only the gray crumbling stone was left. He sighed, but it was right that it should be so. Evidently this was what they called the "new time." People always called it a new time when they washed the blood off their hands.

Only then did he notice the two figures near the archway who stood in the shadow of the lilac bushes: the man with a white, not very clean tunic and the girl who tried to hide a heavy bag behind her back.

"Well, old friend, what do you want here?" asked the man, taking a cigarette from his pocket and lighting it. "The lost time, young friend," was the reply.

The man in the white tunic gazed at him attentively with a suspicious expression. He was still young and his insignificant features showed only the shifty self-assurance of those who stand under the protection of the victors – no matter where they had stood previously.

"You can go on looking for that," he said mockingly after a while. "But beggars are not allowed here."

"Where there is stealing there is not any begging," replied the man in the coat. "Don't bother about your bag," he said to the girl, "I shall not take anything away from you."

The girl cast a contemptuous look at the striped coat which was still hanging round the man's shoulders. "That's all done away with, that about taking away," she said.

"Only the roles have changed," replied the man. "But I would like to know who lives here now?" he added, nodding toward the lighted windows.

"And why do you want to know that?" asked the young man.

"Because it belongs to me, so to say, my young friend."

The young friend took the cigarette out of his mouth and stared at him in surprise. "Two others have already been here pretending that," he said at last.

"Yes, and I am the third," replied the man with the coat. "But it is grand that the other two were here. One does not know nowadays who is still alive."

"I am sorry, Herr Baron," said the young man not very politely, "but now the Amis live here."

"Who are the Amis?"

"The Americans; and a whole staff is quartered here. I help in the kitchen."

"That's a good job," replied the man in a friendly tone, glancing for a moment at the girl's bag. "I don't want anything. I have enough. And you probably have gone hungry for a long time."

"God knows, we have," said the girl rudely.

"I just wanted to see it," the man went on, looking up again at the broken coat of arms. "I have often been here."

"And then?"

"Then I did not come here anymore. I was prevented, my young friend. But the two others you spoke of, do you know where they are now?"

Chapter 1

The young man took the cigarette out of the corner of his mouth and pointed with it over the archway toward the wooded hills on which the moon was shining. "In the shepherd's hut, Herr Baron," he said, and one could not tell whether he was glad or sorry about it. "Do you know the hut, Herr Baron?"

"I know it well," replied the man, "it is a beautiful place up there. I liked to go there in times gone by. Thank you for the information." And he turned to go.

The kitchen hand looked uncertainly at the tall, bent figure which even under the striped coat had the air of owning all this: the coat of arms over the archway, the illuminated castle and the distant sheepfold. He took a cigarette from his pocket, made a movement to offer it to the baron, but on second thoughts he took out the open packet with the other hand and offered it to him. "Help yourself, Herr Baron," he said.

"Thank you, my friend," said the baron pleasantly. "They gave me plenty."

The young servant pushed the packet back into his pocket and shrugged his narrow shoulders with a commiserating gesture. "Perhaps it is just as well," he said with an overly familiar smile, "if nowadays barons have to live for a bit in a shepherd's hut."

The baron did not return the smile, but he raised his hand in a friendly farewell greeting. "Better, probably," he answered quietly, "than if sheep had to live in castles. As time went on, it would not suit them."

At this the young pair looked a little embarrassed, but Baron Amadeus resumed his climb, passing by the courtyard of the castle up the narrow path which led to the heath, the marshes and the peat bogs to where the sheepfold stood. He remembered it all very well, he could have found the path even in the dark. He had not been pleased with these two young people, but he had only gone a few steps when they were forgotten. They were no different from those he had met on his way. No victory and no defeat ever pierced to the roots. Nothing but death reached the roots; and then only if it were admitted to man's vital soul, not simply to the vital point of the body.

But it was splendid that the shepherd's hut was still there – and splendid that his brothers were there – not exactly that they were in the sheepfold – but that they were alive, that they had not been killed in front of a red bespattered wall or under the gallows.

Baron Amadeus had loved but little in his life: music, a few books, his home country and his two brothers. Everything else had sunk as a stone sinks in the sea; but his brothers, even if they had been killed, would only have sunk into the depths of his heart. People had often laughed at them in childhood, and ridicule binds together more closely than pity. Simple people had laughed at them because they were so much alike. Their hair was brown and soft like the fur of a mole, their noses were a little too long and set a little askew in their narrow faces. Others had been amused at the queer seriousness with which they met fun as well as malice, an expression so unusual in immature faces, the composure of which resembled that on the faces of young martyrs or youthful saints.

A wit on a neighboring estate had nicknamed them the "triptych," and that is how they appeared to the unthinking, as if one had only to open the two wings of an altarpiece – and there they would be, standing side by side, three youthful figures from some place beyond the well-known earth, and one of them might well be holding a medieval lute in his long, thin hands, the second a violin, and the third some instrument with which the songs of the Old Testament might have been accompanied. So they seemed to look at the spectator from that sphere with their strange, pure faces without a smile, but with the joyfulness that belongs to those who have touched the hem of God's garment.

In their father's private rooms, which lay in a distant part of the house, each of them, while still quite young, had found for himself some musical instrument, and under the imperfect instruction of a rather unorthodox tutor they had begun to attune these three instruments to one another and to play them with unshakable seriousness. After a few years their mother had commanded them to play before guests for the first time at a birthday party.

They sat down in silence under the candles of the old chandelier and with their solemn faces and stately instruments they had begun to play one of the old masters, perhaps Tartini.

They played until a whisper was heard or a slight smile was seen on the faces of some of the guests, then Amadeus got up with his cello in the middle of the delicate andante, bowed seriously, and left the hall, followed immediately by his two brothers. He had not spoken to his brothers about this occurrence, and from his unmoved face there was nothing to be gathered about the causes that had prompted this action. Before the embittered anger of his mother he had only remarked in a polite and gentle voice that just this andante was the musical interpretation of the thirteenth chapter of the First Epistle to the Corinthians and that this chapter must be well-known to the countess, his mother.

From that time on they had never again played in public.

On the height which the baron had reached by now a soft wind blew which smelled of the peat bogs, and Amadeus sat down for a while on one of the blocks of basalt which lay by the path. The wood was now sparser and more stunted and in the distance the moonlight lay on the bare rock, which shone like silver.

The thoughts of the baron wandered for a little from the thirteenth chapter of the Epistle to the Corinthians to his mother who was called Countess or My Lady by the farmers, and who in respect for her birth wished to be addressed in this way. The Liljecronas who originally came from Sweden had always been a "doubtful" family for her, a family of peasants probably from the dark ages of the Vikings, and she did not consider it impossible that a few hundred years ago they had still eaten horseflesh and had sacrificed human beings to their one-eyed god.

Amadeus did not remember that his mother had ever kissed him, and he could not even imagine how her thin lips would have been able to do so. Only Grita, the old Lithuanian nurse, had kissed him. On holy days she wore seven petticoats one on top of the other, and under these seven petticoats she would hide easily and willingly anything that she wished to protect against Laima, the goddess of destiny – whether it was a young chicken which was to be killed or one of the child-saints of the triptych who wished to hide from the countess. On the battlefields of the children's lives Grita had been the asylum of which they had read in the history of the Middle Ages, the threshold of the sanctuary beyond which the sword did not reach, the peace of God which must not be violated.

Amadeus smoked and remembered the tunes of the Dainos, those Lithuanian folk songs which Grita used to hum in the evenings, when the scent of baked apples came from the oven and the thread of her spinning wheel glided through her old, twisted hands. Eastern melodies, old and melancholy. Amadeus had set them for the three stringed instruments, and Grita had listened to their playing, her white head bent, and then she had raised her face with the peculiar eyes to the playing youths and had smiled as only idols can smile, and had sung in a low voice:

By the Memel's farther shore
Stand three maples fresh and green
Underneath these green trees, underneath their branches
On a day three cuckoos sat.

No, those were not cuckoos three
'Twas not birds were cooing so.
Fellows three were fighting here
Fighting o'er a maiden fair
Under these three maple trees.

Said the first one: "She is mine,"
Said the second: "As God wills."
But the third, the youngest lad,
Was so sore, oh, sore at heart.

Fain would move into the town,
Seek a fiddler for you there.

Chapter 1

Dance, my laddie, full of sorrow,
Dance, I want you to be gay . . .

They had riveted their attention on the song, "the three young fellows," and had shivered with that early foreboding of defenseless creatures under the trampling feet of humankind. And later, much later, Amadeus had gone to the old nurse when she was sitting on the threshold with folded hands in the twilight and had asked: "Grita, what does that mean: 'Dance, my laddie, full of sorrow, dance, I want you to be gay'?"

She had wrapped her large dark shawl around him, for she had felt the trembling of his young, narrow shoulders and she had answered gently: "Leave it now, young master, until you have learned that tears are salt and a kiss is sweet. And that this is better than if it were the other way round."

He remembered that they had played this tune by many cottagers' coffins: "Dance, my laddie, full of sorrow . . ." Their mother had always looked at them through her gold-rimmed lorgnette, as if they were three adopted children who talked to each other in a foreign language – the language of the American Indians or of the Polynesians. But the cottagers' wives had wept, and after one of these funerals as they stood silently at the lofty window of their music room, their father had come in quietly, had stood behind them and said in his gentle voice which seemed as if it came from a distance: "He who builds a bridge for the poor is more than he who builds an empire for kings . . ."

They had pondered about it for a long time, each for himself, for they never discussed such things with each other – and besides, it was such a rare thing for their father to speak to them.

The moon had now sunk to the horizon, and the baron took another cigarette.

Yes, what had the secret about their father been, that none of them had really known anything about him; that nobody had known him, and yet that in some strange way he had been familiar to them? As the outline of a sail on the ocean – that's what he had been like, and nobody knew where the wind would drive him, and whether it was the wind of destiny or an altogether strange and unknown wind. There was a close affinity between them and their father, not only because he had the same hair and the same somewhat irregularly shaped features. There was also the unapproachableness in his face – nothing haughty about it, but a reserve, a remoteness as of one who was different from others – and his melancholy eyes said, as is written in the Bible: "Your thoughts are not my thoughts." But they said so without haughtiness, shyly and almost timidly, as if they knew and could not help it.

To the countess and the well-to-do neighbors he was only somebody who "did nothing"; but how should they know what filled his days and nights? He lived apart, even in his rooms, and Amadeus remembered very well how he had stood there for the first time among books, globes, musical instruments, boxes full of stones, coins, and butterflies. "What are you doing, father?" he had asked. And the baron, raising his eyes from the microscope, had looked at him full of kindness and had answered gently: "I am collecting, Amadeus." "And what are you collecting, father?"

"The grain of mustard seed, dear child, and one day you will collect it too." "And my brothers, father dear?" "They will do so too, Amadeus, you three will. For all the others here" – and he made a wide, sweeping movement with his hand – "all the others collect the fat of the land."

Amadeus had not asked further questions, nor had his brothers, but he had thought it over thoroughly, as he was wont to think. After that he had often gone into the quiet, solemn rooms which were somehow like a warm church, and that was in itself something special, for Amadeus only knew the icy-cold village church. He had knelt for many hours before the old folio volumes and tried to understand the peculiar titles, before he turned the first page: *The whole of the Prophet Jeremiah / in these hard and dangerous times / to teach and comfort pious Christians / interpreted. Item /*

the Prophet Sophonias / interpreted by Nicholaum Selneccerum / Luc. 13 / If you do not repent – you will all perish. Anno 1566.

Then in their last year at school their father had also "perished." From one of his walks the baron had not come home. He had disappeared as a sail behind the horizon or as a cloud in the evening sky, and no trace of him was ever found. He had left nothing but a strip of paper on his desk and on it he had written in his graceful, old-fashioned handwriting: "Lord, thou hast deceived me and I was deceived." Long afterward Amadeus had found this saying in the twentieth chapter of the Prophet Jeremiah.

There had been a great stir in the district, and the countess felt this stir as an unparalleled disgrace. One did not leave the world anonymously, not even if one's name was only Liljecrona. Tramps or saints might do so. "I do not believe that he is dead," she said to her most intimate friend. "He was too awkward for that. I believe that he has gone to Africa, where they still sacrifice human beings – as his ancestors did. There was too much peasant and heathen blood in him."

They searched for him for many months, but he was not found.

The brothers did not speak about this either. But they did not play their trios any longer in one of their own rooms, but in their father's large, forsaken library. "The whole of the Prophet Jeremiah" lay open on the big oak table, and now and again one or the other of them stood before it and his eyes went over the strange words: "And I was deceived."

At that time Grita was still alive, and she was the only one to whom Amadeus turned with a question: "Do you believe that he is dead?" he whispered.

She smiled and stroked his smooth hair: "How should he be dead, as he was so sad?" she replied.

And when he looked at her inquiringly, she took the full spindle from her spinning wheel and turned it in her twisted fingers. "He has spun to the end of the thread," she said, "and now he has taken a new spindle. God has given him a new thread."

This was a great consolation for Amadeus, and he thought it wrong to keep it to himself, and in the evening he told his brothers.

"I have always thought," said Erasmus, the eldest, after a while, "that he sits by the shore of one of the holy rivers in India and smiles. Nobody could smile as he could. Just as if he were at one with God. He had gone through all this on earth, and he had seen that one must start all over again."

With a slight shock Amadeus had noticed how his brother made the same sweeping movement with his hand that their father had made that time when he spoke of "the fat of the land."

"More and more stars," thought Amadeus looking up into the sky. "As if a thousand new ones had been added in all those years when I did not see a star. It will soon be midnight, and I must get up now."

But he sat on, his hands laid together as if they were still fettered.

They had not had an easy time at school. Even their Christian names had been a source of amusement and probably also of ridicule. Erasmus, Aegidius, Amadeus. Evidently they had their origin in their father's old folio volumes and in his veneration of a time when God still bent over the shoulder of the writer. "He still looked at it," he used to say. "He did not look away, as He does today."

But they had got over these years. When they entered the classroom one after the other, tall, slim, with a faraway look in their eyes, it always seemed to the others that emissaries of another nation had arrived, and as if they carried gold and precious stones in their pockets. They answered but they never asked, and the most self-confident teachers lost a little of the brilliance of their diction when these three pairs of eyes looked fixedly at them. "Liljecrona, you always seem to be pretending you have a king's crown under your coat," said one of them to Erasmus with suppressed irritation. "Do take it out so that we can see whether it is made of gold or brass."

"We have no crowns under our coats," replied Erasmus gently and politely. "And if we had, this would probably not be the right place to show them around."

Chapter 1

At the time when the old baron reached his end, the school had tried not to show any curiosity. But at the beginning of winter when there had been a fire in the poor quarters of the little town, and the school authorities thought of helping those who had suffered through it by arranging a benefit concert, the headmaster had called the three brothers to his office and had asked them in a kindly way whether on such an occasion and for such a good purpose they would be willing to play – for everybody knew that they played music together.

Yes, they would do so, Erasmus, the eldest, had replied without having consulted his brothers.

They had chosen a slow and very stately movement by Mozart. None of the audience would ever forget how they sat on the platform with the light of the candles on their music stands falling on their thin, serious faces. They had not looked at their music but straight past each other into a distance which was perhaps filled with quiet faces and forebodings. Those who listened would not forget how the musicians drew their bows across the strings, how they picked up from each other the simple, golden melodies, which fell apart and then wove together again, while they listened to the inner tones of their instruments without any alteration of their general bearing. They only seemed to give out what a distant voice whispered to them, while they were living with and in each other with the same simplicity as in their daily life, and with the same remoteness that separated them from people at other times. It was as if a spell emanating from them fell over the audience, over the unimaginative, nay, over the most ordinary hearts. All felt not only that the melody of the great, dead musician enclosed them in its web, but that they were overwhelmed by the purity and simplicity of these three youths, whose lives were perhaps as strange and peculiar as the life and the end of their father, but no curiosity and no mockery were allowed to touch it, because they sat there as in an altar picture; and it must have been a pious hand which had painted them.

When they had finished and let their bows fall and walked slowly out of the hall, no one stirred, but the headmaster, who was sitting in the last row, got up and bowed to them, when they went past him, and after a pause he turned to the music master who sat at his side and said: "They did not play for the people who have been burned out; they played for their father."

That was the first time they had played in public since their childhood.

"More and more stars," thought Amadeus clasping his hands round his knees. "And I fancied that all light had been extinguished in these years."

Yes, and then Erasmus entered a cavalry regiment as a second lieutenant, and Aegidius had taken over the large estate, and he, Amadeus, in his turn had studied, and sitting at the large oak table, with "the whole of the Prophet Jeremiah" open in front of him, had written down verses and melodies and had slowly gone his father's way of "doing nothing," as the methodical people said.

Yet there was so much to be done, so immeasurably much. For years and decades; and just now under the silent stars it seemed to him as if centuries had passed. For if nothing else could be done, there was one thing that had to be done: to try to find the hidden meaning of a song that fishergirls sang on the sand dunes of Kurland:

Dance, my laddie, full of sorrow,
Dance, I want you to be gay.

Grita had known it even when she was spinning her shroud. But he did not know it, and neither the folio volumes nor the microscope could impart that to him. He who relies only on the intellect must walk with crutches, even though they be set with precious stones, and at the first breath of fate will break like matchsticks.

Of the old people there was now only Christoph, the coachman, left, and often Amadeus sat with him at dusk on the oat bin. On the large estates in the eastern provinces the coachman had always been of special importance, because the horses, too, had been of particular importance. The faithful coachmen were the imperturbable kings among all the retainers on the estate. They drove the babies to church to be christened, the young couples to be married, and the dead in their coffins to be buried, and in the twilight of their stables the young sons learned the wisdom of a long life of service.

Christoph had light blue eyes and a small beard under his clean-shaven chin. The beard, at that time, was already white. He was the only one who addressed Amadeus with the familiar "Du." He said Herr Baron – but then he fell back into the familiar form of speech.

"You must not worry so much, Herr Baron," he said, drawing at his short pipe on whose porcelain bowl there was a brightly colored picture of the old emperor. "Not about his lordship, your father, either. All is well with your father, the old lord, for he has gone to the nether world, do you understand? Some go to join those in the heavenly world, but then we do not hear them anymore. But the others – a man can hear them – if he doesn't go out to look for them."

"Do you hear him, Christoph?"

The coachman took the pipe out of his mouth and nodded. "Sometimes, Herr Baron," he said very quietly.

"Where the three big juniper bushes stand on the moor, before one passes the peat bog – that's where I hear him. The horses get restive there, because a little light stands among the heather. And then I hear him say: 'Well, how are you and everybody, Christoph?' and I answer, 'Things are all right, Herr Baron.' Then we drive past and the light disappears. You see, he has gone down again, Herr Baron."

"You can still do that," Amadeus said after a while. "Your feet still reach into the underworld."

Christoph shook his head doubtfully, pressing the tobacco more tightly into his pipe. "I don't know, Herr Baron, whether it's the feet," he said. "I think it's because we still have faith. Never let anyone drive you four-in-hand, Herr Baron, as the countess does. Whoever drives four-in-hand has lost his faith. Christ went on foot."

Yes, much had flowed into him in his childhood – mysterious and incongruous tales. It had probably helped him to come through the years, the tens of years, the First World War and the revolution, the collapse of a nation and the decay of the Western world. Those mysterious powers of the underworld had protected him, that which was incomprehensible to reason, yes, that at which reason smiled. The spinning wheel and the oat bin had been more to him than the folio volumes. Long before books had been written people had spun – even in the earliest fairytales, and while they were spinning they had sung: "Dance, my laddie, full of sorrow, dance, I want you to be gay . . ." And that's perhaps what he did, even when it seemed to others that he did nothing.

And now at last he got up. The light of the moon still shone over the world and from a distance the wind brought now and again the fragment of a tune from a loudspeaker. It sounded as if a delirious patient were talking in his sleep.

"That's what they have kept," thought Amadeus while he climbed up among the stones. "Victors and vanquished, dancing. But not full of sorrow. Not even the defeated are full of sorrow – to say nothing of their gaiety."

The air had become cooler and the juniper bushes stood like dark pilgrims among the heather, each with its long shadow. The moonlight made everything unreal. A softly sparkling world, but it was unreal and unsubstantial. The dead had as much room in it as the living, and the baron had seen so many dead people.

Then behind a wood of low pine trees, there was the shepherd's hut. Dark and massive, with its steep low gable, and the moonlight shone like silver on the thatched reed roof. Amadeus had no home now and would never have one again, but there might be a roof to cover him in this ruined world, and this, thatched and gray, looked as if it might have space under it for innocent animals and for guilty human beings. It was an old roof, and the shepherd had spent a life under it, and he had learned silence and wisdom. Amadeus had often sat with him on the threshold, from which could be seen a vast expanse of sky and a view over the Vogelsberg on one hand and over the Thueringer Wald on the other. The earth here was poor and barren, but the landscape was grand and lonely, and here the shepherd had had his visions, and his face had been shaped by this country, as these rocks had been shaped by the subterranean fires millions of years ago.

It was from this threshold that they had fetched him. The last he had seen was the tall, lean figure of the shepherd holding up his crook under the drifting clouds. And the last he had heard had been his fearless, solemn voice calling as from a mouth of brass: "He who makes prisoners shall himself be taken to prison. He who takes the sword, shall perish by the sword. Here is the patience and the faith of the saints."

Two of them had only turned and jeered, but the third had looked round and made a threatening gesture with his fist.

Throughout four long years Amadeus had searched for it: the patience and the faith of the saints. He had not found it.

Ah, and now he would see them again, his two brothers, and he was afraid. So afraid that his heart throbbed and his hands trembled, when he saw the feeble gleam of light behind the reed curtain of the small window.

He was afraid for many reasons, his heart was afraid, and reason could not give a name to it. What he first realized was that he was afraid to touch a human being. Not only was he afraid of their words and opinions, their looks and gestures. But there was an actual physical fear of touching them. When a man has slept for a long time on a plank bed with two others, he no longer thinks of the human body as something sacred. When one's habitation has been a dark, airless room filled with the bodies, the breathing, the groaning, and the delirium of human beings, he recoils before men, unless he has "the patience and the faith of the saints." But he did not have them.

As he did not possess them, he wanted nothing but to hide himself like an animal in a thicket. He had been branded and he had not yet got so far that he could transform the mark.

He was afraid because these men were his brothers and he felt that he loved them. He had believed that love was dead in his heart, and now he realized that this was not true. The shy, unspoken love of their childhood, youth, and manhood flamed up in his heart, as soon as he saw the gleam of light. He remembered how they had gone together through the vast loneliness of life, and how different they had been from others in everything: in their faces, their names, the music they played, even in the way they opened and closed a book.

But the other two had remained undamaged, or they would not be here. They had not been free from peril, but they had remained in the cleanliness of their old existence. Their bodies had not been seized, they had not been whipped, and they had not been forced to suffer the feet of tyrants trampling upon them. They could look at their bodies without feeling disgust. They were still clean. They could look in a mirror; there was nothing but the face of their father and behind this the faces of all those who had been like him: quiet, sad, noble, and good.

And there was something that he must know before he stepped over the threshold; and still more it was what they must know before their hands, wearing the signet ring of the family, were offered to him: not that he was no longer good, but that he was bad. It was not important that he was no longer clean, nor undamaged, nor proud, but that he was bad. That with all the power of his blood he hated the murderers and perhaps many of the murdered. He would not mind pointing his revolver at any of those faces with the rigid, sightless masks, at many of those faces arrayed one beside another as before a firing squad. He had already done this with his own hand. And he did not repent it. He held his hand before his eyes and looked at it. The weals and scars showed up even in the light of the moon. It was no longer the hand which had handled the bow in obedience to the tunes which the great dead musicians had devised and written down. It had become a different hand. No lonely hand anymore, only belonging to itself, to a sealed, silent world, but one that had stretched itself out or had been stretched out to the world of violence and evil, and there it had changed. It would not be seen, but his heart knew it. And from his hand the transformation had spread into the innermost recesses of his heart. He had not been incorruptible or this would not have happened. It had not sufficed to live in purity and quiet and "to do nothing." He had closed his eyes against the evil of the world, and the evil had found him defenseless. And if not defenseless, vulnerable and infirm. He had not had "faith," as Grita and Christoph had. His roots had reached into the depths of the earth but not further. And so the blow of the ax had struck into his marrow.

He glanced around – stealthily and hastily – as he had done for four years. There was still time to go. The brothers would never know. He was dead for them, and their last tiny spark of hope would be put out if he did not come back within a few months. They would mourn for him, as millions were mourned in this devastated world. He would remain for them a pure picture broken to pieces by a brutal hand.

He took a step back – stealthily and noiselessly, as an animal when the branches part before it. But at that moment the heavy door of the hut was pushed aside, and Erasmus stood before a dimly illuminated background. He stood there like an apparition which had emerged from mystery into reality, and without making a movement he gazed at the figure in the moonlight.

Then Amadeus raised his hand – in the way they had hailed each other from a distance when they were children – and Erasmus recognized the gesture.

"Brother," he whispered, stretching out his arms.

And then Amadeus stood on the threshold.

It was the small room which the shepherd had used as a living room. With a wooden partition they had divided it off from the large, dark barn and had hung it with mats of rushes. The same clay hearth in whose glowing embers the shepherd used to roast mushrooms stood in the corner and a small peat fire was still burning under the ashes.

But the room was no longer empty and bare as it had been formerly. It was full of old furniture, from centuries gone by, and Amadeus recognized that it had come from the castle. His eyes dwelt on everything, and on the two faces turned to him in silence, and at last they rested on the three music stands on one of which a candle was burning, its calm light shining on the three instruments. Sheets of music stood open on the stands.

"You have . . ." said Amadeus in a low voice.

"Yes, brother," replied Aegidius, "this is what we have saved. This is nearly all."

Then he got up from his seat at the hearth and came slowly toward Amadeus. He did not touch him. He only stroked along the folds of the coat which hung over Amadeus' shoulders. It was the striped coat of which the children had been afraid and from which the eyes of the adults had looked away. Time and again he raised his hand and stroked down the rough, dirty material. It was as if he was stroking something that was alive and needed protection – a sick animal, perhaps, or a child that had been hit.

And under this movement Amadeus slowly closed his eyes. He had fixed them on his brother's face which was quite close to him, and he had gazed into his brother's eyes, which had followed the movement of his hand. He was not looking at his gray hair, nor at the deep lines around his thin-lipped mouth. He only gazed into his eyes, and perhaps he felt without realizing it that he had not seen such eyes for many years. Eyes which in some incomprehensible way had been allowed to retain in this world "the patience and faith of the saints."

Then when Amadeus raised his hand, they took the coat and the haversack gently from his shoulders and led him to the old easy chair by the fire. Erasmus put some wood on the glowing embers, and then they sat with their hands clasped between their knees and gazed into the flames. Their faces between light and shadow were again as the faces on the triptych – faces of young martyrs or saints, strange, cleansed faces without a smile, but one could read in them that they had been in "a fiery furnace."

They did not speak, and only after a long time, when they were smoking the cigarettes which Amadeus had taken out of his pocket, Erasmus bent down toward the fire and put a dark, twisted root in the dying flames and in a low voice recited the verses of their childhood: "By the Memel's farther shore stand three maples fresh and green . . ."

He stopped short, because he felt his brothers' eyes on him, and when he raised his head he saw that in their shy glances was a hardly perceptible reproach.

Then he thrust the dark, twisted root better into the glowing embers and clasped his hands again between his knees, and thus the three remained until a thin white ash began to form over the dying glow.

2

AMADEUS WOULD NOT lie down on one of the beds which the brothers had arranged for themselves, and as he refused with a violence they failed to understand and persisted in sleeping on the floor in front of the fire, they put some cushions on the clay floor and covered them with two blankets.

When they began to undress, Amadeus took a pair of brown pajamas which the American soldiers had given him out of his haversack, opened the heavy door and left the room. His two brothers exchanged a quick, furtive glance, but they did not say anything. The light of the candle was so feeble that neither of them could read the sorrow in the other's face . . . nor was it necessary.

When Amadeus came back, he carried the coat, which was rather like a uniform, on his arm and the heavy shoes in his hand. He looked absent-minded, and his face was shut and withdrawn, as he folded the garment carefully on a chair and put his shoes under it. He went back again and placed them side by side, so that their toes were in line with the edge of the chair. But he did it as if in a dream, and he did not hear the faint sigh with which Erasmus closed his eyes.

When Amadeus lay in front of the hearth, his head propped on his hand and his face turned to the expiring glow, Erasmus put out the candle.

"Good night," said Amadeus in a low voice.

It was now dark and quiet, only a feeble glimmer showed in the gloom from the last sods of peat; a mouse stirred gently in the reed roof. Erasmus and Aegidius had closed their eyes and breathed deep, feigning sleep. But they were not asleep, and from time to time they opened their eyes and looked furtively at the hearth. The attitude of the resting man there did not change, only now and again he stretched out his left hand to light a cigarette at the last embers. But they only saw the dark hand with a reddish shining outline, and the hand appeared strange to them and all by itself, as if it did not belong to a living body. The body did not move, not throughout the whole night.

The narrow beam of light which the setting moon cast through the small window grew longer and fainter. It traveled slowly over the clay floor, until it reached the foot end of the shakedown before the hearth. There it faded away, and the two brothers still looked at the spot, even when nothing was to be seen but the blackness of the nocturnal room. It was as quiet as if a dead man were lying there.

Erasmus was the first who could not bear it any longer. "You are not asleep, dear brother?" he asked.

"No," replied Amadeus gently. In the darkness of the room their two voices also sounded unreal, as if there were no living hearts behind them, but as if they rose from the depths of the earth which lay silently around the house. Such voices, submerged voices as it were, are heard sometimes at night over a swamp, and the belated wanderer stops to listen, shivering in the fog that clings to his forehead.

"I will try to tell you everything now, brother," Erasmus went on, "the little that must be told. It is better to tell it in the night than in bright daylight."

He did not sit up, nor did he support his head with his hand. He remained lying, his arms outstretched on the blanket, and he spoke up to where his open eyes were gazing – up into the high roof of reeds above which stood the stars which could not be seen.

"When you went away," he said, "they were at the height of their triumph. It was the era of the flourish of trumpets. They tried time and again to get me back into the army, but I refused. As a major general I could refuse, even at that time, and besides I was certainly not in good health. The doctors called it coronary disease. I made the most of it; and Aegidius had his six thousand acres, and that was more important to them than one more infantryman's rifle.

"We went from pillar to post for your sake, brother, but it was no use. They held what they had as if in a net of steel. Aegidius volunteered . . ."

"You are to tell only the most important things," Aegidius interrupted quickly. "Night will soon be over."

"Just as you like, brother, though there is nothing more important than to bare one's breast and say, '*Ad sum*! Here I am!' as Isaac did under the knife. Nothing greater and nothing more important. Well, they only laughed. You can exchange clothes for cigarettes, they said, but not a life for a life."

"Brother," Aegidius begged once more.

"It is all right," Erasmus went on.

Amadeus stretched out his hand with another cigarette to the glowing embers, and it seemed to Erasmus as if the hand were not as steady as before. But the light from the fire had become so dim that he might well be mistaken. He waited until he saw the glowing dot appear again before the hearth.

"We had a lot of trouble with mother," he continued. "She resented it as a disgrace, just as when father went away. Not as something wrong, brother, do you understand, but as a disgrace. Something that could only happen to a Liljecrona, because they were peasants and had no feeling for greatness. For the peasant, she said, there was only the sanctity of the pitchfork, not the sanctity of the sword. She too had fallen into 'their' way of speaking.

"But for us she was of some use. Because of her they overlooked many things.

"By the way, when the flourish of the trumpets ceased, she went to her relatives in the Münsterland, to a castle with a moat. There her 'equals in rank' live as in the time of Charles the Great.

"We stayed until the tanks came. They did not allow us to leave before. We drove the cattle together and loaded the sleighs. Christoph sat on the front one – as solemnly as if he were driving to church . . ."

"Christoph . . ." whispered Amadeus.

"Yes, he was much over seventy then, perhaps he was already eighty. But his chin was clean-shaven, and he wore the great wolf-skin coat which his grandfather had worn before him. There were twenty-five degrees of frost, and the east wind swept the snow over the land.

"We drove for a whole day, and then the tanks overran us. It was as dark as in a tomb, but with searchlights playing they drove over the sleighs, over the cattle, over women and children. They went forward and backward several times. It sounded as if the wheels were rolling on wet brushwood. They fired from all the guns, because some sleighs were lying in the ditches and some tried to escape into the open fields.

"We lost each other. We ran toward a wood which showed up now and again in the rays of the searchlights. We fell down – and then we ran again. In the wood we lost each other completely. We went astray and did not find the road again, not even at dawn.

"But I found Aegidius. He had been shot through the left shoulder and was freezing to death. He only told me in the evening that he had been wounded; by that time it was almost too late.

"Then we made our way slowly until we came here. It took us nearly three months. I thought that here we would find some of those who had been with us. They all knew that they were to meet here. But there was nobody."

"The dead rise slowly today," said Amadeus after a while. "And probably the living too."

Erasmus was silent, then he went on in a low, changed voice: "I was no hero, dear brother," he said. "I ought not to have run away, unless I was the last. It all depends on where one is when one runs. But probably my mind was disturbed by the noise when the caterpillar wheels rolled over the sleighs – they screamed so, brother, they screamed so terribly – even the horses screamed . . ."

"We have unlearned there, brother, the obligation to throw ourselves voluntarily under a wheel," said Amadeus after a while. "The wheel will catch up with us, if Laima wishes it. Even if we were sitting on a steeple."

"But they are calling," said Erasmus in a whisper now. "I hear them calling. Every night. 'Herr Baron,' they call, and sometimes they say another word. 'Yes,' I say, 'I am coming!' But I do not come. It is too late; I have forsaken them. Father would not have forsaken them."

"We do not know anything about father," said Aegidius. "We only know that he was good. To be good and to sacrifice oneself are not the same things."

A soft, early light fell through the window, and they heard the first cuckoo call over the peat bog. It sounded like the tone of a distant bell, as if the sacrament were being carried through the early morning. All three listened, and for the first time Amadeus sank back on his cushions, folding his arms under his head.

"How different everything is for my brothers," he thought. "How completely different . . . Those they saw were ten or twenty, struck by war as a tree is struck by lightning. But the others, millions probably, whom they slaughtered as cattle are killed in a slaughterhouse . . . And one cannot tell them, because they might think that one measures the dead by their number. Nor can one tell them all the other things . . . Aegidius did not say either that he offered himself as a sacrifice for my sake . . . '*Ad sum*! Here I am!' That is grand . . . but I cannot lie here and talk about it every night. There was something we found among father's papers: 'He who knows does not speak. He who speaks does not know.' Erasmus was hit in the root so that he ran away into the field. He may be destroyed by it. He still thinks like a nobleman, and he who thinks so nowadays will perish. He is the last aristocrat of the family; neither Aegidius nor myself are. He is the defenseless one. All aristocrats are defenseless today. The tank is the symbol of our time, not the sword. The tank and the whip."

The cuckoo was still calling and Amadeus got up. He took a tin of coffee from his haversack and put it on the hearth. Then he picked up his clothes and shoes and went out.

The morning dazzled him, and he stopped for a while leaning his back against the wall of the hut. Marvelous that the earth could be so new every morning, as if it had risen from the grave after the night.

The peat bog steamed in the morning sun. The rocks in the background sparkled like liquid gold. In the stunted pine trees the spiders' webs were glistening. Nothing moved but the first buzzard, which circled above the peat mounds. No evil had ever been here – not yesterday, not a thousand years ago. Here had always been the harshness of nature and its creatures, but it was too lonely here for the wickedness of mankind.

Only the shepherd had been here, and he had been too old for the vengeance of man. He had not been worth their while. Since they had arrested him, Amadeus, and had led him away from here, all this had remained untouched. Like a bath which the angels had prepared for all those who had risen from the dead. Also for the defeated and terrified, nay, for them most of all.

But was there a healing power in nature? Was there salvation at all in this world? Yes, if Christoph had been saved, everything would be easier. He had had "the faith." One need not have the same faith, but it was beautiful to look at somebody who had it, somebody who needed no staff, no philosophy, but who could see the little light in the heather, for whom there were no limits between the underworld and the heavenly world, who was included in the vast circle and who could say everywhere and at each moment,

"Here I am, oh Lord!" Who could also say it when the caterpillar wheels rolled over his eyes and broke his body. He need not ask, "Why did I run away?" He only said, "Here I am, oh Lord!"

Amadeus sighed and went slowly through the low wood to the small pond at the edge of the moor. The dew wet his bare feet, and the coolness of the earth penetrated to his heart. He looked around for a long time before he undressed and got into the water. The bottom was soft and sandy and only at some distance from the shore became dark and swampy.

The cuckoo was still calling, but Amadeus did not count the years which it promised him. Life was not counted by years anymore.

"One must help him," he thought, "before it consumes him and destroys the roots. Somebody must tell him that I have seen thousands die without moving a hand. One must stop asking, 'Where is thy brother Abel?', because the number of brethren has become millions. Yes, probably one must stop asking at all, instead existing quietly and without any question. The asking of questions has ruined the world since the serpent first asked."

He dressed slowly and went back. The fire was burning on the hearth, and they drank their coffee in front of the door. Erasmus had carried out the small table and three chairs. A heron flew over the moorland and their eyes followed it for a long time. It was as quiet as at the beginning of the world after the seven days of creation.

"How do you manage to live here?" asked Amadeus at last.

"Oh, don't worry, there is always something," replied Erasmus. "They fell trees in the woods, and not everything has been stolen from the castle. The Americans came too quickly. And the things that have not been stolen, we sell one after another, or we barter them. Jakob comes up here every second day."

"Who is Jakob?"

"Oh, a Jew from Poland. You know, we call him Kuba, because that's what we used to say at home. He lives in a camp a good way from here. One morning he came up here, and he maintained that he was an honest man. He only wished, he said, to swap: from the right to the left hand, and from the left to the right. Perhaps he cheats us a bit, but that does not matter – at least he comes alone.

"Besides, we have a friend among the American officers down there: First Lieutenant Kelley, John Hilary Kelley. I like his name Hilary, Hilarius goes well with our funny names. And he goes well with us too. He is always smiling, but his smile is a little sad. War does not mean the same to him as it does to most of them. He speaks German very well."

"And what does he want when he comes up here?"

"Oh, nothing particular, you know. He only likes to sit here for a while and forget his own people. He does not like them very much. He says they no longer have any ears – none of them – but only antennae made of wire. He might very well be a cousin of ours, from another part of the family. He does not think in terms of guilt and punishment as the others do. He does not feel a victor, but like somebody who had to join in the game. And he who joins in the game will get his share of profit and loss."

"But what is going to happen now?" Amadeus asked.

"Nobody knows, brother," replied Aegidius. "Sometimes in history there are short intervals in which nothing happens. At any rate nothing that our eyes can see. So much happened that those happenings have to settle down first before anything new can begin. And then I shall try to find some work – a field, a flock, a plow. It is hard for me to live without a plow – do you understand that, brother?"

Yes, Amadeus understood. Aegidius had been the only one who had "done something" – all his life long. Erasmus and he himself had done nothing, and perhaps they would go on doing nothing; or at least what people call nothing.

"I cannot stay with you very much longer," Amadeus said after a while, shading his eyes with his hand against the rising sun.

"That is nonsense, brother," replied Aegidius kindly. "For really none of us can live without the other two. That was already the case at school, and I am sure it has not changed. You must now try to understand your fate a little. It was hard enough that father went away."

"I can only live alone," said Amadeus in a low voice.

Aegidius glanced at him quickly, and then he gazed over the marshes again. "The times of Orestes are gone," he answered, and there was no doubt in his voice. "And you are not a matricide, brother. We shall play together again, Amadeus, do you hear? We shall play Mozart, and there are no ghosts with Mozart."

"I shall never play anymore," said Amadeus, scarcely audible, gazing at his right hand which lay on the dark wood of the table.

"Why do you say that, brother?" asked Erasmus, frightened, leaning forward. "If I said that, I who have deserted the colors . . . but you who have only suffered?"

"I have not only suffered," said Amadeus gloomily, slowly clenching his fist. "I have killed, too, with this hand. And what is more, or more wicked, as you would say: I would kill again at any time, if one of the faces which smiled while they tortured appeared here. There something within me changed; something that I had was taken away from me – and something that I did not have was added. Nothing has been taken away from you, nor has anything been added. You have remained the same. But if somebody were to paint us now as a triptych – some great artist, who sees the ultimate, all that is really hidden – then people would be shocked at the third among us. He would be different from the other two, and people would say that the evil one was standing behind him."

The two leaned forward and took his hand which lay clenched on the table. They took it in such a way that it lay hidden in their hands. And for the first time they noticed that he did not wear his signet ring anymore.

"Brother," said Aegidius in his soft voice, "if this artist, this great artist, had painted all the Liljecronas in our faces – back to bygone days, and all they thought and believed and did – don't you think that the onlooker would make the sign of the cross on seeing them? Do you fancy that you are the only one who has killed?"

"It is no consolation not having been the only one. The fact is that it was not in our nature. It is something foreign to us, and I have opened the door to it. I have allowed someone with dirty shoes to step over our threshold, and I cannot wipe it clean."

"Tell us all about it, brother," begged Aegidius, "now, this very first morning. You have not quite understood yet, brother, that you are with us again, that we three are together again. And that is as if we were one."

"We are not one," persisted Amadeus. He turned his eyes away and looked past the two faces over the moors. Little white clouds rose above the eastern horizon and began to sail up into the blue of the morning sky. The cry of the migrating cranes was heard from a distance.

Again Amadeus felt that all this might have been the same a thousand years ago. As if nothing had happened, at least not here; that it was wrong for him to sit here. As if he ought to go away quite quickly, so that all this might remain the same for another thousand years. So that at least there would be one small place in this world where nothing had happened and where nothing would happen.

"He was a Frenchman," he began in a low voice, "small and thin and ill. A professor of the history of art at the Sorbonne. According to the lists he had long been dead – heart failure. But we had always saved him. We had falsified the list. That was possible in the last months. Then 'the hangman' discovered him. Of all the murderers he was the most merciless. He held a high rank in the camp. He had also invented the business with the meathook. Did you know about that?"

They both shook their heads.

"Those who had been condemned were hung by the chin on such a hook. It was a dreadful death, perhaps the most dreadful of all. We were forced to lead the Frenchman there. He was quiet and brave, but when we entered the large slaughterhouse, he looked at me once – with eyes that had drunk in beauty for a lifetime, eyes that were filled with the pictures of madonnas and cathedrals – they were so filled with that beauty that these pictures almost covered his death agony. But at the bottom of his eyes, deep below these pictures, I saw it – only I.

"All was already disorganized, because the sound of the enemy's guns was coming nearer and nearer, and some of us secretly carried weapons. I did. When we had led the Frenchman under the beam with the hook, I asked the hangman to turn around. He turned as fast as if a serpent had bit his heel. And he looked into the muzzle of my revolver.

"His face became rigid, for he did not understand. To him it was as if the whole world were breaking into pieces. But it was still a wicked, nay, an infamous face – even in its terrible rigidity. More so than in the relaxation of his daily life.

"He looked around and he saw nothing but the end. There was no pity on any of the faces – only the end.

"He fell down on his knees and begged for his life, and we had not known that human words could come from these lips. We listened as we would have listened if a spider in its web had begun to speak. Or a scorpion. Or a basilisk. We were horrified to hear him speak with a human voice. We felt as if in all these years there had not been a deeper defamation of the image of man than this voice of his. We had thought that there would be the voice of a devil in him or the voice of a wolf, as in the pictures of Hieronymus Bosch.

"The professor begged for the hangman's life, but we shook our heads. The others wanted to lift him on to the hook, but before they could seize him, I shot.

"I could have shot him through the heart, but I shot into his face. Perhaps I thought that with a heart-shot he might get up again, because there was a vacuum in his body where we have a heart. Nothing but an empty space. His life was only in his face, which we had seen smiling. Many, many times. And I shot into this smile.

"He sank down head foremost, but I felt that he did not stop smiling. Do you understand? He did not stop smiling. It was as if his smile were immortal. The immortal evil, and a thousand shots would not have extinguished it. It was as if I had shot into Sirius or into the Milky Way.

"I saw the others drag him away. I was certain, as I had never been before, that this man would rise again. And in his resurrection he would still have the same smile.

"The Frenchman took my hand. The left, not the right. And he said something very remarkable. He said, *'Ceux qui restent ce sont les pauvres.'* Those who remain are the poor. It was so very remarkable, because it was the truth. One of those truths that a man can only pronounce when he has discarded all earthly things: fear, hope, hatred and perhaps love also. *Ce sont les pauvres . . .*

"And that's why I must live alone."

The brothers were still holding his hand. He did not look into their faces, because he knew there would be horror in them. He only looked at them when Aegidius put his hand in a special way over his own, and he saw that Aegidius smiled.

"Don't you remember?" asked Aegidius in a low voice.

"What?"

"Don't you remember when we had a cut in our hand, when we were children? And the blood was not to be stanched, and we ran to Grita? Don't you remember what she used to say?"

"Was it . . . ?"

"Yes, that's what it was. One of her half-Christian, half-heathen verses. She took our hand in her hands – so – and then she said: 'Cover hand, cover death – wake up again by God's breath.' She herself did not know where the saying came from. Probably from her great-grandmother. A spell to speak over running blood. And it always stopped running. Always."

"But this does not stop," said Amadeus after a while.

"It has already stopped, brother," said Erasmus. "It stopped the moment you told us about it. And don't you realize that you saved a life, brother?"

"I did not save it," replied Amadeus gloomily. "The Frenchman died of spotted typhus a few weeks later. After we had been liberated. Are you so sure that one is allowed to save one life with another?"

"I seem to remember," said Erasmus in a low voice, "that he who died on the cross saved many lives with his life."

"You must not blaspheme, brother," replied Amadeus, drawing his hand out of his brothers' hands. "Not even from love of me. Or do you think that my hand was allowed to do what God's hand did?"

"Perhaps that's what it means," said Erasmus still more gently, "that we are created in his image."

Then Jakob came. It was his day. He walked a little crooked and a little bent around the corner of the sheepfold with his half-sly, half-sad smile. *"Djing dobry* to the noble counts," he said, raising his dark cap. *"Djing dobry*, Kuba," replied Aegidius. "Haven't I told you often enough that we are not counts?"

Kuba smiled indulgently and wiped his forehead with a lace-edged handkerchief. "What is a count and what is a baron?" he asked gaily. "Whether the count has seven leaves to his coronet or nine – what is the difference? When a stag has six branches on his antlers and they say that it is a stag of eight branches – that is a mistake. But when I address you as a count, that's not a mistake. For even without a coronet you are a count."

"Ah, Kuba," replied Aegidius, pouring out a mug of coffee for him, "you want a ring or a bracelet, that's why you do not mind about the leaves on the coronet."

"If I want a ring," said Jakob, "I wish for gold, and when I want politeness in conversation I say count."

"We can't give you anything today, Kuba," replied Aegidius. "Call again in a week."

"The gentlemen have a visitor," said Jakob, glancing at Amadeus. "You will have to do business again, for the gentleman, your brother, must also eat and drink and have an American cigarette. The gentleman your brother has his hair cut short?"

"Our brother was in a camp for four years," said Erasmus.

"The Holy One, blessed be he," said Jakob in a hushed voice and raised his cap. "Now I must say prince, and not only count."

"Leave it alone, Kuba," said Aegidius.

Jakob drank his coffee in silence and got up. "Next time I shall bring a bottle of Scotch whisky," he said, lost in thought. "I shall not bring it for gold, I shall bring it for nothing."

He took off his cap and glanced at Amadeus. "If an old man is allowed to speak," he said in a low voice, "this old man would like to say this: he would kindly beg the gentleman to let the Lord our God live in his face and not . . ."

"And not what?" asked Amadeus.

"And not the dead, sir," replied Jakob.

"Thank you, Kuba," said Aegidius.

Jakob bowed, put on his cap, and went away.

Later, when Erasmus carried the crockery into the living room, he found a box of American cigarettes on the window ledge. He gave it to Amadeus, saying, "That's a lot for Kuba, really a lot."

"I shall go out for a while now," said Amadeus when they had washed and dried the crockery. "I want to have a good look at everything. It may be evening before I come back, but I shall come back."

"We know that, dear brother," said Erasmus.

Amadeus took only some bread and a field-flask of coffee with him. He walked toward the west so that he had the sun on his back, and he thought of walking all around the peat bog. These were high moors, just as in his homeland, with stunted pines and birches between the flat expanses of reed and water, and it took a couple of hours to walk around it. At the edges the woods thinned out, everywhere the basalt rocks lay in the moss, and lizards were basking on the warm stones. The sky was high and blue, small white clouds sailed over it, and flights of birds were traveling northward. There was complete calm – not even his shoes made a sound on the soft earth. Only when he passed over dry peat did his footsteps ring a little hollow.

But he did not think of death now. It was as if his brothers' hands had covered death, as Grita had covered the blood. He felt that things were easier since he had spoken. In four years he had scarcely said a word. Nothing was changed, but he felt as if he had climbed out of a cellar.

He no longer knew what it was like to walk without goal or purpose. To have nobody behind who carried a whip or a revolver with the safety catch released. He had forgotten that there was an earth which one was not forced to dig or cart away. Earth which lay there quietly resplendent with the sun, which gave space for his feet willingly and without guile.

And now he could walk across the earth in all directions of the compass, and he could stand still and stroke the smooth stems of the reeds with his hands. He could breathe deeply without feeling a load on his shoulders. He could sit on the dry turf and wait until the lizard came out of the grass again.

In the distance the cranes still called, as they had called in his homeland. He shaded his eyes with his hand, but he could not see the birds. He could only see the sky, the space, the unlimited, silent, marvelous space. Grita would have said that on such a morning one could see God's feet resting quietly and sacredly on a blue footstool.

He got up again and walked on, his hands folded behind his back. This too was something lovely, because for four years he had not known that one could hold one's hands in this way unless they were fettered. Time after time he separated them and laid them together again. It was marvelous to feel how they moved.

Then for a while he thought of his home. Much was lost: the books, the music, the lovely little bricks with which one built up one's day; and the feeling with which the roots of the heart reached down into the cool, damp depths of the familiar soil over which he had run as a child.

That was lost now. Fate had lifted him, at that time, as the wind lifts a seed pod, and some time it would drop him. If there was still life within him, he would take root, even in a foreign soil. Perhaps life was immortal, as evil was immortal. He walked on and on. His shadow was no longer behind him but at his side. The distant mountain chains in the east and west became clearer and clearer, but his eyes scarcely skimmed along their crests. All that was close to him made him happy: the waving grasses, the little pools where the clouds were mirrored. The lapwings circled round their damp hatching places, and he stood for a long time to watch their flight and to rejoice in their wailing cry. He had not seen any birds for so long.

Sometimes he thought of his brothers, but not of the victors nor of his country. No general thoughts existed for him so far. His country drank the bitter dregs of the cup, and that was right. Others had drunk them for twelve long years, and with them, bitter death.

"And not the dead, Herr Baron," Jakob had said. Jakob's people had been most numerous among the dead; his people had gone through the most terrible ordeal since the creation of the world. It was surprising that he could say such a thing. It was more than the small box of cigarettes which they found on the window ledge – much more.

But he, Amadeus, would have to go on carrying his dead. He who did not love could not carry the living. They need love, which carries all.

At noon he was lying at the edge of the moor. Beyond the empty, dazzling plain he could recognize the dark roof under which his brothers were now sitting. They, too, carried the trace of the years, a hard, deeply engraven trace. Aegidius was the only one of them who was not bowed down. That much Amadeus knew. Probably because he had driven the plow. He also was the only one who had been willing to sacrifice himself. He knew that the clod must be turned over. He was far ahead of them. They would never catch up with him. They were no longer enclosed together in the panels of the triptych. They had stepped out. They still held each other's hands, but their eyes no longer looked up to God's brow together.

One of them was called by voices which died under the rolling iron wheels. The other called for the field which had been taken away from him. The third did not call, nor was he called. He was only there. The surging sea had thrown him up on the shore and there he lay, breathing heavily, and the water of the deep dripped down from him.

The dappled flecks of sunshine played between the trees. There was a smell of resin and of deserted country all around, and Amadeus' eyes closed. His hands lay open in the warm moss, and he moved his fingers slowly to and fro. They felt neither the moss nor the earth. It was as if they felt nothing but life, naked life that only existed, that did not desire or suffer anything. Pure existence as a child feels it when he has been forgotten in the sunshine.

After two hours Amadeus got up and walked on. The light above the moorland had changed, the shadows fell differently, but it was still the same earth. An earth without human beings, without question or answer, nothing but space which opened willingly to harbor him. The red kite still built its nest in the high pine tree between the rocks of basalt, and the reed warbler called from the bog where it was deepest. They alone had preserved the burning earth from complete ruin. They alone, not mankind. There was no recurrence for them, nor any change. For them everything was still beginning: the first day, the first fear, the first love.

Amadeus walked on and on; he felt as if he were walking into eternity. He would never get tired of walking over this soft, noiseless earth as long as grass and birds were there, the light breeze, and the vast sky. As long as there were no human beings, no victors and no vanquished. Men always demand something and always stretch out their hands toward the body or toward the heart. But grass and birds did not demand anything from him. They remained in their world. He could walk through them as through water. The water closed behind him and no track was left. And thus without leaving a trace he wished to walk over the earth from now on.

The sun was setting when he returned. His brothers sat on the doorstep waiting for him, as they had done in their childhood. They had to be together before night could fall. The stars had to wait for their meeting.

He sat down at an angle opposite them and looked back over the darkening moorland. He sat on the sawn trunk of an alder tree and supported himself with both his hands on the warm bark. He was tired now and looked forward to his bed before the smoldering embers of the hearth.

"I have not met a soul," he said. "It was beautiful."

"Nobody passes here," replied Aegidius. "None of those who once cut peat here has come back. If any of our people should arrive, they can start at once; peat is nearly as precious as bread."

"Do you still think that anybody will come, brother?" asked Erasmus.

"Yes, I think so, but it's a long way, and probably all their shoes are worn out, or they are going barefoot."

The cuckoo was still calling and the first mist rose slowly. The evening star quietly appeared in the twilight. The frogs woke up. The nocturnal earth began to breathe gently.

"Dear brother," said Aegidius, "we have made up our minds to do what I am going to tell you now, and we beg you to leave it at that. We understand that you must be alone for a while, and it will do you good. We have moved to the forester's house today, it's only a ten minutes' walk. It belongs to us now, and they have two nice, perfectly quiet rooms upstairs. They are very comfortably furnished, better than this, and they take us in very willingly – as a sort of protection. Probably you do not know that the forester Buschan has been arrested. He is in a camp, and I think he played a more or less important part hereabouts. He was a law-abiding man, but he has probably put one foot into the swamp, and he will not get out of the mess for some time.

"We thought that we would come to see you for a while in the morning or evening. You must get used gradually even to us. You can eat with us or alone, just as you like. If you will give me your papers, I will notify the police in the village, and you will get your rations all right. The Americans look after all that."

"You're doing this for my sake?" asked Amadeus.

"Yes, of course, brother. But it is not hard for us to do it, you know. We shall manage very easily, and we don't want you to sleep always on the floor. The most important thing is that you should sleep alone after all these years. We ought to have understood that at once."

"But why do you go there?" asked Amadeus.

"It is near you, brother, and where else should we find any room? The woman was so happy that you had come back."

"Was she?" asked Amadeus.

"Yes, really, I think she was always different from the other two. In their so-called politics, I mean. Only the daughter is difficult."

"The daughter, of course. I forgot – what is her name?"

"Barbara."

"All right, she ought to have been called Brunhild. But at that time one did not know all about these things."

"Don't you like the people, brother?"

"I know them so little. The daughter once beat me on my hand with an osier switch. I thought I would never be able to move it again. She hit with all her might."

"Oh, but why?"

"She had a picture of the 'great dictator' in her hand. One of those cheap post cards, and she asked whether I had ever seen anything more beautiful in the world. Of course, I smiled, and then she hit me. I held the post card on my hand and on that hand she hit me. She was thirteen or fourteen at that time."

"Yes," said Erasmus, sighing. "The girls were the first to lose their heads."

"At least she does not side with the victors like most of them," said Aegidius. "I think she would gladly poison the whole lot in the castle. Don't worry about it, brother. So far you have seen little of what is happening here now. And Buschan has got his punishment. The camps are no paradise, from what one hears."

"I hope not," replied Amadeus.

He walked with them to the edge of the wood, and then his eyes followed them. The shadow of the trees and the wisps of mist enclosed and covered them. It looked as if they would never return.

Amadeus walked back slowly and sat down again on the doorstep. The small room lay in darkness behind him. Nobody was there. He need not hear the breathing of any human being. The peat fire on the small hearth was glowing as it did last night, and as it always would from now on. It was his fire; he need not share it anymore.

He leaned his head against the warm post and clasped his hands around his knees. The evening star was now high above the horizon, and the constellations of early spring gradually appeared over the moorland. An owl hooted in the darkness and a dog barked in the distance.

He was alone; the time had now come when he would learn how to be alone. Horror had taught him how lonely he was. All those who had protected him so far had fallen to dust; gone was all comfort, all security. Man had shown what he was capable of doing when he abandoned himself to the depths of his depravity. Man had become a murderer without passion, without even being at all worried about it. A careless, smiling murderer – and the victims stood on the other side. And in between there was nothing. They might talk and write for years now about guilt and atonement, about freedom and the rights of man. But he who got power again would always do the same, even more carelessly and perhaps more thoroughly. But he who had no power was alone. Gone was the period of childhood, when one stretched out a hand to grasp another hand, that of a mother or that of the law or that of God. You could still stretch it out, but you stretch it out only into empty space. All the victims of these years had stretched out their hands to the last second while they screamed or prayed under the gallows, under the ax, under torture. Nobody had grasped those outstretched hands. Even in death they remained outstretched, open, twisted, alone.

He, Amadeus, would now remain here for a while before this hearth which warmed him, under this starlit sky which shone down upon him as it shone down on the grass and the stones. He had two brothers, and formerly they had been as one, as they had been one when they set their bows to their instruments. But at present they were no longer one. Now each of them was alone, as their father had been alone. So much alone that he had suffered himself to be "deceived." At that time the Lord had "deceived" him, but who should deceive nowadays?

Fate had given him another breathing space, and he accepted it and breathed deeply.

A dog barked in the distance, but it was not one of "their" bloodhounds. He raised his hands and dropped them again. They were no longer fettered. The owl hooted, but it was not a human being that screamed in agony. That's what he possessed and owned now. He had got it as a present without deserving it. It might very well not have been presented to him; he could just as well have been trodden to pieces like the others. The foot of the hangman had passed him by at a hair's breadth. There was no law about it, no consolation, no promise.

There was no future in this evening, except the promise of other evenings to come. He knew neither how much time was granted to him nor what was being prepared for him. He had escaped and he did not know where the next trap was laid for him. He was as lonely as a wolf that slinks through the thicket. And like a wolf he strained his ears to hear whether man was about, the creature with power, the creature with the smile. And he did not know which was the more terrible.

The woman in whose house he sought refuge for a night had smiled. In the second year he had escaped when he was on a work detail outside the camp. It had taken him six months to make his preparations, and he had succeeded, because he had come to a river and had found a boat. The water left no tracks.

But he wore the striped garment and he was nearly starving. At twighlight on the fourth evening, he crept through a wood to a small farm, The farmer's wife was alone with an old maidservant and a prisoner of war. She was young and after the first shock she smiled as a mother smiles over a child gone astray. She gave him food and a small room and stroked his hair before she left him.

In the night she called the police. They bound him while he was asleep and took him back. The woman stood at the door and watched. She did not smile when he stopped in front of her and gazed at her. She only raised her hands, as if she thought he was going to strike her.

But he would not have struck her even if his hands had been free. He only wanted to gaze at her for all the future. Not that he wanted to recognize her, only to find out what two human eyes looked like. "Thank you for meat and drink," he said. "I wonder if you know how I shall have to pay for it." Nothing but that. But she had put her hands over her eyes and had turned away.

They had beaten him half dead after that, and he had been transferred to a penal company for a year. For a year he had stood at the gate of hell. Pious people believed that hell was in a world beyond.

He did not attempt to escape again. He could have done so once or twice but he was afraid. Not of the flight nor of the possibility of being caught, but of the eyes of the farmer's young wife and of the lips that had smiled.

And this fear had remained. The last and most terrible fear of all: the fear of man.

He got up and put dry wood on the glowing embers. He was shivering, and he laid his revolver near his seat by the fire.

Then he sat quietly smoking, until he heard the voices. At first he only heard one, suppressed and imploring. The other was scarcely audible, it was so soft.

The door was still wide open, and he recognized them at once as they stood at the doorstep: the forester's wife with a careworn face and the hostile eyes of the child. She was no longer a child, she was a young girl with dark, loose hair. It would have been nice to look at her, if one could forget the eyes of the farmer's wife.

He made an inviting gesture, and the woman came to the fire. The young girl stood in the doorway and looked angrily at her mother.

Amadeus did not glance at the woman or at the girl. He had clasped his hands around his knees again and gazed into the fire.

"Herr Baron," said the woman, and tears choked her voice from the first words.

Amadeus nodded to show her that he heard what she said.

"I wanted to tell you, Herr Baron, how glad I am," said the sobbing voice.

"I have been told that already," replied Amadeus.

"He is in a camp now," the voice went on, "and I was there once. They stand behind the wire netting. The guards are Poles, and they shoot at the women when they go too near the fence."

"Where I was," said Amadeus, "nobody came to the wire netting."

"I do not complain, Herr Baron," sobbed the woman. "But you must know that he did not do it with a light heart. I implored him at the time not to do it. God is my witness. And he said: 'My heart is heavy, but I have got to do it. I have sworn an oath, and I must do it.' And then he did it."

"Many have done it," said Amadeus. "There seemed to be no harm in it."

"But when he is taken to court," said the woman, folding her hands over her breast, "will you give evidence, Herr Baron?"

For the first time Amadeus turned his face away from the fire and looked at the woman. "I too shall say that I have sworn an oath, Frau Buschan," he replied. "Exactly as he has."

"And you will ruin him," she whispered, staring over the fire into the darkness.

Amadeus glanced at the girl on the threshold, and then he looked again at the woman's face. "I will neither help nor ruin," he said slowly. "I shall only look at the scales hanging in the balance. Just as he looked on, just as you and your daughter looked on."

"But you are a Christian, Herr Baron," she cried despairingly.

"I am not a Christian, but a wolf," said Amadeus in a low voice. "I have been down in the pit, and no one should speak to me."

The woman drew the shawl around her shoulders and turned to leave. But she came back once more and bending over him she whispered, "Is it not enough that I have a daughter?"

He gazed at her for a long time. "Perhaps it is enough," he replied in the same tone.

Then he got up and went with her to the door. The girl was still leaning against the post, as she had been all the time. He stopped and looked into her eyes, which did not avoid his glance. "You struck me once," he said, lost in thought. "Now take care that you do not strike your mother! Grita used to say that a hand raised against one's mother would grow out of the grave."

Her face remained motionless, and there was no flicker of her eyelids, so he did not know whether she had understood.

The light of the moon fell over them as they went away, and it seemed as if they were returning to the dark depths of the moors, from which they had emerged for a transient hour. They did not seem to be going back to any human dwelling.

3

TIME PASSES, PEOPLE SAY. And some say that it rolls on or flies. But for Amadeus it does not pass, it only exists and he exists in it. Sometimes it seems to him as if they were both standing still, sometimes as if they were falling through space into the depths where there is neither space nor time. He and time are not two separate things, they are included in each other, and neither of them is without the other. Things were different behind the barbed wire. Time was there as the hangman or the bloodhounds were there. Not only the time which was shown by the clock on the watchtower: the time for work or sleep, the living time. But behind it, as it were, was that universal, deadly time – something that was not theirs to dispose of, something that was measured out to them. For everything belonged to the people in uniform: work, food, sleep, death. And also time. He who had spent six years there counted as little to them as he who had come the previous day. The victims were shadows without time or name. Only the others had names and time.

But now it is quite different. When the cuckoo calls in the morning, it does not seem to call only today. For it was so yesterday and will be so tomorrow, as it will be in a thousand years. And it is the same with the stars and the evening mist, or with the warm rain that from time to time passes over the moorland like a soft, gray wall. Amadeus accepts it all like a stone lying in the moss. He need not move nor is he capable of motion. He only keeps quiet when all this passes over him: the call of the bird, the mist, the rain, and the stars. He is a creature among other creatures. It is all the same whether he is gay or sad, nor are his thoughts of any importance.

Sometimes he does not know whether he is gay or sad. He only knows that he exists, and what is more important still, that the others do not exist. When he wakes up in the reddish dawn, and the morning light falls into his narrow room, he sits up in his bed with a sudden, wild, breathless movement and listens with strained attention. Like an animal at bay. His heart pounds so that the whole room is filled by it, his hand closes on the revolver, and slowly, quite slowly, the ominous dream-pictures which have weighed down his sleep are shattered: the picture of a dark, closed van, the door of which opens noiselessly to take him in, while he knows that behind the dark walls will be horror, the last, frightful horror that only man can prepare for men.

Or the picture of the young, friendly woman is there, she who stroked his hair in the night when he had sought refuge with her. She bends over him – so closely that he can see the arteries in her throat pulsing, and she smiles down on him as on an awakening child. But the smile changes slowly, terribly, and below her neckerchief something moves, something that he cannot see nor recognize – it may be an animal with a hundred legs and ice-cold eyes – such as the fathomless waters of the deepest ocean may conceal.

Many phantoms drink at his heart in the night, and what they drink is always blood. And whether they assume a thousand forms, inexhaustible as only dreams can be, behind all those thousand forms stands *man*. Man, who stood over him for four years, smiling and motionless, to drain his heart, and only from time to time the hand with the cup is raised to the icy lips. And the cup is filled with Amadeus' blood, his fear, his horror, his life, and his time.

Then he falls back on his bed trembling and breathing heavily, and softly, imperceptibly, time, which he had lost while sleeping, returns and envelops him.

The cuckoo calls and the mice rustle about in the reed thatching. He is so wide awake that he could fancy that he hears the dew falling on the grass or the morning clouds sailing above the reddish moorland. Pliantly, willingly, he is drawn once more into the orbit of all created things. The light blesses him, the call of the bird, and the holiness of the early morning.

Amadeus sits on the doorstep and slowly breaks his bread. He might be the first human being in the landscape, the first and the last. Time does not exist for him. There is no time as long as "the others" are not here. He need not go down to be questioned by authorities in offices or behind counters. Aegidius sees to all that for him. And when they make difficulties there is Kelley, First Lieutenant Kelley, who arranges everything with his capable hands.

Amadeus can waste his day or fill it or leave it empty, just as he likes. The day does not dictate to him, it only gently makes him part of itself.

Generally he goes out early in the morning and comes home in the afternoon or evening. He has formed friendships on the moors, quiet friendships which need no words: with the red kite that has its nest in a high tree above the rocks, with the lizards on the peat mounds, with the quaking ground between the brown water pools on which the cranes have their breeding places, and with the sundew in the peat ditches, with the wild arum and the lady's slipper and with the tall, yellowish orchid which stand like candles in the grass. He often picks a bunch that fills the room with a strange, intoxicating scent.

He does not read much, nor does he think much; he only exists. From the great library of their father's house the brothers have saved nothing but "the whole of the Prophet Jeremiah." Sometimes he opens the book in the evening by the fire, his eyes travel over the large, old-fashioned letters, and he listens to the sound of the great, imploring words which are like the primal complaint of humankind, of those beings created to suffer, born of woman and chosen for all eternity.

"The bellows are burned, the lead is consumed of the fire, the founder melteth in vain."

Or: "Thus speaketh the Lord of hosts, the God of Israel: thou must empty the cup of thy sister, as deep and wide as it is."

Or the word by which their father had suffered himself to be deceived before he went into the unknown.

He reads the words not as wisdom, nor even as revelation. He lets them sink into his ear as he does the voices over the peat bogs, voices which are "above the deep" and sound in the evening under the first stars: the oldest voices of the earth which is trembling with the foreboding of woe, and it matters not whether the tune of this suffering sounds in the mouth of a human being or in that of an animal.

Sometimes Amadeus opens the scores of the old music, which his brothers had saved when they saved the instruments, and he follows the lines strung with black signs and hears the sounds as they were when he was his former self. This great riddle of life: that a black sign can stand for a sound and the sound in its conjunction with other sounds can convey the mood of the heart – its sadness or its sparkling joy. A cadence can mean a girl's lament or the dance of a young fellow though he is sad. The great riddle that the vibration of a string is also the vibration of the heart, and yet the quivering of the string is nothing but a physical law, which can be expressed in a formula, while the vibration of the heart can only be expressed by a smile of the lips or a tear on the eyelash.

But even there, even with the tunes, Amadeus is alone. Everything is for him as it was on the first day. He remembers the past, but only as in a dream. The marshes are new to him, the grass, the sky, the fire, everything. He must conquer the world anew, just as children conquer it. And he does so with infinite caution. Once he fell into a pit, and he walks as if expecting the next pitfall to await him just by his door. As a child he had known sorrow and melancholy, as all children do. But he had not known horror, and now, knowing horror, he is a marked man. His greatest pleasure is to put his hands on moss and to open and close his fingers in the sun. This is the gesture of freedom for him, of rescue, yes, of salvation.

Since Amadeus is out all day long, the brothers come in the evening. They sit on the doorstep or on the warm trunk of the alder. They had not known about the forester's denunciation, but now his wife has told them of it. She wept and they consoled her. They do not speak of it to Amadeus, but in the twilight they search his sealed face to know whether the dead are still there. The dead have installed themselves in that face, and if they were not the dead one might say that they are installed for a lifetime.

Amadeus, too, watches his brothers. When they get up, Aegidius looks as if all this still belonged to him, and as if he would stride over the moors as before he strode over the fields. But Erasmus looks like a tree a little bent over, at the edge of a desert or on the crest of a dune from where one sees nothing but sand. He is the only one in whose face still lingers a trace of childhood: of the helplessness, the uncertainty, and confusion of those early years.

When they have gone away, Amadeus thinks most about him. He is the only human being whom he would like to help, the only one for whose sake he can forget himself for a while.

When Jakob comes, he arrives in the early morning. He just looks in on him on his way to the forester's house. He does not come to exchange anything from "the right hand into the left." He knows that the baron will not barter, yes, that he is so poor that he has nothing to barter – neither material things nor things of the spirit. And it is on account of this poverty that Jakob comes, especially for the poverty of the baron's spirit.

Jakob himself has overcome everything so completely that bargaining, exchanging, and adventure give him pleasure again. Even the early morning delights him, and when he stands at the edge of the moor and the lapwings call in the distance, he can even think of his lost home, of the little village with the thatched roofs where his parents were killed more than thirty years ago in a pogrom.

His people have come through so much in two thousand years that it has passed into the blood of the later generations. At one time the sickle-wheeled chariots drove over them, then there were the crucifixions and death in the flames. They wandered and sang. Then the caterpillar chains of the tanks went over them, they suffered torture and died in the fiery furnace. They wander again and sing again. They sing and trade and sometimes they dream of the Promised Land. Once upon a time they sat by the waters of Babylon when the Assyrians ruled over them, and now they sit in the camps of the victors waiting for their fate to be decided. They have learned great fearlessness and great patience. None on this earth has greater patience than they.

Some of them are tired and some are wicked, and some are as full of hatred as their torturers were. But not many, and Jakob does not belong to those. Nature has created him without hatred, and he has remained so pious that there is no room for hatred in his heart. He has become even more pious than he was in his homeland.

"The Holy One, blessed be he, wanders again," he says to Amadeus and clasps his hands around his thin knees. "He is wandering and looks for a place where he can rest. He looks into the faces of men and goes past. The face of the Herr Baron is not yet a place where he can rest. The face of the Herr Baron is still occupied by the dead and by himself. You must put aside all that belongs to yourself, so that the Holy One, blessed be he, can find a place to rest."

"And you yourself, Jakob?" asked Amadeus after a while.

"I have put everything aside, Herr Baron," answers Jakob, gazing over the moors with his melancholy eyes. "I have put aside father and mother, and I have put aside a young wife and two children whom they burned in the fiery furnace. I have made room in my face, and when the Holy One, blessed be he, wants to visit me, he can visit me or not visit me – just as he likes."

"And how did you do that, Jakob?"

"I have done nothing, Herr Baron. I thought of my young wife and the two children in the fiery furnace, and I thought that they sang. And how should I lament or cry when they sang? My distress was insignificant, Herr Baron, and the distress of Herr Baron is also insignificant. As long as others are in distress in this world, our own distress is not much."

"I have seen them," said Amadeus after a while, as if speaking to himself. "Their distress was not small, Jakob."

"What is small and what is great, Herr Baron? It is not good for a man to look at himself with a magnifying glass, Herr Baron. We ought to look at ourselves with a soldier's field glasses holding them the wrong way around, so that we may see ourselves as small as if we were far away behind the marshes. Then we will see ourselves as the Holy One, blessed be he, sees us: so small, so small, Herr Baron." He picked up a dry blade of grass from the floor, cut it to pieces with his fingernails, put the smallest bit on the palm of his hand and blew it into the air like a speck of dust.

"Herr Baron ought not to think so much about himself," said Jakob, getting up. "Herr Baron must not think that he has got to carry the dead on his shoulders. There is the Holy One, blessed be he, who carries the dead, and he has not asked either Herr Baron or me to help him."

Jakob picks up his cap and bows. "Herr Baron will forgive me," he says politely, "if I speak to him as if we were equals."

Amadeus' eyes follow him for a long time while he walks around the sheepfold into the wood toward the forester's house, a little crooked, a little bent, the sack over his shoulder, as his people walked a thousand years ago from village to village, from country to country, despised, spat on, and hated, and yet they had not forgotten to "make room" in their faces for their God, who had been to them a stern and jealous God through all the generations.

But when the thin, bent figure has disappeared behind the pine trees sparkling with dew, the face of the baron closes up again. It has no room yet. He does not yet live for others – neither for God nor for men.

"Time passes," people say, but Baron Erasmus does not know whether that is right. When he sits in the warm moss at noon, leaning his back against a rock and gazing through the smoke of his cigarette over the shimmering moors, he looks like somebody who really lives beneath the rocks and who has only come up for a little time to observe a strange world. He has the saddest eyes of the three brothers, though he rode for many years at the head of the Uhlans: first at the head of a squadron, then at the head of a regiment, and at last at the head of a brigade. He loved his men and his horses with the temperate but reliable and unswerving love of a nobleman.

He was not born to be a cavalryman. From childhood his heart had been full of dreams in which he was a great benefactor, like the old, rather weary magicians in fairytales who put their wealth into needy hands. Erasmus had always been a little uncertain, somewhat oppressed by fear, when he was away from his brothers. He was like a precious stone broken out of a ring. In order to be whole he needed someone to walk at his right and at his left. Not just anybody or someone grand or powerful – just his brothers. With them at his side there was nothing striking in him any longer, nothing special. Then he was nothing but one panel in a triptych, and if he did not want to be looked at or spoken to, the wings with the pictures of the brothers closed above him and he was hidden away.

He had only expected to grow old in a quiet, beautiful way. He would become intimate with the families in the old manor houses of the district, as a guest who appeared now and again, to read aloud to the women and to tell fairytales to the children. A rather peculiar but beloved guest, a last relic of times gone by, when respect and even worship were due to women. He would not have done anything outstanding in life. He would not have won a battle, nor written a book. He would have discovered neither the poles of the earth nor a new star. But if somebody had been in need under the old roofs of his homeland, he would have been remembered, his delicate hands which drew the bow without pretension over his violin, his kind eyes which, in spite of their melancholy, spread radiance over all that was dark. If it were a matter of honor or discord or pain or some insoluble problem, he would have been called on as a calm, great judge of the troubles of the heart. Such were Erasmus' thoughts when he retired from the army, and now he sits in the warm moss, his back against a boulder, listening to the black woodpecker beyond the moors. He had been called upon – though in a different way from what he had imagined – and he had not heeded. He had not been called upon as a calm judge, but for help when anguish was at its deepest – as one who could save and heal – and he had not heeded. He had run over a snow-covered field in unworthy haste, he had run to a dark, sheltering wood and behind him the screams had died down – those of the men and those of the horses, the terrible screams of those who were forsaken and lost. "Herr Baron," they had called – "Herr Baron" – and then it was only "Herr," as the cottagers used to cry in their deepest need: "Lord – Lord . . ."

But he was already far away under the dark trees from which the snow fell on his brow, a hunted man and a deserter, and later when shame began to burn in him, he could not find the road again, the crimson road where blood had dyed the snow, where snow fell into the staring, open eyes of the children.

Time passes, people say, but for the baron Erasmus time stood still. A frozen time, and it froze on that road under the gnarled willow trees which stood like ghosts at the edge of the road. Time froze with the dead, the dead took it in their twisted hands and did not give it back again. Baron Erasmus had failed in the hour which fate offered him. He failed, and now time has expelled him from its quiet, constantly progressing march, and he sits there leaning against the rock and sees the sun travel, sees how the clouds sail above him and beyond him, and he is left behind, as the frozen victims were left behind, though he ran away, yes, just because he ran away.

His hair is nearly white now, and sometimes in the morning when he glances into the small looking glass, he feels as if he had paid with his hair. But he knows that one has to pay with one's heart, not with the hair on one's head.

He chose this place in the wood because from here he can overlook part of the road in the valley. It is the road that leads to the castle, and he who wants to come up to the brothers must walk along it. He sees how the trucks of the victors leave a cloud of white dust behind them, or he sees a cyclist or now and again a single wanderer who carries something on his back. But no van comes loaded with furniture, no children run at the sides of the wheels, and he imagines that those whom death and frost have spared can only arrive in this manner; just as in his homeland they have always moved from one estate to another, when by chance they had to change masters.

He remains there until night draws near. The moorland grows dark, the wood, the road. Wild ducks fly in the glowing evening sky over the peat bog, and the reed warbler begins to call. The first, white, misty cloud appears above the reed patches, the day shrouds itself in darkness, the evening star mounts above the horizon.

Then he gets up, sighing, a tall, thin, bent man, and returns to his room in the forester's house, where his brother is waiting for him, so that they can go together for a little while to the sheepfold where the other brother lives, the third and youngest, of whom the song of their childhood said: "But the third, the youngest lad, was so sore, oh, sore at heart."

But when Erasmus remembers these verses, he shakes his head gently. For the third, this youngest one, has faced the consequences. He did not miss the hour. He did not run away across the field. And when they sit on the trunk of the alder tree or on the doorstep of the shepherd's hut, Erasmus glances out of the corner of his eye at this youngest brother and asks himself why this face is so gloomy and frozen instead of beaming with happiness, with the happiness of him who has exclaimed, "*Ad sum!* Here I am!"

* * *

"Time passes," people say, and Aegidius is the only one who experiences it mornings and evenings. He cannot see any field from the moorland, but he feels that the meadows are being mown now and that the grain is ripening. He does not hear the real bird call of the day and of the night, nor the call of the lapwings nor the hooting of the owls. Waking and sleeping he only hears the voice of the corn crake, which used to fill the harvest nights in his home country. That inexhaustible, warning call to praise God, the harvest, and the daily work. The call to the tune of which the scythes were sharpened in the crimson dawn while dew still covered the sleeping earth.

He does not mourn for men, but for the earth, for the lost fields on which thistles will now be growing, for the wheat that falls out of the ears, and for the hands which have nothing to do, neither to sow nor to reap. Empty hands which idly hold a pine branch when he stands at the edge of the wood gazing into the veiled distance toward south or southwest to where the land slopes away and where the fields of Franconia or the blessed Wetterau are ripening in the sunshine.

He is the only one of them who now and again leaves the moors for a day or even for a few days. Jakob managed to get him a bicycle for some jewelry, a well-worn vehicle rattling in all its spokes, but for Aegidius it means just as much as a carriage and four, and on it he roams through the plains at the foot of the mountain range wherever they are making hay. There are only a few large estates, mostly the property of some lord of the manor; and there he sits under one of the apple trees which line the road, or on the bank of a ditch near the bushes, his hands clasped around his knees, and watches the machine as it goes through the field wet with dew, or the scythes as rank on rank the scented grass falls over them in level swathes.

The farmhands in these fields are not so happy as they were in his home country, where harvesttime was still half pagan. Most of the young people he sees wear ragged, dirty uniforms without badges, and most of them glance at him suspiciously as he sits hour after hour beside the ditch watching them. The country is full of pillagers, people from all nations who sit workless in the camps and for whom other people's lives and property mean as little as they meant for their deposed taskmasters.

For Aegidius it does not matter to whom this land belongs, and still less that it does not belong to him. Only work matters to him, and he likes to gaze at a man who drives a mowing machine or handles a scythe, and if he were not so shy he would ask someone to let him use a scythe.

At the edge of one of the large estates where they have been mowing the grass for days on end, he can at last get up and lend a hand. Something has gone wrong with the machine at his feet and the bailiff, a short, quick man who always scolds in a loud voice, showers a hail of curses on the driver, who bends over the sparkling blades. "I wonder if I can help," says Aegidius politely and walks around the machine. He does not listen to the hostile question as to who he may be, and after a while he asks for a wrench. It is not difficult for him to find what is wrong, and while he screws on a new nut, he tells the bailiff that he must watch to see that this is always screwed up tight, because it has to bear the main weight of the whole machine.

Aegidius does not hear exactly what the bailiff answers; but it strikes him that he speaks politely, and when he draws himself up, wiping the sweat from his brow with the sleeve of his coat, a woman is standing near the machine, in a cotton frock and with a large straw hat shading her sunburned face. She looks at him in a friendly way, says, "Thank you," and nods at him.

The horses begin to pull again, the grass is mown, and Aegidius' eyes follow the machine as it drives along the edge of the high grass evenly and quietly. "Machines cannot be put in order by scolding," he says, turning again to the woman.

He only really looks at her now, and is a little taken aback by her majestic appearance as she stands here in the meadow, a formidable figure. He tries to think of a gentler expression, but does not find one. She is as tall as he, but broader and more powerful.

Only her large, friendly, blue eyes under her broad hat are kind and moderate her rather overpowering size.

He walks back with her to the road, where her dogcart is waiting for her, and they start a friendly, rather reserved conversation. She is the mistress of these fields and meadows since her husband was killed in Russia, and she has a lot of trouble with the bailiff and the farm hands.

Everything has changed, not only the times, but with the times men and conditions. In answer to her cautious question Aegidius said that he was but a looker-on. "I have got to cycle almost seventy kilometers to be able to look at fields, but I do not regret that. I cannot sit up there on the moors all day long with folded hands."

"Where is that – up on the moors?" He tells her, and when she asks for his name, he tells her that too. She knew his cousin and the castle, and she looks at him out of the corner of her eye. "Will you come and have a cup of coffee with me?" He thanks her politely; he has to start on his way home now. His brothers are waiting for him, and in a few words he tells her about them. With her eyes on the ground she draws shapes in the dust of the road with the stick she carries. "I am sorry," she says in a low voice, which is remarkably gentle for her heavy build.

A fleeting smile crosses his face, and then he looks back at the meadows where the distant machine now creeps through the high grass like a big, awkward beetle. "One must only give sympathy, not receive it," he replies and helps her politely into the small trap which dips down to one side as she gets in.

Then he takes his bicycle out of the grass and starts on his way home. He has not learned her name.

In the evening it is he who has great things to tell in front of the sheepfold. His brothers listen to him, glancing at him furtively, and even Amadeus' lips smile awkwardly. "They have started the haymaking too late," says Aegidius, lost in thought while he looks at a green blade of grass which he has brought home. "And the bailiff is not worth anything. It was quite simple, but he could do nothing but swear. One ought not to swear at harvesttime."

But Aegidius avoids cycling the same road again. He is worried that he mentioned his name, for he does not like to be invited from the ditch side to a cup of coffee. He is fully aware that he has got to learn and to unlearn a few things, but he does not wish to do it just there.

Time passes; the young birds of prey now wail at the edge of the moors, and the cuckoo no longer calls so many times that one could live to be a hundred years old.

Time passes over the moors and the sheepfold and over the three brothers, one of whom wishes to forget the anguished voices, and the other the scent of the meadows which are being mown, and the third the fear of men and of their smiles. Time takes much away: the yellow orchid in the damp wood and the wildflower for which Amadeus stoops and which he holds long in his hand, while his eyes gaze deep into the little white bells. But time does not take away those memories which the brothers wish to forget. It has enclosed and carefully preserved them and directly a thought touches them they open their eyes wide and stare at their victim. They are there and cannot be avoided.

Nothing happens up here until midsummer. The forester has not come back yet, and his wife with the impassive face looks after the brothers as if they were two princes whom the marshes held in their spell. The girl sits for many hours at the edge of the rocks gazing down upon the road like Erasmus. Her face is gloomy, she looks much older than she is, and when she is alone, her face becomes careworn and hopeless. She, too, is waiting, evidently not for her father, but for the secret armies which will arise somewhere, perhaps in the Alps, and march up here to bury under their tanks the so-called victors and their laughter and their noise.

Jakob comes, and Kelley, but they go again, and it seems as if the summit of the mountain were above the world of humans; no trace is left on it by strange feet.

Only at midsummer something happens. A visitor comes to Amadeus in the evening. He hears an unknown step at the door, a slow, hesitant step, and like a wolf from his lair he is on the threshold. It is only a strange woman, big and heavy, with a straw hat hanging on her arm and a stick in her hand. She looks like one of the giants' daughters whose fathers once played here with the rocks, when fire still broke through the earth. Amadeus stares at her in silence.

It is good that she does not smile. She only scrutinizes him, knitting her brows a little as if she were thinking of engaging him for some work, and then she asks in her gentle, low voice whether Baron von Liljecrona lives here. She would like to talk to him about something, and as there is no post, no telephone yet, she has come herself.

From what Aegidius had told him, he knows who she is, and with rather a forced politeness offers to show her the way to the forester's house.

She thanks him, but asks to be allowed to rest a little here. The way up has been rather tiring for her. She sits down on the trunk of the alder tree, and as Amadeus cannot prevent it, he remains standing at the door of the shepherd's hut, leaning his back against the doorpost with his arms folded over his breast. Seven locks seem to close his face, and it does not make it any better that he notices that the woman considers him, without curiosity, only with a quiet, friendly attention.

"I am sorry," she says at length, as she had said once before. He, too, is struck by her soft voice, but he only shrugs his shoulders and goes on looking over the moorland on which the shadows grow deeper and deeper.

"I have come," she says after a while, "to ask your brother to help me. The bailiff has made off with a lot of money, and within a week the rye must be mown. I cannot manage that alone anymore."

"Who should be able to do it, if not you?" thinks Amadeus.

"Do you think that he would be willing to come?" she asks, and her voice sounds almost shy.

Amadeus shrugs his shoulders once more. "I don't know," he replies, "but I think he would be willing to go to any harvest, even if it were on the moon."

"Thank you," says the woman, smiling. But after that her face becomes serious again, and like Amadeus she gazes over the moors. "If I could help you at any time," she says after a while, "I would like to do so. The winters are severe up here and not good for the heart. There will always be room in my house for you."

"Thank you," replies Amadeus, "but I have room enough here."

"Perhaps it is not quite right," says the woman modestly, "to blame everybody. Everybody is a poetical conception, but not a conception of daily life. Nor is it a kind of conception . . ."

"Neither poetry nor life have obliged me to be kind," replied Amadeus.

"We can only oblige ourselves to be kind," says the woman gently. "Anyone who looks rather out of the ordinary, as I do, knows something about that."

The first shadows of night fall over the earth. Above the western part of the moors the sky is burnished in the setting sun. It looks as if there were a conflagration beyond the earth.

"I have no children," said the woman gently, "and sometimes I feel happy about it."

When she is about to get up, Erasmus and Aegidius come out of the wood to the sheepfold.

Erasmus is so bewildered that the woman cannot help smiling, and before she says what she wants she gazes for a little while at the three brothers, at one face after another. They are standing side by side against the wall of the sheepfold; the light of the setting sun reflected in their eyes shows up the almost touching likeness of their features and impresses the stamp of deep, almost painful loneliness upon the three figures.

With some anxiety the woman feels that perhaps none of the three might be able to face life alone. That if she were to take one of them into her house, she would have to take all three. But the next minute she begins to doubt the idea, when her eyes return to Amadeus. He has stood the test alone, and more than blindly has given her to understand that he does not wish to grasp her hand. She sighs a little and then she says what she has come for.

Aegidius does not hesitate for a moment. He even thanks her for having thought of him.

"Of whom else should I have thought?" she asks with her friendly smile. He promises to come quite early the next morning, and now he will accompany her down to where her trap is waiting. It is not too safe for a woman to be alone on the road at this time of the day.

She shakes hands with the two others, and Erasmus kisses her hand according to the old custom. She blushes a little, but she looks at Amadeus. "The victors cannot always make the peace," she says as she takes leave.

He only bows in silence.

They remain sitting at the door of the sheepfold and wait for Aegidius.

"I feel as if he is going to Queen Semiramis," says Erasmus after a time, and follows with his eyes the smoke from his cigarette.

"He will go into her field," replies Amadeus, "not into her hanging gardens."

"A mighty woman," says Erasmus, lost in thought.

When Aegidius comes back and sits down between them, they can no longer distinguish each other's faces. The stars sparkle in all their splendor, and the owls hoot above the moor.

"I was so happy," says Aegidius at last, "but now I feel how hard it is to leave you. It will only last over the harvest."

"It will last much longer," replies Amadeus without any reproach.

Aegidius meditates for a while. "I do not know," he says. "Perhaps one can get used to her superhuman scale."

"The ancient Greeks would probably have called her 'the cow-eyed,'" says Erasmus smiling. "But it was a goddess they called by that name."

"I shall come and look after you as often as I can manage," Aegidius continues. "She has a trap, and I am sure I shall get permission to use it. She likes you very much."

"You must not think of us, brother," says Amadeus. "It is a good thing one of us has got something to do, and there was no doubt that you would be the first. Probably you will be the only one." He said it without bitterness, but Erasmus bends forward and with particular care he presses out his cigarette end. "I am sure we shall manage all right, brother," he says, "provided that the forester's daughter does not kill me."

"I don't think that she has a special design on your life," replied Aegidius smiling. "For her you are only an apparition from a 'decadent age,' as we all are. But probably you most, because you are kindest to her."

"Kindness is the gold of the dispossessed," said Erasmus gaily. However, he felt very lonely when Aegidius had left. He now had both the rooms on the top floor; he had opened the door between them and walked for hours from one room to the other, avoiding the threshold, which creaked at every step. Or he stood for a long time at one of the small windows, his forehead pressed against the pane, gazing over the low forest into the distance, which always remained void for his eyes.

Sometimes at twilight he saw strangers under the bushes at the edge of the wood, young men with open shirt collars, and he saw the forester's daughter talking with them while she glanced back at the house over her shoulder. But he did not pay any attention to it.

Not until one morning three American soldiers came into the house and he was summoned into the kitchen and questioned as to whether he had noticed any young men coming frequently to the house, did he remember it and look at the girl, who was leaning coldly and proudly against the wall as if she were St. Joan about to be burned at the stake.

"I have not been watching," he said politely, "and I am out of the house almost all day long."

The sergeant looked at him thoughtfully, then asked: "Are you a fugitive?"

"Yes, one may call it so," replied the baron.

"And you were a general?"

"That's right," said the baron smiling. "But I took my discharge twelve years ago."

The sergeant turned over the leaves of his notebook and shrugged his shoulders. "You ought to be a bit careful," he said to the girl then, and got up. "After all, we are the victors."

"Child-murderers are no victors," replied the girl, looking past him as if a rubbish bin were standing there in his stead.

He frowned, but the two others laughed, and the youngest raised his hand and in fun stroked the girl's cheek. The girl hit him so hard that he took a step back and glanced flabbergasted at his hand.

"Look here," he said angrily.

Then they went.

"You ought to be careful," said Erasmus before he turned to leave the kitchen. "Even if I don't pay attention, I see many a thing. A girl should not try to run her head against the wall. If it is not bad for the wall, it may be bad for the girl."

She cast a searching glance at him and then went out of the kitchen.

The soldiers report their visit, and though most of the listeners laugh, the officer of the military police takes it more seriously. One morning when Amadeus locks the door of the shepherd's hut to walk over the moors, he sees the girl and three soldiers step out of the wood in front of the forester's house. The girl goes between them through the dew-covered grass and they walk slowly past Amadeus.

The soldiers are merry and carefree, and the girl walks between them as if they were cannibals. She sees Amadeus standing there looking in silence at the four as they pass, but she only returns his gaze with icy contempt.

In the evening Kelley tells Amadeus in his smiling way that it had been a remarkable hearing. If they had caught a wildcat it might have been about the same. It seemed to him throughout that the girl was about to jump over the table and strangle the first lieutenant. "What a pity," he said in conclusion. "So nice to look at and so thoroughly stupid."

"She has got a month's prison for contempt of the dignity of the American Army. Personally I cannot imagine what a girl of seventeen has to do with the dignity of an army of millions."

After four weeks she comes back, and it is said that the warden of the prison, a pious man, had promised a big wax candle for the church of the little town – if after these four weeks he were still in office and alive.

At this time, when Aegidius is already busy with the wheat harvest, a loaded van drawn by four quite exhausted horses drives with many pauses for rest along the narrow winding road which leads up to a mountain that people call the Wasserkuppe. The van is loaded with old, much-broken furniture. Women in dark shawls which almost cover their foreheads sit in the straw of the van. They sit there quiet and bowed, and the eyes of the people of the district follow them for a long time, as if they were the ancient Fates of the legend, wandering now since the roots of the world ash tree had been sawn through.

There are children walking in the dust beside the creaking, rattling wheels, each holding a stick, and the people in the fields have to look hard to see whether these are really children and not dwarfs from the Kyffhauser or the Riesengebirge. They seem so old and subdued.

In the front of the van on a narrow board covered with a sack sits a tall old man with clean-shaven chin and a white beard the cut of which is unknown here, holding the reins of the four horses in his left hand. He sits upright and straight, as if he were carved out of wood, and his light-blue eyes are the only ones that gaze into the distance, instead of into the dust of the road – as the eyes of all the others do.

4

WAS IT CHANCE OR fate that Baron Erasmus had been sitting for more than a hundred days by the rock gazing in vain down upon the valley road – or had his melancholy eyes prepared the highway for the van with the four horses? One can ask for a highway, even when it is difficult to understand the language of the people who live there, and no magic is needed to find it in the end.

For, one morning in August, Amadeus awoke at the sound of the fire crackling on the hearth. He left the heavy door of his room open at night now, because the small window did not let in enough air, and he entrusted his light sleep only to the great solitude of the moorland.

He sat up as quickly as when he had one of his bad dreams and stared at the figure that knelt before the hearth and blew into the feeble glow. The feet of the figure were wrapped in rags such as the woodcutters in his homeland wore, and of the head Amadeus could only see the white hair that fell long and smooth over the coat collar. The coat was blue and reached to the knees.

"Christoph," he said in a low voice, and he felt the hands on which he leaned tremble.

"Just a minute, Herr Baron," replied the soft voice. "Let me blow the fire up. You must try to get some small pine twigs, so that you will not have so much bother in the morning, Herr Baron."

When the fire burned and filled the room with its crackling, Christoph rose, supporting himself with one hand on the hearth. Then he carefully wiped his hands with a gray cloth, came to the bed, and sat down gently on the side of it.

"So you are here, Herr Baron," he said, gazing with his bright eyes full of affection into the face of the baron, "and we did not know whether you were still alive. Only down at the castle they told us."

He spoke as if he had piled up the wood in the hearth the previous night as well as on a hundred previous nights. But he took pains to control the quivering of his chin, which trembled a little as with children who are nearly crying. "Four years, Herr Baron," he said, counting it off on his fingers. "In four years a tree can bear fruit."

"I have not borne much fruit, Christoph," replied Amadeus. "But how many of you have come through it all?"

Christoph counted once more on his fingers. "Worgulla," he said, "and he was the man who looked after the farm horses. Donelaitis and Skowroneck, and they were day laborers, and their wives and five of their children got through. Two others were frozen on the road, and one was shot by bandits when they tried to rob the van. They were German or Polish robbers. And one baby starved because the mother had no milk and the peasants would only give milk in exchange for a horse. But we needed the horse, and when we had made up our minds to exchange it, it was too late; those were German peasants."

"And the others, Christoph?"

Christoph folded his hands on his knees. "The others died, Herr Baron – there – on the night when our Heavenly Father drove us out."

"It was not God who drove you out, Christoph," said Amadeus gently.

"The sin, Herr Baron," replied Christoph. "And those who sin are driven out by our Heavenly Father. Not on account of the sins of our fathers, but the sins of our sons and daughters, the sins of all of us, Herr Baron."

"Did they suffer, Christoph?"

"Some did, Herr Baron, but not many. Most were broken by the iron tanks, but some of them were only half killed. The frost got them after a few hours. We could not bury them."

"And you, Christoph?"

"I was lying in the ditch, Herr Baron. I could not run in my big wolfskin coat. Those who ran across the field were shot. Then we put the horses into the vans again. There were just four left. We waited until the morning, and when nobody came anymore, we drove on. We have been driving for a long time. Sometimes they held us up, and sometimes they sent us the wrong way. I have been driving all my life, Herr Baron, with two or four or with six horses. But never as I had to drive now, never. I don't want to hold reins anymore, Herr Baron."

His face looked tired and drawn in the morning light, and a thin film passed over his eyes as over eyes that are going blind.

Then he drew himself up again, as if he were sitting on the coachman's box and had to drive the countess. "The water is boiling," he said. "Have you got coffee, Herr Baron? We have only barley, but anyhow it is homegrown."

Amadeus dressed quickly and went out. The country was sparkling in the morning sun, and he saw them at once in the golden light: a battered remnant. They huddled at a little distance from the sheepfold, where some big stones lay among the heather. But they neither sat nor lay there – they crouched on the stones and around them, and only a few children stood at their mothers' knees and looked toward Amadeus with their old eyes. They crouched there quietly without moving, as if night had drawn all life out of them. As if they had been here for many days and nights, without hope and without a plan, waiting for what should be decided about them. Their clothes were old, their shoes torn, and most children stood barefoot in sand and dew.

But Amadeus thought that the most terrible thing about them was their eyes. They looked as if they did not contain nor reflect anything. There was not even curiosity in them; there was nothing in them. They had seen so much that they neither wanted to say nor to see anything more. It would not have been so terrible had they been blind.

They got up as Amadeus came to them, and he saw that their lips even tried to smile. The women kissed his hands, and when he put his hands behind his back, they kissed the hem of his coat. The men stood there with their arms hanging down and looked at him. They did not look at him as they used to do, when he had visited them in their cottages or spoken to them at the edge of the field. Formerly he had been, as it were, of their own kind, a being of the same world, standing high above them, as if standing on a mountain. But now he had been removed beyond their reach to a gloomy realm beneath the earth, and they had not known that he would return once more with a human face.

Then the women began to weep, and that was more terrible for Amadeus than anything else. He stood in their midst and tried to pat their hands or their shoulders, as he had done when a child, but he did not succeed. He was bewildered at their wretched appearance as they stood there, and that they had been crouching silently around him while he had been asleep, perhaps throughout the whole night; that for them he was still the master, gifted with magic hands that could lift them out of their accursed fate. He was no longer a master and he had no magic. He was only full of fear. They did not know that he had been humiliated and beaten, that he hid and veiled his face from the earth and from time. That he could not bear so many eyes about him, so many outstretched hands, so many hearts that pressed hard upon him. Everything that once had been and had united them was lost in the depths.

Not even suffering linked them together, nor homelessness, nor death. They stood before him like shadows, like the departed who had risen once more from the rigidity of death from that nocturnal road under the willow trees over which the clanking caterpillar chains had rolled.

He tried to smile and did not understand why the women's eyes were filled with so much fear, even with some horror as they hung on this smile – as if a smile did not become him anymore. He did not realize that this smile distorted his face, because only the face smiled, not the heart.

He led them into the little room around the fire and spread all his provisions before them. Then he saw for the first time that Christoph still wore the long, blue coachman's coat with the silver buttons stamped with the coat of arms and the seven-leafed crown. And below that the rags that he had wound around his feet, and above it the smooth, white hair that fell over the collar of his coat. Now he understood why the people at the roadsides, at all the roadsides, had stared at him as at an apparition. That's what he was – an apparition from another century, much further back than the year of his birth.

He charged Christoph to care for them all, and he also put a packet of cigarettes on the table. He would now go to fetch his brother Erasmus who had been waiting for them every minute of the day and the night. His brother would know what should be done for them.

He went off quickly as if he were afraid that the children or the women might hold him back by his sleeve, and not before he had arrived in the shelter of the wood did he stand still and look around, as if he thought they might be following him. His heart beat painfully and heavily, and he felt as if behind each tree somebody was standing and looking at him, somebody who did not want to do him any harm, who only stretched out his hand gently and without saying a word, because he trusted him. The wonderful confidence of the past, the confidence of the poor in the hand and the heart of the master.

"I have lost so very much," he thought, deeply troubled, "so terribly much."

"You must come now," he said gently to Erasmus. "A few of them have come back."

Amadeus had to help his brother to put on his coat and his shoes. Erasmus was like a child that had been lifted out of a wolf's pit. But later he was able to speak to the forester's wife, to ask whether she would give them the barn for the time being. Then he would look after everything himself.

The woman was even willing to give them the house, all that he might ask for. She understood what this meant for Erasmus.

Then they returned, and now Erasmus talked almost without a pause. "Aegidius will know what to do," he said. "He will take them to the estate. People who can work are needed everywhere."

Amadeus stopped before they came to the last bushes. "I am going on the moors for a bit," he said. "It is rather much for me . . ."

Only now did Erasmus look at him. "Forgive me, brother," he said gently. "I have only thought of myself; I am afraid it has always been like that with me."

"You need not say that," replied Amadeus. "They did not come to me, none of them. They did not even know whether I was still alive. I am only a kind of ghost to them, and they will have to get accustomed to me."

"They will come to you, too, brother," said Erasmus in a sweet voice. "Somebody will be the first to come. We do not yet know who it will be."

When Amadeus came back about noon, the space in front of the sheepfold was empty. Something colored was lying among the stones, and he picked it up. It was a child's doll, or the remains of one. It was made of some coarse material, even the face. It had yellow eyes and one was torn. A tiny, yellow rag hung down from it. It looked as if a stone had hit it and as if it was running out.

Amadeus held the doll long in his hand, pondering what its name might be. Children always saved the most important items, he thought, in a fire or in any other emergency, while grown people always snatch up the most unimportant things.

He took the doll and put it in the farthest corner of the hearth, where the clay did not get warm. Its half-torn, yellow eyes, which the child was sure to have called golden, followed him now when he walked about in the room or picked anything up. So little could make up a home.

They had to carry on their backs everything with which the van was loaded, and it took them two days to do it. They also led up the lean horses. The gay, clear voice of Baron Erasmus was to be heard until late in the evening.

Then all became as quiet as it had been before. Christoph came in the morning and in the evening to the sheepfold to light a fire and to be at hand. Sometimes he was allowed to sit by the fire and Amadeus listened to him. Amadeus was not afraid of him. He seemed not to belong to this life anymore. He asked and required nothing. He was as one who got leave now and again from the underworld to sit with men and hold a chip of pinewood in his hand which he split with a big, old-fashioned knife. Even the knife looked as if it had been lost in the sand in pagan times.

Christoph did not speak of the days when they had been happy together. In his tales he went much further back, to the times of his father and grandfather, when something like serfdom still existed and when at the age of six he had started to polish the head harness of the carriage horses. His round Slav face became more and more absorbed in himself, and his bright blue eyes beamed with a light that did not come from the things of this earth but from the visions which were behind these things. His mouth had become a little twisted in his old age, and his lips drooped to the right where for a lifetime he had held his short pipe.

"Yes, the old families, Herr Baron," he said, taking the pipe from his mouth to press the glowing tobacco down with his forefinger. "Where the pictures hung on the walls and the children grew up with the dead. So much happens in these old families, Herr Baron – and in those times, you know, everything was different from today. Life was not as nowadays when everything can happen in one way just as well as in another; no, what happened then had to happen just as it did. Our Heavenly Father still looked at it, you know. He stood above the roof at night and looked on, and then everything happened as he willed. Do you understand, Herr Baron?"

Amadeus understood very well.

"The masters were not always quiet, Herr Baron," Christoph went on, lost in thought. "Some were wild and some were also hard. It is long ago, but my grandfather still remembered it. All of them, however wild, could be stirred.

"One of them gambled, you know. He gambled for ten years. And when the father of my grandfather stood with his sleigh and six horses in front of the house where the master was gambling, he did not know whether in that night the horses and he himself would be the stakes. At that time the masters even gambled away their men. At midnight, when inside the house the gamblers shouted and made a great noise, my great-grandfather peeled off one after another the rugs in which he had wrapped himself and went upstairs, whip in hand, as the baroness had ordered him to do. Then he stood behind the master in the golden hall, pulled him by the sleeve, and said, 'Pray excuse me, sir, but the mistress is waiting.'

"The master did not look up from his cards and his gold. 'Let her wait, Christoph,' he said. 'Back to the horses with you!'

"Then my great-grandfather went back to the horses.

"But after an hour he stood again in the hall, pulled his master by the sleeve, and said, 'Pray excuse me, sir, the fields and the cattle are waiting.'

"The master did not look up. 'Let them wait, Christoph,' he said. 'Back to the horses with you!'

"Then my great-grandfather went back to the horses.

"But after an hour he stood again in the hall, pulled his master by the gold-embroidered sleeve and said: 'Pray excuse me, sir, but our Heavenly Father is waiting.'

"Then the master laid the cards down, stuffed his gold into his pocket, and got up. 'Hold me by the belt, Christoph,' he said, for at that time the masters wore belts round their coats, 'and hold me fast so that I do not turn back.'

"Then they went out. My great-grandfather held his whip in his left hand, and with his right he led his master by the belt downstairs to the sleigh. That's what they were like at that time, Herr Baron, do you understand?"

Amadeus understood that too.

Christoph took a glowing cinder out of the hearth with his fingers and put it on the tobacco in his pipe.

"And once," Christoph went on, "it was in the early dawn, they saw a beggar standing on crutches at the roadside. He stretched out his hand. 'Drive on, Christoph,' called the master.

"But my great-grandfather stopped the six horses and waited.

" 'Drive on, Christoph,' shouted the master and stood up in the sleigh.

"But my great-grandfather undid his leather belt, unbuttoned his wolfskin coat and took a coin out of his pocket and gave it to the beggar; 'For Christ's sake, brother,' he said. Then he buttoned his coat again, buckled his belt, took up the reins and the whip and drove on. When they had been driving for a while the master said, 'What did you say to him, Christoph?'

" 'I said to him "For Christ's sake, brother," Herr Baron.'

" 'Drive back, Christoph,' commanded the master.

"And they turned around and found the beggar by the roadside, and the master poured all the gold he had won in the night into the beggar's cap. It was so much that some of it fell over the rim into the snow.

"Yes, the old families," concluded Christoph, and gazed into the fire, which was burning down on the hearth with a sighing note.

Christoph never said anything to show that he was worried about Baron Amadeus, and that his anxiety determined the choice of his stories. But when he got up and put the chips of pinewood on the hearth he sometimes said, "So it went with the masters formerly, Herr Baron. They could be aroused – and sometimes our Heavenly Father chose a simple hand . . ."

Amadeus liked to listen to him.

It was as if Christoph's hands turned the globe and this continent sank down, so that others, strange ones, might rise above the horizon. And with this continent that sank down, the last years sank down too, yes, perhaps all his own life, and it seemed as if nothing were left but the long line of the generations, all that was common to them and encompassed them. As if the baron Amadeus were only an unnumbered page in the great book which gently opened by itself, and that the triptych was something nameless, just as the father who had suffered himself to be deceived. Nothing was left but the character of the family, and God leaned down over the old roof, now long fallen in, and looked at it. This family, the members of which could in bygone times be "aroused."

Then Baron Amadeus remained sitting at the other side of the fire, his elbows propped on his knees while the last gleam from low flames fell on his idle hands, which he tried to warm at the golden embers. Only once before Christoph said goodbye he stopped by the baron, lost in thought, as if he were about to pluck his sleeve or to grasp his belt, and with his deep, kind old voice he said, "You poor, frozen master."

But Amadeus did not answer.

Nor did he ask much; he only sat there waiting. Old people like to talk. Christoph had had neither wife nor child, but only the horses and his masters. The horses were lost, but the masters still existed, as well as the whip which he had saved. There was no other token of office for a coachman of the nobility. The whip was for him like the scepter in the hand of a king.

Even without his horses he was still indispensable to these "young masters" whose hair was gray or already white, but who sometimes were as children at his knees, just as in times gone by, when he had sat on the oat bin and had given them the fruits of his life's experience: a serving life, poor and within narrow limits, but through serving his life had become so rich that there was not its equal in the manor house.

Now the two "young masters" lived up here, and they were as poor as he was. But Christoph saw very well that poverty did not oppress them. For the real aristocrat, poverty was neither a burden nor a disgrace. But he saw very well, too, that they were sometimes afraid. He did not know how great or how small this fear was, nor what they were afraid of – his eyes were too simple for that. But he realized that they were afraid like children. No wisdom was needed to console children. They only needed a pair of old hands which put the glowing cinder on the tobacco in the pipe, quietly and without trembling, even if the outside world came to an end.

He felt, too, that they were not afraid of the things that humble people feared. They were too noble, too high-born, and he knew well what that meant. They were afraid because their door was no longer locked, the door to the room where they could be apart. Because the door was forced, and because everybody could step over the threshold: the military police or a cattle dealer or a farm hand who asked for higher wages; afraid because they were still living in an aristocratic world and now suddenly nobody was obliged to wipe his shoes before stepping over their threshold. Not that they had ever asked anybody to wipe his shoes before entering their door, but they expected that this should be done in honor of the world in which they lived; a stately room perhaps, furnished with books and pictures. Or in face, their narrow, reserved features which were only in part their own, the other part belonging to the noble family whose name they bore and whose honor they had always upheld.

So Christoph was not surprised when Baron Amadeus asked him one evening by the fire whether he was afraid.

Christoph took the pipe from his mouth and bent down a little to the fire.

"When I was a small child, Herr Baron," he said, "so small" – and he held his hand with the pipe a little above the floor – "I was afraid as children are afraid. At that time we were still told of the Man in Black, the Corn Woman, and the Moor Witch. At that time the wood owl hooting in the oak tree predicted somebody's death. At that time little lights were to be seen on the peat bogs, and Queen Mab made plaits of elflocks in the manes of the horses. Perhaps it is still so today, and I believe it is so. But my eyes see it in a different way, Herr Baron, do you understand? My eyes are full of faith now, and he who is full of faith is not afraid. Our Heavenly Father can send the Man in Black to you, for he can send everything, but the Man in Black does not exist for his own sake, do you understand? Our Heavenly Father holds him on a thin thread and pulls him back, when it is enough."

"And our Heavenly Father?" asked Amadeus. "Would you not be afraid of him, if he were standing at the threshold?"

"Why should I be afraid, Herr Baron? If he should say: 'Are you there, Christoph?' I would put my pipe down on the hearth and answer: 'Come in, O Lord, here I am. But stoop a little, because the door is so low.' Do you think that it can give him pleasure to frighten me, Herr Baron? An old man with white hair? Who never stole any oats from the oat bin and has never lost his whip?"

"But if it were not our Heavenly Father who stood on the threshold, Christoph, but a human being? A friendly-looking man, but one whose clothes were transparent and you could see the knife around which his hand had closed in his pocket? Or you could read on his lips the words which he would speak before the court, lying words and words of betrayal? Or if you knew or believed that any man whom you know, everyone indeed, could stand before your threshold like that?"

Then Christoph raised his left hand which trembled a little and put his finger tips cautiously and gently on the folded hands of Baron Amadeus. And with a kind, quite beautiful smile he said,

"Can you believe, Herr Baron, that Christoph could stand like that before your threshold?"

"No, not you, Christoph, not you. But . . ."

"And even if it is only your old coachman who would not stand there, sir," said Christoph, "is it not always true that our Heavenly Father would have room to stand there? You see, sir," he went on gently after a while, "we, too, have had fathers, grandfathers, and forefathers. Many of them in far-off days were fettered and were whipped and some were whipped to death. But we do not carry it as a burden anymore, sir. Our Heavenly Father has taken the load from us. He has even taken to himself those who used the whip. I believe that he was more grieved about them than about those who shrieked in pain. Do you think, sir, that his hand is so small that there is no room for you in it – even though you are a baron?"

He sat quietly thinking for a time, then he took a cinder from the hearth and put it on his pipe.

"If God crucifies," he said gently, "he must take into his hand the one who is crucified. He does not stretch out his hand in vain, sir. He does not trifle, not he."

The fire died down, but the last crimson glow was still reflected on their faces.

"I am going to tell you something now, sir," said Christoph after a while. "When everything had come to an end at that time, we drove westward. We could not bury the dead, because the earth was frozen a meter deep. Snow had already covered them, when we had harnessed the four horses. We drove only by night; by day we camped in the woods and lit a small fire.

"We drove around the villages, because there was death in the villages. Once under the full moon we came to a village which was burned and deserted. It lay low, where there were only woods and lakes and marshes. One could think that it was the world's end.

"But it was not altogether deserted, for a dog was howling around the chimneys which were left standing. It was terrible to hear it, Herr Baron. The sky was crimson all around, and there was no living being on the earth, not a vestige of life. Only the dog was howling. The echo resounded from the wood and you might fancy that another, a second dog was howling there. And these two were all that God had left alive.

"We had no more oats for the horses and I left the others on the outskirts behind a wall and went into the village. I and my shadow – a big shadow, for I was wearing the wolfskin coat. I thought the shadow was too big for myself and for the burned village. I was afraid of my shadow.

"I found nothing; all was burned down to the foundations – except the church. It stood a little off the road on a hillock and was not burned. Perhaps they had not had time to climb up the hillock.

"I went up there. I had not found the dog, it always crept away when I came near. It may have been afraid of my big shadow.

"The church was built of wood, and I stopped in front of the door which lay in deep shadow.

"Then I got a shock, sir, yes. I was frightened to death. For somebody was sitting on the threshold. So wrapped up that I could not recognize whether it was a man or a woman. But it was a woman. At least it had been one. Now she was nothing but a ghost. She held something in her hand that looked like a child's toy, a rattle or some such thing. She raised this hand toward me. I believe lepers must stretch out their hands like that.

"But she was not a leper. She was only distraught. Something had crushed her, and she had been left lying in the snow. I only saw something white where her face was. I did not know whether she was alive, and yet she had raised the hand with the toy.

"I asked her many questions, but at first she did not answer. Then she told me everything. She may have been afraid of my coat, until I told her who we were.

"She told me everything. 'I am the only one left,' she said, 'I alone, I and the dog. We had done nothing to them. They killed men and women. The women screamed before they were killed. I heard them, because I did not scream. The girls had poisoned themselves beforehand. The doctor had given them poison. We had a great doctor in our village. He defended himself and they shot him dead.'

" 'And the children?' I asked.

" 'They drowned the children in the cesspool. They had to break the ice first, and then they drowned them.'

"Oh, sir, the words came from her white face as from the face of a dead woman; and all the time the dog was howling.

" 'Come along with us,' I said. 'You cannot stay here. There will be room for you on the sleigh.'

"I saw that she shook her head. 'I cannot come,' she said, 'for I am with child. By those who have slain. Many children. I don't know how many. It shall grow up under the cross, it cannot grow up otherwise, or it will be cursed.'

" 'What cross?' I asked.

"She lifted her hand out of the black shawl and pointed to the church door. It was in the shadow. 'Are your eyes blind?' she asked.

"I raised my eyes, sir, and I saw. A man was nailed on the church door and his head was bent. I may have cried out, for she shook her head. 'You must not cry,' she said. 'He did not cry either. He is our vicar. I cannot take him down, for he is frozen fast.'

"The dog was howling and I trembled, sir. I trembled in my wolf-skin coat.

" 'Now go,' she said. 'It shall grow up under this cross. A village must have children, or God wipes it out.'

" 'Come along with me,' I pleaded, 'for Christ's sake, come.' But she drew the black shawl around her again. Nothing was to be seen of her face after that. The dog was howling.

"Then I went off, sir, I and my shadow." He was silent, and his bright eyes stared into the dying fire.

"Thus it is written in the Bible," he went on gently after a while: "In the same night two will lie on a bed; one is taken, the other is left. Two will grind grain together; one is taken, the other is left. Two will be in the field; one is taken, the other is left. Thus it is written, sir.

"I asked her for the name of the village, but I have forgotten it. It may have been the village Nameless or Nowhere.

"Then we came into a district which Worgulla knew well. There were three burned villages one after another, but the signboards with the names on were not burned. The name of the first was Adamsverdruss, and I gazed at this name for a long time. The second was called Beschluss, and the women were afraid of it. But the third was called Amen, and it was there that we lost the wolves' track. Then we could drive by day, if the airplanes did not come.

"And now ask me once more whether I am afraid, sir," said Christoph. He got up and dusted the ashes of his pipe from his long coat. "Was the woman afraid who remained sitting there below the crucified man? And are we to be less than a cottager's wife in the village Nameless?"

But Amadeus did not answer this question either. He looked at the child's doll with its yellow, half-torn eyes that was propped in the corner of the hearth, and he did not hear that Christoph went out and gently closed the door behind himself.

The next morning one of the children stood at the door of the hut, a girl about six years old, timid and silent, her right forefinger in her mouth, and stared at the doll on the hearth.

"Is that yours?" asked Amadeus.

The girl nodded.

"What's her name?" asked Amadeus.

"Skota," answered the child. And Skota meant Goldie. Amadeus took "Goldie" from the hearth and gave it to the little girl. The girl wrapped it in her shawl and pressed it to her. Then she left without saying goodbye. Always from now on when Amadeus entered his room, he looked first at the comer of the hearth. But it was always empty. Goldie was gone.

Aegidius came the third day after the arrival of the cottagers. He had not been able to leave the wheat harvest. He sat on a bundle of straw in the barn of the forester's house and distributed the food and the clothes he had brought with him. He suggested that he should take them all the next evening to the estate of which he was now the bailiff. They needed workers as they needed their daily bread, and he would be a kind master to them. They would be responsible to him alone, only to him.

His face tanned by the harvest sun was beaming, and he looked from one to the other as they stood in front of him with their faces marked by fear and privation.

But then something strange happened – they did not want to come. Donelaitis spoke for them while he held his cap quietly and modestly in his hands.

They did not want to come because they wished to remain apart. They did not like other people, but they were fond of each other. They had never quarreled on the way. Donelaitis had looked around immediately after their arrival. There were a few wooden houses by the peat bog, well and solidly built, with clay hearths. During the war there had been much activity there with foreign workers who had lived in these houses. Peat was like gold at this time, and they could live there. In winter they could fell timber. So much timber had to be felled. He had spoken about it to the forester's wife. They would not suffer want. And they would be together.

Aegidius looked at him thoughtfully. "But you will be in the wilderness, Donelaitis," he said at last.

"Is not the whole world a wilderness today, Herr Baron?" asked Donelaitis. "And here it is a little like it was in the old days. It smells as it smelled at home, Herr Baron.

"But if you could help us a little, Herr Baron, with bedding and kitchen utensils, for instance, and with some wood so that we might have a bed and a table?"

Aegidius was not satisfied, but he had to give in. He went to Kelley, to the commissioner for refugees, and to the Landrat, and after two weeks the cottagers moved in. Christoph remained with Baron Erasmus in the forester's house.

All, even Amadeus, could not fail to realize that Erasmus had woken up. His hair had not turned brown again, and the lines around his thin-lipped mouth had not disappeared. But his eyes, his smile, his gait had changed. In the depths of his eyes there was no longer the snow-bound road with the willow trees and the twisted and frozen dead. It seemed as if there was a little life in their depths – twilight still, as at the bottom of some moor pool, but ready to light up when the sun shone.

He was on the move the whole day, after Aegidius had gone back for the winter tillage. He was to be found in all the offices of the district with Germans and Americans, and even though he always came to beg for something, nobody could bear him a grudge. They knew that he had been a general but they could hardly credit him with such a rank. His eyes were so kind and his shy voice had such a power of persuasion. Nor did he ever ask anything for himself. That was a great deal in times like these, when a defeated people rushed savagely and without consideration of those next to them to get to the few lifeboats left over from the catastrophe.

What he gained most quickly and without any trouble was the heart of each secretary, even the hardest, and he gained a lot with it. The old-world, rather touching courtesy of a long chivalrous life overcame all opposition. When he bowed in his reserved way, his soft eyes fixed on an impassive face and asked for a permit to buy a few bowls or a pair of working shoes, it seemed to those whom he addressed as if he were fetching them to a minuet in a hall hung with gilt-framed minors, and as if he felt it a distinction that he was allowed to make his request just to them.

"I shall be obliged to marry, brother," he said one evening to Amadeus. "It would be best to marry an American with slaughterhouses in Chicago, so that I can build a house for each of the cottagers and buy a piece of land for them. They cannot dig peat and fell trees all their lives."

"I don't know, brother," replied Amadeus seriously, "if that will be good for you."

"You think not?" asked Erasmus thoughtfully. "I don't think it can be so difficult. You see, the rate of exchange of generals stands rather high, even in the new Germany – unfortunately – even if they were such bad generals as I was. And the same is the case in Chicago where a baron is concerned, in spite of all their democracy. Liljecrona is a beautiful name for Mrs. Backwoods or whatever her name may be."

He smiled and looked gaily down at the enameled bowls which he had brought with him and had put on the floor.

"They would pull off your last coat, brother," said Amadeus, "and lead you through the streets with a placard tied on to you."

"Oh yes," replied Erasmus, "they are quite capable of doing that, but I could send dollars to the people on the moor. We have got to think that over well, brother."

Amadeus cast him a sidelong glance, but he could not find out whether he really meant what he said.

If Erasmus was not going about on errands, he stopped all day long in the small wooden houses on the moor. There was so much work for him to do that he never had any time to spare, especially with the children who had no other toy but Goldie, and there was nobody who could comfort so well and stroke their hair as he could. His whole way of living changed from day to day, and full of surprise he watched this transformation. Sometimes when he stood at the edge of the moor looking over its brown expanse, he seemed to see a cavalry regiment, his regiment, the sparkling of the head trappings of the horses and the soft fluttering of the pennants on the gray lances, and he himself on horseback at the head of them, rising up in his saddle, waiting for the bugle note which would call them to the charge.

A strange picture, so strange that it nearly made him smile, gently and a little sadly, as a man will smile when he looks back on his childish games. And something else was changed: he was no longer wrapped up in himself, as one might say.

Books, pictures, music, visits to the estates of the neighbors, the great, quiet office of a justice of the peace, the gentle aging in an environment of comfort and security, had not been granted him.

There were no hands to kiss and no perplexity of the heart to be disentangled here. He had to drive in nails, to make a kneading-trough, to provide new clothes for Goldie, and to make a boat of pine bark, in which a little mast could be fixed.

In the evening he had to sit by the fire and persuade the tired people that home was wherever they had a roof and a hearth and where they went to their daily work with a brave and sometimes even with a joyful heart. The world was not so secure as they had all thought, nor the yard fence, nor money. Not even the fatherland. The only security was in their hearts, which beat through good and evil times, and in the work of their hands, no matter whether they cut wheat or dug peat. Only he was lost who no longer felt the beating of his heart or who stretched out his hand in vain for an ax or a spade.

"God bless you, Herr Baron," said the women, when he stood up and smiled at them in farewell. When had anybody said this to him before? The young lieutenants had not said that when he had ordered them to appear before him for an interview, nor had his books nor his pictures, among which he had spent his days. Books and pictures had been silent, and the young lieutenants had said quite different things from "God bless you, General" or "God bless the general," as the official regulations would have worded it.

It was a beautiful farewell greeting to carry on his homeward way, and only sometimes did Erasmus stand at the edge of the moor, before he walked into the wood, and gaze back over the moonlit or gloomy wilderness. Mist hung over water and reeds, a night bird called out of the vast, starlit space and the shadowy shapes of twisted willow trees emerged and stood out against the luminous distance. Then the baron laid his hand on his beating heart and listened to hear whether he could distinguish one of the many voices that he heard above the depths: a voice different from those he had heard this evening; a distant, forsaken voice, one that had not been taken along with the rest; one that had been forgotten and that raised itself above the stir of the day and called far over the earth to those who had gone on, to those who lived and lived in security.

It was as if this voice knew that Baron Erasmus stood there at the edge of the moor, quiet and lonely, and that he must hear it, even if it was but the voice of a child that called out of the shawls in which it had been wrapped to protect it against frost and snow.

Then Baron Erasmus shivered and looked up to the full moon, as if from there balm might be poured down on his sore heart, the "balm of Gilead." But nothing poured down except the mild, cool, ghostly light, in which the willows cast their twisted shadows, as twisted as the hands of men that clutch at the last hope.

Then the baron turned away with a sigh and went into the darkness of the wood, where the voices were no longer audible. In the forester's house he went gently into the room where Christoph slept and sat down on the side of his bed, until Christoph woke up or pretended to wake up, for he never went to sleep before the baron had come home.

"Do you think that they have forgiven, Christoph?" he asked in a low voice. And in the dim moonlight Christoph could see how he folded his hands.

"It's their turn now to ask for forgiveness, sir," replied Christoph calmly. "Or do you think that the dead enter into the courts of heaven like a farmhand who thinks that he has not been paid enough wages? That they say: 'It's us, but we still have a reckoning to discharge down on earth'? There is no reckoning on earth anymore, sir. That has been puffed away like chaff. Suppose that one of them stretches out his hand with the account, don't you think that our Heavenly Father will lead him to one of the windows in heaven and say, 'Now look down!' And the man with the account will see a moor, exactly as it was at home, and a few cottages near the moor, and some men digging peat and some women cooking the dinner and some children for whom a baron carves a boat of pine bark. And the man will say, 'Are those the people, oh Lord?' And our Heavenly Father will answer, 'Certainly these are the people.' The man will look down for a while, will crumple the account in his hand and say gently, 'Forgive me, oh Lord!' And our Heavenly Father will smile and take the crumpled paper and will put it in the pocket of his grand, golden garment and lead the man back to his place, where the bowl with buckwheat groats stands and will say, 'I suppose the groats won't be so rich down there?'

"Oh, dear sir, is there anything a man has to forgive when he is allowed to touch with his hand the grand, golden garment?"

Then Baron Erasmus got up slowly, bowed as he did when he entered an office, and said, "Thank you, Christoph; you know it all as well as if you had been there."

"I have not been there," replied Christoph gently, "but I shall go there one day, if our Heavenly Father will have mercy on me."

5

WINTER IS THE TIME for the lonely – both among men and among wolves – and for those who live on the borderline. It covers the life of the solid ground and reveals the life to which we must lift our eyes. It is not the time of animals, nor of flowers, but the time of the stars. Snow does not grow up from the earth, it falls from the stars. It is cold and pure like the stars themselves.

There can be no hiding of tracks in winter, neither by man nor by wolf. Whoever walks over the snow must answer for it. Snow does not spring up again as trampled grass does. In the landscape a man towers as high as the pillar of fire in the wilderness. He who marks out the first track through the waste of snow must have courage. He who can face this winter desert must know inner harmony.

The only live thing in winter is fire. It rules evening and night. Whoever sits before it must have dismissed the specters that live in the heart or they will stare at him out of each flame. He must have forgotten the cries of the past or he will hear them in the low hum that each fire makes. A man must have gained his white hair in peace to be able to sit quietly by the fire, his hands clasped around his knees and the shadows of familiar objects about him.

Winter is the time of long nights, and everything casts big shadows. When the cock crows, it is as if the earth begins its first circuit. Nobody comes to the lonely and they go nowhere. They are alone with themselves as in a dungeon. Death stands behind the door.

Some write verses or play a melody. Some read books or look up to the stars. Some grind the grain of the past and weigh the flour in their hands. Some draw pictures of the future on the wall, and their eyes follow the footprints which go over a dream field.

All who live in the silence of loneliness are serious and most are truthful. There is nobody before whom they could act a part. Nobody before whom they could pretend to smile when their heart is sad. Nobody to whom it would be worthwhile to tell a kindly lie. The mirror in front of which they live is incorruptible. There is no applause for them and no curtain calls. This is not theater time for them, but the time for judgment. The judges sit veiled, their hands lie still on the dark cloth. They do not speak, they only listen.

The lonely man speaks, alone, without witness or audience. A fire burns on the hearth and casts its shadows. There is no future in the small room, only the past. There are hands that move, eyes and lips that smile. But they do not watch him. They are but shadows that glide past, and the lonely man follows them with his eyes. The judges are veiled, and it is not possible to know whether they can see.

The lonely man can get up and walk about in the small room. He can go to the little window and watch the moonlight on the dead wilderness of the moor. It is as dead as the moon itself. It might be a reflection of that cold satellite. He can pause in front of the cello and touch a string with his finger – there is a low, dying sound; it is there, and then it is not there. It has no meaning, it is not part of a melody.

There is danger in such a room in winter, that the things and the shadows may overpower the lonely man as the wolves overpower a sick prey. As the things in a prison overpower the prisoner. The lonely man must be able to raise his hand and exorcise them like a magician. He must be able to say, "I will walk over the moor tomorrow, but not where you want me to go. I will not go with you into that room with the gullies in the floor for the blood to flow away in."

He must not only say it, but do it. He may admit that he was broken, but he must will to rise again, even with broken feet. He must believe that they have broken his feet but not his heart. Much is needed to break a heart, and it rarely happens in four years. A whole lifetime is needed for that, and even then it rarely comes to pass.

When Amadeus closed his eyes and they were no longer filled with the shine of the fire, he sometimes saw before him the shrouded face of the woman who was sitting under the frozen and crucified man and perhaps was still sitting there. He heard the dog howl and the snow drift against the church door on which hangs the crucified man with his bowed head. His hair was white with snow, the sockets of his eyes were filled with snow. He was as dead as the wood to which he was nailed, and yet an immense power emanated from that head and, radiating for hundreds of miles, streamed into his room. A symbolic power and neither death, nor rigidity, nor decay can subdue it. The power of victory, victory over the shadows. Because he did not scream – the shrouded woman had borne witness of that. Because he probably smiled – dumb, kind, invulnerable. A young, simple vicar of the village Nameless.

Amadeus remembered again the words the shepherd had pronounced as they led him away: "Here is the patience and faith of the saints." He had raised his staff high under the great, sailing clouds and had given him these words to bear him company on his hard way. He had not understood them, nor had he gained patience and faith. Perhaps he understood now what patience means – "the cup for joy" – and if so he had gained much.

He opened his eyes again and looked around. The things were still there and their shadows, the movement of the lips and the hands. But they did not have power over him now, as they did in the beginning. Other shadows had stepped in among them: his brothers' shadows and Christoph's, who, whip in hand, stood at the gate of heaven.

Baron Amadeus had been given a pair of skis by First Lieutenant Hilary Kelley, and now he ran on them over the moor. The swampy ground was frozen hard and he could run over it in safety. Space was not limited for him. The sun cast his shadow on the even whiteness, or the drifting snow enveloped him. He was alone in a wonderful way, more completely alone than in summer. In the distance he heard the strokes of the cottagers' axes felling timber in the wood, and presently he saw the turf sledges to which the women had harnessed themselves. They used to go down into the plain to sell the peat and they would be home again before noon.

When the driving snow had covered the tracks of the previous day, Amadeus harnessed himself to the first sledge to make it easier for the women. It no longer cost him a struggle to go down with them into the villages. The inhabitants were not surprised to see a man among the women, although in some way he looked different. So many strange sights were pictured in the minds of these people that they no longer took much notice of what happened around them.

The women, knowing that he was unwilling to talk, did their heavy work in silence. At first they felt oppressed when "the master" put the harness over his shoulders, but then they accepted it. They were shy with him, but that was their heritage from the past. They knew that he had suffered, and that deepened their shyness. Masters ought not to suffer, according to their old-fashioned ideas.

Some time later Aegidius sent back one of the horses which he had taken to the estate when there was no food for them in the forester's house. After that it was easier for the women. The horse could draw peat to the villages and bring back firewood to the cottages, and that was Christoph's work.

None of them was alone now except Baron Amadeus. Not even his brothers. They had begun to take new roots, and a soft breeze already blew through the fresh young foliage. One had to be careful and cautious with them and must not lean too hard against their young growth, but they stood once more in time, and time began to heal them slowly.

Only Amadeus was still without time. He lived between day and night, as all earthborn things must live, but time was still something outside himself; he had not yet taken it into his blood and heart.

Sometimes Kelley came to see him, and then they would sit by the fire and talk.

But when he had left, time once more fell away from Amadeus.

They could talk about the things of the world, but they could not hold them in their hands. Or they only held them as playthings, and after a while they put them aside.

"Write it down," Kelley had said one day. "As I shall write it down. You free yourself from what you write down. You drive it out of your blood and put it on the threshold. Sun and wind will dry it, and then it becomes something different, no more a part of ourselves, but a product that has sprung from us. And after the labor pains comes calm. Write it down."

He had said it very seriously, and the baron thought much about it. Kelley, too, had been rushed into something that was against his nature, yes, something that he abhorred. He had not gone under, and he was only waiting for the time when he could climb out of the pit and cleanse himself. He was much younger than Amadeus, but he had not lost himself. He intended to retrace his footsteps to the starting point, and when he had reached it, he would begin anew. The fog had not bewildered him, nor the battle, nor the propaganda slogans. He had worn a uniform and carried a flag, but his heart was not changed. He had safeguarded his heart, and that was a greater victory than the saving of his life.

And one evening Amadeus began. He got up once to see whether the heavy door was firmly closed, and then he laid the white sheets on his knees and wrote. What he wrote was not verse and not a dream. It was reality, a naked and uncompromising y; but it was not a copy. This reality was only the raw mate- which he tried to mold, and he realized that this raw material ched back far into the past, beyond the picture of the shepherd no had raised his staff to the words of the revelation – back to the song which his old Lithuanian nurse had sung: "But the third, the youngest lad, was so sore, oh, sore at heart . . ."

And probably still further back to that Liljecrona who had ordered the coachman to turn about, because he had said, "For Christ's sake, brother."

The baron smiled perhaps, when he read the first pages, but later he did not smile. The judges had veiled themselves, but they were listening. He felt that they listened because somebody admitted and confessed.

The room was peopled with other shadow companions. No one was there to whom he could call, and yet the whole room was full of their potency. He saw the old Lithuanian nurse there, and the shrouded woman who sat under the crucified vicar, and beyond them he saw Christoph, whip in hand, and the figure of the little girl who pressed Goldie to her heart.

Amadeus learned the blessing and the fascination of work. How one becomes submerged as an island is submerged, and how, as one sinks, so disappear space, time, one's own breath, and one's own heartbeat. And how there emerges soundlessly and mysteriously another existence – a different space, a different time – hands that lift the cloth from faces, hands that open and close, lips that begin to speak. But they are unsubstantial, and in the light of the fire they fade and die away.

With his mind's eye Amadeus saw them so distinctly that no space and no time could take them away – they lived with a super-reality which penetrated even into his sleep.

Now only the girl Barbara was alone on the moor. Perhaps nobody but Christoph, whose eyes saw so much, knew it, but he was unwilling to speak about it. In the morning when she put on her skis, he saw her proud, rigid face. And behind this rigidity he saw the child's face that was as terribly lonely as the face of the woman on the threshold of the church.

Only he had "the patience of the saints."

Barbara had sent away the young men who in summer used to stand about with her behind the bushes at the edge of the wood. She despised people who cut telephone wires but were afraid to blow up the castle – it might have been done in the evening when the victors were sitting before their golden dishes. Who despises is alone. She loved nobody but her father; he was behind barbed wire, and she had realized long ago that her hands were too weak to set him free.

For many years, since her childhood, she had lived in a state of tension, with high-flown, intoxicating ideas which made her kneel down before idols like a fanatic. Now the idols lay in the dust and she hated, because there was no reason for kneeling anymore. She hated those who had overturned the idols as much as those who had not safeguarded them. But most of all she hated herself, for her faith was faltering. She was too intelligent to take for lies and propaganda all the statements that the victors now circulated. She felt that her roots had been cut by somebody, and as she could not recognize who had done it, she hated everybody, for everybody could be "somebody."

Most of all she hated those who had not knelt down and who could now pretend to have been right. And the deepest hatred of all she felt for Baron Amadeus, because she once had struck him. She did not yet know that she hated him because she hated herself. She was not too young for passion, but she was too young for discernment.

She skied over the moor, because the vast space and the silence suited her thoughts, and when she passed over the half-covered tracks of Baron Amadeus she pressed her lips together, as if she were passing over his life.

Until one day in a snowstorm he glided out of the juniper bushes and stopped in front of her.

He looked at her without anger as he said, “I do not wish you to ski here; I want to be alone, and there is quite enough room for you elsewhere.”

He saw that she gripped her hands about her sticks as she replied, “Are you still a master, that all this should belong to you alone?”

“Perhaps no master as you understand it, but perhaps somebody who ought to be left alone.”

“And I?” she replied with a sudden savageness in her face and voice. “Who am I that I cannot be left alone?”

He pulled off his right glove, took it in the left hand and looked at the snowbound solitude as if searching for an answer there. “You are a poor child,” he said kindly, and lightly stroked her face, which had turned deathly pale. “Not because you are suffering, but because you make others suffer.”

She still stood there long after he had disappeared behind the bushes. She stared down at his tracks, which were already covered by the driving snow, shivering as if he himself were still standing there. Only when she began to shiver in the cold wind did she turn around and glide slowly back to the forester’s house.

When her skis were dry, she greased the runners with wax and took all her gear up to the attic, where she kept it in a dark cupboard.

Erasmus and Aegidius talked it over with each other and decided that Christmas Eve should be celebrated at the shepherd’s hut, and that the cottagers should be there with them. Amadeus did not agree, but Erasmus pleaded with him so earnestly that he had to give in. “When our hair turns gray or white, brother,” said Erasmus, “we do not light the candles for ourselves, but for those who need their radiance. And you believe that they need a little, don’t you? Who else shall give it to them, if not their ‘masters’? You see the so-called masters of the last years did not just prohibit it, but they jeered at it, and that was hard for poor people. Things that made our hearts glad when we were children ought not to be mocked at. Now they have only got us, us three. In all these years God has left them a little in the shade, but we are still here. They can see us, we are reality to them, don't you agree?

"A master is not somebody who thinks of himself first. A nobleman always thinks of others first, and a brother always thinks first of the two other brothers, is that not so? Even though one is sad, one must not make others sad. You were away for so long, dear brother, that now you may well be with us for an hour, don't you think so?"

Thereupon Amadeus had given in.

Erasmus decorated the tree, and Christoph handed up the shining trifles which they had got in exchange for wood and peat and the things that Kelley had given them. Amadeus sat by the fire and looked on. Christoph's face was as attentive as if he were driving a coach and four, and Erasmus looked as if he would have liked to hum a tune, but he did not sing. He only stepped back, considered what he had done, and nodded to Christoph.

"Be sure to bring the girl along," said Amadeus, before they went back to the forester's house. "She needs it most."

Before twilight Jakob came and put three parcels under the tree. He only raised his hand when Amadeus thanked him and then sat down by the fire.

"It's not our custom to celebrate Christmas," he said, "but I feel the solemnity of it. How they fled to Egypt with an ass, and the soldiers of Herod searched for them – that was the beginning, Herr Baron. They also searched in these years, and they found not only those who were two years old. And they will search again in two years or in two thousand years, and they will find again. But there will always be an ass, Herr Baron, that will carry a mother and her child. Always.

"As I walked through the wood I saw the first star standing above this sheepfold. I knew that there would be no infant and no crib here, but that a man would be here whom the Holy One, blessed be he, has hidden from the soldiers of Herod. In the face of the Herr Baron there is a tiny little resting place now, no bigger than a little bird needs for its foot in the snow. The star above the sheepfold will shine upon this place in the face of the Herr Baron. Jakob will return happily to the camp, where they get parcels from all over the world. He will feel as if the angel of the Lord has smiled down on this roof." He got up and bowed.

"And you, Jakob?" asked Amadeus, as he had asked before.

Jakob gazed at the sparkling tree, and his old, sad eyes lighted up. "Jakob escaped King Herod and his soldiers," he replied, "but he lost the ass and what it carried on its back. Jakob is alone and his track is like a narrow ribbon in the desert. But the star will shine even on the smallest track."

Amadeus stood at the door of the shepherd's hut and his eyes followed Jakob. It was no longer snowing, and stars were sparkling in the canopy of heaven. A dog barked in the distance, and Amadeus could see the dimly lit windows of the cottages on the moor.

"Only he who realizes the insignificance of his own suffering can perfect himself," he thought.

Then he lit one of Kelley's candles and waited.

They all came, even Aegidius and Kelley and the forester's wife with her daughter. Erasmus led the two women in, and they sat down in a corner of the hearth where it was darkest, and where one of the old beams which supported the roof half hid them. They both wore black frocks, and the woman had drawn the shawl far down over her forehead.

There was room for all of them; the children stood at their mothers' knees, and Kelley sat on the wood by the hearth. The cottagers' parents used to take off their shoes when they were led into the hall of the manor house for the Christmas celebration, but these people could not do so, because snow lay high before the threshold; but they all looked as if they would have liked to respect the old custom.

Christoph had not yet arrived. Then they heard a little bell ringing in front of the narrow window – just as in their childhood. At first there was only a gentle tinkling, but then it rang quite close, as if the sound came down from the stars. They all knew that now the children should recite some verses, but there had been no time to learn verses, nor had they known that Christoph would remember this old custom.

They looked down at the ground, shyly and sorrowfully; then the forester's wife stood up in her dark corner, put her hands together, and in a low voice recited the verses of the hymn, as if she were a child called on by the bell to give evidence of the piety of her heart:

After fear and calamity,
after shivering and shaking,
after war and great horrors
which frightened the world

Give me and all those
who long – oh so eagerly
for Thee and Thy mercy
give us a patient heart.

Close the gates of the vale of tears
after all that cruel bloodshed
let streams of joyfulness
flow happily along.

The solemn words which had come down from the days of the Thirty Years' War still lingered in the little room long after she had sat down again, like a child that has performed her task.

The daughter had not moved. She had leaned her head against the rush-hung wall and with wide open eyes she stared into the shining candles.

Then Christoph came in, and Erasmus and Aegidius took the violins out of the cases and gently tuned the strings. The eldest brother looked entreatingly at Amadeus, but he only shook his head.

Then they played old Italian Christmas music, and without

realizing it Amadeus moved the fingers of his left hand, as if they were lying on the strings of his instrument.

After that Baron Erasmus as the eldest of the brothers read the Christmas Gospel. They had no Bible, so he read it from a sheet of paper onto which he had copied it. The candlelight fell on his white hair, while his face was in shadow, but Amadeus thought that his face was shining brighter than his white hair.

Amadeus had never known whether his eldest brother had faith or not. Even at this moment it seemed to him a matter of indifference. There was so much "faith of the saints" in this voice and around these thin lips. And if it only brought consolation and hope into the hearts of the needy, even then it was "the faith of the saints"; perhaps it was more than that.

There he stood, the man who had spent half his life on horseback, commissioned to train young soldiers in the military profession, to teach them how to kill and how to conquer – and now he read the words about the child in the manger as if the angel who had witnessed it were standing behind him. Erasmus stood there as if no roof but that of a shepherd's hut had ever been above him, and no other floor but its clay floor had ever been under his feet. There he stood, free from all sadness like one who has divested himself of all earthly concerns and must be cheerful because the eyes of the sorrowful are fixed on him. One who has to care, but not for himself. One who has lost, but who does not stoop to search for what he has lost, but for what others have lost.

Then he spoke to the cottagers, but what he said in his low voice had nothing to do with piety, nor with the homeland, nor with all that had been lost in the war, but only with the children. He reminded them that only a few had been saved, and that these children were the harvest of this whole year and of all the years of their lives. They had saved the helpless, and now they must take pity on all the helpless. All – he repeated it. They ought to be joyful as long as there was a single child among them. As he said this, he glanced at Goldie, which looked at him with its torn, yellow eyes, while the child pushing close up to him pressed the doll to her heart.

When he had finished and had put the sheet of paper with the Gospel on it into the pocket of his coat, he retired for a little time into the dark corner behind the hearth and sat down quietly with the two women dressed in black, who sat there motionless like two shadows.

While Baron Aegidius distributed what he had brought from the estate, Kelley stirred the contents of the bottles, which Christoph opened one after another, in a big, iron saucepan on the fire. They drank the hot punch out of mugs and earthenware bowls, and the children carefully ate the biscuits which the "big woman" had baked for them. They did not speak much, nor were they particularly cheerful. They gazed into the light of the candles and listened when the foreign lieutenant told them about the Christmas customs in his homeland. But they felt at home here. The endless roads of their flight were lost in the fog above which the stars glistened. The missing and the dead had disappeared, and the moaning and sighing were heard no longer. Their masters were here – that which for them was unshakeable in life. These masters had not expelled them nor had they let them sink. They held a shield over them as they had done for centuries. They did not care whether there was a new order in the world, with no rulers and no servants; they preferred to remain in the old order. They did not yet see "rivers of joy," but they saw a roof above the candles, and as they were going home under the stars, they would see their own roof, and after that night under the twisted willow trees a roof was something marvelous – just as the stable had been something marvelous for the mother of Christ.

Then one of the women who sat in the shadow said: "If the masters will permit it, tell us a story, Christoph."

Christoph sat on the edge of the hearth next to the forester's women, smiled, and filled his short pipe with fresh tobacco. His

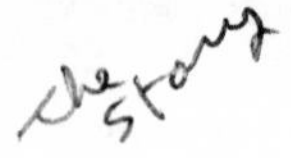

threadbare coat of blue cloth was properly brushed and the light of the candles shone on the buttons with the coat of arms and on his white hair. Behind him his shadow fell large and silent on the bright wall.

He smiled at the brothers, one after the other, and then he looked into the lights and shadows of the tree.

"My grandfather told us this story," he began. "When his father's father drove the horses, they had a master who was strict and sharp with his tongue; he had been long in military service, right back to the time of Emperor Napoleon. He was not a hard master, but he had seen much that was hard and cruel during his campaigns, and he was used to order and not to obey.

"One Christmas Eve the grandfather came driving with him from a little town, and he drove fast, for it was already time to light the tree. They had been delayed and the snow was falling fast. At that time there were still wolves in the forest, and they had lit the lanterns on the sleigh and the master held a rifle on his knees.

"When they drove out of the forest and were in sight of the dimly lit windows of the manor house, the grandfather all of a sudden stopped the four horses, for in the light of the lanterns a child stood by the road. It was a small child, a boy, and snow lay on his shoulders. The grandfather said that he was amazed, because there was no snow on the boy's hair, only on his shoulders. And it was snowing fast. But the boy's hair was like gold, without a single snowflake on it.

"The child stretched out his right hand, palm upward, as if he wanted to have something put in it. He looked like a laborer's child, only more delicate. He had a happy, smiling face, though he was all alone on the edge of the deep forest, and now when the bells of the sleigh were not ringing anymore, they could hear the wolves howl in the distance.

"The horses stood still and were not frightened.

" 'Drive on, Christoph,' called the master impatiently. 'It is late.'

"But the grandfather did not drive on. He had folded his hands in the fur gloves over the reins and gazed at the child. Later he said that it had been impossible to take his eyes off the child.

"'Drive on, Christoph,' shouted the master and stood up in the sleigh.

"But the grandfather did not drive on. He took the rug from his knees and lifted it a little, and the child put his foot on the runner of the sleigh and sat down at the side of the grandfather. The boy was smiling all the time.

"The master was so angry that he forgot himself. He was not angry over the child, but because the grandfather had not been obedient, and the child had been the cause of the disobedience.

"So the master stood right up in the sleigh in his splendid uniform and his fur coat, grasped the child's shoulders, and tried to throw him into the snow.

"But the child did not move. There he sat smiling and gazing at the horses and their large shadows thrown by the light of the lanterns. The grandfather, holding the reins, looked on. He said that he could not raise even the little finger of his hand. He was rather taken aback but he was not afraid.

"Then the master jumped out of the sleigh with a terrible curse, a curse which perhaps he had learned in the times of war and death. He stood at the side of the runner and raised both his arms, meaning to pull the child out of the sleigh.

"But the child did not move. He even raised both hands as if he wanted to show that he was not holding on to anything. And he smiled.

"The snow was still falling in the light of the lanterns, and it was so quiet that the grandfather could hear his heart beat.

"'Get in, sir,' he said in a low voice, 'for Christ's sake get in.'

"And the miracle was that the master obeyed. He got in and they drove on.

"The grandfather could move his hands again. The child sat quietly at his side. No snowflake was to be seen on his golden hair. But when they drove into the courtyard they were very much afraid. For in the moment when the sleigh drove below the coat of arms on the archway all the windows suddenly were lit up: the windows of the great house and the windows of all the cottages and the stables. It was so bright that the whole yard was bathed in light – a brightness, the grandfather said, that was not of this earth. All the cottagers came out of their houses, and the animals' heads appeared at the stable doors, as if the beasts had been untied: the horses' heads, the cows', the sheep's. Without making a sound, the people and animals gazed at the sleigh, which drove up in a sweeping curve and stopped before the flight of steps in front of the manor house. And they all saw the Child – all of them. There was not one who did not see him.

"The Child was the first to get out of the sleigh. But he did not step down, said the grandfather, he floated – without weight – like a snowflake. He turned round once to the sleigh and smiled, and then he went across the courtyard to a cottage where a little boy lay dying. They all knew that he would not live through the night.

"And when the Child from the sleigh stepped over the threshold of the cottage, the lights around the yard suddenly went out, and the people were as if dazzled and groped their way to the stables to tie up the animals.

"But the grandfather got down from the sleigh and helped his master up the steps, for he could not walk alone. Inside in the large hall where the tree was and where the antlers and the pictures hung on the wall, and where the stuffed birds stood, the master looked about him, as if he were in a dense, unknown forest, and in quite a strange voice he said, 'I thank you, Christoph.'

"But the cottager's child was well again by the morning.

"Yes," concluded Christoph in his low, gentle voice, "that was the night when the grandfather drove the Christ Child."

He got up, took a cinder from the fire for his pipe, and sat down again by the hearth.

The candles burned down without a flicker, and in the hush they could hear how the frost was splitting the trees in the forest.

After a long pause a woman spoke up again: "If the masters will allow it, tell us another story, Christoph."

Again Christoph glanced at the brothers and took the pipe out of his mouth. "My grandfather told this story," he began. "When the grandfather of his father drove the horses, they had a vicar at the church on the estate who was a shy, humble man and very poor. And he had seven children. In the castle there lived after a good master whom they had called 'the saint,' a harsh master, as happens now and again in wild times. It was still the time of serfdom.

"On Christmas Eve, because he felt lonely, the master had detained the vicar in the manor house and had kept him back, as if he were a sort of toy which he could take out of a box or put back when he was so minded.

"When the master had drunk a great deal of the hot punch, he wanted to play at dice with the vicar for a couple of gold coins, although he knew that the vicar was as poor as a church mouse.

"The vicar refused. As long as he had been on the estate he had never refused anything, and he knew that it was dangerous to have a will of one's own. He did not refuse because he was poor. He refused – so he said in his humble way – because the soldiers had cast lots for the garments of Him who was born this night and had lain in a manger.

"The master looked long at him while he shook the dice in the leather box.

" 'Cast the dice, vicar!' he said.

"But the vicar shook his head.

" 'Once more I say: cast the dice, vicar!' said the master, and his lips were pale and thin.

"But the vicar shook his head and only folded his hands on the white tablecloth.

" 'If you do not cast the dice – and thus refuse to do what your master commands you,' said the master, 'I shall have you whipped like any disobedient servant, and you will be given as many strokes with the whip as I shall throw pips on the dice out of this box. Once more: cast the dice, vicar!'

"But the vicar shook his head.

"Thereupon the master got up slowly, shook the box, and let the dice roll on the white cloth. He kept his eyes fixed on the vicar's face, and only after a long pause did he count the pips on the dice. 'Seven, vicar,' he said. 'As many as you have children; for each child the whip will strike you once.'

"He roused all his household and all the serfs on the estate, men and women, and ordered them to come into the large hall. 'This man,' he said, 'has refused to play at dice with me, and thus has treated me, his lord, with contempt. Bind him so that I can have him whipped, seven strokes, one for each of his children, and so that you may learn what it means to treat me with contempt.'

"But none of the people stirred. The grandfather in the foremost row heard how the men groaned and the women wept. But they did not move.

"The master looked sharply at each one of them and then he smiled. 'Your turn will come, too,' he said. And then he called the overseer. The overseer was a hard man, even harder than the master himself, and he stepped forward.

"He bound the vicar to one of the two columns which supported the ceiling of the hall, tore his clothes from his shoulders and struck him seven times across his back. The blood ran from the vicar's white skin, and the men and women went down on their knees and prayed. They had covered their eyes with their hands. The vicar did not utter a sound.

"When they had unbound him, he walked to the table and looked down on the dice which still lay there as they had rolled out of the box – two-three-two – and then he looked at the master: 'Pray,' he said in a low voice, 'that the Child may look at you tonight, or it will never look at you again.'

"Then he went out of the hall with the others.

"The next morning the master drove to church, as had been the custom since time immemorial.

"He did not walk, though it was not farther than one could throw a stone from a sling. The grandfather went behind him into the church and left his grandchild with the horses.

"The church was crowded, and the master sat in his carved pew and had folded his hands in their white gauntlets over his prayer book. It was as quiet as the grave.

"The vicar was pale, but otherwise there was nothing to show that anything had happened to him.

"After the prelude, when the little organ began to play the melody of the opening hymn, the vicar raised his eyes from his folded hands and looked at his congregation. For the congregation did not sing. No mouth opened, and everybody's eyes were fixed on him. They heard how the master stamped his foot once. They heard it, because the wheel of his silver spur clicked.

"But then the master sat quiet and sang. He sang the three verses of the hymn in his high-pitched, melodious voice, and he sang alone with the vicar. No other lips moved. The grandfather said that few events in his life had been as awful as this.

"But the vicar did not look at him who alone sang the Christmas song with him.

"He saw his seven children who sat with their mother opposite the pulpit, and the mother was a thin, bent woman.

"Then the vicar read the Christmas Gospel according to St. Luke; everything was as it always had been. When he had finished reading, something happened at which the hearts of the faithful trembled once more, for the vicar did not go on to interpret the Gospel, but in a low voice began a solemn memorial address on the life and body of the late Hjalmar von Liljecrona, and the deceased man was sitting opposite him in the old, carved oaken pew and staring as one whose senses God had darkened.

"'He died,' said the vicar, 'because he had thrown dice for the swaddling clothes of the Child in the manger, and because the

Child had turned his eyes away from him. He died, because he had not only thrown dice for the clothes of this holy Child, but for the clothes of seven poor children of this world, and with them for the clothes of seventy times seven children.'

"'And he had died in such a terrible way that he was walking about like a living person without knowing that he was dead, while everyone in the congregation beheld his living corpse and turned away from him shuddering, because he was stinking like the dead man in the story of Lazarus.'

"And the vicar had got so far, when the master jumped to his feet with a frightful curse, pulling his sword out of its scabbard. 'Take back that word, you devil of a vicar!' he shouted in a hoarse voice. 'Take back that word!'

"But the vicar did not heed him any more than he would have heeded a breeze wafting through the church, and he folded his hands to pray for the dead and asked the congregation to do the same.

"Then the most terrible thing happened; the master sprang to the foot of the pulpit and, grasping his sword in the middle of the blade, hurled it at the vicar's heart.

"Now, beautifully carved in wood in the wall of the pulpit was the mother of Christ, holding the Child in her arms and lovingly protecting him. And the sword – though hurled from so near – missed the vicar and buried its point in the heart of the Child Jesus, quivering there for a time, like the shaft of an arrow. Then it slowly sank, drawn down by the heavy baskethilt, fell on the pine boards of the floor and broke into a thousand pieces. And my grandfather as well as many others saw a thin trickle of blood run down from the wound in the wood and drip onto the floor and onto the steel of the blade, which turned crimson.

"Then, for the first time that morning, the vicar looked at the master who stood below him. He did not look at him angrily – there was not even reproach in his glance. He only looked at him in deep sorrow, as one may look at a picture of someone who is dead, and he remained so when the master had fallen on his knees and covered his face with his hands in the long, white gauntlets.

"And so the vicar led him out of the church, slowly, step by step through the kneeling congregation. When the master refused to get into the sleigh, they led him through the snow to the manor house, the vicar on one side, bareheaded, and my grandfather on the other side, the whip in his free hand and an expression of consternation on his face.

"From that hour the master was a changed man, as many of his line before him had been changed, because it lay in their blood.

"Yes," concluded Christoph in his low, gentle voice, "that was the night when they cast dice for the Christ Child in the old house."

Then he took another cinder from the fire for his pipe and sat quietly on the edge of the hearth, looking into the candles which were burning down.

Soon after the people started for home, and as they slowly walked through the snow it was as if the old stories went with them, the stories of the old, gloomy houses where so much happened but where men could still be changed, if a voice could touch their hearts.

They did not go away in a sad mood. They only felt as if they had been lifted out of this strange land for a while and put back into their lost homeland, where the Christ Child could still stand at the edge of the woods, or could be struck by a man's sword without being harmed by it.

The brothers still sat on by the fire for a time, and Erasmus was the first to break the silence. "If we consider," he said, pondering, "If we consider what our ancestors were like – and I am sure they were like that – then I can only say that it's a miracle how we have come through it all."

"Do you know that we have come through it?" asked Amadeus.

Erasmus smiled and put his hand on Amadeus' knee. "Dear brother," he said and his voice was full of love, "we are such that it does not take a loud voice to change us. We make it easier for them, also the child Jesus."

"Are you quite sure?" asked Amadeus.

"Yes, brother, quite sure, and so are you without knowing it, and so are you."

When the brothers left, Amadeus' eyes followed them from the door of the hut, and he saw how one of them walked down the mountain and how the other disappeared in the shade of the wood in front of the forester's house. A winter moon stood high above the sparkling moorland, and, in the south, Orion's belt glittered above the snowbound woods. The dog barked again on the lonely farm, and for a while Amadeus thought of the village Nameless, of which nothing had been left but a woman, a dog, and the crucified vicar. Probably none of the three was there now; perhaps they had become symbols – raised above their mortal state.

For a short time the baron also remembered last year's Christmas tree. "They" had put a real tree on the parade ground of the concentration camp. On its strong branches, lit up by flares, three men had been hanged, and a cold wind stirred the three bodies gently. The prisoners, men of almost all nations, had been forced to stand around the tree for many hours without moving, while the symbols of a "new time," with sightless eyes, had looked away over them into the distance that was not lit up by a single ray of light.

Erasmus had been so certain that it did not take a loud voice to change them, so terribly certain.

But Amadeus, as he closed the heavy door of the hut behind him, was not quite so certain.

6

THEY ALL GOT THROUGH the winter, all of them. Some got through it as one gets through an illness – with hope and patience – and some as one gets through a time of solitude which rests the heart and thoughts after one has lived for a long time in turmoil or at the edge of turmoil.

The cottagers felled the trees and went to their work at dawn, their feet tied up with rags, the ax or the saw over their shoulder, as they had done in the woods of their homeland. Their breath froze on their lips, and at noon they lit a fire and the blue smoke rose quietly over the tops of the trees.

The women sold peat and firewood in the village, and nobody could read in their quiet faces whether they thought life and times hard or easy. But marriage had always put an end to a woman's youth, and used as they were to heavy daily work they could scarcely remember a time when life had blossomed, so it was perhaps easiest for them to put up with the great change.

Only Erdmuthe, the young wife of Donelaitis, sometimes loitered behind the sledges, put her hand over her eyes so that the sun might not dazzle her, and looked around in the shimmering wilderness, as if she expected to see somebody on the horizon, a messenger perhaps, coming to them with great tidings. Her beautiful, young face with the fair hair falling around it looked neither happy nor sad. It looked only as if she ought not to be gazing here over the moor, but from the crest of a sand dune on her native seashore toward the distant horizon, to see whether some sail appeared, a narrow, white or brown triangle like a bird's wing; and this bird would shine in all the colors of the rainbow, like the birds in the fairytales of her homeland. Like her husband, she came from the shores of the Curonian Lagoon, where the fiery beams of the lighthouse circled through the darkness of the night and where the passions of men were less tamed and more unbridled than in the quiet security of the inland province.

But when the women called her, her hand dropped and she followed obediently in the tracks of the others. The women never asked her what she had been thinking about.

The children grew up in tranquility and roamed about freely, and slowly, very slowly, they ceased to start up in their dreams screaming until the mothers took them to their hearts and with their hands wiped from their eyes the terrible pictures which hung there as in a gloomy, bloody hall.

The forester's women also got through the winter, and Baron Erasmus, as well as Christoph, helped them a little. The baron now no longer believed that the girl had designs on his life, but every morning he could see anew that she looked right through him as through a wall of glass. The wall did not mean anything to the girl, only the pictures behind the wall, and the baron had not the faintest idea what they were like.

Baron Aegidius worked day and night to rebuild the estate which had fallen into ruin, and the lady of the manor neither hindered nor encouraged him. Without a word she yielded to all his plans, and with unfaltering kindness she spoke to him, gave him free play, and surrounded him with warmth and gratitude.

As for Amadeus, outwardly he had not altered his way of living. He no longer came across any stranger's track on the moor, and in the evening he sat bent over his sheets of paper and tried to disentangle the threads of his life and of the times, and it appeared to him to be a miracle that one could pin down the passing of life in scrawled handwriting, by a continuous movement of the hand, as it were – not only life's pictures but also what had existed behind the pictures: his own heartbeat and that of many other hearts, and the immeasurable, uncountable variety of thoughts, emotions, hopes, and despairs that had flowed through the blood with this heartbeat.

As it was an incomprehensible miracle when under the cello's bow the invisible world emerged from the instrument – that which cannot be expressed on any sheet of music, because the writing conveys to the human ear nothing but the vibrations of the strings, clear vibrations which can be calculated mathematically, but which have nothing to do with what sinks from the ear into the heart, to evoke there the miracles of existence and to reconstruct a whole universe, vast and enchanting.

He did not long for any other work, for instance that of "reconstruction," of which the newspapers wrote so much. He had already experienced after the First World War how the flood of words poured down over the ruins, and how in a disastrous way people forgot that the reconstruction of their own small lives was the most urgent and most important work laid before their hands. And so, out of the thousand-fold multiplicity of the small, unreconstructed lives, the disaster had arisen which had devastated the world – and the hearts of the world.

He did not mind that for the time being he did "nothing," as they would call it outside, and as they had always called it. He accepted it calmly, because each hour he was dimly conscious that something great was awaiting him: to sink his severed roots once more into the soil and to mature. To attain a ripe old age appeared to him an enormous task, and he believed that in a ripe old age the grains would fall to earth as quietly as in a wheat field which had not been reaped in time; and perhaps it made no great difference whether these grains became the food of birds or of people. It only mattered that they existed, and that they were not hollow, and above all that they had not grown bitter.

Even in his seclusion he could clearly recognize that the country as well as the period was filled with bitterness, and it was not only the bitterness of the defeated and exiled. A cup for which they had stretched out their hands had been snatched from them. They had been deprived of the "riches of the earth." Very few understood that they had not been deprived merely of food. The face of humanity had been changed in a decisive way. What the times and their devilish instruments had left behind was a human face that could no longer mature, that was ageless and consequently without any future.

Those who lived in barracks and caves were not disconcerted because they had neither house nor bread nor clothes, but because there was no quietude in which to mature. They could not imagine the bench under the evening sky, where they could rest with folded hands, where children sat on the ground with birds around them waiting to receive their evening meal.

The victors were troubled because the reward of their victory fell to pieces in their hands as a temporary and perishable reward, and there remained nothing but fear of the world, of the terrible face of the world turned to stone in its loneliness. A world that might bring upon itself the next catastrophe even tomorrow, for catastrophes cannot be averted by guns and airplanes but only by the calm and almost sacred power of those who have become mature and benevolent. The victory of arms, even if it had been gained by intellect, was like chaff on the threshing floor of the earth. But the victory of the heart was the only one which could master the demons.

But where was the victory of the heart in this world? Thus Amadeus was not concerned with whether he did anything or nothing. His only concern was whether he could change himself or become changed like those whose stories Christoph had related as an example to him. Not that he could change from a wolf into a lamb, but he would like to be a master over wolves and lambs – not a master through force, but through the realization that wolves and lambs both belong in the great circle of creation, and that maturity does not mean the hatred of the one and the love of the other. He was concerned to bring it about that evil should, as it were, emigrate from the world, because it has become alien to the world, and it is no longer necessary to fight for a lamb.

In the silence of the moor and over his sheets of paper, the baron also recognized that whoever became hard in hard times did not master the times, but became a partner with them and consequently their slave. These did not win any grain; they only won booty or gold. And those who were indifferent did not win anything either, nor did the orators, nor the prophets, nor the victors. But Jakob had won his grain, though he had lost those who sat on the ass to escape into Egypt. He had won a little room in his face, where God could rest when his feet had grown weary. Times were such that even God's feet could grow weary. Jakob had not only won room, he had also lost all fear. He had been more deeply and lastingly victorious than all the victors of this war. He was a ripe ear in a field of unripe and hollow ears.

Amadeus remembered something that he had long forgotten. He remembered the face of the girl when she had come to the sheepfold with her mother for the first time. When they left he had said a few words to the girl, but he had forgotten what they were. He only remembered the girl's face when he said these words. He had felt that it looked like a frozen face and that hatred had made it freeze. It was quite unimportant what kind of hatred it had been and what had been its source. In his mind's eye he only saw a face in which hate was the master.

When she had gone away, he had taken up the little broken looking-glass, one of his possessions, and had gazed into it for a time. Then he had thought that he would not want to look like that girl – never – and especially not in his old age. At that time he had not yet considered whether he should hate or not hate. He had only thought that he would not like to live with such an expression in his small room or on the moor. Probably he could not avoid being afraid of people, but he would not like to be afraid of himself. What kind of life would that be, if one were afraid of one's own face?

He remembered it now, and he was filled with a little hope that he remembered just this. It had not fallen through him as through a sieve with too large a mesh. It had been stored away and had emerged at the right moment.

What he learned about the happenings in the world did not make him more sociable. It did not make him uncertain either. Jakob and Erasmus brought him the gossip of the day, and Kelley brought him newspapers and books. He listened and he read the papers and books. Now and again somebody called on him under the pretext of some official occasion: the commissar for fugitives or perhaps someone representing "the victims of the Nazi regime." He looked at them while they spoke, and he listened. But he felt that they were "on the further shore"; a wide river was between him and them. He did not know exactly whether it was the river of time or how one should term it. But there it was: dark water flowing mysteriously, and he saw neither bridge nor ford.

What in the beginning had been like a foreboding in him, he now realized more and more clearly as a fact: that with the victory of arms nothing or next to nothing was gained. That the acrobats and jugglers and conjurers – those of politics and of art, those of the weltanschauung and those of words – especially those of words – were still standing on the stage, as they had probably stood for a couple of centuries. That the enormous gulf between word and life had not been filled up. That the jugglers juggled with words to convince the onlookers that their words meant life. Then they left the stage, their hands full of gold, but not full of corn, in order to make room for other jugglers. Something deeply shrouded sat in the background – perhaps the woman on the threshold of the church, before whose white face all jugglery came to an end.

And so Baron Amadeus "did nothing," he only wrote and meditated and paid little attention to the expression of his face. He only tried, unheeding of the jugglers, to recover the life which he had lost. He did not attempt the task with placards or titles – with the placard of "democracy," for instance, or that of "freedom" – he did so without any title, just from his heart. He did so after considering the variety and the sum of what his ancestors had left behind and had bequeathed to him, and with the simplicity of times gone by, those times in which Christoph's forefathers had driven the Christ Child, and in which men had "heard the call," men who had never dreamed of being changed.

With such considerations Amadeus also got through the winter, even though he did not believe that immediately after the last snowstorms his wheat would sprout and bear fruit.

There happened, when the snow had melted, two or three things on the fringe of his life which cast their shadows on the doorstep of his hut. The first was that the victors left the castle, and the local authorities requisitioned it for the displaced persons. The second was that Aegidius told them one evening that he intended to marry the woman on whose estate he was bailiff. The third was that the "dark one," as the people of the district called him, appeared at the edge of the moor.

In the matter of the displaced persons, Erasmus showed himself to be the second of the brothers who could "do something." He undertook the discussions with the authorities, a host of discussions. He shared out the rooms, had them cleaned and put in order by the women, and with their help and Christoph's, he carried the necessary furniture from one wing of the castle to another. He also accepted the offer of the authorities to live in the two small rooms which they were willing to give him. Christoph was to move to the castle with him, but for the first time he refused. He wished to stay with the two women who needed him, as he said. He did not wish to live in a castle; that was not for him. And he did not want to be so far from the youngest master, who might perhaps need him some time. Erasmus gave in at once to this last argument.

Now and again Erasmus came up to the sheepfold in the evening and sat on the threshold in the warm spring air and told about his experiences. "You cannot imagine, brother, what it is like," he said with his kind, rather melancholy smile. "How our Heavenly Father managed about everything in Noah's Ark, I don't know. But then, he was God Almighty. But what is assembled and installed down there, that is beyond my imagination and power: I am trying to lead it, but how can you lead a squadron which is ready to bolt? There are businessmen and tramps, dignitaries and cigar merchants, acrobats and scientists, a real count and a real poet. They flap about like fish out of water, and like fish they snap for air. That is what strikes you first. Each does it in a different way, but most do it in a noisy way. I did not know how noisy it can be in such a small corner of this earth."

"And why do you remain there?" asked Amadeus.

"Well, I feel it is a kind of duty, brother," replied Erasmus, gazing into the sunset glow. "You see, I am perhaps the only one who does not want anything for himself, not even my small rooms, for it was much more beautiful with the forester's women. But I think when they see that I live in peace, it might help them a little to long for peace, too."

"Do they not live in peace?"

"They would like to tear each other's hair, brother. Especially the women. I did not know how much activity can be bottled up in a woman."

"You might have learned a little about it in the last twelve years," said Amadeus smiling.

"I know, I know," replied Erasmus. "You see we are people who do not like to go to fairs. We sent our bailiff or our men with what we wished to sell, but we did not like to go on a merry-go-round, did we? We did not like the music, and we did not like the people who sat on the little horses to the right and left of us. I suppose we were too proud, brother."

"I don't think that we were proud," said Amadeus. "We were only quiet, and quiet people don't like fairs. We have missed many opportunities to learn, and we must make up for it."

"Do you think so, brother?" asked Erasmus doubtfully. "All right, I will do what I can, and I am trying very hard. But you see, when one of the women comes to me to 'get her rights,' as they call it, and she has a floor cloth in her hand, I cannot help thinking that she has come to kill me, to stuff the floor cloth into my mouth and to look comfortably on while I suffocate. They have eyes like wolves, brother."

"In the forester's house you also thought that the girl had designs on your life, brother," said Amadeus. "I don't think that anybody wants to kill you."

"That's what you say," said Erasmus pondering. "You haven't seen them. I dream of them, and yet I cannot go away. Once I ran away, and now I look upon this as a sort of punishment. He is a severe and righteous God who has imposed it; I notice that now. That is how it was in the Old Testament."

"You will have to console yourself by knowing that I would not be able to do what you do, brother," said Amadeus. "You are better than I. Though it was not our habit to make comparisons between ourselves, perhaps there is some consolation in it."

"To be better than you will never be a consolation for me, dear brother," said Erasmus, getting up. It was as if he had forgotten everything: the women and their floor cloths, the noise, the confusion, as he stood there, his whole face radiant while he looked down upon Amadeus with a smile.

Then he was buried in thought again, and after a while he said, "I think it is because they always appear in numbers. Do you understand, brother? There never seems to be one just alone by herself. It is as if envy or greed or hatred makes all people akin; then they look so frightfully alike. When the women come to me, I always see thirty or three hundred, and they have six hundred eyes and six hundred hands and three hundred floor cloths. It is too much for me, and I am very lucky that Christoph is there most of the day. He looks so calm and strong with his white hair and his blue coat with the silver buttons. He who has so often driven six young horses is also a match for six women. I am afraid that we have paid our toll to the centuries, yes, to time in general. We were not afraid of six morning stars or six halberds or scythes, but we are afraid of six women. Our nobility has become decadent, you know, too susceptible. We have worn gloves too long."

"I think we have not quite kept up with the others, brother," said Amadeus. "The others went on too fast. We have stood and looked about too much: at a child that was sitting with sore feet at the side of the road, or at a passage in the Bible, or at something that father said. Others don't stand and look about, they move along with the times. They smile a little over those who still question their hearts. Such people were also the ones who had fewest difficulties in the camp. But even if we have lagged behind, brother, let us not be ashamed of it! So much is thrown away and lost on the road of the so-called times, that it is all right if there is somebody to pick it up. I always fancy that the day will come when people suddenly discover that what they have lost lies behind them, not in front of them. That a moment may arise in their lives when they put the short stories or the bestsellers aside and remember the verse of a hymn which they learned when they were children. That they will switch off the radio for a while, and in the vast silence which ensues sit there like forsaken ghosts and, when they look around, will see nothing but other ghosts who sit like themselves before the silent contrivance for noise. A refrigerator is not the same as the black silk skirt of their grandmother, in whose pleats they could hide their faces when they were frightened children.

"And fear is on the way, brother; its first cold breath is already here. The appalling fear of the terrible loneliness of the human race, which has set aside the grandmother and has dethroned God Almighty and instead splits the atom to create a bomb or shoots rockets to the moon.

"And when that time comes, brother, they will look around as ghosts look around, and then perhaps they will go to those who picked up from the dust of the road and safeguarded those ancient things. 'How was it formerly?' they will ask. 'Is it really true that it was different then? Open your hands so that we can see how things were formerly.'

"Perhaps, dear brother, we shall be the ones who will open our hands, we or our grandchildren. It need not be the nobility who safeguard what has been found and who will then open their hands. But it will be easiest for them, because they were brought up in awe of the past. Their families watched over them best. The old families held the scales in their hands, not the people who wrote the leading articles. They also remembered the verses of the hymns, the old songs, the old melodies – and they also remembered the old laws. Not the law that the weak must be exterminated, but the old law that they must protect the weak.

"Not all of us have been faithful; perhaps very few. But you ought to know, brother, that I thought it beautiful to look at your hands when I came back. In the world today there are few hands which have remained quite clean – neither among the victors nor among the defeated. However, the hands of soldiers or of politicians are not the most important. Much more than hands is at stake.

"You see, when I read the books that Kelley brings me, I always ask myself whether the people who wrote them became better through writing them. Do you understand that? Perhaps they all were happy that a great work was finished at last, and that they would get money and fame. But had their faces become purer, their hearts and their hands? That ought to happen to the writer of a good book. I believe that Claudius or Bruckner or Mozart had beautiful faces when they put down the pen – like an angel's face when he has delivered his tidings and is unfolding his wings again.

"But I cannot believe the same of the writers today. I can only see them smiling, if anybody speaks of such a thing to them. As they would smile if their grandchild were to ask them whether they were good. Not a kind smile, only a smile of the times. Not as Christoph smiles when he tells of the great-grandfather who drove the Christ Child.

"But you have still got it, brother, you have it even when the women with the floor cloths come to you. That's why nobody will kill you. Because yours is an eternal and immortal smile."

Erasmus was still standing there as he had stood from the beginning, his eyes fixed on the setting sun. But when he turned around to Amadeus, it was as if his face had absorbed the whole evening glow. "You suppose me to be better than you are, dear brother?" he asked gently. "Don't you know that Aegidius and I only go on as we always have done, while you are being transformed?" He bent down to the sitting man and looked at him. "The Christ Child would climb into the sleigh with you," he said.

Then he nodded to him and went down the mountain.

One evening Aegidius came up to the sheepfold and brought Erasmus with him. Erasmus and Amadeus both noticed that Aegidius had something on his mind. The old calm and security no longer emanated from him, and they were both rather perplexed. He had been – as it were – the unshakable axis of their lives. One who had sown and reaped wheat all his life long, while they had been tangled in the web of their dreams.

Aegidius wanted to sit by the fire, though it was calm and mild. The stars had not yet come out, but the evening was filled with the vast beauty of the moor, above which the woodlark was singing.

"You will be surprised as I myself am surprised," he began at last, gazing into the flickering fire on the hearth. "But I feel that none of us has the right to step out of the triptych without further ado. I always felt that two of us have been father and mother to the third, no matter which of us was the third. And now I must ask you a question. Formerly this was called a sanction, among staff officers for instance, and I would now like to ask you for a sanction."

"I think you want to get married, brother," said Amadeus calmly.

"Yes, that's it. And the peculiar thing is that she herself suggested it. Don't think that she did it in a selfish or aggressive way, rather very quietly, as if it were a matter of course. She said that it would be difficult, probably impossible, to keep me in her house otherwise. But she would understand perfectly if I did not want to. She would understand that a Liljecrona would prefer to show himself with somebody who did not look as she did. She said it all very quietly, but I noticed that it cost her a terrible effort. Yes, that she went through fire, so to say."

Amadeus kept his face unmoved, but Erasmus was quite overwhelmed. Not only that he was frightened, no, he looked with a sort of despair at his brother, as at somebody whom he loved and whose face death had marked now.

"Do say something," said Aegidius after a long silence. "It is by no means easy for me when you don't say a word."

Erasmus cast a sidelong glance at him, and then his lips smiled again, even though it was a rather painful smile. "You must not ask us, brother," he said. "Who are we that you must ask us? Without asking anybody you have always known when it was time to sow or to reap; you are sure to know now what to do. It is only that I am a little bit afraid, brother. Not that you will be going right away and will only be a visitor with us, but that you have undertaken to solve the insoluble. And that you take it on yourself quite alone. We should not be able to help you if you are in need of help. Women are such dangerous creatures, brother."

"She isn't dangerous," replied Aegidius quietly.

"I know, I know," said Erasmus quickly. "She certainly is a good woman, but is there not something threatening about her – something of the ancient world, I would call it?"

Aegidius looked at him and smiled. "You need not throw the spear with her, brother," he said, "nor the stone. Nor will she cut off your head when you come off second-best. What I would like is that you should give her your hand and say: you are welcome among us. Do not say, 'I welcome you,' but rather, 'You are welcome among us.' For we are brothers, Erasmus, real brothers, almost as in a fairytale, rather than brothers in an enlightened century."

Erasmus felt ashamed and stretched out his hand. "Forgive me, brother," he said. "Everything is all right now. It's a failing of mine that I don't question the heart first. Perhaps it is because of my profession; nor do I know what your heart says to it. But I need not know that."

Aegidius made no reply and continued to gaze into the fire.

"My idea, brother, is that you are going to marry the fields, not the woman," said Amadeus at last.

He said it without any reproach, but they could see that it went home. "No doubt there is some truth in that," replied Aegidius. "That's why I have come. You always said that I was the strongest, the calmest, and the most reliable. But I'm not. Perhaps I was so while I had the fields. Fields give you calm and strength. But when I lost them I was without roots; I know it best myself."

The fire burned slowly down, and through the open door came the voices of the night birds circling over the moor or traveling to the north. The brothers listened to their cries dying away in the distance and silently looked into the fire. They knew that it was as grave an hour as the one in which their brother had been fettered and led away, or in which they had harnessed the horses to the loaded sleighs. They did not know whether they would see each other again – sufficiently unchanged – to take their former places in the triptych.

"Is it honorable?" asked Aegidius after a while, folding his hands between his knees.

"Do you think that you could do anything dishonorable, brother?" asked Erasmus. "It has always been a noble duty to till the field and to protect the defenseless."

"Even if I killed a man, you would say it was noble, brother, noble for me anyhow. You are the purest among us, so pure that out of a rag you would be able to make part of a golden crown."

"I don't know about that, brother," replied Erasmus with a smile. "Anyhow, I haven't yet made crowns out of floor cloths in the castle."

"But with me, brother, with me, that's the important point."

When the moon had risen, Aegidius got up from his seat.

"Thank you," he said. "When she does come, let her sit by the fire as I am doing. She will be more afraid than I."

"She need not be afraid, brother," said Erasmus. "She who will bear your name need not be afraid."

The third thing that happened was that the "dark one" appeared. The people who had seen him had given him that name, because his face was blackened and he wore a mask. He appeared at night on lonely farms, knocked at the door, and demanded admittance. If he was admitted, he asked for food and everything else that he needed, put it into his haversack, and disappeared. If he was not obeyed, he blasted off the door lock with a revolver and seized what he wanted. If he met any opposition, he shot without hesitation and without warning. It was easy to see that the life of a human being was no more to him than a grain of wheat that can be blown from the hand.

To judge from his way of speaking they supposed him to come from the north of Germany. People only knew that he was tall and slim.

Twice he had been seen at twilight, once in the morning, once in the evening. Both times at the edge of the marshes where, according to the experience of the people of the district, the bog was inaccessible and extremely dangerous.

Once or twice American soldiers surrounded the moor, slowly beating across it. But there were large stretches where a man could not find a solid footing and which were hidden because great patches densely covered with reeds surrounded them. And then, looting, plundering, and murder were still so much the order of the day that the emergence of the "dark one" did not mean anything out of the ordinary, except for those who were affected by it. People thought that he was not an alien robber from the camps, but a "native," and they suspected that he was one of the "great" hangmen of the past years – that was the reason why the victors bothered about him.

Amadeus only heard of it from Kelley, who asked him to take some interest in the matter, as nobody knew the moor and the peat bogs as well as he. If the Atlantic Charter was unsafe with the victors, he said with his half-ironical, half-melancholy smile, he would like to put it for safekeeping into the hands of Baron Amadeus, before he had to return to the States.

"For your sake I will help with the matter," said Amadeus, "not for my own."

"Perhaps neither for one nor the other," replied Kelley seriously, "but for the sake of the children who do not sleep quietly at night. 'Freedom from fear' is a beautiful phrase, and perhaps it is in better hands with you than with an American general who has little time to trouble about children." So Amadeus promised.

But he was surprised that he was affected by it in a different way than he would have been a year ago. He could only think of this man as a wolf or another beast of prey. He could not imagine that the "dark one" was a human being. It seemed to him as if the great shadow of the present time was already cast over all that was human. It was not for him to judge the hangmen, even if this were a hangman. They had already receded into the background of his life. They had become the hunted, and he had never been a hunter.

He was only concerned with what Kelley had said about the children. Children had had their share of suffering and horror and ought to have done with it by now. It might even happen that the "dark one" appeared one day at the cottages on the moor and stole Goldie, for instance. And Goldie was the symbol of an impoverished child's heaven, which should not be made any poorer.

So Amadeus began to roam anew over the moors and marshes. He knew well those parts of the marshes where a wolf might live, even though he did not know their depths. And so he lay in ambush between the juniper bushes at the edge of the moor for many hours before dawn and before dusk, and also under the full moon at night.

Chapter 6

It was beautiful when the earth grew quiet or still lay in the silence of early morning. There were the soft sounds among the heather, where invisible creatures were wandering; there was the soft morning breeze in the tops of the trees from which the dry needles fell. There was the glimmering mist which rose or was wafted to and fro among the little birches. There were the brilliant stars which gradually penetrated the darkening sky or slowly faded away. There was the barking of the dog in the distance and the booming of the bittern from the depths of the marshes.

And how beautiful it was when a warm spring rain fell and, after it was over, still dripped from the trees. There was the soft whispering of the young leaves, of the needles and the mosses, that sounded around him like a special language, disappearing and reappearing: the language of unknown creatures whispering a message or an order to one another, a language that was above and below the earth, spoken without fear, for the human being that crouched or lay there did not understand it.

It was also beautiful to breathe the scent of the young leaves, which had in it something of "once and never again," something that cannot be described, as a color or a sound cannot be described, but which was there in its unshakable existence. At its edge man was only as a stranger or perhaps as a guest before whom a door was opened, but who realized that behind the one open door a thousand unopened doors remained, the thresholds of which the little beetles could cross or the lizards or the birds – but never man, the so-called lord of creation.

How unperturbed, how splendidly unconcerned this nature was about all that had been happening to humankind! And also about that which now was hiding away in some safe place and for which another was waiting and watching – a man or a wolf, a hunter or the hunted. The drops ran down the blades of grass slowly, without a sound; that was the important thing for the earth, nothing else. The sky grew more and more crimson, the cranes began to trumpet, the day rose again above the mysterious work of the earth. Amadeus got up and walked slowly back, and his thoughts did not dwell much on the man who might or might not live behind those walls of reed.

But his thoughts dwelt for a long time on the realization of how much in such hours fell away from his own being, as if the rains had included him, too, in their great work of cleansing and sterilization.

In the end he felt that he was lying in the moss for those many long hours only for his own sake, not on account of the "dark one." As if those hours were only there so that spring could take, as it were, compassion on him. So that it should be shown to him that there were other ways to pass from disorder into order besides those of the intellect, for instance, or those of work or of faith.

Then one gloomy evening, made still darker by deeply rifted clouds, it happened that reality started up in front of him, something that the eyes saw and the mind could not simply ignore by not thinking about it. This reality took the shape of a girl who stepped out of one of those patches densely covered with reeds, a long stick in each hand, with which she seemed to be groping for safe ground. She looked around cautiously for a long time before she turned her head back once more, lifting one of her sticks as a greeting. After that she walked slowly, step by step, over the deceptive surface toward the wood where the baron was kneeling among the juniper bushes.

Long before he could recognize her face, he knew that it was the forester's daughter, but he tried to divert his thoughts from this recognition and its consequences and only fix his attention with clear accuracy on the windings of the narrow path along which she advanced with extreme care.

And only when he had seen that the path ran on solid ground between two peculiarly shaped juniper bushes which he engraved deeply in his memory, did he think that he must not be seen, and he kept hidden in the shade of the alder bushes until the girl, quickly now and without hesitating, started to walk along the other side of the bog.

Only then he meditated carefully, like a detective who from a few clues has to build up a case. He had not expected this and he thought of it with some bitterness. He had looked upon this which had settled itself here – as an alien hunted animal settles itself for a time into a thicket or a cave – as on something foreign to the district.

But now it had found an accomplice and friendship and had attached to itself what was untouched and innocent in this landscape. It had gained a sort of home, and a human being of this sphere had lent a hand to it. Not to the life of a homeless person or a fugitive but to that of a murderer. And so it was not true that the dreadful times had slowly fallen away from this land and its people, so that they might regain the standards of the past. That time had returned, unchanged and bloody as before, and despising the old laws as in the past.

It would have been different if one of the men or young fellows of the neighborhood had lent a hand to it. It would have lain in the nature of a man who cannot dispel poison so quickly from his blood, who gets used to a bloody trade as quickly as to an unbloody one, and who will even find some justification for it.

But this time a girl had been the accomplice, and that made the distortion of nature more terrible and impressive. It was unimportant for the moment that the girl's name was Barbara and that he knew her. Yes, that during the winter not far from here he had laid his bare hand upon her cheek.

It was only important that this was somebody created to bear children and to hold them at her breast. Somebody predestined by nature to shelter, protect, and console. And who now had laid her hand on the hand of a man before the muzzle of whose revolver a child was nothing but an insect, and who in the past years had perhaps crushed such an insect smilingly a thousand times.

It was thus that the evil time had arisen again around the whole moor, around the room in the shepherd's hut, around the course of one's thoughts: that bloody, lawless, and terrible time. That it took away the peace, the small, painfully gained shred of peace that was as helpless and susceptible as a newborn lamb.

From this evening, Amadeus did not go to the two juniper bushes anymore. He did not quite understand what kept him from it.

Probably he thought that it was not his business to heal the times and certainly not to heal them with a revolver. Evidently it was a feeling of aversion, yes, of disgust at sitting there watching until the girl should come out of the reeds alone or with him in whose life she now had a share. It was an aversion against hunting human beings that filled him, and even for the sake of the children he could not master it. Perhaps it was also the dread that he might see in the man behind the reeds a repeat of past times, at whose beginning he himself had once stood.

But while he was still pondering whether it was his duty to inform Kelley without delay, something happened that showed him a way out of it. The young wife of the worker Donelaitis, who after curfew had gone to the edge of the moor to look for mushrooms to sell, and had forgotten about the time, had been attacked in the twilight by somebody who according to her description must have been the "dark one." She would have been lost if she had not carried in her hand the small, pointed knife with which she cut the roots of the mushrooms. She thrust this knife at her aggressor and hit his face and gained time to escape and hide before the pain allowed him to molest her again.

Amadeus asked her to show him the place where all this had happened, and in the dawn of the next morning he stood with Donelaitis in front of the two juniper bushes. "He is sure to come here," he said. "I have established the fact that there is no other path but this. I would like to give you my revolver, but then you will have trouble with the Americans." "I do not need a revolver," said Donelaitis, gazing over the moor. "In my homeland a long time ago, we caught and strangled the wolf with our naked hands. He who touches my wife, be it a wolf or a man, will fare badly."

Amadeus glanced at his set, gloomy face, and then returned with him to the cottages.

He waited in front of the shepherd's hut until Christoph passed by on his way to the castle. "You must stay there for a few days, Christoph," he said, pointing to the forester's house, "and see to it that the girl does not leave the house. Will you be able to do that?"

"Guarding girls is more difficult than guarding horses," replied Christoph without surprise, "but it shall be as the master commands."

And he went back without asking a question.

7

SO MEN ARE WHO are created in the image of God: a vacillation of time, a mutation of the world axis can transform and hurl them down – as in the beginning some of the angels were transformed and hurled down. Not only man, who has always been irresolute, always given to violence, can revert to long-forgotten, bloodstained ages, but woman, too, who is formed to love and preserve, can be detached from the old order of nature, divested of charity, and allied to death so closely that her hand can sow the seed of death with the same coldness, yes, with the same devotion of heart of which man is capable when law has been overthrown and the road is open before him as in times when men stoned each other for a piece of bread.

Thus it can also happen to a girl a few decades after the time when women's education taught them nothing but to paint pictures, to make a little music, to sit over an embroidery frame, and with their album of verses in their lap to wait for the predestined or chosen one who was to continue the unwavering line of the families on well-arranged paths, accompanied by tradition and the blessing of the church and the parents.

Thus a girl now starts marching instead of dancing, carrying a flag in her hand instead of a sunshade and despising, yes, hating all those who do not want to belong to the new order.

Thus a girl can fall to an abysmal depth the very moment the flag is hurled down, because she has devoted the sum of her existence to this flag. And it is as difficult to awaken the dead as to lift her out of the bottomless pit back to the ancient, despised order with its old, despised laws of love and charity. A dim realization of what she has lost may touch her slightly, perhaps when she sees children's eyes reflecting the Christmas candles, or when a man strokes her cheek with his hand gently and consolingly.

But this glimmer of truth will only last until the dream-phantom of recent years emerges from the mist. Perhaps in the shape of a lonely, unbent man who has gone through victory and defeat unbroken, and whose hands still seem to her to hold a fragment of the crown, the blood-stained crown, which once was lifted out of the dark waters, and whose dread-inspiring shimmer had begun to spread its light over the whole world from the shores of the ocean to the snow-covered summits of the Caucasus, and from the midnight sun of the North Cape to the crumbling pyramids of the river Nile.

And before the eyes of this "preserver of greatness," this one who has remained, the vision of the children's eyes and that of the caressing hand vanish. This man recognizes nothing but the will to power, the strength to break laws, even the law of a ridiculous Jewish God. Before these eyes each death is justified if it can win one a piece of bread or a cup of water, because only the inferior are killed, the race of the old and the subhuman who must be exterminated, so that the master race can rule the world, as it was predestined from the very beginning.

There had been no hesitating for the girl Barbara when, one evening in the twilight, the man had stepped out of the reeds and had told her of his past life, of his plans and of his aims. He was altogether different from the young cowards who had been afraid to blow up the castle. This man would be willing to blow up the whole earth if he had the power and opportunity, and under its ruins he would bury all those who had betrayed the Führer, his idol. But the gallows were waiting for him if he were caught, and to protect him from this fate had now become the girl's one object in life. He was like the ancient god to whom the virgins of the land sacrificed themselves – and each sacrifice promised lasting, eternal bliss.

When Barbara wanted to leave the house in the evening and the old man in the long blue coat barred her way, she did not regard him as somebody who restricted her freedom, but as a being from the realm of Loki who stood between herself and the light-god, a demoniac being from the bowels of the earth with the poisoned arrow in his hand, and she struggled with him as she would have struggled with one from the underworld, until he carried her into her room, locked the door behind her, and nailed the heavy shutters across the windows. It was of no avail that she beat the wood and the walls with her fists and shouted for her mother.

For the woman sat by the cold hearth, wrapped in her shawl, and only nodded when Christoph said that what he had done was done at the order of the master, and that she might be sure that this order saved the girl from something worse. Evil was afoot on the moor, and he thought that one victim was enough for this house.

Moreover the imprisonment lasted only a day and a half. At the first hour of dawn of the succeeding day, Donelaitis stood by the bedside of Baron Amadeus, wet to the hips with the dew of the high grass, but as composed as if he came from mowing a meadow. He reported that he had caught the wolf and that he was going to the village now to lead the Americans around the marshes to some place to which they could drive in their cars. The baron should wait for him by the two juniper bushes. He would tell him everything else later.

By the time Amadeus arrived at the bushes, the sun already stood high above the marshes, the mist was dispersing, and the dew sparkled under the blue sky.

He saw the "dark one" lying in the heather, just between the two bushes, and from the distance he thought that Donelaitis had killed him. But then he saw that he was alive, not dead, yes, that apparently he was without wound except for the mark which the little knife had left on his right cheek.

But when Amadeus stood right in front of him he saw that Donelaitis had actually caught him as a wolf is caught. A heavy iron trap had closed over his right knee, one of those which are called "swan's neck." The chain of the trap was fastened to the trunk of the nearest alder tree, and the prisoner lay on his right side. His arms were tied together and bound behind his back. His eyes were open and he gazed at the baron.

Without the experience of the past few years Amadeus would have passed by this face without any particular attention. He would perhaps have thought that its home might be somewhere in the region of the northern or northwestern coast of Germany, a face which belonged among the old peasant families who had settled there since time immemorial, a fair-skinned, hard, lantern-jawed face – as work and history had formed it.

But now he looked at it in a different way, because he had seen many people with such faces. In former times they had been bowed over a plow which they had to drive through heavy soil and they still looked as if that was the work they had to do. Only that now they no longer had to drive the plow through a long field but through the living bodies of human beings who were lying before the plowshare in thousands, one bound to the next. The clods were turned as in a field, but the plowshare became red, and the plowmen looked down on this red plowshare as imperturbably as if it were lifting the wheat stubble.

The baron gazed down into these eyes for a long time. They did not close before him, nor did they avoid him. Motionless they looked up at him, not as at an unknown man's face in which might be read a life or death decision, but as at a cloud sailing across the sky, or at a spider's web suspended between two reeds, or at some other of the thousand phenomena of the marshes, of the vegetable or animal kingdom which one meets in the course of the day. They gazed as at something of such absolute indifference that one could not be sure whether the retina of those eyes received the picture at all, to say nothing of the man's ability to classify it and make it his own.

It would not have been correct to say that these eyes were especially hard or cold – that for instance they resembled the eyes of a beast of prey. They were neither greenish nor lashless, nor were they essentially different from the eyes of a man who at dawn lies at the edge of the moor, looking up into the blue sky. The only thing that distinguished them from other eyes was their detachment from the surrounding world. It was by no means a sort of blindness, for the objects of this morning hour were reflected in them, but only on the surface, and there they remained and did not penetrate to the depths, to brain and thought. Yes, one did not even know whether there was a depth below the surface at all – perhaps there was nothing, just as there is nothing beneath the surface of a metal mirror.

If the baron had perceived such a depth and had seen hatred, cruelty, or essential evil in it, he would not have been so frightened as he was at the cold emptiness of these eyes, because this emptiness was, in the truest sense of the word, inhuman.

It seemed to him as if in this emptiness the total of the past four years was rising up anew, the total of all their torture, agony, and death, and as if it gazed at him with the cold certainty of something which would never perish. As if this last year of security had been only a dream, and it was not true that the past was defeated and overcome. He felt as if he had been living for this whole year in a death chamber, living quietly and cautiously, though without danger, because evil had lain on a bier in the darkest corner of the room.

And now when he looked around for the first time, he realized that the corpse had had its eyes open all the time, and that these eyes had followed him: every movement, every breath he breathed in this presumed security, while the rigid lips had not thought it necessary to show by the faintest smile that they were not dead. Thus it would remain for all time, for ever and ever. Even if they were executed and rooted out from the face of the earth, even from its darkest corner, someone would always be left over as this man was left over, who looked on at the extermination as one looks at the idle flames of a wood fire. It would remain so – not because a human being was left over, but because evil, primal evil was left, which at God's will had been woven into creation at its foundation, and now not even God's hand was able to pluck it out of the tissue. It was a part of the world order, not only at its fringe, but intertwined with it, as if it had been driven into it by suffering, as pain is driven into the tissues of a body and so merged with it that no separation is possible.

The baron took a few steps and sat down on the stump of a tree so that he could look over the moor and would only see the prisoner at the extreme edge of his field of vision. The sun had mounted in the sky and the contours of woods and mountains stood dark and sharply outlined in the clear morning light. The herons flew from the trees where they had slept to the fishing grounds, the ants at his feet scurried to their work, and on all sides rose the melancholy song of the lark over the radiant earth. The space of the horizon was filled with the age-old order of things, but at the edge of this space the "dark one" lay motionless in the heather, and the baron knew that his wide-open eyes were staring at him as at a stone or the trunk of a pine tree.

Even if this "dark one" were put out of the way, into a jail or under the gallows, it would go on, here or somewhere else on the earth's surface – there it would be and it would remain forever, just as night goes on, without which there could be no day.

No, it was not at all easy to change oneself, thought the baron, clasping his knees with his hands. If the dark forces of the world could not be changed, how should a man be able to transmute the darkness within himself – since it was but a part of that great, universal darkness? "The patience and faith of the saints," that was the great word at the beginning as at the end.

Then he heard the cars drive up and stop among the bushes. He caught sight of the colored stripes around the steel helmets of the military police and got up. He explained what there was to explain, and with Donelaitis he cautiously opened the heavy iron trap. It seemed that the bone above the knee was not broken, but they laid the prisoner on a stretcher and carried him to the waiting cars. He did not utter a sound, and his eyes passed over the faces of the soldiers as they had passed over the face of the baron.

When the noise of the motors had died away, Donelaitis unfastened the chain of the trap from the alder tree and gave his report. When they first came to the forester's barn, he had noticed the trap in a woodshed there, and he had remembered it in his present need. It was always dangerous to catch with bare hands a man who carried a revolver. The first night he had dug the trap in – quite flat – between the two bushes. Even this was risky, but he had to try it.

At dawn the fellow actually approached on the path leading toward the marshes, so he must have been out and about. "I had nothing," Donelaitis went on, "but the old shepherd's sling which we used when we were young – a split piece of wood with a round stone in it. As a boy I could hit a crow on the wing with it. But I didn't need it; the man walked into the trap as he would into an open door. I was on him in an instant, before he had time to grasp his revolver. Even people like that get a bit of a shock when an iron trap closes on them." That was all he had to say.

They went back together, one behind the other, and Donelaitis without pausing took his ax and saw and went to the clearing where the men were working. His face looked as if he had just been putting a fence around his little garden.

Amadeus went to the forester's house and found Christoph in the kitchen. "You need not guard her anymore," Amadeus said. "We've got him."

"That's good," replied Christoph after a pause, and went up the narrow stairs.

Amadeus was still sitting by the fire with the deeply worried woman when Barbara came into the kitchen. He noticed that her face had grown older, but then he did not look at her again.

"You need not go there anymore," he said. "He is no longer there; we have caught him."

She leaned against the wall and stared at him, as if he were an apparition. "Murderer," she whispered at last. "You murderer."

At that he raised his eyes to her white face and gazed at her for a long time. No, those were not the same eyes, and a load was lifted from his heart when he realized it. Those were eyes filled with hatred and a shade of mortal terror, but they did not look through him as the eyes at the edge of the moor had looked through him. Those were eyes which one might, perhaps, with the patience and faith of the saints, call back to life one day. They were not like a blind mirror. There was still some life at the back of them.

"I have already warned you once not to strike your mother," he said slowly, "because she is a poor, defenseless woman. And I would not like to touch a hand that strikes the defenseless. And my hand has touched many things in these years."

She did not speak as he got up and went toward the door, but her eyes followed him until it had closed behind him.

The hearing took place in the chief town of the district before the highest military court. The Intelligence Corps had a photograph of the "dark one" and knew the details of his past life. It had led through most of the camps and had left the bloody trail of a wolf behind it. But he was not condemned on account of this trail of blood and suffering, but only for what he had done during the recent months which he had spent among the reeds of the marshes. In spite of the mask he had worn, all the witnesses recognized him. He himself was silent, and his cold eyes glanced at those who passed sentence on him, as they had glanced at Amadeus: unmoved, indifferent, uninterested.

Only when Donelaitis and his wife were called did his expression change, and he looked at them with a kind of deadly curiosity, as if he were quietly considering what traps and what manner of death might be most suitable for them.

But when the man from the Einodhof stepped forward, whose wife and child he had shot because she had offered resistance and because the child had screamed, and when the man pointed his finger at him as at a beast of prey and asked in a trembling voice, "But the child – why the child?" then the thin lips of the prisoner moved for the first time, as if for the first time he was going to give an answer. But it was only something that might have been a smile that distorted his lips. A contemptuous semblance of a smile, completely disinterested, as detached as the little ripples which at a breath of wind run over the surface of a pool. As if the man's question and his charge were so incredibly stupid that they could only be answered by the semblance of a smile.

The man stepped back when he saw the smile, and for some time there was deadly silence in the hall, as if for one heartbeat they stood before the chink of a door through which they beheld the awfulness of the beyond. The baron, too, had noticed the smile and his eyes searched the hall. But the girl was nowhere to be seen and her name had not been mentioned.

The "dark one" was sentenced to death, and a week later he was hanged.

Donelaitis was offered a sum of money which he refused.

Now and again one or the other of the soldiers who had driven him and his wife to the court appeared at the cottages on the moor; they would sit on the bench in front of Donelaitis' little wooden house, distributing chocolates to the children and trying to draw Erdmuthe into talk. But she only shook her head, smiled in her absent-minded way, and with unmoved face watched the visitors depart.

Sometimes in the evening she stood on the moor and gazed over the brown expanse into the great sunset glow which lay like a distant fire over the earth. Only when Donelaitis came home from work and called her, she went slowly back with him and would answer his questions, but in such a way that she seemed to linger still in a different world.

The women thought that she was homesick, but Donelaitis did not know this word. Perhaps he knew the feeling but not the word. One morning before he went to work, he told her in his taciturn way that he did not like the soldiers' visits.

She cast a sidelong glance at him as if he had said something peculiar, shrugged her shoulders, and replied that it was not up to her to prevent an American soldier from coming to the moor. Besides, she did not speak to them, as she did not understand their language.

He had already taken hold of the handle of the door and did not turn around, but stopped short, gazed down for a time on the brown wood under his fingers, and said slowly that it was not a matter of language.

And then he went. She stood still a moment looking after him through the closed door, as if the wood formed no obstacle to her glance. Then she smiled in her reserved way, a smile which revealed nothing of its origin, and set about her morning's work.

So after a while the soldiers stopped coming, and she went to the woods as usual in the afternoon to collect mushrooms, which she sold or bartered in the castle.

Quite slowly the ripples which had been set in motion by the fate of the "dark one" grew fainter and fainter and then subsided, as if he had been but a stone cast into calm water. The scene closed again around time, around people and their daily work. A year passed, and a year is a long time for one who has so much to forget. Yes, to forget: for instance the winter road with the gnarled willows or the cries fading away in the snowstorm, or the white face on the threshold of the church, or the barbed wire around the place where death ruled.

They were not responsible for either remembering or forgetting. Sometimes the memory was buried in darkness, and sometimes it rose out of oblivion. Sometimes they believed that its features when it arose grew fainter, more distant and unreal, as the features of the dead which can only be remembered with difficulty. And sometimes when they started out of their dreams, it was so near that their hand could reach it.

They had to let the matter rest there. The daily work did not need the dead, and it had to be done as their forefathers had done it. Their forefathers had not asked for happiness, because only the masters were entitled to happiness. Time had passed and happiness had been taken away from the masters, too, and it seemed as if they were nearer to them now, since they had only their daily work and not happiness.

And then it had turned out without their will or knowledge that Baron Amadeus stood nearest to their hearts, because time had left him the least happiness and the least daily work. He was the poorest, even poorer than they. Without a wife, without a child. He had only one suit and one coat, and moreover the coat was a striped one with stains that could not be rubbed out. And he smiled more rarely than any of them, and when he smiled it was a sad smile, involuntarily sad, just as it came from the depths of his heart, so his deepest heart must be sad.

His two brothers had their feet planted in time once more and in their daily work. One of them managed an estate, plowed and gave orders, and the other was attempting to keep a confused mass of human beings well in hand. But Amadeus had remained without time and without work. He lived in a shepherd's hut and walked over the moor or sat by his little fire. But when he stood or sat with the cottagers, or looked on while they were working, they realized that he was the poorest of them all, for he was not tied to life as they were, neither by day nor by night, and that his roots had been cut. As they watched him when he was standing in the twilight at the edge of the marshes, he seemed to them to be pondering whether he could take root there like an old, transplanted tree.

Just because he had suffered so much, their hearts were moved. The two other brothers had been in peril and had had to flee, as they had, and were now poor as they themselves were. But where suffering was deepest, and where one had to carry it all alone on one's bowed shoulders, there they had not been. In all of them still moved a dim memory of the centuries when their forefathers had been in the depths of suffering, under the yoke of arbitrary and capricious power and violence, in complete hopelessness. What serfdom meant, only Amadeus had experienced, that was why he was like one of themselves. He was one whom God had marked, as He had formerly marked lunatics, saints and beggars. One should not reckon accounts with them, nor bear them a grudge, because no one knew what God intended to do with them. It had come down to them from their forefathers that they had to be open-handed to such people.

Nor were they surprised when one day the baron started to dig the soil around their little, wooden houses so that a dark square lay around each cottage. Nor that he strewed seeds out of little paper bags into this dark soil. When the women stood still by his side, he only said that the children ought to have some flowers in front of their windows. Men's eyes had a different look, if they had seen flowers in their childhood.

He divided the soil into small beds and told the children how they should be shared out. Goldie got a bed all to herself.

The men as they came home in the evening from the wood or the peat bogs glanced at him as at one who is playing an idle game, but they thanked him, and when they sat for a while working in front of their houses, they looked down awkwardly and thoughtfully on the black soil at their feet, into which the baron had put the seed, and they talked a little about him and his loneliness, and that he seemed the one of the three brothers who was most like the old baron. So much so that perhaps one day he, too, would disappear into the underworld.

All of them were invited to the wedding of Baron Aegidius, and Amadeus was the only one who stayed away. He had asked his brother not to take it amiss; he was not yet able to come.

He stayed all day long by the empty cottages and looked at the first sprouting leaves of the young plants, and in the evening he watered them. For the first time he became aware how lonely and forsaken the moor was without the smoke from the chimneys and without the children's games in the heather.

He stood still, the watering can in his hand, and looked around him. It seemed as if with this awareness something great had happened within him, something that he had never thought possible. As if while wandering round and round in a circle he had come to a new gate, and he only need raise his hand and open it to behold beyond the habitual circle a new stretch of the earth's surface.

This impression affected him out of all proportion to the rather insignificant idea which had given rise to it, and he sat down on a bench in front of one of the houses, spread his arms right and left along the back, and gazed over the moor. Even the familiar sight of the great, silent, lonely expanse had been transformed for him into something that was not altogether outside his life, existing only for itself. Something that was not only a place across which one could walk as across other places, but something that was attached to life, that was connected with life, and that now, this evening, had become especially silent because the cottages were silent. Something that people had raised up out of the great silence by their work or their light laughter, or perhaps just by their existence. Something in which they had struck root, and with which they had transformed the alien earth, so that it had come nearer to their doors and windows.

He remained there for a long time meditating why he, too, felt part of this slow transformation. Whether the reason was that he had dug a piece of this earth, or that he had dug it for the children's sake.

The stars had already risen while he still sat on, probably the only person stirring and watching at the edge of the moorland, rather as if he were holding a dialogue with the owls that hooted to one another above the plain, over which by now darkness was gently stealing. Sometimes a shooting star shot into the depths, and unthinkingly his eyes followed its narrow, golden streak which flared up and faded away, like the handwriting of a distant, unknown being, a god who did not heed him at all.

As he climbed up to the hut he thought for a while of his brothers, how each of them was shaping a life of his own, more active than the one he, Amadeus, was leading, for he only wrote and strewed flower seeds on the earth. But the thought did not make him feel lonelier. They had always left each other ample room, just so much that they could always hear one another's gentle call – and so it would always be. Nor would Aegidius' wife be able to change this fact, and Amadeus remembered how forlorn she was the first time she sat with him, and he knew that she had not been so far from his heart as he had fancied. Yes, the reason for his remoteness was perhaps that he kept his heart aloof from other hearts, and it struck him that perhaps he was the only one who had cast a shadow on this day.

But the next day Erasmus was full of talk and news, as if he were well aware of this shadow, and as if he wanted to tell his brother so much that the shadow would vanish, no longer oppressing him who had cast it nor those over whom it had fallen.

Aegidius' wife let two weeks pass before she called on Amadeus. He had not expected her visit and felt ashamed. She sat on the chair by the hearth, on which the fire had gone out, and quietly folded her hands in the lap of her dark dress. Her eyes looked slowly around the room, without curiosity but with a sort of calm sympathy; then they rested on Amadeus' face.

"He was very sorry," she said in her gentle voice, "and so was I. Perhaps I regretted it even more than he did."

"It was not meant impolitely," replied Amadeus. "It was too soon for me. I can't do it yet."

She nodded. "I knew," she said, "and I did not expect it. I know that you three are joined as in a circle, and it is difficult for me. I feel that I am deeply indebted to you."

"There is no question of such a thing," replied Amadeus.

"I have been able to revive his courage," she continued in a low voice. "It was easy with him. But I cannot do the same for you. It's not for me to attempt it; besides, it would be beyond me. But I wanted you to know that I would like to do so."

"Thank you," said Amadeus. "I have always known it. I have not borne you any grudge for taking him from us. If it had not been you, it would have been someone else. The soil called him, the fields, or whatever name you care to use. He could not remain with us forever as if we lived in a fairytale."

"I don't know," she replied, "whether it has not remained so. The happiness of a woman rests on frail foundations. A woman would give her last field for her happiness. A man would not."

"But she would never want this happiness for herself," replied Amadeus, glancing at her.

"I don't know," she said in a low voice, gazing into the cold ashes on the hearth. "I really don't know, but I am grateful that you say so. I have drawn up a deed by which everything is to be his property, even if one day he should no longer care to have me with him."

"You ought not to think of him in that way," said Amadeus.

"I do not think it of him. I am thinking of men in general, not particularly of him. Sometimes men are nameless."

When she got up, she looked around the room. "I came to ask you to live with us. But now I realize that you couldn't do it. Of you three only you have gone to the end. When you call there will be no echo."

"As long as there is sorrow in this world," he replied, "no one will have gone on to the end."

He accompanied her to the narrow path that led down from the hill and said, still holding her hand, "The last time Aegidius was here he asked us to say to you, 'Welcome among us.' He need not have asked, we would have said it of our own accord."

Before he could prevent it, she lifted his hand impulsively to her cheek, then let it go and walked quickly down the hill.

"How is everything going over there, brother?" asked Amadeus in the evening, when Erasmus was sitting with him. "She came to see me today, but she did not seem to me to beam with happiness."

For a moment Erasmus did not understand him; then he shook his head. "She will never beam with happiness as others do," he replied. "There are women in whom joy or what we call 'happiness' works inwardly. What our eyes behold on the outside is only a reflection. It is as if they hoarded it in their hearts for times of need. They know, too, that happiness is not a permanent thing. Permanent is only that into which we have changed it."

"Ah well! I suppose it's a school of wisdom you have down there in the castle among all those women?" remarked Amadeus smiling.

"Yes, perhaps it is, even there," replied Erasmus. "They have overcome their difficulties better than the men – although only with a floor cloth. For quite a few men do not even have that. They have nothing at all, do you understand? They have only hunger. When the tablecloth has been pulled away from under their plates, they only ask, 'Whose fault is it?' But the women stoop and collect the broken pieces."

"That is a great truth, brother," said Amadeus.

"Where seventy or eighty people live together, some crumbs of wisdom always fall from the tables," replied Erasmus. "But as to her, brother, we must be especially good to her. For she really does not know whether he married 'her.' And the splendid thing about her is that she did not know it right from the beginning, nor did she want to know it."

"Yes, it is not easy to deal with us," said Amadeus, "even if we are not hungry and do not search for the guilty one."

As he was going, Erasmus told his brother that among the men in the castle there were a few who wanted some kind of work to do. The idea occurred to them that they would like to try their hands at cutting peat up here. Why, he did not know. He did not even know whether they had ever held a spade in their hands. Probably they only wanted to escape from the so-called communal life. The people up here might well lend them a hand; after all, the whole thing would only last a few days.

"The cottagers will not be pleased," said Amadeus. "But the peat bog is so large that they need not interfere with one another. You may safely send them up here."

It turned out as he had surmised, that they actually stayed only a few days, and the fruits of their labor looked rather forlorn as they lay about at the edge of the peat holes. The children played with them for a time, and then heather grew on them, and the cottagers forgot that people also lived beyond the peat bogs.

But one of them did not stay away. He did not come every morning, and sometimes a week went by before they saw him again. But then once more he stood there at the edge of the bog, where they had given him a place as far away from the cottages as possible. And all day long they could see the flashing of his spade when the sun shone on the metal. Sometimes he rested for a while, leaning his hands on the spade and gazing out over the marshes as Baron Amadeus or the young Frau Erdmuthe would do, and there in the cottages they said jokingly that he was counting his turfs. But he certainly was not doing that. His quiet face, serious and furrowed, was not the face of one who reckons. It only relaxed from the hard work and let the great silence of the landscape fall into it. Then it seemed detached from daily work and was only there for the sun to shine on – as it shone on the marshes and the wood. It looked gay and happy in spite of its many furrows – almost like a child's face that looks up from play to see how large the world is.

The people could tell Amadeus nothing about him, and one evening he went himself to find out who it was that had entered into his world as quietly as if he had come home. His steps were noiseless on the soft ground and he came up to the man from behind without being heard. The man stood leaning on his spade as usual, gazing into the distance, and when the baron had almost come up to him, he heard to his surprise that the man was singing in a low voice. His hands were folded over the handle of the spade, his head was inclined to one side, and he was singing to himself. Without words, only the melody, and it was obviously a hymn tune. Amadeus did not remember the words, but he remembered the melody, and he stood still and listened without moving. The man stood there like a figure in an old picture, absorbed in something that only his eyes could see. It was not clear whether it was something gay or sad, but it was obvious that it was something certain, something of which he did not doubt and to which he sang, as if he were sure some answer would come from it. An echo of the melody which he was singing and, with this echo, a reverberation of the words to which this melody had been written.

Children might stand so, oblivious of themselves, and sing out their half-unconscious life into space. Amadeus was immediately deeply affected by it, as if he had not seen such a thing since his own childhood, and he was ashamed to be standing like this behind the man, a witness to that which was not intended for him.

Then the low voice became silent, as if it had now sung everything: joy, sorrow, or homesickness, and as the man turned to his work again, he saw the baron standing behind him. He was not startled, he only smiled in a friendly way and nodded to him, as if he had known him a long time.

From near at hand Amadeus could see that his hair was already gray. What struck men when they looked at this face were not the many furrows, nor the mouth but the eyes. Large, very serious, rather deep-set eyes of an extraordinary, almost blissful warmth, eyes which seemed to be brimming full with the sunny landscape with which he had just been communing. They looked at the baron neither with astonishment nor with timidity, but with some joyful recognition, as if he had met him long ago, long before he had held a spade in his hand.

The tone of his voice, too, was warm and familiar, when he said how pleased he was to see the Herr Baron, because he would probably never have had the courage to call on him in his hut.

"Do you know me, then?" asked the baron, surprised.

"Yes, how should I not know you," replied the man, "as I am living in the castle under the protection of Baron Erasmus? Besides, I see you almost every day walking over the moor to find the evening."

"To find what?" asked the baron.

"The evening, Herr Baron. For nowadays many of us only go through the day to find the evening. The evening used to be there as a matter of course when the morning had been there, and one did not have to look for it. But nowadays nothing exists of its own accord. So much has been lost that people are afraid even time may get lost. Or at least the course of time, so that they are not even sure of their evening. And yet there it is, so wonderful, so certain, and so entirely for everybody that one must sing for joy that it has come."

Raising his right hand from the spade he described a circle above the marshes as if to show to the baron the evening which he had discovered.

"Are you an exile?" asked Amadeus at last.

The man smiled. "Not more than others," he replied. "Not more than we all are, since the angel with the sword stood at the gate of Paradise. But men have only remembered his word since they have had no roof of their own above their heads."

"And you remembered it earlier?"

"Much earlier, much earlier. That's why the roof of the castle is as good for me as my own roof was in times gone by. Perhaps even better. Just as the roof of the shepherd's hut is much better for the Herr Baron than his former roof."

"Are you quite certain about that?"

"Not quite as certain as most men are about what they say or, for instance, about their opinions of life, or that they are right and the others wrong. But fairly certain, anyhow, as certain as I am that this is beautiful." And again he described a semicircle over the moor with a sweep of his arm.

"What did you do before this?" asked Amadeus after a while. "Before you were driven out a second time? What was your profession?"

"A parson, of course," replied the man with surprise. "What else? Did you not notice it?"

"How should I have noticed it?" asked Amadeus wondering.

"Well, quite simply: by my way of speaking. Each trade, each profession can be recognized. The cobbler by his thumb and the sailor by his walk. There is nothing contemptible in that, there is not even anything comic. Jacob Boehme, for instance, was not comic at all. But parsons have their own way of expressing themselves; that is because they have taken such pains with the Bible. As judges with the *corpus juris.* Besides their turns of expression, they have a confident way of speaking which no other profession has. If somebody comes to them and unpacks his load of worries, they always know what to say. A word out of the Old or the New Testament. You will notice with many of them that they once sat on the school bench side by side with our Heavenly Father. And mostly 'go up one' as school slang has it."

"You never 'went up one'?" asked Amadeus.

"Oh no, Herr Baron, always lower, much, much lower; mostly I was the last among my colleagues."

"And now?"

The parson smiled. "Now I am having a bit of a holiday. Not from God, but from my church duties. You know as well as I do that there are no holidays from God.

"At first I thought I must get a congregation again as quickly as possible. As children think, when a wheel of their little truck breaks. But wherever I put in an application they cast sidelong glances at me. They did not look down upon me, that would not have been so bad, because that happens where man is set above man. Though it ought not to be like that in the church, where only Christ is set above us.

"But a sidelong glance is worse. Dangerous people are looked at sidelong, not inferiors. Those who stand outside, in front of the windows, for instance, to watch what is going on inside. Or the sick, or still more the abnormal people who live in their private worlds."

"And why did you seem dangerous or abnormal to the others?" asked Amadeus.

The parson smiled again, stuffing a short, very unhandsome pipe with tobacco, which he collected with his fingers out of the pocket of his coat. "Oh," he said, "I said one or two things that seemed to them rather strange. 'I would like to go somewhere,' I said, 'where I can serve.'

"'We do that everywhere,' the bishop said, gently reproaching me.

"'Oh no,' I said, 'we do not do it everywhere. Many serve the state, and many serve the church, and some serve the Golden Calf.' That put the lid on it, of course, and they said that for the time being I had better remain in the castle; there was plenty for me to do there."

"And that is where you are now?" asked Amadeus.

"Yes, that's where I am."

He struck the spade into the black earth and sat down on a stack of dry peat. "You must excuse me, Herr Baron," he said, "but I am tired. We were not taught this at the university, you know. The Heavenly Father whom they knew was not at home on the moors."

"And now?"

"Now he is more at home here than in the castle, Herr Baron. It is too noisy for him there."

"Do you do that for your own sake – the peat-digging, I mean?"

"For my sake? Oh no, I do as little as possible for my own sake. I do it for the people in the castle and for God's sake. The old ideas are gone for good, Herr Baron. The people in the castle don't like to see a man, with or without a surplice, get up and talk to them. There has been so much talk that they are fed up with it for a time. They are filled with distrust. Not only of the Heavenly Father, but likewise of those who call on him from the pulpit. They want bread and water. They do not like their parsons to have white hands."

"And now you are here, to show them that your hands are getting brown?"

"Certainly," replied the parson without a moment's hesitation. "'Do you pray out there on the peat bogs, parson?' one of the women asked me yesterday. She did not ask it in a very friendly spirit. 'No,' I answered, 'I want to cut so much peat that one of your children need not be cold all through next winter.' That's my way of life, Herr Baron. In two brown hands can lie much power of persuasion. Yes, even a bit of the gospel may lie in them. 'The glad tidings,' if one may paraphrase it like that. If the ancient times have returned, something like primitive Christianity may also return."

"You think that the ancient times have returned?"

"Certainly," said the parson again. "At any rate, crucifixions have come into fashion again, and they were always a sign of the ancient days."

Baron Amadeus looked away far over the moor, because in a flash he remembered the bowed head on the church door. "But have the crucifixions not come to an end at last?" he said after a long pause.

The parson shook his head. "They are only beginning," he replied. "The noisy ones are over, and even those not everywhere. But the silent ones are only beginning, those of hearts, not those of bodies. And in such times the parsons must not stand above their congregations, high up in carved pulpits, but among their congregations. They must be the poorest, the poorest of all, do you understand, Herr Baron? For only then will the people believe in them. Only when they cut peat will people believe in work, warmth, fire. Only when they go barefoot will people believe that

Christ went barefoot. Only when they are looked upon as fools will people believe in the wisdom which was proclaimed two thousand years ago. There is no other way, Herr Baron, no other way, even if the churches are crowded."

He knocked out the pipe on the torn sole of his shoe and trod out the red-hot tobacco. "I must go now," he said getting up. "There are some sick folk, and I must sit with them for a while."

He put the spade over his shoulder and looked around him once more. "There is the evening that we have been looking for," he said, smiling. "As quiet as God's word before churches existed."

They walked up to the sheepfold together. The baron asked whether he was all alone.

"Yes, all alone. Only then can one be a fool in peace. Two fools together constitute a danger, and probably they are also a little ridiculous."

"But you were not always alone?"

"Oh no, but the others are at peace now. We stayed till the last minute on the Baltic coast where I had my congregation. Then we went off together. The children froze to death. Three. Two girls and a boy. And my wife was machine-gunned from a low-flying airplane. Her mind was already distraught, and I considered it a mercy for her. She cursed God – and that is hard for a parson."

"And you believe that they are at peace now?"

"Certainly," replied the parson, again without any hesitation. "At that time God stretched out his hands over the roads by day and by night to take the human beings to his heart. When people refuse to believe in him, he always stretches out his hands."

The parson stood at the door and glanced into the shepherd's hut. "So, that's what it looks like," he said. "I have often wondered what it would look like here."

"From now on you can always come and sit here as often as you like," said the baron. "Very few do sit here."

The parson nodded. "There will soon be more," he said with his usual quiet confidence. "If those who suffer do not attract men, they suffer in the wrong way."

"And you think that I am suffering?" asked the baron.

"Who else?" replied the parson. "Who else? But it will get better and better. It will get better the moment you start cutting the peat for this small hearth yourself. It always begins with the hands."

"But if it does not begin with the heart, the hands will not begin either."

"Our Heavenly Father looks after the heart," said the parson, shouldering the spade again. "You may be quite sure of that, Herr Baron. In spite of bishops and churches. But we must look after our hands ourselves, see that they get a little brown, you understand, don't you?"

He smiled in his childlike way, an innocent smile devoid of all ill feeling, and all his features seemed to share in it. The essence of his whole being was in this smile.

Then he nodded to the baron and slowly walked down the narrow path.

8

THE PARSON'S NAME WAS Wittkopp, and he became a great help to Baron Amadeus, as far as one man can help another. He was as great a help as Christoph, although he did not tell stories about the old families. It was just that he was there, and his calm, quite unobtrusive presence was secure and certain like the certainty of the evening of which he had spoken, while they stood together at the peat bog. It was not the self-assurance of those who always had a text ready from the Old or New Testament whenever a load of pain and worry was unpacked before them. He seldom quoted the Bible. He even said that they had forfeited that right for a time, because they had used the words of the Bible like conjurers to support men and opinions that ought not to have been supported. A church that had sent its clergy into the war ought to be absolutely silent for some time, he said, so that it could relearn the Ten Commandments, especially the fifth commandment.

So he told no stories and did not quote the Bible. The secret of his power to help may have lain in his fearlessness, just as Christoph was without fear. They were the only two round about the shepherd's hut of whom Baron Amadeus could say this, and because of it they were, for him, the only two completely mysterious beings. Only he did not know whether this mystery had quite the same origin in both of them.

But he became very well aware that neither of them blew his own trumpet – and then he happened to remember that Jakob, too, belonged to them. So there were three in all, and three seemed to him a great many in his narrow sphere of life. Perhaps the reason was that time did not exist for them, which meant the loud, noisy doings of the day, that only longed for the evening and for nothing else. The loudspeaker time in which men thought that they must get help out of the ether, and when the loudspeaker was switched off there reigned the terrible silence of ghosts. People knew that the ether was always filled with voices, but with a turn of the hand they could be silenced. This time was in man's power, and with a movement of his hand he could conjure it up, in order to forget the other time, the great, powerful untouchable time that stood silently in the background.

And those three lived in that untouchable time. The parson called it "the primitive age," and Jakob and Christoph probably gave it a different name. But it was the same element and it gave them their sense of calm security. From this sense of certainty arose their power to perceive those among the uncertain who were in danger, just as Jakob had seen that the baron Amadeus was in danger. Just as Parson Wittkopp, when, very gradually, he had become familiar with the people on the moor, had recognized that the young Frau Erdmuthe and the forester's daughter were both in danger. "You must keep an eye on those two," he told Amadeus. Intuitively he felt that those two were more endangered than the others. He could not exactly explain it, but he was reminded of the eyes of his wife before they were darkened. He had not forgotten them. Such eyes still saw the things of this world, but they saw them only as pictures, and behind the pictures they saw the wall on which the pictures hung.

"We," said Wittkopp, "see things in space, and there is room about them. But the others no longer see the room around because there is a wall behind. They do not yet know it is the wall against which they will knock their heads. We must take them by the hand, yes, as a matter of fact, we ought never to let their hands go."

"Do you know the origin of all their trouble, parson?" asked Amadeus.

No, that Wittkopp did not know. Perhaps it was because they had been deprived of security in their lives, that which is indispensable to us all, and which, of course, was different for each individual.

It was as if a child were running through a familiar room, when suddenly the floor opened beneath his feet and he fell into an abyss. Sometimes only the legs were broken, and broken legs could be healed. But sometimes the heart, as one might say, was broken, and that was not so easy to heal. That was what happened to his wife when they had to leave the parsonage and journey along the roads, for the parsonage had been God and the world for her. For Frau Erdmuthe perhaps it had been her homeland and for the young girl the so-called Reich. But he was not sure of that. All he knew was that the floor had opened up before their feet, that he could read in their eyes. His wife's eyes had been just like theirs, and the children's eyes, too, when they were cold and terrified on the sleighs. Dilated eyes, into which the whole world had been hurled – not only carefully selected bits of the world such as were generally provided for children. They had indeed been "overwhelmed" – that was the right word for it.

The Baron Amadeus was very worried and meditated about it for a long time, but he did not yet know how "to take them by the hand."

He rather thought that things would go better now in the forester's house, because the forester Buschan had been discharged from the camp. He had heard the news from Christoph, who had lingered for a time on the threshold of the hut after he had told it. "He will now have to appear before the court," he said, looking past the baron over the marshes. "They are very much afraid of it. I would be afraid, too, for I have never had to stand before a court – not before an earthly court. These aren't even judges, either."

"And what are they then?" asked the baron.

"Oh, sir," said Christoph, deeply worried, "they were struck, and now they strike back. But a real judge has not been struck first."

"But right has been struck, Christoph."

"Right cannot be struck, sir. Nor can God be struck. You can strike a horse when you are drunk or savage in your heart. But you can't strike God, because your arms are too short. They could crucify the vicar in the village without a name, their arms were long enough for that. But they could not crucify God. He smiled, do you remember, sir? God smiled in the vicar's face."

He started to go and then turned around again. "Do you remember, sir," he asked gently, "how the Christ Child sat on the sleigh and the master could not pull him down from the seat? Nor will the judges be able to pull him down, for he is still on his way to a cottager's sick child. Today, sir, just the same as ever."

The forester came on the evening of the next day, and the baron, who was sitting on the doorstep, signed to him to sit down on the trunk of the alder tree, where Jakob and the woman and his brothers had sat. The baron could see by the resemblance in their faces that the girl was of the same blood as the forester, but his face had developed under different influences. This was a simple face, more easily read than the girl's, and it reminded the baron of many faces he had seen during the past years. It looked as if it had been broken, and the man held the pieces together only with difficulty. It was devoid of hope and had not in it that hatred which in his daughter's face seemed to unite the features, as it were, and to bind them into a whole.

"I have not come to justify myself, Herr Baron," said the forester at last. "Perhaps not even to ask you to forgive me – I only wish to tell you that I did not want to do what I did that time, and that is the truth."

He picked up a piece of wood from the ground, turning it in his hands while he was speaking. Now and again he lifted his eyes to the face of the baron; otherwise he looked down on the wood in his hands. His daughter would have sat there very differently.

"How do you know that I am aware whether or not you did it?" asked Amadeus at length.

The hands stopped their restless movement and the eyes stared blankly at the questioner.

"You did not know it, Herr Baron?" he asked at last in a low voice.

"I may have suspected it," replied Amadeus. "Nothing more. Have you spoken about it?"

The forester shook his head. "My wife and my daughter knew it," he said, "and the district leader to whom I wrote it."

"They say that the district leader is dead."

The forester was still staring at him. "And Herr Baron thinks that I could . . ."

"Of course, you could, Buschan," said Amadeus. "Or is there anybody else you have harmed?"

The forester shook his head. "I did my duty; I was not one of those who wanted to do harm."

He looked down at the piece of wood in his hands. "I was not interrogated there," he said after a while. "They only despised us. That was all they did. But it was the worst."

"There were worse things," said Amadeus.

"I know, Herr Baron, I know. I do not wish to compare myself. But Herr Baron had something that compensated for all that. I had nothing. No one had despised me until then."

"I do not despise," said Amadeus.

"But I have done harm to the Herr Baron, I have stolen four years of his life from him."

"Not life," said Amadeus. "Something quite different. Life cannot be stolen. And as to the other thing, well, I suppose you had lost control of it, and then it ran on of itself."

"The Herr Baron ought not to console me," said the forester, and now his voice was full of despair.

"Do you think I should have come out as the others did?" asked the baron. "I did come out like that, but now a year has gone by. Your wife has wept much during this year."

Children were singing around the cottages on the moor in the distance, and the forester raised his head to listen. It was long since he had heard children's voices.

"I am afraid; I can't do it," he said after a while, when the children had finished singing. "You have opened a door for me, Herr Baron, and I might escape through it. But I could only do it secretly, and the Herr Baron would follow me with his eyes."

"I wouldn't follow you with my eyes," said Amadeus. "I would take care of your wife and your daughter – she is still very young."

"It would not be right," the forester went on. "There must be a court of justice for everyone, and for me too."

"The court of justice was here," said Amadeus. "The trial is finished. But I was not judge."

"Who was?" asked the forester in a low voice.

"Where a man confesses, there is a court of justice. I only listened."

The forester got up. Twilight had fallen and the goatsuckers called from the edge of the marshes. "I am a simple man," he said. "I would like to live among trees again. I went off the right track. I listened to the voices of men."

"There are periods," said the baron, "when men believe in barbed wire, victors and vanquished alike. It's a primitive belief. We must start to believe in something different."

"I have started," said the forester, "I have started this very evening, and I thank you, Herr Baron."

Amadeus remained seated on the doorstep and waited for the stars. The forester had disappeared in the darkness like a shy animal. For the first time Amadeus thought that much had happened in this year. After all, it did not seem to be true that time did not exist for him. When he sat on this doorstep a year ago he had been different. A year ago he had spoken in a different way to this man's wife. He did not know what was the cause of it – perhaps his brothers, perhaps Christoph. Perhaps no human being was the cause at all, but something that he could not fathom. Something that had arisen from the past history of the family, as when the Christ Child had climbed on the sleigh. Perhaps he had let himself "be deceived" as his father had been "deceived."

He did not know. He only realized that he was himself like all his ancestors described in Christoph's tales, the kind of man who can be changed. It made him feel insecure, for he had thought that he was beyond all transformation, that he was stamped even though not cleansed. There was so much confidence in the utterances of the victors that he too ought to have become sure and confident. But he had not. Probably the victors had not either. But their words were confident and he had no kind of security. Words did not delude him any longer; that was why now and again a word could so terrify him. One of the parson's words or Christoph's. Because these were old words from a time when a word still meant something. "In the beginning was the Word." At that time it was truly real. And when Wittkopp and Christoph spoke, it was as if their words had their origin in that time. In that time of few words which they called "the primitive age," when no newspapers or books existed. "Right cannot be struck –" that was such a phrase. Today they would quote a thousand proofs against it and yet it was a phrase of "primitive times," unshakable and unconquerable. An old coachman knew it better than all courts of justice and better than the victors, and better than he, Baron Amadeus, himself.

He felt that such words guided him. He was open to them, he heard them in his heart. A year ago he would not have heard them. And when would he be so old that he would not only listen to them but speak them himself? They had not been in a camp, neither the parson nor the coachman. They had only lived their lives and finally they had trod the bitter road of flight and loss. So the camp was not the last stage, nor was suffering the last. There must be something yet in store which was more than all this. But he could not give it a name. No, he had not even discerned its features. But he was straining after it. This was a beautiful, old word, which was used in the Bible too. He had not yet reached completeness; he was far from it. One had not only to grow old. That was a natural process, without merit or dignity. Man could even grow old in a half-hearted, yes, in an ignominious way. Man could also suffer in an ignominious way without influencing or attracting others who were suffering, as the parson had said. Suffering just for themselves, as it were, as one could rejoice just for oneself. As many in the camp had eaten their bread in corners of the barracks stealthily, because of some unforgotten shame of possession.

The man who had sat here was a simple man. He had only gone "off the right track." He had listened to the voices of the times, to the voices of the loudspeakers. The baron had opened a door for him, but the simple man had stopped on the threshold. A voice within had whispered to him that one must not sneak away, that there must be a law for everyone, that it would be a despicable way out to sneak off. Where had that voice come from? It could not have come from his own world. For more than ten years that world had led him along the easy path which was "off the track." He had not been guilty, he had only believed in God or in a particular world order, blindly, as all faiths have to be believed; he had believed in "what man does not see."

Besides, much had been presented to him: men, words, and flags. It was not his fault that those were false gods. He was a simple man. He had not learned to distinguish and to weigh up last things. He had let himself go with the current. Now people were crucified and burned, as the church had crucified the heretics. The judges broke the wand. Judges who were selected according to how much they had suffered. He who had suffered was allowed to judge.

He was not asked how he had come through his suffering. Most had come through it with hatred in their hearts. They judged as they had been judged a few years before. They struck back. They did not know that right does not strike back.

Amadeus remembered how the woman had come to him a year ago, and how he had answered, "I will only watch how the scales move up and down." Today he did not wish to look on. The others did so and it gave them pleasure to look on. But it no longer gave him any pleasure. In Christoph's hands the scales would keep in balance, and Amadeus did not wish to be less than his old coachman. He did not wish to cast the dice, as his ancestor had done.

The stars had already come out and were sparkling above the marshes. The dead did not stand at his elbow any longer. The bad dreams came more rarely. The flowers that he had sown around the cottages were now in bloom, and he had not struck the man who had sat with him an hour ago. It was not much that he had reaped in a year, but when he put grain on grain it might well be a handful. And a handful was much for a time when one had "done nothing."

He did not see the forester again for a long time. The brothers, having consulted Amadeus, had taken him back into their service. The woman had anxiously awaited his return from Baron Amadeus, but he had told her nothing. He had sat for a while by the kitchen fire looking into the flames, and he only said, "He is the first who has not hit back." The woman was silent, but the girl broke into a laugh. "He will make up for that," she said. "He is not the kind who forgets."

The forester had glanced at his daughter and shaken his head. "You must not be so certain," was all he said. "It was no good to me, being so certain."

It was not long before Buschan noticed that it was not only the victors who had despised him. He had not expected that one of his own blood would despise him, and he was deeply hurt. They had gone through all the past years together united in the same faith. The child had often supported him when he had wavered. And now she despised him. She did not say so, but he felt it in her eyes which would often not meet his own, in the atmosphere of unapproachable aloofness which she set up around herself. Above all in the fact that she did not contradict him whenever he owned that he had made a mistake, that the whole nation had made a mistake. She did not contradict him, as one does not contradict a person who is ill or who is blind.

At first he had tried to convince Barbara, but then he held his peace. He accepted it as his punishment, the hardest that could have been imposed upon him. He had led her as a child, and at a time when she could have been led along any way. He had led her the wrong way and she had gone so far along it that there was no turning back for her anymore. She was blinder than he was, but she was prouder. Her pride had not been broken, and probably it could not be broken without tearing her life to pieces.

There was much he did not know. He had heard about the "dark one," but nobody but Baron Amadeus knew that he had been the light of her life. A light that had suddenly gone out, the glare from a terrible mistake. She could not be blamed for the fact that in her eyes the baron was a murderer, not a saint as he was in her poor father's eyes, a murderer who had caused her hands to be tied so that there might be no witness of the murder. A murderer who was to be hated more than anything else on earth. Something that had to be exterminated so that one could breathe again, so that the heart did not beat like a hammer in one's breast by day and by night. Nor could the forester know that a child lived under this confused and darkened heart. His eyes were not schooled to detect the secret of a growing life before it became apparent to all. Even if he had known it, he would never have understood how it was that this child could transform the life of the young mother, could spread over it so terrific a darkness that the local name the father had earned for himself got its real sense and meaning through it. He would never have understood that this child seemed to be alive and to grow only to warn her and call to her mind somebody whose life had ended on the gallows while according to the ideas of the mother he ought to have sat on a throne. He would never have understood that this child was not the calm fruit of bliss and love, but was to be the voice of vengeance and retaliation, that it spoke while still under its mother's heart, long before it was given the speech of men. And that while she was lost in the dreamy contemplation of an unreal future the young mother lent her ear to the low, whispered, scarcely audible words without knowing that these were only her own words which her darkened mind put into the mouth of her still unquickened child. And these words whispered or sometimes only breathed to herself demanded that judgment be passed before the child opened its eyes. So that the first half-unseeing glance of these eyes should see the judgment, not the judgment of the murdered one, but the judgment of the murderer.

The listening, brooding woman did not yet know where the blow would fall, but probably the spot would be on the moor, somewhere near the place where she had found solid ground underfoot again, where she had stepped out from shifting ground and had left behind her all her memories, and where they had set the trap which had caught wolves in former times. Somewhere there it would happen, so that the same sun might shine into the dimming eyes of her enemy that had shone on the face of the hangman.

There was no one who could take her by the hand and lead her back into reality out of her confused and bloody fantasies, no one to whom she could speak, no one on whose breast she could cry out her heart. While still a child she had become accustomed to harsh and ferocious pictures and ideas. Every tear had been looked upon as contemptible in her world, and she had been taught to hate at a time when she ought to have been playing with dolls. The wheel had carried her along; the glitter of the turning spokes had dazzled her, and in her confusion her hand still clung to the axletree which had been hurled into the abyss long before.

She was not ashamed that she was with child. She had been taught that there was nothing a woman should be more proud of than of bearing children – not for a husband or a lover but for the Reich alone. And if the Reich had been shattered for a while, she herself was as a sacred vessel wherein the seed of the future was stored.

It was not that she was intoxicated with these words; for her there was no more intoxication. There was only a gloomy resolve which she turned over and over in her mind. Nobody understood a word of her language; she was left over, a relic from a period of hysteria which had swept her along. There was nobody whom she could love. She could only despise and hate. She had to despise her father, who had been broken by a year in prison, whose eyes were so clouded that a murderer appeared to him to be a saint. She had to despise most of those who once had peopled her Valhalla, and who by now had managed to sneak off with false names, with forged papers, or with poison for a last emergency. She was left quite alone, but she had allowed herself to be the vessel of the last fruit, before the fearless one had been torn out of her arms.

So now she sat again as before on the outskirts of the moor, hidden among the juniper bushes, and watched Baron Amadeus disappear among the young birches, then emerge and disappear again. She was crouching in the heather like a hunter lying in wait for game. She did not hear the cuckoo call and did not see the shadows of the clouds as they sailed over the marshes. She felt neither sun nor rain. She felt only the new life stir within her and heard the faint whispering which she knew so well, but to which she bent down ever deeper and deeper to learn still more surely its secret message. Her young face gradually altered, not only because of nature's work beneath her heart, but because of what was going on in that heart. She could not keep the reflection of all that obsessed her mind from showing in her face and from slowly changing it. Nor did she perceive it when she looked each morning into her little mirror, for her eyes had changed too. She no longer had any conception of beauty or disfigurement; to her only time still meant something, time which each day left its imprint on her features; and each morning in her little mirror she could look at the new sign, and the whispering voice would ask, "When . . . ?"

There was nobody who could tell her that she lived a dreadful life, that she was a mother who was poisoning her child before it was born, that the voice she heard was not the voice of her child, but her own voice which in her willfulness she lent to the one unborn.

It frightened her that it was Christoph whose eyes had recognized that she was with child, long before her mother saw it. For one morning before he went to the castle, he had stood still when she walked past him, raising his hand as if he wanted to stop her. "Don't go to the marshes, young mother," he said, "where the folk of the netherworld live. Better sit on the doorstep, so that our Heavenly Father may find you."

She recoiled before his raised hand and stopped, for her knees were trembling. But he had already turned and gone away.

Why had he said "young mother"? Why had he seen what nobody else had yet seen and what nobody should see before its time? The hand which he had raised was as much a murderer's hand as that of the baron or of the Lithuanian laborer, and he had better not raise it, so that she might not remember it too distinctly. He was already on the verge of death, and she would let him have his brief term of life. She would have patience with him. It was not worthwhile to forestall death, as he was so old.

When the eyes of her mother recognized her condition, she was no longer frightened. Steadily she looked into the face that had become strange and unfamiliar and nodded. "Yes, that's how it is," she said, "but nobody need help me."

She did not say "Forgive me" or "Help me!" She only looked at her mother as if she had been eavesdropping, with a slight disgust, as a girl may look at her mother when she has found her unkind or rough.

But she grew restless now that she was not the only one who knew it, and for a few days she did not sit at the edge of the moor but climbed down the wooded slopes into the plain and only came back in the evening.

The forester said nothing. Once he tried to stroke her hair as she was sitting on the doorstep when he came home from the woods. But she evaded his hand. "It's mine, only mine," she said, as if with this awkward gesture he had tried to claim a share in the child.

Apart from these two it was only Baron Amadeus who heard about it, and he was told by Christoph. At first he would not believe it, but later when he thought it over, he was not surprised. It filled him with a slight horror, which he tried to overcome but without success. For him it meant the immortality of evil which nothing could destroy.

It was as if evil had become master of the new generation, no matter whether it had been condemned or not. It had become invulnerable because it had found a vessel in which to preserve itself from death. It was not only laid in store here but in a thousand unknown vessels, which were hidden away until the time came to reappear.

He had not been able to prevent it. He had just sat on his doorstep pondering about his own life. He was as guilty of this child as Wittkopp or his brothers or Christoph. He had not drawn the suffering to him because he had only thought of his own suffering. He did not even know whether the child which the girl carried under her heart was a joy to her or a burden. But he remembered the smile with which the "dark one" had looked at the upraised hands of the mothers whose children he had killed – killed at the very time when this child had been conceived. Probably this child would smile in the same way as soon as it knew how to smile.

The baron had never before thought how awful it could be to inherit a smile – as awful as to inherit a blemish or a disease.

He did not speak to anybody about it, nor did he go to the forester's house. It seemed to him as if the child would confront him there, as if long before it was born it would smilingly look on as he struggled to find his way out of the evil of the times, back into what the parson called the primitive age. Or to find his way into something that was above the present and the past, into a period where man was neither wolf nor lamb but was master of both.

He was not yet aware that the child had long since set out on the road to meet him, although it was still unborn.

It was a hot and oppressive summer on the moor, and Wittkopp got his brown hands well before the expected time. In the afternoon heavy storms hung above the hills and their dim-colored fringes appeared above the marshes. The woodlarks were silent, and the little birches stood as motionless as if their leaves were made of metal. The bitterns' boom was heard more than ever before, as if the bogs were opened and more ready than ever to lure and swallow up lost travelers. At dusk when the lightning had faded away and raindrops fell from the trees, little will-o'-the-wisps hovered over the marshes near the dense reed patches, where the "dark one" had had his abode. The cottage women said they were the poor souls of children that had not been baptized.

There was much illness among the children, and even Goldie was not spared. Her child-mother came to the baron and said that the doll with the yellow eyes had spotted typhus, and the women had told her that only the baron knew something for certain about the sickness. That was quite correct, even if the baron knew more about the sickness than about the way to treat it. However, Goldie got an old scarf tied around her neck and soon found herself on the road to recovery.

Christoph called it a plague year. He maintained that there were years when the earth was angry, or if not the earth, then those who lived beneath the earth. Years in which the grubs came to the top and destroyed the meadows, or gardens fell prey to the fen cricket, or when the bark beetle ravaged the woods. Years which were but a mirror of the hearts of men when the poisons secreted in plants sank down to their roots. But down there, he said, the evil of hearts was cleansed and purged, and men and earth began anew in the light of the sun, as if both had made atonement and had drawn up a new covenant.

About this time he began to come away earlier from the castle, which he declared was a "wasp's nest," and he sat on the doorstep of the hut until the baron came home from his excursions. It was noticeable that the heavy summer oppressed him, too, and that now for the first time his old, quiet hands began to tremble a little. Amadeus first saw it when these hands put the red-hot cinders on the tobacco in his pipe.

"You ought to take it a little easy now, Christoph," he said then. "The castle isn't the right place for you now, and my brother will learn how to get on without you."

"The Herr Erasmus has always been slow to learn," replied Christoph. "He mustn't be left in the lurch. There are too many women in the castle whose grandmothers still rode on broomsticks."

As he left for the forester's house he took once more a long look over the moor on which an ominous, livid light fell from behind the distant clouds. "You ought not to walk there so often, sir," he said gently. "When the earth is angry, it will not tolerate men. It wants to be alone while it heals itself."

But Baron Amadeus did not feel that the earth was angry. It was different, and there was more often than before an oppressive, brooding silence when the walls of thunderclouds slowly rose up over the horizon. Then the black woodpecker called louder than was its wont and the tall pine trees stood motionless as if under a spell.

But the baron was about to write the last sheets of his manuscript, and as in a dream he roamed about through the day filled with visions of the past and endeavored to link them to the present time. He had not the gift of premonition; he did not meet anyone on his wanderings who could have awakened him out of his far-off world.

It was a day like all other days, when one late afternoon he stood between the two juniper bushes, where the trap had been buried, shielding his eyes with his hand against the sun. He had not been to this spot since the man had lain here in the heather, and he did not know why he had come. But as he gazed over the sparkling marshes above which a heavy wall of clouds rose slowly and noiselessly, a strong desire took possession of him to track out the path by which the girl had come that time, when she stepped from between the reed beds, and if possible to find the reed hut, which the "dark one" had probably built himself there. And perhaps he would be able – before the thundershower began – to set fire to the hut and so wipe it from the face of the earth. Perhaps by so doing he might clear away the evil that had had its abode there, and perhaps the girl and her unborn child would feel relieved when the place became what it had been before, a home for cranes and no longer the refuge of two exiled, forsaken beings who had clung to each other in their terrible loneliness, and who in all their downfall and ruin wanted to have a child so that it might one day continue the tracks which now ended in this wilderness.

And so as he stood there, his hand above his eyes, lost in thought, the first bullet struck the baron. He felt a sudden pain in his left shoulder, before he heard the shots – many shots as it seemed to him – and he felt the second bullet in his arm, before he was aware of what was happening.

He let himself fall on to his left side so that his face was now turned toward the wood behind him, and in falling he drew the revolver out of his pocket. He saw the bushes and the trunks of the tall pine trees above them, and between the trunks half hidden by them, the forms of two or three people, young, as it seemed – who were already about to make off before he fired shot on shot at them.

He seemed to hear a voice, a high-pitched, clear, authoritative voice which was familiar to him, but familiar, as it were, only through a mist. Then the figures were gone, in the distance boughs broke, and the forest stood again as it had stood before – empty, silent, lit with a brassy light.

Amadeus turned on his back, for his left side was very painful, and now only the blue, slightly veiled vault of heaven was above him, a vast dome below which hung a bird of prey, but he could no longer recognize what kind of bird it was.

He moved his lips a little, but there was no taste of blood. A deep, heavy, almost blissful fatigue fell upon him, as if it fell out of the vast canopy of heaven, and he slowly closed his eyes, before which appeared a serene, purple light.

He wanted to think, but his thoughts flowed away like water through a sieve. The shots and the voice had receded so far that all that had happened seemed years ago, and he was only conscious of the fact that he now lay where the other had lain, on the same spot, as if time had repeated itself. As if it had played a trick with them, and neither of them had known it or been aware of it – not he himself, not the other.

And so, gently, under the wall of clouds which was rising higher and higher, his eyes closed, and the last he thought was that now his heart would stop beating, too, and that he must keep that in mind, so that he could tell Christoph what it felt like when the heart stopped beating.

When he awoke he did not know how much time had elapsed, in fact, he was not even conscious of time. He lay there in a world without space and time. The wall of clouds had not risen higher. It had broken up and was flecked with pale patches, as if rain showers had poured down beyond the moor. The air was much cooler around his temples.

He slowly turned his head to look at the wood, and then he saw the girl. But he remembered Christoph's expression – it was the "young mother" whom he saw. She was sitting in the heather a few paces from him, her hands clasped around her knees like someone lost in the contemplation of a landscape, and she was gazing at him.

He laid his head more comfortably, as far as his pains allowed, and then their eyes met. He did not yet connect her presence with what had happened. He only tried to take in her whole appearance, and the first thing he realized was that her eyes had changed. They were without hatred now. He realized it as quickly and distinctly, as if all that had happened had only occurred so that he might realize this.

They watched him without moving, with a sort of calm curiosity, as children will watch a grown person who is occupied with work which is new to them. There was no fury, no pity in them, but they were not like the eyes of the man who had lain on this spot before. They were neither cold nor withdrawn nor aloof, they had not yet been set on any of the horrors of life. It was as if they were looking at something they had never seen before.

"What are you doing here?" he asked at last, scarcely moving his lips.

The answer was indeed surprising to him. "I am watching to see how you die," she said. She said it as calmly as if she were telling him that the sun was setting.

At first he was surprised, but later he was shocked. Not at the words she used, for the meaning of the words had not yet come home to him. It had not occurred to him that he could die here. But he was shocked that she was sitting there to look on. That a girl who carried a child under her heart, who was herself still a child, sat there in the heather stained red with blood at her feet and was waiting for his last breath and would then go back into the routine of everyday life just as if she had been picking berries and her little basket was filled to the rim.

His mind worked slowly, probably because he had lost a lot of blood, but he did realize that something terrible was happening here. Not that they had shot at and hit him, but that apparently the "young mother" had arranged and managed it all. That she had dismissed her workmen, and now sat there to look at her work as calmly as if she had had a stage fitted up and now sat there waiting for the performance. And the performance consisted in the dying of a man, in a lonely monologue which had no other witness than this "young mother."

Perhaps after all it was the plaguy earth, as Christoph had called it, that had produced all this, that had designed this sort of recurrence, so that the past might be extinguished by the present. A man had been caught and condemned here between the two bushes, and now the earth caused the other to be caught and condemned, so that a balance might be struck and it might be cleansed and exculpated.

There, Christoph had said, under the roots, the wickedness of hearts would be cleansed too. And so Amadeus was not appalled at what had happened to him and was still happening. He was appalled that something was left over that was not purified but was only looking on. For that which was looking on was not yet purified, the earth had not got hold of it, had not drawn it down into the workings of its roots.

With his right hand he cautiously fumbled for a cigarette and pushed it between his lips. "Light it for me, please," he said.

But she shook her head.

It took him some time to get the matches out of his pocket and strike one. He did not have to cough; evidently the lung was not hit. But this was unimportant to him at the moment.

"Have you looked on before?" he asked, as if the words had only just been spoken.

She shook her head.

His eyes followed the blue smoke as it rose in the calm air.

"I have often looked on," he said, "very often. It is not easy. It needs a strong heart. Animals go into the thicket so that nobody can look on. Animals are wise."

"I don't need to be wise," said the girl quietly.

"But you must come nearer," he said after a pause. "It's too comfortable looking on from an easy chair. You must be near enough to discern death's handwriting. His handwriting is very small."

"I'm quite near enough," said the girl.

He gently shook his head. "One must be near enough to see the gray film that comes over the eyes. Like the first evening mist over the marshes. There is no other opportunity of beholding the work of the Hand from Beyond."

"I am sure I shall see it quite well from here," replied the girl.

The baron gazed long up into the evening sky that became slowly clear and pure. "Now I need not search for the evening any longer," he said. "It was so easy to find it. Wittkopp made it so hard for himself."

The birds woke up once more after the storm had passed over. The woodlark sang and the black woodpecker called again from the depths of the forest. The baron listened intently, and he would have liked to know whether the "young mother" heard the voices of the birds too. But he did not ask.

"You are aware," he said after a pause, raising his right hand which had again grasped the revolver, "you are aware that it would not be difficult for me to look on while you die, instead of you looking on at my death."

"I know that you will not do that," said the girl.

"You are quite right there," replied the baron. "Because the bullet would go through you and your child."

For the first time her expression changed. She had not known that he was aware of how things stood with her. A deep flush passed over her face, so quickly that Amadeus could not tell whether it was anger or shame that gave rise to it.

"You are not a child-murderer," she said sullenly.

The baron nodded. "No, that I am not," he replied. "It's enough that you are."

"I am not," she cried out, pressing her hands into the heather as if she were about to jump up.

"Certainly you are," said Amadeus. "You allow it to look on. You are not the only one who is looking on. Don't you feel that its eyes are open and it's looking and looking? When there was slaughtering to be done on the farm at home, we were packed off; our father did not allow us to be on the scene. That was in the old days that have gone for good. But even nowadays this shouldn't be. It's as if the child were to be accursed, and you ought not to curse it. It should be the sun to you – your sun which has set for the time being. No one should curse the sun."

She had got up and was staring at him. Her face was blanched.

"It would be easy for you," he went on in his low, even voice, "to take my revolver and make an end of me. My hand is weak, probably I wouldn't even try to defend myself. But you'd better not do that, because the child would look on at that, too. You must not embroil it, it will be the only thing left to you. After this evening nothing else will be left to you. Your hatred is dead already, I see that by your eyes. They are filled with anxiety, I see it. And you used not to be afraid."

She wanted to speak, but she only went on staring at him, as if a great transformation was taking place in his face.

"Many things are beyond our strength," he continued gently. "We think them out in the confusion of our hearts, but when they are there, they are beyond our strength. Nature is stronger than the will of our heart, and it protects children when the mothers do not care to protect them any longer. It is a pity, for I had thought of looking after this child. It will be so poor, so terribly poor. Like a child who has got lost and has to be suckled by a she-wolf."

The sunset shone above the marshes, a wide gate glowing in deeper and deeper crimson into which the herons flew. A marvelous silence reigned over the world; it made all words superfluous and meaningless. It was as if distant gods rose up above the horizon and looked down on all that had happened without their will.

"You ought to go now," said the baron. He no longer looked at the girl but into the sunset, and his eyes were filled with the quiet, red glow. "Best of all go to Christoph. He is the calmest and cleverest of all. He will best know what to do. He will be able to tell whether it is still worthwhile to do anything for me, better than any doctor. He can see death, the real death. Just tell him where you have found me, nothing more. You must only think of your child now, so that it may forget what it has seen."

She glanced around the silent moor; her face was now deeply distressed and utterly forlorn, but the baron did not see it, as he did not look at her.

"One more thing," he said as if in farewell. "See if you can find the cartridge cases. And take the revolver with you. Give it to Christoph. It is forbidden to have arms, and Kelley must not have worries over me."

She stooped obediently and groped about in the heather, as if she were blind. She put the cartridge cases into the pocket of her dress and took the revolver. She held it as a child holds a weapon.

"Don't run," said the baron, closing his eyes. "You mustn't run anymore now, it might harm the child. But don't walk too slowly either, so that you get home before dark. Be careful not to make a false step and go tumbling down. You must look after yourself very carefully now."

She hid the revolver under her apron and went. After a time she began to run. She ran straight across the marshes, because it was the nearest way, though it was not without danger for her.

Christoph saw her coming and went to meet her. Later, he said that she had suddenly appeared out of the sunset like a ghost. She screamed at him, though he stood just in front of her. She screamed like a poor, dying animal, but he had understood what she wanted to tell him. Then she had collapsed at his feet and had lain there as if she were dead. He had sent the women to her, and then they had gone across the moor with a stretcher. Goldie's little mother had run to the castle to fetch Baron Erasmus.

9

AMADEUS LAY QUITE STILL. When the girl's footsteps had died away, the immense silence returned. There was no longer a purple light before his eyes, and he could again see the grandeur of the sunset. It seemed to him that only now he had found "the evening," as Wittkopp put it; quite different an evening from all those that had gone before, the ultimate in time that could be found, and as solemn as nothing had ever been before.

Perhaps it was because he was lying, not standing or walking. Because he saw the world from a different angle. Perhaps because he could not simply get up and go. Twilight was falling and the goatsucker wantoning above in playful circles flew closer and closer down toward him. He watched it so that he always saw it framed against the grandeur of the evening glow. He did not turn his eyes from this glow, which was always there as the chief beauty of this evening.

He did not think much. His left side was so painful that he could not piece together his wandering thoughts. He did not think overmuch about the girl. He only saw her sitting there, as if she had not gone away, but he did not consider how she happened to be there. Probably he should have taken her "by the hand," as Wittkopp had admonished him. He had not found the way into her walled-up heart. But anyhow she had gone now – the revolver under her apron – to fetch the others.

Mostly he thought of the way in which he had shot at the three escaping figures. This alone was the riddle of the evening. His hand and his eye had been perfectly steady and accurate. And yet he remembered that before he pulled the trigger he had shifted his aim by a hand's breadth – for all the three shots.

He turned the question over and over in his mind. Why had he done this? He had done it automatically, at any rate without thinking. His hand had done it; he did not know who or what had guided his hand. The natural thing would have been for the hand to take aim and hold it firmly. It had certainly taken aim, but it had not held it. Not from weakness or uncertainty, no, it had not wanted to hold it firmly. Something had happened within him that he could no longer recall. He thought a long time about it, but he did not find an answer.

He still had three cigarettes, and these would probably suffice if the girl had really gone to find Christoph. He shivered suddenly, for it was borne in on him that she need not do that. He had not thought of this possibility till now. She might just as well have gone off and left him to silence and the night frost. She might have thought that she had seen enough of his dying, and that the dew and the mist and the cold of the earth would do the rest.

But then he dismissed such thoughts. They were contradicted by something he had seen in her face. It was as if in place of hatred he had seen dread – the immeasurable dread of a child before the unknown. There was no blood track behind her as there was behind the steps of the "dark one." Perhaps the course of her thoughts had been bloody, but not that of her actions. Between those two there was a towering wall which had to be climbed, before a thought could become an action. Evil was different from the idea of evil. Pulling the trigger of a pistol was quite different from picturing the action. It was like the step from the parapet of a tower into the abyss. It was the ultimate decision and there was no return from it.

He was chilled through by this time, and the heather which he touched with his right hand was cold and damp. The evening star had come out, and the first owls were hooting. How beautiful the world was before night enveloped it! A secret life awoke in the forest and all around. The light feet of the beetles and mice slipped over the mosses. The lonely dog began to bark again in the distance.

The baron closed his eyes and listened. He did not think about whether he would soon hear the steps of the men coming across the moor with the stretcher. He only thought that he had not accomplished all that he had wished to accomplish, and this filled him with a gentle melancholy. He had not taken the bow of the cello into his hands again. He had not made the hard way for his brother's wife easy enough. He might have made Goldie a better bandage when she was ill. He ought to have said to Jakob that the donkey had not lost its load, that it had only put it down in an oasis in the shade, and that it would be back again when the time had come to take up the load again.

No, he had not been transformed quickly enough. An impulse from outside had been necessary – these shots, for instance, two of which had hit him. An impulse from within ought to have sufficed, from out his heart and not from out the bushes of this wood, where the accomplices had stood and escaped as soon as they thought that they had done their duty.

But now everything was all right again. Especially as he had shifted the barrel of the revolver before he had shot. He did not yet know why he had done so, but he realized that it had been good, good in a deep, mysterious, inexplicable way.

He smiled faintly and opened his eyes again. It was not easy, for the lids were so tired. But now he saw the stars, all the countless stars, just as they were that night of his homecoming when he had been amazed at their number. A sparkling vault under which he was lying so that the radiance fell into his eyes.

It was comforting and so marvelous that he was no longer afraid. He realized it suddenly without any warning. It dispelled his fever and calmed his thoughts. It enveloped him like a warm mantle. It was as if a miraculous form had knelt down beside him, close to his heart – this was what he had striven for so long, so long, and now it was there without his raising a hand, without his hearing its light steps: the sense of being at home.

It did not matter whether the girl had fetched the men or not. Even if he had to lie here the whole long night under the rising and setting stars, the sense of being at home would remain. It would neither rise nor set. It welled up from sources which were hidden from him, but he felt that it would not leave him no matter whether he lived or died. It was not attached to the body, nor to the beating of the heart. It was there as the canopy of heaven was there. No human hand could reach and touch it, as nobody could reach and touch the stars. It had come to him as if it had found the place in his face, the place of which Jakob had said that God was to live there.

He smiled again and it seemed to him as if this living space warmed and grew larger with his smile. As if a smile without fear was the only way to create this living space, where neither he dwelt nor the dead, but just that other whom Jakob called God.

Now he heard the steps of the men coming up to him from behind the wood. He could not see the light of the lantern, the reddish circle that glided up and down the trunks of the trees. But he could feel the brightness which came toward him. And in the center of this brightness was not the stretcher, nor Christoph, nor perhaps Erasmus, but the quite marvelous certainty that the "young mother" had not been silent but had spoken; that she had said, "There he lies! Fetch him before he dies!"

"Oh, my dear young master," said Christoph, and knelt down by him. His hand that held the lantern trembled still more than before.

Amadeus only smiled and closed his eyes before the bright light, until he heard Christoph's deep sigh.

"He is not here, dear master," said the soft, distant voice, and Amadeus knew well what Christoph meant when he said this. "Now I shall have room in my face," he was still thinking as a beautiful weariness overcame him. "So much room."

Then the faces faded away, the light and many stars, and a vast, splendid darkness slowly closed over him.

He only woke when they put down the stretcher for the first time to change the carriers. They had not gone across the moor but had taken the nearest way down to the castle. The wood had been left behind them. The air was cooler and smelt of fields and meadows.

They had put the lantern on the ground and stood around him in silence.

"Why are there so many, brother? Why are the women here?" asked Amadeus in surprise.

Erasmus bent down to him and in the light of the lantern Amadeus saw his frightened face under the white hair, but his smile was kinder and sadder than ever. "Did you think that they would leave you alone, dear brother?" he asked. "Don't you know what you mean to them?"

"What do I mean, then?" asked Amadeus, surprised, looking into the faces of the women who knelt by the stretcher. "And you are there, too, Erdmuthe?" he said in a low voice. "Hold my hand now, as the parson said."

The men lifted the stretcher again, and Erasmus bent down to Amadeus once more. "Did I not tell you that she would kill one of us, brother?" he asked.

But Amadeus shook his head. "You must not say that," he answered. "She has not killed any of us, do you hear?"

For four weeks Amadeus lay in the small white room of the hospital. He saw the surgeon and the nurses; they all seemed to look after him with kind and cheerful faces. But they were nothing more than apparitions who glided about the quiet room. For behind him he always saw that other room, that room in the shepherd's hut on the moor; and there the most important thing of his life was going to happen, and he must go back to it as quickly as possible. Not much was done by healing his body and by the doctor's promise that the fingers of his left hand would rest on the strings of the cello as easily as before. Nor by his testimony to Kelley and the secret service of the victors that according to his opinion those fellows, certainly foreigners, had come from the camps and it would be useless to search for them.

It was only important that he should be able to go home to the solitary threshold where, after this, everybody who had been overwhelmed by fate should find help.

He learned that the "young mother" had been lying unconscious in a high fever ever since she had collapsed at Christoph's feet, and he knew that his was the only hand toward which she would stretch out her hand when she awoke.

He himself longed to see again that grand evening glow in which fear had left him. The room where he had to live here was too small; only in his hut could he finish reflecting on what had filled his mind while he was lying at the edge of the marshes between the two juniper bushes.

He had many visitors, and he looked attentively into the faces that bent down to him. These faces seemed to be changed likewise, as if they, too, reflected the warm evening glow that had changed him.

The parson was the only one to whom he spoke about the fact that he had shifted the barrel of his revolver before he touched the trigger. Wittkopp saw no riddle in it. "It is always present within us and looks on," he said. "Mostly in silence and without a movement. But then comes a moment when it lifts its hand and touches our hand. We scarcely notice it, but it suffices that we say a different word from what we intended to say, that we walk a different way from the one we intended to go. Those are the great decisions of our lives, which, we imagine, are so magnificently dependent on our so-called free will. It is as if this hand within us lifted one of the tablets of stone, for instance, the one on which is written: Thou shalt not kill. Or better: Thou shalt not kill anymore! But it does not lift it without further ado, just as it pleases. The tablet is only lifted when we are mature enough to read it. Do you understand, Herr Baron? It only lifts the tablet when we have won different eyes. Generally we have won these different eyes without knowing it. As often as not we ourselves have become different. The hand only wants us to recognize what we already know."

"You think that I already had different eyes while I was standing there on the moor?"

"Yes, did you not know?" asked the parson in surprise. "Did you not know that you had lost the taint of evil?"

The baron studied his face for some time, then he looked at the high window through which he caught a glimpse of the distant sunset. "Have I lost it?" he asked gently.

"You had already lost it," replied Wittkopp, "when for the first time you stood behind me on the peat-bog to search for the evening. Evil seeks only the night, as the 'dark one' sought it. You tried to appear evil for a time, because you had planned it and because you were afraid. He who is afraid feels safer in evil than in good. But now you are no longer afraid. You have stepped over the threshold. When the shots fell, they only hit your body, not your heart. Paul was only afraid as long as he was Saul, not afterward."

"But I am not Paul," said Amadeus deprecatingly.

"He who is on the way is Paul," replied the parson with his simple and perfect confidence. "Ever and at all times. I suppose you know by now that God also took the girl by the hand, don't you? Only a blind person would not see it."

His brother's wife sat with him, too, and the kindness in her face was so great that it seemed to brighten the whole room. "I feel that you have suffered for us alone," she said. "So that we could live in peace. That you have also suffered for our child, so that it may remain untouched."

"I did not know that you were expecting a child," replied Amadeus. "I think now the scales are balanced."

She did not understand him, but he shook his head.

"It will be a sunny child," he said, "and it will make things easier for the "dark one" I think I shall come to the christening; I would not have thought so a few weeks ago."

She bent forward quickly, as if she were going to kiss his hand, but he took hers and laid it to his face. "It's beautiful to pay off debts," was all he said.

The most peaceful times were when Jakob sat with him. It always seemed as if he lived in the neighborhood, not as if he had come from a distance. Yes, as if he took up his abode wherever there was sorrow, so that he might help immediately. There was about him, always, an atmosphere of such spacious calm that nobody could imagine that he came from a camp where thousands of people were fighting for space, money, or the future. He put down his bundle by the bed, bowed and sat down, small and unpretentious, in the old armchair which the sisters had placed ready for visitors. His sad, brown eyes glanced quickly and unobtrusively at the face of the baron, and then he smiled. After a pause he said, "God loves the Herr Baron" – or something similar that Amadeus had not expected, that surprised him and made him happy. "When the Herr Baron has come back to the large shepherd's hut," he went on, "he will have much, very much to do."

"But I don't do anything, Jakob," replied Amadeus.

"The Herr Baron will be a light above the moor," said Jakob. "It will be seen from a distance, and then a man can raise his hand and say: Thither will I go."

"But I am not a light, Jakob."

"Perhaps the Herr Baron is no light, but somebody has lit a light within the Herr Baron, and that is the same.

"The Herr Baron has tried to hold his hand around the light so that nobody might see it. But the Holy One, blessed be he, saw to it that the hands of the Herr Baron sank down into the heather, and after that the light was to be seen all over the moor."

"Do you believe that God did it, Jakob?"

"Did the Herr Baron think that the girl did it?" asked Jakob. "Who is a girl that she can take the darkness out of a human face?"

"How is it that you know so much, Jakob?" asked the Baron after a long silence.

"Do I know, Herr Baron?" he replied. "I don't know. I only listen. My life has been such that I have had to listen by day and by night to hear whether they were coming along with spears or bars to destroy us again. Some hear when a door is opened, some hear when it is bolted or unbolted, and some hear when the angel turns a page in the great book."

He stooped and took some tins of fruit out of his bundle. "I have thought this will do the Herr Baron good," he said.

"I have never done anything for you, Jakob," said Amadeus, ashamed.

Jakob had already got up and tied his bundle. He made the last knot and looked at Amadeus. "Five hundred years ago," he said in his modest way, "the Barons von Liljecrona, to gratify their love of power, caused us to eat soap, if there was soap in those days. Or they pulled out our beards, or they took our daughters for a night of pleasure. Five years ago our rulers did the same. The Herr Baron did nothing of the kind. He gave of his bread to those who were without, and he allowed those whom the big fish had spat out of its belly to sit on his doorstep. The Herr Baron has acted as a brother to his brother."

He bowed, put the big chair back in its place, and left the room gently.

Then came the evening when Christoph fetched away the baron. Amadeus had wished that it should all be done very quietly. Christoph had got a carriage with a pair of horses, and in this carriage he drove the baron to the castle. He sat straight and upright on the coachman's box in his long blue coat, the buttons of which he had polished, holding the whip in his right hand. He had no cap now, and his long white hair was ruffled by the evening breeze. They drove slowly, and the baron could hear the larks in the fields. It seemed to him that he had not had such a drive for fifty years.

Donelaitis was standing under the broken coat of arms and took charge of the horses. Then they climbed slowly up the narrow path to the hut. "If you had a belt, dear sir," said Christoph, "I would hold you by it, as my grandfather held his master when he led him down the steps."

"One does not always need a belt to be led, Christoph," answered Amadeus.

A golden light was already falling on the quivering birches when they sat at last on the doorstep of the hut. The smoke stood still above the cottages in the motionless air. The men had sunk a draw well, and the heavy beam towered, dark and massive, up into the evening sky.

"I will never go away from here, Christoph," said the baron in a low voice.

Only after the equinoctial gales were spent did the "young mother" awake from the dark night of her fever, and nobody who saw her could doubt that her reason was disturbed. She went about and talked; she talked more than before. And she smiled, but in a way that frightened most people, for the smile came from the disturbed depths of her mind. Her face was quite changed. It not only had the abstracted, almost foreknowing remoteness of one who will soon be a mother, but hers was a face absorbed in something that nobody else could see but which was always there; something so radiant that its reflection illuminated her whole face.

She recognized those who came to her, and she talked to them as one talks to a guest. But it seemed as if all the past were extinguished from her memory; as if life began anew every day, and as if it were only there so that the day might come when the child would be born.

For this she remembered, yes, it was almost the only thing she remembered: that she was going to have a child. A miracle had been created within her, an immaculate conception, and no one confronted with those eyes fixed on faraway things dreamed of questioning who the father was.

When the autumn sun shone upon the marshes, she wound her way softly singing as she went, smiling and lost in thought, between the trunks of the tall pine trees. She stood still to examine the resin drawn out of the bark by the warmth of the sun, or she listened to the black woodpecker which called from the deep forest. Then she seemed to be hearkening, her head inclined, her hands folded over her pregnancy. The smile on her lips seemed to come from her childhood days.

Or she sat on the threshold of her father's house, her head leaning against the doorpost, her hand stroking the silky coat of the dog, which had put its head on her lap. She did not do any work, nor did she make any clothes for the coming baby. She was like one of the flowers by the forester's fence, which nobody had sown and which nobody tended. She knew nothing about her roots there in the depths, nor about the sun which shone down on her. Nor did she need to know anything about them, for the earth, the animals, the sun were there, whether she knew of them or not.

When she was told that Baron Amadeus had recovered and was living in the hut again, she raised her head listening, as if it were not her mother but some distant voice that was speaking to her. "Amadeus?" she whispered. "Who is Amadeus?"

Then she got up and went into her room.

The forester's wife was the first who came to Amadeus. She sat by the fire in her black shawl and wept. She looked as if she had come from the depths of the forest after burying her children – all her children – there; yes, as if anybody wishing to paint a picture of the nation to which she belonged need only paint her, as she sat by the little fire wrapped in a somber shawl, without speaking, silent tears welling from her eyes.

"At first, Herr Baron," she said, breaking the silence, "when she had a high fever she talked all night long words which I did not understand – names which I did not know. She spoke rapidly, as rapidly as if she were driven by whips. And she was afraid, so terribly afraid. I was a stranger to her, a perfect stranger. She did not know that she had a mother. She was as if she had not been born of a woman. Then she sang, Herr Baron, she sang for two weeks. There can never be anything more terrible on this earth for me,

Herr Baron. Her eyes were wide open, and she was trembling with fear. But she smiled while she sang, she smiled in a terrible way."

"What did she sing?" asked the baron in a low voice.

The woman looked around timidly, as if somebody were standing behind her, and then she softly sang the verses into the fire. Her eyes were opened wide and she trembled so much that it was as if it were the daughter who sat there and sang. It was a monotonous tune, such as children sing to themselves when they are alone.

Sleep, sleep, baby dear –
Your father turns in the wind without fear –
He hangs above our garden.
The birds sit all around him,
They do not sing, they do not sing –
They are waiting, waiting, waiting.

Sleep my baby in thy cot,
The birdies all are sent by God,
He sent them to him
To peck out his dead eyes –
They are mute when they rise –
They pecked out his dead eyes.

The baron shuddered and he raised his hand for her to stop. But the woman did not see it. She sang as if the flames on the hearth could burn the words to ashes, and then they would no longer exist.

When the birds have flown away –
We will find, we will find
That my child is blind, quite blind;
Sleep well, sleep well, my little blind . . .

At last the woman was silent. She drew her shawl closer around her shoulders, as if even before the fire she were cold. The door of the hut was open and they both heard a nightbird call as it circled over the marshes. It was as if it had caught up the song and now was carrying it above the sleeping world.

"And then did she stop singing?" asked the baron gently.

"Yes," replied the woman. "Then she did not sing anymore, and now she is happy."

"She will come," said the baron after a while. "Don't worry and go home. I am sure she will come."

The woman got up and he accompanied her to the threshold. The bird was still calling, farther off than before, and she stood for a moment to listen. "If you had a child, Herr Baron," she said, "and you heard it calling out there, you would go at once to look for it. But where am I to go?"

She was shivering in the night air, and then she glided away like a shadow.

Nobody had foreseen what was going to happen, and again Christoph was the only one who knew of it before the baron. He often sat with the "young mother" on the warm threshold of the forester's house in the evening, when he had come home from the castle, he and the dog. She did not remember that Christoph had once carried her upstairs and locked her in the room. Perhaps he had become for her what the good giant of the fairytales is to children, and she used to gently smooth his white hair, ruffled by the evening breeze.

She did not make her meaning clear, for there was never anything really clear in what she said. Everything was floating as on dark water, and as on water there was always a picture and its reflection.

Nevertheless, he understood her, and he nodded at what she said. There was such bliss in her smile that he could not do anything else, although it frightened him. In the simple world of his imagination he felt that he would destroy her if he did not nod.

But after she had gone upstairs, he went once more to the shepherd's hut. He walked quite slowly, lost in thought, but when he stepped over the threshold his face was as cheerful as ever.

As usual he introduced the subject by telling one of his tales. After he had put a cinder on the tobacco in his pipe, he began: "When I was a child, sir, there was a man in the village who believed that he was the old emperor. He came from a family where such ideas did sometimes come up. He had once seen the old emperor in some war of the time, and when he became queer he hung on to this picture with his poor remaining senses. He bought an old blue uniform and shaved his chin like His Majesty.

"He did no harm to anybody, and he was pleased when the young farmhands in the fields presented arms with their pitchforks as he passed by. That was all he wanted.

"But we had a young teacher who didn't like it. He had just come from college and thought that there ought to be no silliness anywhere about him. He called it that because he was very clever.

"And so he tried to rid the man of his strange fancy. He did not want anyone to live in a false, make-believe world. He started in a serious way, showed him pictures of the old emperor, and when this didn't help, he began to make fun of him. He mocked at the man, and then he jeered at him. And as he was the teacher, the children copied him.

"At first the man grew angry, but after that it got worse and worse. Then he grew shy and sorrowful, and one day he went into the bog; he did not come back. Probably he thought that it was not worthwhile living if he was not allowed to be the old emperor."

"Why do you tell that story?" asked Amadeus.

Christoph looked into the fire and nodded, as if he had given the answer already. "You see, sir," he said at last, looking at the baron, "she believes that you are the father of her child. And she believes it as if it were gospel truth."

The baron stared at him, and for a moment it seemed as if he were going to smile. But only for a second, and not even Christoph could be quite sure of it. Then his face grew very serious and he knitted his brows, as if he had to think something out with all his might.

"You are not mistaken, Christoph?"

The old man shook his head. "If one says such things, one must not be mistaken."

The baron got up and walked to and fro in the small room – from the hearth to the door and back again.

Although he could not collect his thoughts, he felt instinctively that this meant a serious change, that behind the cloud of the fever something had happened that nobody could have foreseen, and that the girl took it for "Gospel." Perhaps it would dissolve and disappear like most fever fantasies. But perhaps it would last on – the one narrow bridge over a terrible abyss. And the least thing he did or said, or which he did not do or say in the right way might hurl the "young mother" into the bottomless pit – the mother and the child.

He stood still by the hearth and looked down on Christoph's white hair. Christoph had put the short pipe on the hearth and had folded his hands between his knees. His hands were trembling a little, and he did not look up at the baron. He looked into the fire.

Amadeus did not need to ask anymore. He knew now why Christoph had told his tale.

"You must not say anything, sir," said Christoph at length, "I know it isn't you, but others will not know it as I do. Perhaps they will be pleased to believe it. People always find pleasure in such things. Now, sir, you have the hardest burden of all to take on your shoulders. It may be harder than the camp. Jeering can bend the shoulders lower than violence."

"You talk as if it were a matter of course to take this on my shoulders, Christoph?"

The old man raised his head now and glanced at the baron. "You know it as well as I, sir," he said calmly. "Or do you want her to go into the marshes?"

"But she will wake up one day, Christoph!"

"It's up to you now, sir, to see that she awakes cheerfully. It's up to us, too, but most of all to you. Actually that's the reason why the bullet did not hit you half a hand's breadth deeper. You know that, I suppose, dear sir?"

No, Amadeus did not know it, and this, too, he thought over for a long time.

But then he shook his head. "Perhaps they ought to consult another doctor," he said after a while. "This is beyond our power."

Christoph made a gesture as if pushing something aside. "Have you read in the Bible, sir," he asked, "that the possessed were healed by a doctor?"

"Why do they urge me to be something that I am not," thought Amadeus. "He speaks as Wittkopp spoke about Paul. They have high ideas of me, but I have only got up out of the heather."

"It's what Jakob told you, sir," said Christoph getting up. "God loves you, that's what it is."

But the baron was afraid when, about nightfall a few days later, he saw the "young mother" coming. It was a different fear from the one he had lost under the juniper bushes. It was no longer fear for himself, and he felt that this was more serious and harder to cope with.

The "young mother" saw neither the baron nor the sheepfold, nor the setting sun. She walked very slowly, looking down upon what she carried in her hands. It was a little basket plaited of willow twigs, half finished, and she was plaiting it while she walked. Her face was calm and she smiled as if she were talking to some good and kind friend who walked beside her.

Amadeus noticed that a great change had come over her face. He had last seen her sitting in the heather, her hands clasped around her knees, and then she had wanted to look on at his dying.

She did not raise her eyes till she stood in front of him. These eyes were not frightened, they were not even astonished. They were as if she had lived with him for many days and nights and had just returned from the forest where she had gone for half an hour's walk. These eyes were filled with a deep, quite natural love.

"This is where it will sleep at first," she said smiling, and lifted the basket up high with both hands. "Do you think it will be large enough?"

Amadeus was sure of it and stood aside to let her cross the threshold. But she did not want to go in. She glanced into the half-dark room and knitted her brows slightly, as if she were trying to remember something. Then she shook her head and sat down on the threshold. She pointed with her hand to the empty place at her side, and Amadeus sat down beside her.

For a time she gazed out over the moor, over which darkness spread slowly. The children were singing again around the cottages, and she listened with a happy smile. Her face was not devoid of expression as is so often the case in those whose senses are darkened. Her face was completely absorbed, and the world in which it was absorbed existed only for her; others had nothing to do with it. For her it was the real world, no make-believe, no phantom world. It was as real as the evening moor was real to Amadeus.

She started again plaiting the thin osiers, and it appeared to Amadeus as if the illness had also changed her hands. They had become transparent like the hands of saints in old pictures. Those hands could no longer carry a flag. There was a touching fragility about them, the defenselessness of a human being who can be pushed over into the abyss by the slightest touch.

When she felt Amadeus' eyes on her, she stopped working and leaned her head against the doorpost. Then she raised her left hand and began gently stroking his hair, as she had stroked Christoph's and the dog. Perhaps she thought that she was sitting on the doorstep of her father's house.

Amadeus accepted the caress without moving. He did not resist it, as he would not have resisted had Goldie's little mother been sitting at his side. But it was a strange, almost solemn emotion that he felt. He could not remember anybody touching his hair since Grita's death. He was now without fear. He felt that he only had to keep still, and it did not matter what she was thinking or who she believed he was. She had no fear, she had confidence in him. She felt more at home with him than she had probably ever felt with anybody in all her life. Christoph had said that he had only to see to it that she should awake cheerfully. That was all.

She stayed with him until it grew dark. Her arm lay on his shoulder, and her hand glided up and down, always up and down. But when the night birds called, she shivered a little and her arm dropped.

"You must now think about its name," she said, when she got up. "I would like to have a simple name, quite simple."

He promised to think about it.

Then she put her left arm around his shoulder, stood on tiptoe, and kissed him. Her lips were cool, and Amadeus thought that they smelt of some autumn fruit – of blackberries, perhaps, that had been ripening in the sun all day long.

He heard her footsteps, soft and light, die away in the distance like the steps of some shy animal. He stood for a while there where she had said goodbye to him.

It was as if he had been in an unreal world for some time and now had to wake up gradually. As if he had been somebody else – a dream-person, not himself – but there was no fear in this unreality anymore. It was difficult to be, as it were, double, no longer single. As if he had to give himself up for a time and be what someone else wished him to be. Not an actor, but a shadow perhaps that glided over a screen.

The feeling that this was something difficult gradually ceased, too. From now on she came every evening, as a child comes to listen to a fairytale before going to bed. When it grew colder she sat with him by the fire on a heap of cushions, which she put one on top of the other so that she could lean her head against his knee. When the little basket was finished, she brought other work with her, or rather another toy. But when she had busied herself for a while with it, she dropped it, clasped her hands around her knees, and gazed into the flames on the hearth.

There was so much peace around her that it enveloped not only herself but also Amadeus. Yes, it was almost a spell that fell over him, because for a time he, too, could forget what had happened: the "dark one" and how she had sat like this by the juniper bushes, her hands clasped around her knees. Only then her eyes had not been fixed on the fire but on his face.

And each time when she said goodbye, she stood on tiptoe and kissed him.

It no longer troubled him, whether people knew it and smiled at it.

He was only troubled by the idea that one day she would awake and that – according to Christoph – she must awaken cheerfully.

Once when he came home late from the moor, he found her standing by the cello, lightly touching the strings with her fingers. Her head was inclined so that her hair fell over her face, and she listened to the soft sounds that faded away with an abstracted, serene countenance. She seemed to be listening to the heartbeat of her child, but he saw that it did her good. Yes, that it filled her with something new, something that had not existed up till now. He did not know whether he was doing right, but after some time he got up, sat down behind the hearth in the shadow of the beam where she had sat the Christmas before, and began to draw the bow carefully over the strings.

It was something new for him, too, something that he had not done for long years, and he was so affected by it that he forgot everything else for a time. He listened to the sounds, as if his hands had had nothing to do with them, as if it were only the immaculate purity of the wood that had begun to speak, as a forest begins to speak in the wind. As if after all something had persisted throughout these dark years that they had not been able to destroy – melody, one of the greatest miracles of this earth.

And not until he looked into the young face illuminated by the flames of the fire did he remember that he was not only playing for himself. There was no restlessness nor curiosity in this face, nothing but a blissful radiance, as on children's faces that are turned to an old chiming clock. The eyes followed the movements of his hands but they did not take them in. They only took in the sounds that emanated from under his hands; it was these sounds that transformed her face.

Amadeus tried to find in his memory the simplest tunes he knew; they were the songs that Grita had sung and the hymn that the forester's wife had recited here. He drew the bow over the strings more and more gently and at last he let the melody die away, as a breath of wind loses itself in a great forest.

Barbara said nothing, she only leaned her head against his knee when he sat down again by the fire, and now it was Amadeus who for the first time gently stroked her hair. He was suddenly afraid that with the tunes she might remember the song she had sung in her fever, and his hand stroked her hair so that she should not remember.

From that time he played every evening.

When she had left, he went on sitting by the fire and thought it all over. He did not know much about the illnesses of the mind, and his thoughts always went back to the evening when he had been lying in the heather and she had sat there to look on. The root of it all must be there. Much had gone before, but there the deciding factor had lain, and the fever had only been the result of this factor. It was important to preserve this decisive factor until the moment when she would awake. One could not live permanently under an illusion or in a false conception. A day would come when the curtain must split, and then it would be apparent whether or not Amadeus was stronger than the powers of darkness. Whether she would leave her head resting on his knee, or whether she would raise her face and look at him with the old hatred.

He understood with perfect distinctness that, in these months of darkened consciousness in which she could be deluded, he had to imbue her with his own being to such a degree that on awakening she would not feel deceived. That the world would not appear a split world to her and she would not have to decide where to put her foot, but that it would be one world in which she could be as much at home as in her make-believe world; where it did not matter who the child's father was, but only who had watched over the child like a father; not who had given life to the child, but who had kept it alive, had seen to it that its life was without hatred, blindness, and death.

But how to do it Amadeus did not know. Sometimes it came into his mind that he would need "the patience of the saints" for it, and for the first time he recognized the deep meaning of this simple expression. What he did not recognize was that he had by now long ceased to live for himself, as everybody ceases to live for himself who cares for the happiness of another heart.

He did not know whether his brothers or the people on the moor knew anything about all this. He only seemed to feel that they were particularly considerate to him. But this they had always been since his return.

The parson was the only one to whom he spoke about it. In any case, the parson knew it, for he dismissed it with a wave of his hand.

"Did you ever consider, Herr Baron," asked Wittkopp, supporting his head in both his hands, "that it happened there where the other had lain? At the same spot, and as it were, in the same posture? And that only a slight break in the chain of thoughts and conclusions was needed to bring about a substitution? A sort of proxy? That the second picture laid itself above the first so exactly and so congruently that the first was covered? Yes, that it was put out and disappeared? That's how I tried to explain it to myself. The sane person still recognizes the first picture below the second. At least he knows that it is there, even if he does not see it. But those who are sick in mind do not realize it anymore. For them only the last picture counts, for they live in pictures. There is no doubt that she was already sick in mind at that time.

"But this has nothing to do with the duty you have to fulfill. Neither its beginning nor its origin. That is something for the doctor – a case, a phenomenon. You have got to cover the picture of a man so completely that not even the smallest bit of the outline of his picture remains visible for those distraught eyes. You have to extinguish the 'dark one,' Herr Baron, do you understand? To extinguish him from her memory and from the present so completely that even the future cannot awake him. That she may remember his name and what he looked like but not what he meant for her, not his significance.

"You have stepped into his place, not only when you were shot at and were lying there, but also in all that concerns the child. You have sucked up the 'dark one,' as it were, into yourself. But if you offer resistance, everything falls to pieces again. The 'dark one' is back again, the evil is back again, the vicious is back again. Do you understand what God has chosen you for? I so much want you to understand it. You need not call it God, but you must know that what is laid on you is so beautiful that I myself can only call it God. For it is beyond all human invention."

"So that's what you mean," said the baron, resting his eyes meditatively on Wittkopp.

"Yes, that's what I mean, Herr Baron. And I know besides that you are the only one in the whole neighborhood on whom such an obligation could be laid, because you are the only one among us who can make himself good enough for it. But you should also realize that you must not do it out of generosity. You must realize how much you owe to the poor girl for the opportunity to perfect yourself. Without her it might have been impossible for you. Did you know that to become good we need evil?"

No, Amadeus had not known it.

"When I saw you standing on the moor," he said after a time, "leaning on your spade and singing that hymn, I understood for the first time how beautiful life can be if man has made his peace with time. With the good and sorrowful of time – perhaps I understand it now for the second time, parson."

"And a third time will not be necessary, Herr Baron," said Wittkopp, getting up. "This will be sufficient for your whole life, even if it should last a hundred years."

10

THE TRIAL OF THE FORESTER Buschan took place in the first week of Advent, and his wife and Baron Amadeus were summoned as witnesses. Because of the girl's mental condition it was decided that she should not be called.

Amadeus was much concerned lest the "young mother" might get to know of the proceedings, but he refused to have her prevented by force, should she wish to go to the trial.

He saw her the moment he entered the little hall in the district town. She was sitting between Erasmus and Christoph, wrapped in a dark shawl like her mother, and gazing at the judge's seat with a calm, faraway smile. Nobody unacquainted with her story would have thought that she was not normal.

Amadeus sat down on one of the benches at the back. The hall was packed and the people looked as if they had come to see a play and were waiting for the curtain to go up. Amadeus thought that two or even five years ago they would have looked just the same. Recent times had not stamped their faces except with the signs of hunger or even of want; the catastrophe had not shifted their hearts out of the routine of daily work.

The public prosecutor sat at his table and turned over his papers. He was a short man, looking depressed and worried, perhaps a foreman in one of the ammunition factories, and Amadeus had been told that he had spent two years in a concentration camp. He would have known it anyway by his face, which was bad and full of fear, like so many faces he had seen at roll call. He was "in power" now, and the expression in his eyes showed how much he despised all those in the hall who had not been behind barbed wire.

When the president, with the assessors, came into the hall and sat down behind the long table, Amadeus looked at him long and earnestly. He was the former editor of an unimportant newspaper with socialistic tendencies. He had been beaten up in the first days of the seizure of power and had been led through the streets with a placard around his neck. Then he had been submerged, nobody knew where he was, until the surf had thrown him up again onto the shore. He had lost his wife and children in the air raids. But his eyes were quiet as they looked at the people in the hall, as if he did not remember the past years.

The assessors sat there with round, apathetic faces, as if it was their appointed role to sit there, and as if they had been sitting in this small hall for years in order to sentence those who had little chance to sit still on chairs but had been continually on the march.

The accused and the witnesses were called, and then the forester was cross-examined.

Buschan in his clean, plain suit stood quietly at the bar, and with his calm eyes he looked at the president and the prosecutor. People could see that he had settled things in his own mind. He did not halt in his answers, he did not look about him, he did not have to hesitate when he was questioned.

He did not deny that he had believed nor that he had been mistaken. He spoke so simply that there was no room for doubt.

The prosecutor failed to prove against him that he had oppressed the woodmen or that he had ill-treated the prisoners who worked in the forest. He had obeyed orders, but beyond that he had not done any harm.

It was easy to see that the prosecutor regretted that the forester had neither shot at nor killed anyone.

But then he pushed aside the papers on his table, glanced quickly over the hall and asked how things had gone with the Baron von Liljecrona. He made it plain that for him all the questions up to this point had been unimportant and of no real significance, and that he only began to perform his official duty now. It seemed as if he were pulling the cloth from the face of a murdered man and were raising the head with one hand so that everybody in the hall might see the dead eyes.

The forester unconsciously clasped his hands together and for the first time lowered his eyes and stood silent before the court. But then he looked up, directing his calm eyes not at the prosecutor but at the president. "I have confessed everything in the shepherd's hut, where the Herr Baron lives," he said, "and the Herr Baron will confirm it. I have confessed that I wrote the indictment very unwillingly, but that I thought then it was my duty – and that I repent it."

All was silent in the hall except for a low sobbing which came from the corner where the forester's wife sat wrapped in her black shawl.

"What were the terms of the indictment?" asked the president at last. "It cannot be found and the court has to rely on the evidence of the accused."

"The president can rely on it," replied the forester and their glances met. "I went into the forest with the baron to examine the traps we had set and a fox was caught in one of them. As we stood in front of it the baron said, 'You had better not set any more traps, since the whole nation has been caught in a trap. We ought not to do to animals what the state is doing to human beings.' That's all! I wrote it down and posted it."

"And you realized what the consequences would be?" asked the president, and he did not look at the forester but at the baron Amadeus. The forester considered for a moment, then he answered in a low voice that he must say "yes" to this question, though he had not been able to foresee all the consequences in detail.

The president made no comments on this statement. He was playing with his pencil, trying to balance it on the narrow edge of the glass lid of an inkpot which was in front of him on the table. He could not do it. "Has the prosecutor any other questions to ask?" he said finally, without looking at the man to whom he spoke.

"It should be sufficient," replied the prosecutor in an injured voice.

Frau Buschan was called and did not refuse to give evidence, as most people had expected her to do. She had pulled her black shawl down over her forehead and looked as if she had come to a funeral. Her face was so full of pain and sorrow that the assessors felt uneasy when they looked at her, and the president offered her a chair.

But she shook her head. She had only to state that she had not read her husband's letter, but still she had implored him not to send it. He had been a good husband and father and was good to the workmen, but he was laboring under a delusion.

"And your daughter was in the same state, is it not so?" asked the president in an undertone.

"She is suffering, sir," whispered the woman. "I beg you not to disturb her or she may scream."

"It doesn't sound altogether credible to me," said the prosecutor without lowering his voice, "that you implored your husband not to send the letter as you say. In such cases husbands usually obey."

The woman turned her eyes toward him and gazed at him for a long time. "I don't understand what the prosecutor means by 'altogether credible,'" she said at last. "At home we either believe or don't believe. I still read the Bible."

The prosecutor shrugged his shoulders and glanced at the president.

Frau Buschan was dismissed, and the other witnesses were called, one after another. They had no further evidence to give, except that the forester had been "a supporter of the Hitler business," as a timber merchant put it. However, it was quite correct that according to the evidence of all he had not harmed anybody.

Then Baron Amadeus was called and sworn in.

This witness was closely scrutinized by the members of the court. But whereas the two assessors watched him narrowly with a sort of shy horror, as if he were still a captive in an iron cage – as if such a thing were beyond belief – the prosecutor's face expressed a certain disapproval – disapproval that here was a member of the Junker class, one of the exploiters, who had been put by fate on a level with the suffering proletariat. In some obscure way it did not fit into the prosecutor's system that an exception to the rule had now appeared, and without a doubt he would have preferred to see a miner or some sort of laborer here in the witness box instead of a baron.

The president asked the baron whether he had known about the part the forester had played in his case. No, he had not, because he had never been interrogated after his arrest, and nobody had informed him why he had been arrested.

"So that," the president continued his interrogation, "as the indictment cannot be found, the forester could have denied the facts of the case, just as his wife could have refused her evidence."

"Yes, that is true," replied the baron, "and it is also true that I suggested the idea to the accused, when he came to see me for the first time."

A tremor passed through the hall and the president waited until it had died down.

"And what did the defendant reply, Herr Baron?" asked the president then.

"He replied that he could not go through the door that I had opened for him, because right was right, and because a man must pay for his mistakes."

"But that is beautiful, is it not?" said the president after another pause.

"Yes, that is certainly beautiful," replied the baron.

The prosecutor begged to be allowed to ask a few questions. He laid his pencils in straight parallel lines, cast a sidelong glance at the baron, then looking again into the hall he asked whether it was clear to the witness that with this so-called open door he would have withheld the accused from the course of justice.

No, that had not been clear to him, replied Amadeus, looking at the prosecutor. It was an established fact that nobody but he, the baron, had suffered from the measures taken by the forester.

"Right had suffered," replied the prosecutor sharply.

"I would like to know what right is," Amadeus went on. "First in general, and then in this particular case."

The prosecutor expressed surprise that anybody who had been in a concentration camp for four years should ask such a question.

"Four years ago," said Amadeus, "it was the right of the state to arrest me. Today it is the right of the state to arrest the forester Buschan. This fact alone is alarming. But right ought to reassure, not to alarm."

"Does the witness wish to indicate that he would be alarmed if the defendant now were to be sentenced according to the accepted idea of right?"

"Yes, very much alarmed," replied Amadeus. "When the forester came to see me and made a clean breast of what he had done, I was reassured, altogether reassured. Anything that would take the matter beyond this point would very much alarm me."

"Would not the witness do well to give up thinking so much about his personal point of view?" asked the prosecutor.

"That I would willingly do," replied Amadeus, "if the prosecutor would be good enough to think less of his point of view. I have seen many like you," he went on after a while. "Four years is a long time. There were many in the camp among those who were struck, who struck back to avoid being struck again. And I would not like it if people are still being struck. Right is not aggressive; judges are aggressive."

The assessors gazed at the baron with consternation, as if he were speaking a dead language that had fallen into disuse many centuries ago. The president looked quietly down at his pencil which seemed to be balanced for a time.

The prosecutor asked angrily whether the witness meant that he, the prosecutor, had struck anybody.

"Of course I don't mean that," replied Amadeus calmly, "because I don't know anything about it. Perhaps other witnesses may know or may not know of it. It is not important either. It is only of importance to know whether the forester Buschan honestly believed, and whether he has given up his belief. A man who is sentenced today for his belief is laid under the same suffering as we who were sentenced for our belief. The same things ought not to happen again, but different ones, better ones, or we shall have suffered in vain."

"You yourself, Herr Baron," asked the president, putting his pencil down on the green tablecloth, "you do not harbor any grudge against the accused?"

"Not the least," replied Amadeus. "I only thank him."

"What do you thank him for, Herr Baron?"

"For this, that he has shown me where alone judgment can be passed."

"And where is that, Herr Baron?" asked the low voice.

"Here," replied Amadeus, laying his left hand on his heart.

The president looked long at him; nothing could be heard in the little hall but the soft breathing of the assembled audience whose eyes were riveted on the judge's table.

"*Ad sum.* Here I am, oh Lord!" said a low voice in the background. It was Wittkopp's voice.

The president turned his eyes from the face of the baron and looked in the direction from which the voice had come, but he said nothing.

"If there are no more questions," he said at last turning to the prosecutor, "I think this evidence should suffice."

The prosecutor shrugged his shoulders.

When in half an hour's time the president with the assessors came back into the little hall he pronounced sentence: that the accused, in consequence of his straightforward words and his repentance, was declared a "Nazi sympathizer"; that he had to pay costs; and that for the duration of two years he was not to be allowed to occupy a public post, but his post with the Barons von Liljecrona was not considered a public post.

Then the president looked down for a while on the green cloth of the table and then, looking up at the baron, he said in a low voice that the court would not like to omit to express their thanks for this trial and all that had transpired in it, just as the last witness had expressed thanks to the accused. It is true that this was not customary, but the proceedings had not been customary either. He and his two assessors felt as if the last witness had also opened a door before them through which they might go calmly, even though the accused, be it said in his honor, had not gone through it.

They all drove in Kelley's car to the great gateway of the castle. Then Baron Amadeus and the forester's family climbed up the narrow path to the shepherd's hut. During the journey and during the walk nothing was said. Buschan and his wife walked in front, hand in hand, looking at the bushes deeply covered with snow on either side of the path as they went.

Then came the "young mother," humming to herself like a child; her smile, too, was like that of a child walking through the winter woods to a Christmas party, or perhaps walking a long way to the cottage of the seven dwarfs. When she stopped and turned around to look at the baron and the valley at her feet, Amadeus could not tell whether she was smiling at him or at the valley, or whether she was recalling the voices in the hall which she had just left. Hers was a timeless face, except perhaps that time which lay between this moment and the birth of the child.

They had left the thin fog below them, and the sun shone on the roof of the hut and on the wide expanse of the marshes so brilliantly that their eyes were dazzled.

The forester and his wife were about to say something, but Amadeus shook his head and stood still, and so they went with their daughter past the hut into the snowbound woods in front of their house. The daughter turned around once more and waved her hand; then she, too, disappeared.

Before Amadeus opened the door, he gazed once more over the moor. There, at some distance from the cottages, at the edge of the moor, was a woman's form, motionless, as if she stood there only to feel the rays of the sun. Her shadow lay black and sharp behind her on the untrodden snow. She stood as still as one of the juniper bushes around her. She was the wife of the young Donelaitis. Amadeus recognized her by her fair hair, which shone in the sun.

He sighed a little, then he went in to light the fire on his hearth.

This was the second Christmas to be celebrated here, and nothing much had changed to all outward appearance except that the room was a little more crowded. Aegidius had brought his wife; the parson and Buschan, who had not been here last year, had also come.

But when they thought back, they realized how much had happened and how much had changed. And to most of them it seemed that the ground under their feet had become more solid; to most of them, but not to all.

Jakob had come and had brought some little parcels and had not been able to take his eyes off the sparkling tree. Christoph had rung the bell at the window. His hands trembled, but his face was serene and happy as always, and from time to time he glanced at the "young mother" and nodded to her.

Amadeus thought that the eyes of the young expectant mothers beamed in a special way, as if in them the light of the candles was reflected more warmly and more deeply than in all the other eyes. But while his brother's wife sat quietly near the hearth, her hands folded on her lap, as quietly as if she were part of the miracle of the birth that they were celebrating, the "young mother" knelt in front of the low-hanging branches of the tree and pushed the little basket she had plaited in the autumn into the soft, half-lit shadows. She had lined it with moss and decorated it with little silver stars, and over the moss and the stars she had spread little cushions, made of remnants of colored material, which she pushed to and fro, as if at any moment the angel might bring the child to the window, as he had brought the bell down from the dark winter sky a little while before.

All the time the calm, blissful, rather empty smile played around her lips and in her eyes. Everyone looked at her in silence, especially the children who were a little afraid and yet felt pity for her, until she got up and looked at the tiny crib once more and then settled down on the floor and leaned her cheek against Baron Amadeus' knee.

The second unexpected thing was that when the brothers began to tune their violins, Amadeus got up and sat down beside them with his cello, looking quietly into the soft light of the candles as he drew his bow gently over the strings. Just as if he had done so every night since they had found each other again.

When they got up and his brothers glanced shyly at him, he only smiled as if it had not been anything special, as if nothing in this room had been unusual: neither the fact that the forester and his daughter were there, nor that Aegidius had a wife. Nor that they had a parson who did not want to preach a Christmas sermon, nor that they had one of the victors among them who sat on the clay floor near the hearth, who smiled like a child and hummed to himself, "Come unto me all you children on earth . . ."

Nothing particular, because it was only that time had gently passed through the forest for the year's cycle – a particular time, primeval time perhaps – and it had brushed by and transformed each one of them, whether he had been holding a spade or a revolver or only a few of the gleaming yellow flowers which grew along the edges of the marsh dikes.

Nor was it anything particular that the Christmas Gospel was not read by the parson but by Baron Erasmus, as father of all the afflicted. This time he did not read it from a sheet of paper, but from an old Bible which the parson had given him.

At the solemn and simple words about the crib and the swaddling clothes they looked down at the little basket under the branches.

And again there was nothing particular in the fact that there were among them two for whom these words seemed specially written, as they are for all mothers in this dark world, because time had not only led Death by the hand, but also Love, and they are as brother and sister, when they are woven together into the stuff of human beings.

The frost split the trees in the forest, as it had done a year ago. They raised their heads and listened, but they did not think of what people call fate, that which might already be standing, a dark shape, at the edge of the forest, and might be looking at the house and the shimmering expanse of the moor. This, too, was a fantasy, to imagine fate and all that depends on it as a dark, lonely figure – that fate which in reality filled their hearts and wove them together with other hearts in a bright or dark tissue which could never be undone.

For even if their thoughts went back or into the future, the unknown future, their life was filled most with what was given them here and now, with this roof above the star at the top of the Christmas tree, with the light of the candles and the flame of the hearth, with the words of the Gospel and the notes that had come from the three instruments, and with the hope that the ice over which they walked still held, and that a tomorrow would be as certain as today and as yesterday had been.

There was no doubt that they were more cheerful than the year before, though more sorrow was gathered in this room than at that time. Perhaps because there was more sorrow, and because they had not excluded it from this room, to be just to themselves, but had included it, that it might be lessened under their happy eyes.

They even accepted the fact that the "young mother" sat on the floor next to Baron Amadeus, leaning her cheek against his knee, and nobody referred to it – neither the parson, nor his brother's wife, nor the baron himself. Perhaps they knew something; in any case they would not have asked a question. Since they had carried Baron Amadeus on a stretcher from the moor, there was nobody who would have taken the liberty of asking him a question if he did not speak of his own accord.

However they recognized this, that the web was not yet complete, and it made them a little afraid. Perhaps they understood vaguely that the "young mother's" eyes saw visions and forms that they themselves did not see. That she was still in a sort of sleep, and that no one knew how she would be when she awoke. The circle of the year was not closed by this evening, it linked over into the next year, and through all this happiness a secret tremor ran, as it used to at their home before the ice broke up on the great lakes.

But they did realize that Baron Amadeus had altered since last year, and this joy was not dimmed by any anxiety. None of the brothers had awed them as he had, for he alone had been at the open gates of hell. They did not yet know much of what had happened there, but they knew that millions had not survived it. Even the conception of a million was something they could not grasp and which was not of their world, like that Queen Mab who now and again put her hand on their hearts at night, before she plaited the manes of the horses.

It was from there he had come back with tight lips and with eyes which only a year ago had looked through them as through glass. But then he had dug the soil around their cottages and had sown flowers. He had put a bandage around Goldie's neck and had helped them to draw the turf sledge. He had lain in the heather and the flowers had been reddened by his blood. He had not trampled the forester down; he had raised him as the prodigal son was raised.

And now this evening he had drawn the bow over the strings of his cello, whereas a year ago he had only shaken his head. Now he sat by the fire with the girl at his feet, and when he looked at the cottagers his eyes no longer went through them as through glass, but right into them, right into their hearts, as if they wanted to say, "Be happy, as long as it is still granted to us to be happy!"

Two brothers had gained what they had not had the year before: the one a castle, the other an estate and a wife who was expecting a child, but Amadeus had only the small room below the reed roof, the bread he broke, and the fire that warmed him. He had less than they, but he was content. He wanted to stay with them and not to go away anymore. He was the master he had always been, and if one of them had to stretch out his hand for help or for consolation, he would stretch it out toward Amadeus as toward a light in the darkness.

The candles burned slowly down and the shine of the silver stars on the green moss in the little wicker basket stood out from the darkening shadows. Then one of the women plucked up courage and said: "If the masters have nothing against it, tell us a story, Christoph!"

Christoph took the pipe out of his mouth, looked at the brothers and then at the "young mother" and said, "My grandfather told this story: When the master whom they called 'the Saint' lived in the castle, and when my great-grandfather drove the horses, there lived on the farm a laborer's widow and her daughter. The young girl was beautiful, even if she was rather proud and cherished the thought that she would marry a prince. People laughed at her in their good-natured way, and when one autumn they noticed that she was with child, they urged her to tell them who the father was so that they might be wedded before her shame was plain for all to see.

"But the girl refused. She was no longer proud and vain, and often in the evening she stood on the moor gazing far out over the dreary waste, as if he were about to cross it who would come to her with a golden crown in his hand and would lift her up out of her shame and heartbreak.

"But he did not come.

"She had a hard time in her home, for her mother was a strict, harsh woman; and when she spoke of the child she only called it 'the accursed one.'

"When it was born shortly before Christmas, it was a child like any other child, and its little, quiet face did not betray whether its father was a prince or a serf. When the old woman looked at it she was never tired of finding some new defect in its tiny features; she would make the sign of the cross before it and would ask her daughter whether she did not see that its left eye was blind, or, another day, that it had a harelip or a birthmark on its forehead.

"Although the daughter did not see anything of the kind, each time her heart stood still with fear and horror, and she often got up in the night and, holding the little oil lamp above the sleeping baby, searched its face to find out the truth.

"But on Christmas Eve as dusk was falling, she wrapped the child in a dark cloth, crept out from the farmyard, and hurried to the deep gravel pits in the great forest. It was snowing and the branches of the pine trees hung heavily laden above the narrow path. The young mother was silently weeping, but she did not stop until she was at the edge of the pit and below her was nothing but darkness. She knelt down, drew the cloth from the face of the sleeping baby and gazed down at it. All at once she believed she saw everything the old woman had seen, the harelip and the birthmark, and if the child woke up and opened its eyes then she would also see its blindness.

"Then she whispered, 'Have mercy on us!' and bent over the edge of the pit.

"But as she bent forward a boy stood between her and the blank space. There was only enough room for the feet of a bird to rest on, but the child stood as securely as in a garden. He was not more than three or four years old and was dressed in an old coat which was much too large for him and reached down to his naked feet, but he smiled sweetly and raised his right hand.

"'Were you going to do that?' he asked. 'Don't you know how deep it is?'

"Then the mother wept and told him of her distress. 'A mark?' said the child in surprise, putting his hand on the baby's forehead.

"And afterward the mother told how the child's hand had gleamed, as if a ray of the sun that had set long before was shining on it from between the clouds.

"When the boy took his hand off, there was no mark to be seen, however closely the mother looked at the little brow; there was only something like the silvery reflection of a flower, the flower called Christmas rose, and even this delicate gleam slowly faded from the pure skin.

"And when the mother looked up to thank the boy he had disappeared, as if he had flown away over the yawning pit, and she said later that the last she saw of him was his smile. The boy was no longer to be seen, but his smile was still there, as if the low-hanging snow clouds were smiling.

"Then the mother got up, wrapped her child again in the shawl, and went back through the wood.

"But when she passed out of the darkness of the trees, her heart stopped beating, for she remembered that her child had other blemishes still besides the mark on its forehead. She opened the shawl quickly and looked down at the little face. Its forehead was as immaculate as it had been by the gravel pit, but her eyes dimmed by tears saw the harelip, as if her mother were standing at her side pointing to it with her old, crooked finger.

"Then the young woman looked around her in the white, cloud-covered world in which it was snowing, snowing; and then she hastened over the moor to one of the ponds where the water stood dark and motionless.

"But when she knelt down at the edge of the pond and bent forward, whispering, 'Have mercy on us!' behold, there stood the boy between her and the deep water on such a narrow space that there was only room for a bird's feet, and he smiled his sweet smile and raised his right hand. 'Were you going to do that?' he asked. 'Don't you know how deep it is?'

"Then the mother wept and told the boy of her distress. 'A harelip?' asked the child in surprise, and put his hand gently on the half-open mouth of the sleeping baby.

"And when he took his hand away, there was no blemish to be seen, however closely the mother looked; instead the sleeping child began to smile so beautifully that its lips looked like the petals of a flower opening in the sunshine to reveal the golden center.

" 'Do you see its lips now?' asked the boy, getting up. 'But if you still know of some secret blemish in it, tell me now, for many a mother is waiting for me tonight.'

"Then the mother told him of the left eye which might be blind.

"The child only smiled, passed his hand once over the eyes of the sleeping baby, and the eyes opened. A lovely smile was on the baby's lips, and its blue eyes beamed, and the mother as she bent forward saw that both eyes followed the movements of the hand with which the strange boy wrote circles and signs into the darkening air.

" 'If anybody finds a mark on it again,' said the boy, 'only say that you will take it to me, for with me, in the realm of love, all men's blemishes vanish.'

"Then the mother bowed low before the little boy, and when she raised her eyes he was gone; only the marshes flashed up once again as if under the glow of a belated evening sun.

"Then the woman went home, and when she came into the courtyard she could see the candles alight behind the lofty windows of the castle, and she went quickly up the flight of steps so that she would not be too late. When she opened the heavy door of the hall, all the people of the estate stood silently by the wall, and her mother was in the front row. She saw that all of them looked at her with surprise, even with fear, and the master whom they called 'the Saint' came up to her, bowed, and said, 'Thank you for coming and for having made yourself so beautiful for this night.'

"Then she looked down at herself wonderingly, and she saw that the shawl in which she had wrapped the child was full of Christmas roses, so that the smiling face of the child seemed to lie in a blossoming garden, and nobody could turn his eyes from it. Not even the old woman who had called it 'the accursed one.'

"Yes," said Christoph, taking his short pipe up again from the edge of the hearth, "that happened in times when the Christ Child still went about on Christmas Eve to have mercy."

The "young mother" held her eyes fixed on Christoph's lips all the time, but her face was unchanged, quiet, and happy. Only Baron Amadeus noticed that her shoulders shivered slightly, as when a breeze blows over a young forest, and he laid his hand gently on her hair and left it there.

The brothers did not say much when the others had gone and they were left alone with Christoph. Above all they did not speak about the forester's daughter. Only when they said goodbye, Aegidius' wife said to Christoph, "Will it also be like this some other evening, though it is not Christmas Eve?"

Christoph took the pipe out of his mouth and smiled, as one smiles at a child's question. "It's always Christmas Eve for a mother, Frau Baronin," he answered, "for every mother."

The cottagers and their children had already left at noon, as they wished to go to church in the district town. Only Donelaitis' young wife did not want to go. She had shaken her head and had followed them with her eyes from her threshold.

It was still not dusk when young Erdmuthe knocked at the door of the hut. She had tied a scarf over her fair hair and she carried a small bundle in her hand, as the women of her homeland did when they had to journey across the country.

The baron looked at her for a while and then invited her to sit down by the fire. "Are you going to meet them?" he asked.

But she shook her head. Then she undid the knot of her scarf, so that it slipped down from her hair to the nape of her neck, and she looked quietly into the flames. She kept her hands folded in her lap, as if she were holding a hymnbook between them. Her face was not unhappy or distressed. It was much as usual, only that it had a faraway look.

"I have come, sir," she said gently, "so that the others shall not think I have gone into the marshes."

"And where are you going?" asked Amadeus.

"Away," she said, "home."

Amadeus was startled. He knew that he would not be able to hold her back, even though he did not know why she was going.

"You have never been at home here?" he asked.

She shook her head.

"Not even with your husband?"

She shook her head again.

"Has anything happened?" he asked in a low voice.

"No, sir," she said. "Nothing has happened. He will think that something happened with the Americans, but it is not true; that isn't it. Tell him that it is not true. Last summer I thought now and again that something ought to happen with them, so that at any rate something should happen. But it wasn't the right thing, not the right thing for me. They were from a different part of the world – also in this. It wouldn't have helped me."

"And in what should it have helped you, Erdmuthe?"

She looked at him for the first time, and for the first time Amadeus saw that in this hour of decision she had the eyes of a child, a child that kept everything to itself, that lived quite apart and quite absorbed in itself.

"You were a good master, always," she said. "You were good even to the girl who wanted to kill you. There is nobody here that I could speak to except you. That's why I have come to you."

"Have you not come too late, Erdmuthe?" he asked.

She shook her head. "He is good, too," she said, "but I cannot speak to him. I can cook his dinner and lie with him at night if he wants me to. But he isn't the kind you can speak to. I don't know anything about him. He can set traps and catch men, and if I had forgotten myself with one of the soldiers, he would have set a trap for me, too. But I cannot warm my hands at him when they are cold."

"But he has been good to you," said Amadeus.

"He was as good as men in my homeland are to their wives, and the wives are content, but I am not. You don't know anything about us, sir, not even the cleverest of you. Sometimes you yoke us to the plow as in old times, or we are just a plaything for you. You don't know how we give ourselves to you; you don't know how humble we are, and you know nothing of our pride. You don't know how lonely we are when we have given ourselves, and when you begin to think that it is your right – a right and a habit."

"And do you know more of us?" asked Amadeus.

"Much more, sir, much more. Even the youngest of us knows much more, even among simple folk."

"And now?"

"I am homesick, sir. I thought that he had brought along everything that I needed, everything, the whole of my homeland, but he brought only himself. The rest was left behind – all of it. If I had a child I would stay here. With a child you don't need a homeland. But I shall not have children. I don't know why, but I shall not have any."

"And what will you have there?"

"Oh, sir," she said softly, and fervently pressed her hands together in her lap. "Do you have to ask that, sir? Don't you know what a homeland is?"

"I believe I do."

"Look at the others, sir. They live like shadows. They have their work and their daily bread, they have a roof and a hearth. You have sown flowers for them, and perhaps you sometimes think that they are happy. But in their sleep they are not happy, sir. In their sleep they weep, and when the women stand on their doorsteps in the morning gazing over the moor, you can still see the tears in their eyes, if you stand in the shadow and they do not notice you. But they have their children and when the children are awake, it is easier for them."

"Everything has changed, where you want to go," said Amadeus. "You must not go there believing in a fairytale. There are no more fairytales in that country."

"I don't want to find a fairytale, sir. I want once more to sit by the river where the nightingales sing. I want once more to see an elk on the moor. I want once more to see the lighthouse in the night. I want once more to see the colored crosses in the churchyard. I want once more to smell the meadows when they are mown. I want once more to sit on a doorstep and sing into the evening glow. There I grew up, sir; there I played as a child; there at Easter I strewed the floors of the room with sweet calamus."

"You will not strew them anymore," said Amadeus gloomily. "They will put you in prison or they will kill you on the way."

"Not on the way, sir, not on the way! I know that I shall have to pay so that I can get through. But then I shall be there. If I am only there for a single day, sir, yes, if I am only there for a single hour. Only so long that I can take up the white sand in my hand and let it run through my fingers, only so long, sir."

The fire crackled on the hearth and the blue flame slipped along the last log of wood. There was a low humming sound above the glowing fire. Grita would have said that the Fire Man was singing. Amadeus bent forward, his hands between his knees, and looked into the crackling wood. He knew that he could not hold her back, neither with pictures of life nor with pictures of death. He had not taken hold of her hand, as Wittkopp had advised him to do. There had been too many hands, or he had been too weary. And the call of her native soil was stronger than his hand – the river, the marshes, the songs – nothing could withstand it. Even if one knew that it wasn't there any longer, that it was changed or effaced, even then nothing could withstand it. They would not have leveled the dunes, not even the victors could do that. There would always be a handful of sand left which she could pick up and then let it run out through her fingers. That was all the homesick needed, those who felt that real, deep homesickness that consumes the whole being, that could not be stilled, no, could not be appeased even by a husband. It could only be appeased if she had a child, but she was not to have a child, neither a fair nor a dark child.

The young woman tied the scarf around her head again and took up the bundle which she had put on the floor. "Don't worry, sir," she said gently and got up. "It's different with you. You have been where none of us have been, and you have to care for many. They think of you as fishermen up there think of the lighthouse. Even the girl and her child will think of you like that. Pray for me, sir, pray that I may hold a handful of sand. Nothing else, only a handful of sand."

He gently stroked her cheek and went with her to the door. "If I bound you by force," he said, "you would have to stay, but it would only be for an hour."

She shook her head. "You wouldn't do such a thing, sir," she said. "He who has once been bound does not bind another. I knew that when I came to you."

Snow was falling fast in big flakes as they stood on the threshold. It was already twilight. The silent horizon had come close up to the house. Beyond it was the end of the world.

Into this twilight she walked, her bundle in her hand, never to return.

Amadeus stood there and looked after her until her footprints in front of the threshold were filled with snow. When her footprints were covered it was as if she had never been there. And snow fell until it whitened Amadeus' hair, but he did not notice it.

11

NIGHT HAD ALREADY FALLEN when Amadeus went down to light the fires in the various cottages. It was still snowing and no footprint was to be seen by the doorstep. Walking would be difficult, even on the highroads, but she who walked there alone need not turn around to see whether anyone was following her. Snow covered her, and snow protected her. It fell in thick folds over all that had been. Behind her steps it blocked the old year; it blocked all the past.

The last fire Amadeus lit was that on the hearth of a man who now would sit there alone. Amadeus did not know how he would sit there, whether his thoughts as he sat would be gloomy or sad, or whether he would have no thoughts at all. But he did know that Donelaitis would not follow his wife. That, the men of his country did not do.

Amadeus could only try to tell him why she had gone away, and it was not certain that he would understand it. He would only understand that she had gone and would never come back. And when he had understood that, he would never speak of it again till the day of his death.

Nobody would ever learn what he thought about it. Most likely he would go on with his work and would sit by this fire in the long winter evenings. He, Amadeus, had sat so too, and nobody had known anything about his thoughts. But he had been different, because he could still be "changed." Nobody would change this man.

Amadeus heard the churchgoers come home and then Donelaitis entered. He saw the baron by the fire and looked quickly around the room. Perhaps he understood at once.

"Sit down a little with me," said Amadeus. "She is gone."

Donelaitis did as he was told, and obediently he took one of the cigarettes which Amadeus offered him.

"She has not gone into the swamps," Amadeus went on. "She has gone home – to the great river. She went alone. She came to see me before she went."

The fire crackled; that was the only sound. Not even the man's breathing was to be heard.

"You know that she did not go anywhere else, sir?" he asked at last.

"Yes, I do know. Perhaps she did think of it last summer, but not now. Perhaps you did not talk enough to her, but even that would not have helped her much."

"Up there we do not talk to our wives – after the wedding," said Donelaitis. "We talk to our horses and sometimes to the sails, when we are on the sea; but not to our wives; that's how it is with us."

Amadeus nodded. "Most are content with it," he said. "But now and again there is one among them who is not content. You have found such a one."

"She will never get there," said Donelaitis after a pause. "How can she get there when the world is full of rogues?"

"She knew," replied Amadeus, "but she wanted to hold the white sand in her hand once more."

"You could have bound her, sir," said Donelaitis, "until I got home."

"I told her that, but she knew that I cannot bind anybody since I was bound myself. And then she would have gone into the swamp. You could not have bound her day and night. You can bind hand and feet, that is all; you cannot bind the heart."

"Formerly they were beaten," said Donelaitis gloomily, "with the bridle or with the belt. Men did not think anything about it, nor did the women. I would not have beaten her."

"You would not have beaten her and you could not have held her. She was like a bird on a string. I dare say most women are like that. She would have stayed, if she had had a child. But she felt that it was denied her."

"The fog witches have denied it to her, sir. Too often she stood at the edge of the moor in the evening. She was never here. She did not wait until the Christ Child came. Perhaps he would have come, because he comes to such as her, too."

"She would not have seen him, Donelaitis. She would not have believed that he could be about here. In her homeland she would have believed it and would have seen him, but not here. You brought her with you but without her heart. Her heart was left there. Now she has gone to look for it. Nobody can live without a heart. The conquerors do not know how many hearts they have torn to pieces."

"Who will wipe the snow off her scarf?" asked Donelaitis, stooping deeper down over the fire.

"You are not going to follow her?" asked Amadeus.

The man shook his head.

"We do not follow a woman in our homeland," he replied. "A man goes after a horse that has run into the wood from the field, or after a sheep that has gone astray on the moor. But a man does not go after a woman."

They sat there and smoked until the fire went out. Nothing but a reddish glow came from the embers. There were two men, but the room was empty. They only needed to look around where shadows stood in the dark corners to realize that it was empty. Even death could not have made it more empty.

"Formerly we tried to seize good luck at this time, sir," said Donelaitis. "That's what we called it. The women had baked and had put it below the plates. We were allowed to lift three plates.

There was bread under one and a cradle under another. Then there was money, the key to heaven, a ring, or a death's-head. There were twelve things which lay under the plates. I do not know what she found when she lifted the plate. What am I to find when I lift it?"

"Lift the spade, Donelaitis," said Amadeus gently, going toward the door, "if there is a spade under one of them. And if there is not, we two will make it and put it under a plate. It's a good talisman for both of us. The spade is not homesick, except for the earth."

It was still snowing, and it was hard climbing up to the hut. Surely it was midnight by now, but no bells could be heard. They had taken the bells down from the steeples and melted them. The conquerors would probably discharge a volley and let off fireworks, but the snow muffled the noise and the light. It covered all footprints – those of men and those of animals. It covered the old year, as was befitting. The homeless, displaced persons might lift the plates as they used to do when they had their homes, but the snow fell even on that which was under the plates: on the bread, the cradle, the death's-head, and also on the spade which they had both pictured.

Christoph was waiting for him in the hut. "I didn't want to go away, sir," he said, "because the old year is nearly at an end."

He listened attentively while Amadeus told him what had happened. "It is slipping out of our hands, sir," he said, "like the sand which she wants to hold. Don't grieve, sir, you cannot hold sand nor men. Now perhaps the earth has worn out its anger. On this last day of the year it has perhaps worn it out. The evil and the grief of hearts have sunk down to the roots and there they have been cleansed. A good time will come for all of us, not at once, but presently it will come. My eyes will still be able to see a little of it."

"What sort of a good time will it be," asked Amadeus gloomily, "when snow will fall on her scarf and one day the dew into her dead eyes?"

"The good snow time," replied Christoph in his quiet, confident voice, "when a heart can turn in on itself, and the good thaw time, in which the Child with bare feet stands before wanderers to stroke away the mark and the blemish. And the best time of all, when two children will be born and nobody will know which is the bright and which the dark child, because the Christ Child on the moor will have laid his hand over the source from which they have both sprung.

"That will be a good time for all of them, for then and not until then they will have two children to look after. This will come easily to those who do this work, and so the grownups also will get their share, and most of all those who have a heavy heart."

In the New Year something quite unexpected happened. Baron Erasmus, sitting one evening by the fire in the hut suddenly declared, without any warning and with deep embarrassment, that he, too, was going to get married.

"Dear brother . . ." said Amadeus after a while, but Erasmus raised his hand, as if he did not want to hear anything. "You see, brother," he said gently, "I am feeling very lonely just now. Two children will be born this spring, and though neither of them is yours, they will be near your heart. And that is quite right. But the nearer they are to your heart, the farther away I shall be from you. You must not shake your head. I know that it will be so.

"Previously I thought of marrying so that I could help the people here, and perhaps it was more than half a joke. But now I am afraid of being so lonely. You know that I have always been afraid. In a way it seemed as if you, too, might suddenly step out of the triptych and disappear beyond the frame, and I would be left standing there all alone in a frame much too large for me.

"Besides, I fancy that I shan't hear the children's voices any longer, or only from a great distance – as if with marriage I could make up for what I did so wrongly – that is, if there is any way at all of making up for a wrong deed."

"Are you doing it only for that?" asked Amadeus.

Erasmus shook his head. "No, not only for that. You see, I wouldn't like to live there like an owl among crows until the day of my death. I would like to have something a little brighter, brother. Things have been pretty gloomy all this time, don't you think so too?"

"He is another that I have not looked after," thought Amadeus, taking a sidelong glance at Erasmus as he sat hunched up in his chair, his hands folded between his knees. He did not look like a happy bridegroom.

"We have never wanted anything for you except what would make you happy, brother," he said in a low voice. "Forgive us if we have not had time enough for you."

Again Erasmus shook his head, as if such things ought not to be said. "She is not a dollar-princess," he went on, a little embarrassed, "but anyhow she has a number of factories up there which her husband left her. Cigars or such-like. Perhaps it will be enough to buy a few homesteads for our people. That was important to me. Not that I want to smoke her cigars, but our people ought to have a better life sometime. She is rather of the demimonde, you know. I think that's what people call it. But I believe she loves me. Yes, I certainly believe that." And he eyed Amadeus as if his brother had doubted it.

But Amadeus did not want to doubt anything that concerned his brother's happiness. Certainly "of the demimonde" did bewilder him a little. Erasmus was not in the habit of using such expressions. They talked it over and agreed that Erasmus and his fiancée should come to see Amadeus one evening, for they were already engaged. "Not that you are to judge her, brother," said Erasmus with a shy smile. "But all those who wanted to come into our lives have sat there by the fire, haven't they? I feel that here is something like a court of justice of hearts."

"Here is no court of justice," said Amadeus gently, and helped him to put on his coat.

He stood on the threshold and his eyes followed Erasmus for a long time. He could not deny that he was deeply troubled. His brother had given too many explanations and reasons, yes, even excuses. One does not need excuses if one loves, Amadeus thought. If only one loves. His eyes still followed his brother's tall, bent figure after it had disappeared in the darkness, for he felt that it was enshrouded in sadness and danger, and that it might be too late to prevent him from taking the step "off the track." If his brother took such a step off the track, it would be a big step. He would not first grope with the point of his stick to test whether there was solid ground before his feet. He was probably too much of a nobleman to do that.

The very next afternoon Daisy arrived at his door, and she was alone. The baron did not much like the name Daisy, but it was perhaps more usual in the Hamburg district than it had been in his homeland. Nor did he like her second name, Knolle, although he blamed himself for this dislike, for that had been the affair of her first husband, and she could not do anything about it.

After having introduced herself she filled the little room with a strong perfume and with that which Erasmus termed demimonde, and this, too, Amadeus disliked. He disliked it thoroughly from the very first moment, and his face and attitude only changed when he noticed that Daisy was afraid. He could not say how he noticed it, but it filled, as it were, the background of her eyes, as fear can fill the eyes of a child who is lying with calm assurance.

He offered her an easy chair by the fire and asked her if he could get her a cup of tea or coffee.

No, she did not want anything. She had enough to do to watch this "wonderful" brother.

She laughed – perhaps her laugh was a little too loud and a little too shrill – and she looked at him with eyes under brows which were nothing but a mere streak, and these eyes seemed to be so clear and frank because she did not want him to notice her embarrassment. He considered her appearance thoughtfully. It seemed to him that these eyes had already faced many men, wonderful and less wonderful men; and now he was rather sorry for her – sorry that she had climbed up this hard path to him, that she had schemed out how she would be able to fascinate him or how she would be able at least to sit with him in such a way that he should not detect her uneasiness too soon.

The baron offered her a cigarette, and now he did not dislike it quite so much when she inhaled the smoke deeply and breathed it out again, puffing like a child's toy engine. He was not pleased with it, but he only looked quietly on and was glad to see that smoking seemed to ease her tension.

He tried to ask her a few questions about her past life, her stay in the castle, her plans for the future. But her answers were lost in empty space. It was as if the knob of a wireless were slowly turned, and from all the stations of the world fragments came in reply: the beat of a melody, a sentence of a sermon, a review of a film. Each might have its own sense, but there was no time to follow up the sense because the voice of the next station interrupted immediately. There was something ghostlike in this overcrowded ether, as if even the ether were no longer infinite between the constellations, but were filled with the shadows of the dead speaking in whispers to themselves on their illimitable journey to the narrow tomb, where at last they would be allowed silence.

It seemed to Amadeus as if she were afraid of saying too much, of saying things which might be brought up against her later. As if she had come straight away from those packed towns where eavesdroppers stood on every corner, where the sirens might wail at any minute, and where in crumbling cellars there were strange faces before which one had better be on one's guard, particularly when they asked questions in such a friendly way as he had.

"He is one of the best men in the world," he said presently. "That must be known by anybody who wants to walk at his side."

She smiled a little, but she nodded emphatically. "There are a few others who are good," she replied, "the parson for instance. Nearly all the others are riffraff."

Amadeus shook his head a little reproachfully. "Not to my brother or to the parson," he said. "They have been struck down through their own fault or not through their own fault – and they must really be given time to raise themselves again."

"Yes, you are marvelous, you Barons von Liljecrona," she said, smiling at him. "All three of you are marvelous. But probably you are the most difficult."

That he did not know, replied Amadeus with some reserve. One thing she ought to know before she stepped in among the three brothers – that their ways were still those of times gone by, and that they were in many things old-fashioned, as people would call it nowadays.

Perhaps even she might be glad to become like that again, she hazarded thoughtfully.

Then the baron relapsed into silence; he was sinking into an ever-increasing melancholy and listened without attention to the ether – voices which forced themselves on him from between these red-painted lips. Although most of it was meant seriously, or was just helpless or uncertain in tone, most of it was disjointed and without that consistency which even the simplest life ought to have. Sometimes it seemed to him as if it might as well have been a bird of paradise sitting there, brightly colored and very pretty to look at, which was waiting for the lump of sugar that would be given to it.

But Amadeus could not give it to her. He thought that it would perhaps all turn out to be a tragicomedy, but more likely it would turn out to be a tragedy. An infinite pity for Erasmus and for this woman came over him, a poignant realization of how lonely, how lost, how unhappy they both must have been that they should reach out and grasp each other's hands. It seemed as if his brother's balance had been upset, and as if he had grasped the nearest railing to hold himself up. They had not been near enough – Aegidius and he – for Erasmus to grasp their hands. They had not been good brothers. They had not had vigilant hearts.

Perhaps one might still try to hold him back and guard him – not only against this marriage, but also against his entering upon it in order to forget something and to gain something, but in no way to give anything. Probably it would be a deadly blow for him to have his double error revealed. The children still called to him from the snowbound road, and this woman would certainly not have children.

"It's terrible; it's terrible," he said, lost in thought.

As Daisy had just finished a description of the air raids on Hamburg, she took his sigh as sympathy with her experiences and got up. It was a suitable conclusion to her visit, and in any case she had not felt very comfortable all the time. She had seen very clearly that her charm had not worked. Yes, it was even possible that from time to time she had forgotten to exercise it. This reserved man was certainly the most uncanny of the three brothers. Aegidius, whom she had seen for a quarter of an hour, was the simplest; he had only looked at her as he would a wheat field, wondering if it would pay for the sowing. It had been easier there, as his wife had been sitting with them, his wife who looked like a giantess in disguise.

But this one was uncanny because nothing impressed him and one never knew what his peculiar eyes really did see. What he had said was full of riddles, and it would be better to hurry up with the wedding so that this man with the striped coat could not suddenly drive them out of the castle. Terrible things had happened up here, and one had to be on one's guard. Here was the old, no longer remembered world of the eastern boundaries of the Reich, and to her it was as incomprehensible as a book in a foreign language.

But when she said goodbye she smiled in spite of these thoughts, for she was glad that her visit was over, and in her lightheartedness she was foolish enough to ask him whether his "sister-in-law to be" did not deserve a kiss. But she repented it at once, because the baron stared at her without the trace of a smile, as if he regretted that she had overstepped the limits of familiarity in such an unseemly way. With an unmoved face he replied that one did not kiss in this room, and he said it as if she had suggested that they should forge a will together.

However, she did not show her feelings, and when she walked in the glow of the evening sun over the heather to the footpath, she did look like a bird of paradise that had flown astray but had found its way again.

Amadeus' eyes followed her, too, from the threshold, and it came into his mind that from this spot his eyes had followed many people and their destinies. As if these forms had risen from the depths, and after a time they had gone away again; and very rarely did he know what the world was like to which they had descended.

Nor did he know it of this woman.

He dreaded his brother's next visit, and Erasmus noticed his anxiety immediately.

"I'm not a judge in these things, brother," said Amadeus after a time. "I know very little of men and still less of women. They are like butterflies which you never catch, and even if you only try to see their colors and the beauty of their wings, they shut their wings together and you only see the colorless side."

"Perhaps I see both sides, brother," said Erasmus shyly.

"Then it will be all right," replied Amadeus. "Aegidius and I will be near you, nothing will be changed."

"All will be well, when I have a child," said Erasmus after a long silence. "Then they will not call anymore, and all will be well."

"I am sure all will be well, brother. One married for a field and gained a wife. The other is marrying for a child, and he will fare just as well. Now only I am left, but you must not ask me what I am going to marry for. Because I shall remain alone."

"You are the richest of us three," said Erasmus. "Many sorrows have been brought to you by this fireside, and you have always seen to it that the poor left you rich."

"Not always," replied Amadeus, "not always."

"Will you give me the pleasure of coming to my wedding?" asked Erasmus at last.

"I shall certainly come, dear brother. You may depend on it."

When Erasmus went, Amadeus did not know whether he had gone away from him rich.

Some days later he set out on the long journey to Aegidius to have a talk with him. His sister-in-law now expected the child any day, and for the first time Amadeus saw in her ungainly appearance only her face. A beautiful, quite peaceful face shining with an inner light which was but a mirror of the miracle that was taking place within her. "I may have hurt you now and again," Amadeus said when he was sitting alone with her by the fire. "I beg you to forgive me. I was then still at the stage of life when one criticizes." He bent forward and kissed her hand. She did not withdraw it. She only said, "Now I am no longer afraid."

Aegidius was worried, but he, too, thought that they had better not interfere with Erasmus. "You may have thought," he said after a pause, "that I have gone away from you both, and that I only live for all this. But that is not so. I have only learned to look on quietly. You learn that from the fields, where the seed sprouts and grows without us. But I have realized, too, that none of us can step out of the ring that encircles us. Then I believe sometimes that father is still alive and watches over us.

"Let us not interfere with Erasmus. It looks as if he were leaving the ring altogether, but that is not the case. That's why we mustn't be worried. Don't forget how worried you were when I came here. He will come back, probably very soon, and we must only let him know that we are always here waiting for him. Perhaps he will be ashamed when he comes back – quite wrongly – and we must only make it clear to him that each of us ought to be ashamed also. We have spilled enough milk already.

"What do we know after all about the poor creature who thinks to gain a seven-leafed coronet now? What price is she paying for it, and what has she been through to be willing to pay it?"

"Sometimes I believe," said his wife gently, "that only in fairytales people behave and live as you do. Three brothers who go into a dark wood, and each hears the other's voice whenever he is in need – over hills, over mountains. Always when I see one of you, I have to think: Once upon a time . . ."

"But my wheat grows well," said Aegidius with a smile.

"Perhaps," said Amadeus, "it is all because we come out of the East; and perhaps because time has touched but not conquered us. We still have our own time. Many nowadays will smile at it, but it is easy for those to smile who have no time except morning and evening. There beyond the mighty rivers life went differently – more broadly, more peacefully, and no doubt in many ways more primitively. It was not a fairytale, but I understand that it may appear so to many."

A difficulty arose at the last moment, for Daisy had no documents; she was nameless and homeless. Her last trunk had been stolen on the way, and where she had lived the last few years all was destroyed and burned down. But two young fellows in the castle with whom she was friendly witnessed her name and home, and as at that time there were many displaced persons without any papers, the registrar finally gave in.

But when Amadeus saw the two "young fellows" at the wedding dinner, he thought that a marriage ought to be more securely based than on their testimony. Over this wedding dinner in the castle there certainly was not a propitious star. It was a black-market dinner; that alone did not please everybody. Most of the guests disquieted Amadeus. He only knew Wittkopp. Aegidius sat politely and obligingly at the side of the young wife, and Christoph in his blue coat stood behind the chair of Baron Erasmus, as in the old days, and supervised the serving and clearing away of the courses.

Opposite Amadeus sat the old count, pallid and plastered with decorations. Probably as a result of an illness, he could not open his eyelids as he wanted, and only when he was addressed did he open them with a great effort, like a sleeping owl. He ate and drank with little moderation, and for some unknown reason spoke only French.

But the young fellows in sweaters and without jackets behaved with as much assurance as if they were the young wife's brothers. They were only referred to as soldiers, without any other profession, flying officers the young wife declared, and she explained that they were "marvelous heroes."

The young wife wore a real wedding dress and the count an old-fashioned tail coat, and when Amadeus looked round the table, the idea came to him that they might well be sitting in a puppet show arranged by unskillful hands, and that when the man behind the curtain laid down the cords, they would all stiffen suddenly and become dumb, rigid, and lifeless.

"C'est la canaille," said the count in his high-pitched voice to one of the young men, and he lifted his eyelids. *"Toujours la canaille . . ."*

But Amadeus could not decide who really was *la canaille,* the rabble.

Much was drunk, the laughter grew louder, and the young wife upset her champagne glass without heeding it. Nor did she heed that the young men's talk began to overstep the limits of decency.

Christoph's face was the most imperturbable. He still stood behind his master's chair looking down upon the table and the guests as his forefathers might have looked down upon the gamblers' table covered with gold coins. The only thing that was missing was the whip in his left hand. It appeared to Amadeus that Christoph's right hand did not tremble any longer, the hand that would have to take his master's belt to lead him down to the sleigh.

Christoph paid no attention when the Count beckoned to him with his forefinger, nor did he pay attention when he called him. He was not at everybody's beck and call. He certainly did not understand the words *toujours la canaille,* which the count now addressed to him.

Amadeus got up when one of the young fellows started to drink out of the bottle and the other began in a loud and somewhat hoarse voice to show his talents as a singer – accompanying himself on a mandolin. "The sea was sparkling far and wide . . ." he sang, while he fixed his dimmed and already rather lifeless gaze on the young wife. Amadeus stood still for a moment, pondering what the connection might be between this song by Schubert and this half-drunk fellow, other than perhaps the words, "the unfortunate wife." But he could not fancy that she had "poisoned with her tears" any of her companions, not even this obscure minstrel with the wine stains on his sweater.

The face of Baron Erasmus was so overly happy when he said goodbye to him that Amadeus believed he could recognize the deep sadness below the features, and he could do no more than nod to him without a word. It was like the face of a child who sits in a swing flying through the air, but the higher the swing goes the more the happiness disappears from the face, and its place is taken by an ever-growing fear, which stiffens the happiness into a mere mask – fear because he realizes that it is too late to get off. While he was still on the stairs, Amadeus heard the last phrase "poisoned with her tears" and the wild applause. Then he stood in the courtyard and saw the stars in the canopy of heaven. "So many stars," he thought again and walked slowly across the great dark courtyard.

He stopped once more under the massive stone archway and looked up at the broken coat of arms. Here he had stood then, the dead behind him, and here he stood again now. The dead had stepped back again into their shades, and change had gently passed its hand over the living. Evil had been abroad on this portion of the earth, too, but at any rate, they had tried to set good against it. They had not annihilated evil, for it was immortal, but they had gained a small space where they had hoisted the flag of good. They had perhaps erred and been overhasty in much, but in the end they had gained what was great: they no longer criticized and no longer passed sentence. They had become quiet in a world of noise. They had no more "programs," nor a weltanschauung. They did not say: "This is good" – and certainly not: "This alone is good!" They had not solved the world's problems. They had become modest and a little skeptical and a little resigned. They were no longer so convinced of the splendor and might of man; they were rather more convinced of all that which lay beyond the might of man, even though they had no name or had different names for it. It was no longer so important to them who was the victor and who the vanquished, who belonged to this nation and who to that. For the nation of those who had good will recognized no frontiers. They did not want to conquer nor to rule; they only wanted to help and heal: the ruined towns and the ruined faces, the hands that had killed and the eyes that had looked on at killing, the hearts that lived in hatred, in darkness, or only in negation.

Again Amadeus raised his eyes to the illuminated windows, to "Belshazzar's Castle," where the "marvelous heroes" drank out of a bottle, and where his brother might well have stepped "off the track." But where, as in primitive times, Christoph stood – as his forefathers had stood – behind his master's chair, ready to seize his belt if the time came. Always provided that he would recognize when it was time.

And as Amadeus climbed up the mountain and heard the night birds calling above the moor, he only thought of the two children who would so soon be born. And then he thought of the young Erdmuthe, of how with the bundle in her hand she walked over the roads of the devastated earth to behold once more the reed roofs on the river Memel, the colored crosses in the churchyards, and the lighthouse on the spit, whose beams of light circled over lagoon and ocean through the night. Probably she would not reach these things, but only the night of prison and death; and evidently she was so constructed that only death could still her longing for home, the great longing for home of the simple people who had been driven and beaten like cattle under dictatorship as under democracy, under serfdom as under the dominion of the rights of man.

They had not been able to hold her back – not even Baron Amadeus. They had no power over homesickness – nor, so it seemed, over the heart of her who sat on the threshold of that church below the crucified vicar, nor over the hearts of those who walked toward the shore of the river where stood "the three trees, three maple trees."

A week later a son was born to Baron Aegidius, and with the invitation for the christening Amadeus was informed that their mother had written from her moated castle that she, too, would come to see them on this occasion.

It was a big piece of news, and the most bewildering that Amadeus had received this year. It was as if a picture on the wall suddenly began to move, as if it wanted to step down out of its frame and move about among human beings. Amadeus was shocked to realize how remote his mother had become, not only remote in space, but remote also from their hearts, whereas he who had passed out of their ken and had disappeared since their childhood, when "the Lord had deceived him," had remained so near that one only need open a door to be with him again.

It did not appear to him as a fault, neither on the one side nor on the other. It was only as if the earth suddenly widened before his eyes. How far a being could move from the heart and the consciousness of another and yet still live on the same earth! And how much greater its emptiness could be!

He had never offended, blamed, or hurt her. He only had not loved. She had borne him, but he was not of her blood. It was as if she had only adopted him, and then, when he could walk, she had sent him away, not only him, but all three of them. As if she had never looked at him solely with her eyes, but always through her gold-framed lorgnette – even when he was in the cradle.

He sighed a little, but then a faint smile played around his lips. When the hair had turned gray, they could not well play mother and son together if they had failed to do so in childhood. Certainly she would not feel the slightest inclination to do so. She would go to Aegidius' house in the same way that she would go into a peasant's house where a child had just been born, and where a gold coin or a silver spoon would be put into the cradle. Probably she would inspect this daughter-in-law through her lorgnette as she would the giantess at a fair. How she would inspect the other daughter-in-law, the sophisticated one, Amadeus could not picture to himself.

Only this seemed comforting to him, that nobody would drink cognac out of the bottle and that probably no "heroes" would be there.

They had hired a carriage and two horses and Christoph drove them. Erasmus and Daisy sat behind, and Amadeus sat on the coachman's box by Christoph. It was easier for him not to see his brother's happy face and his shy eyes which begged: "Don't ask any questions, brother, please don't."

Amadeus did not want to ask.

Daisy wore an expensive fur coat but she was quiet, and now and then she shut her eyes as if she were wondering how things would be at this festival. Probably not so merry as at her wedding dinner. The figure of her mother-in-law appeared to her to resemble the marble statue which she had seen in some opera – *The Magic Flute* or something similar.

Christoph still had no cap, and now and again he pointed with his whip to the young wheat or to a flight of wild geese and said a few words to Baron Amadeus. And the baron answered as he had answered as a child when they drove across the country. The sun shone warm and the smell of the earth was strong and clean. Amadeus asked in a low voice whether Christoph believed that the earth had worn out its anger.

Christoph gently shrugged his shoulders. "Wait a little yet, sir," he said. "Where we are driving to, it has worked itself out, but otherwise it still has a good deal to do. It will be a good year, sir, for the fields and for us."

They were sitting at the top of the flight of steps in the sunshine when the carriage drew up. Amadeus saw that his mother got up and looked at them from the topmost step. Her hair was snow-white but she held herself as erect as she had in his childhood. She wore a long, lilac-colored dress and a fur cape round her shoulders, and she stood there as if all this belonged to her: the house, the estate, and Christoph, for he was the first whom she addressed. "Where have you left your hat, Christoph?" she asked in her high-pitched voice. "Does one drive to a christening bare-headed here?" She asked as if inquiring why a child had not done its homework.

Christoph lowered his whip as a sign of greeting and looked at her from the height of his coachman's box. "The hat got lost on the way, my lady," he said politely. "They did not send it after me. But with our white hair, the baroness and I don't need hats anymore."

"Your white hair is not my white hair," replied the baroness, as if correcting a mistake in an account, but Christoph was already looking straight over the horses' heads.

Erasmus and his wife went up the steps first, more slowly than was necessary, and all the time the baroness viewed the new daughter-in-law through her lorgnette. Not kindly and not unkindly, merely attentively, as she would have looked at a new lady's maid. She kissed Erasmus on the forehead but even while she kissed him her eyes did not turn away from the young woman.

Then she gave her hand to Daisy to kiss, who in her embarrassment obeyed without hesitation. "So this is you," said the baroness thoughtfully.

Daisy nodded.

"And formerly your name was Knolle?"

At that the young woman nodded again.

"Well, that's not your fault," said the baroness and drew her fur cape closer around her shoulders.

"Just as little as it is our fault that our name happens to be Liljecrona," remarked Aegidius with a smile.

It was his wife who suffered most during these introductions and her eyes searched his face for help. Aegidius had been a little amused at the whole scene and if Daisy had raised her eyes, she would have seen that he gave her a little nod. Such things were not so new to him as they were to his wife.

Then the baroness brushed a kiss on Amadeus' forehead and kept her eyes fixed on him for some time. "You are the one most like him," she said, "and you, too, fell into the pit, just as he . . ."

"Yes," responded Amadeus in a friendly tone, "but at least my brothers did not throw me into it. They did not want to sell me."

"Why that?" she asked, at a loss. "Why should they sell you?"

"Into the land of Egypt," said Amadeus, and he smiled. "Like Joseph."

She shrugged her shoulders. "Always these old tales," she replied, cutting him short. "That at least you ought to have unlearned in all these years."

"These years would not have been, if we had unlearned less," said Amadeus. "I am not one of those who unlearn."

"Yes, exactly like him," she said once more, reflectively. "He, too, always went along as if there were no stairs in this world. And when there happened to be some, he did not notice them and went down into empty space – headfirst."

"You did notice them," rejoined Amadeus. "But you did not notice that they, too, led into an empty space."

"I never find myself in empty space," said the baroness, dismissing the matter.

Aegidius' wife invited them into the breakfast room. It was nearly time for the parson and the guests to come.

The christening was to take place in the manor house. Aegidius was the only one who showed gaiety which was superior to the occasion. Nothing affected him: neither the categorical opinions of his mother, nor the embarrassment of his sister-in-law, in whose demeanor a little defiance began to show, nor the uneasiness of his wife, nor even the face of his brother Erasmus, who was talking a great deal and hurriedly and yet looked, to those who knew, as if he had not only lost the children on the wintry road, but had lost his regiment, too, and was now halting, a solitary rider, at the edge of the battlefield.

For Aegidius it was a solemn day, the happy solemnity of a man who had gained not only a field but also a son for that field, and who looked with a chivalrous gratitude on his wife, who had given him the field and son. He was living in the present but was also living in the distant future, and the people around him appeared to him not only as witnesses who were participating in this festivity but also as symbols of destiny, bearing within them more than the ordinary life of every day. He already saw the woven fabric and not the threads alone, and he knew that the present tangle would straighten itself out and fall smoothly into place. In his brother Erasmus' face, too, those threads which did not belong to the fabric would fall off in due course and would be stored up for a different cloth, even those of that pathetic, dressed-up woman. Even those of his mother, who was neither a mother nor a grandmother, but only a poor baroness who according to her own opinion did not live in "empty space."

"She is a female Cyclops," said the baroness to Amadeus, who was sitting beside her, and she hardly troubled to lower her voice. "The only difference is that she has two eyes. But I think the child will have only one eye in a few weeks' time. You have gone back to the old tribal god, you Liljecronas. He, too, had only one eye, and I would not be surprised if they were to sacrifice a human being to this child today, a cottager's child or something of the sort."

Amadeus glanced at her out of the corner of his eye, but by now he too had become infected by his brother's sober gaiety. He was not indignant, he only smiled. Why should only good and evil be imperishable? Why not also rigid and fixed ideas? Haughtiness or poverty of thought? She was a poor woman, but she did not know it. She had lost everything: husband, sons, and property, but she had not realized it. She was in a dreadful vacuum and her heart was empty, but it did not seem like that to her. She sat at the head of the table and she was the head of her own family. Even in death she would take the lead and would ask the ferryman why he did not wear a cap while he rowed her over to the other shore. She would not give him a coin but would explain to him in her high voice how he ought to conduct himself with such passengers, even if his hair was already white.

While these thoughts passed through his mind, Amadeus remarked that he would inquire whether they had already chosen a child. Otherwise she and he would have to do it.

She raised her lorgnette and looked at him, though he was sitting at her side. "One does not joke with one's mother without permission," she said as if she were sitting in a nursery. It was not said sharply, only in an offhand way, and with this she dismissed the faux pas. She was sure that he had taken it to heart.

"And this other creature," she went on quietly, "*cette courtisane secondaire, cette soi-disante Knolle,* where did he pick her up?"

"She has factories," said Amadeus, smiling. "At least she says so. Cigar factories. And at any rate this is a golden or certainly a gilded trade."

"Why did you not prevent it?"

"We no longer prevent anything," said Amadeus. "We only look on, until the time comes."

Then there was still a quarter of an hour in which to walk through the park in the sunshine. The baroness also looked through her glass at the daffodils, but she had no fault to find with them. It was impossible to tell whether they belonged to an inferior race.

The ceremony was solemn and beautiful. The baby did not cry and still had both his eyes, though the baroness gazed at him attentively throughout the proceedings. Moreover not one of the laborers' children, who stood open-eyed by the walls of the great hall, spring flowers in their hands, was sacrificed – although the baroness examined them too, attentively, one after another.

Only the district administrator and one or two of the neighboring proprietors had been invited, and they looked on with friendly surprise when after the christening the three brothers moved the palms aside and sat down to their music desks, which had been hidden by the plants.

This was Amadeus' idea, and even the mother of the newly-christened baby had not known of it. But hers was now the face that shone with happiness as she sat in her easy-chair, the baby in her arms, looking at the players. As if now after a year of waiting, Baron Amadeus had opened his arms and admitted her into the inaccessible domain of their heritage and of their three hearts.

They played a slow movement by Mozart, but for her it was unimportant what they played. While she felt the warmth of the little body at her heart, she looked at the players with wide-open, surprised, almost enraptured eyes. Life seemed never to have granted her a more beautiful, more sacred hour than this. It was as if she had been transported out of the darkness of a world of scorn and isolation into a world where there was no scorn, and as if these interlacing notes which upheld and supported each other were a guarantee that henceforth she would never be cast out again.

Of the three faces, her husband's was the brightest and gayest, and while he drew his bow to and fro across the strings, it seemed as if he only played what his heart was longing to express. As if it were his music, not that of Mozart or any great composer of the past.

It was not the same with Erasmus, whose cheek was held closely against his violin, and who looked as if he had been ordered to play. He played with the obedience and devotion due to the task, but the music had not yet loosed itself from his inner soul to soar upward in beautiful, buoyant freedom. For him there was no serene happiness in this hour, and not even Amadeus knew what stood before his brother's eyes; whether the women in the castle who came up to him with their floor cloths to get their rights, or the woman with the large, curious, almost frightened eyes who watched him as he drew his bow over the strings. Whether it was the despairing children on the snowbound road who had called to him so long, or perhaps the yet unborn child that he awaited as the saving grace of his life.

Amadeus, though he was not the gayest of the three brothers, was the one who best understood all that had gone to make up the present time, all that lay between the concert in the school hall, where they had played for the people who had been burned out of their houses, to this hour when they were playing for the little, new life.

He understood those years which at first had moved along with them and then over them, tearing down and obliterating so much of their world; those years when whole nations had been put under the yoke like animals, and history, as it is called, had been made. Decades in which death had had its fill as well as the god with the fiery belly whom the ancients called Moloch.

And yet some things had subsisted throughout their course: grain grew again on the earth and children were born, and some people still remembered what the Bible and the old families had called "good." This melody which he was playing with his brothers had not been destroyed, because no power on earth could destroy it, since it once had risen from a childlike, gifted heart. No matter if evil did persist and always would persist, it was not the only thing left on earth, for there was always something they could set against it, though it be nothing more or nothing less than this perfectly pure and completely balanced melody, that even the hand of a god could not have brought forth in a more perfect form than the young musician who had composed it.

Amadeus glanced once over his left hand at the faces of the listeners – at his mother's cool, critical face and the happy face of his sister-in-law, at the guests' still shyly astonished faces, and then at the spellbound faces of the cottagers' children, who gazed wide-eyed at this marvel. Then at Christoph, who stood in the midst of them, leaning against the wall, his white hair falling over the collar of his blue coat, gazing at him as if Baron Amadeus had now at last made the new covenant after the Flood from which they had all been cast up, and as if he, Christoph the coachman, could now go down in peace, into the grave, as it was written in the scriptures.

Amadeus had gained neither a field nor a wife nor a child, and when they got up and he put his instrument aside his hands were empty again, and yet it appeared to all the others that his was the most radiant face. Probably this was so, because while he was playing he was not thinking about the care of a little human being, not about the rejoicing over a little human being, but only about the infinite continuity of existence and about the covenant which was contained in this melody – in every melody which rose up from a pure heart – the covenant which was made when such a melody was created, albeit such a melody might never be created again.

It was because of his radiant face that the brothers after they had put aside the violins did not stay behind their chairs but came up to Amadeus, one from the right, the other from the left, so that now, after so many years, they stood again as in the triptych that at one time had so amused the people.

But nobody smiled now. Neither the baroness who had seen them standing in that way after the school concert, nor Christoph, who also remembered it, though perhaps in a different way. None of the brothers failed to notice that their mother refrained from making any remark but stood for a time at one of the high windows and looked out over the verdant park.

At last Amadeus went up to her and offered her his arm. "I think we must go in to dinner now," he said. "They are already waiting for us." He said it very gently and considerately, as if he must not disturb her in her reverie.

"How long ago it is," she said at last, looking out once more at the bed of daffodils. "So terribly long ago."

"So splendidly long ago, mother," replied Amadeus. "So splendidly long ago."

It was a merry dinner in the large garden room, even though nobody drank out of a bottle and no songs were sung; only the young wife Daisy might not have considered it very pleasant. She sat throughout the meal like a bird on its feeding perch, her anxious eyes turning to right and left, ready at any moment to fly off in case of danger.

But there was no danger for her. Her neighbors at table were attentive, even though a little cautious and reserved, and when the young woman wanted her glass filled time after time, they only showed a little surprise by a scarcely noticeable raising of an eyebrow.

After a time she grew merry, and when her high spirits became noticeable, the hostess rose from the table.

Coffee was served on the terrace, and when Daisy suggested "a quiet game" Erasmus said that it was time to start if they wanted to get home before dark.

"I am afraid," said Aegidius' wife in a low voice as Amadeus was saying goodbye to her. But he only shook his head and smiled. "Now you must not be afraid any longer," he replied. "Now you have a child, you must never be afraid again. We shall see to everything when it is necessary. Have a room ready for him, so that he can come at any time. Probably he will come with a heavy heart, and certainly he will be ashamed, and that will be the bitterest for him. You see, he wanted to get rid of his shame and to forget it – or what he had imagined was his shame."

The baroness was now standing once more at the top of the flight of steps where she had stood in the morning. It was not clear whether or not she still remembered "how terribly long ago" it was. She gave the brothers a farewell kiss and looked closely for a while at Erasmus. "You are the eldest; take care that you do not become the youngest," she said coolly, without admonition in her tone.

He did not understand immediately, then he blushed and, bowing slightly, he turned away.

As they drove home Daisy went on talking for some time in the carriage, chattering much and merrily. Then as the evening glow deepened, she became quieter, and at last she fell asleep, her head leaning against the high cushions of the upholstery.

Amadeus turned around once when he heard no more talk behind him. Daisy's mouth was half open and it struck him that even asleep she looked like a bewildered child. He nodded to Erasmus, who was looking past Christoph into the growing darkness of the evening; no one broke the silence.

For Amadeus it was as it had been in his childhood, when they drove home after a visit to some neighbor. Then, too, they had been silent and only the creaking of the horse collars and the head harness was to be heard. No, for him it was not "terribly long ago"; for him it was quite near, at the edge of the road, where the dew was already falling, in the plantation of young firs from which came a low bird call, in the evening clouds below which a heron was flying to the moor. Quite near, just as Christoph was quite near, who held the reins and the whip and on whose white hair the dew was falling.

"That was the bright child, Christoph," he said in a low voice.

Christoph nodded. "The other child will be bright, too, dear sir," he said. "The earth means well with us now. Take a deep breath, dear sir, so that you can notice it."

Amadeus obeyed, taking many deep breaths, and he realized that Christoph was right.

Now his hard time would come, his, together with the "young mother's," and he did not yet know how he would be able to change it into a good time.

But he was quite sure that the power would be granted to him. It would not come from his reason but as an inspiration, even as the melody of today had come as an inspiration to the great master. It would come to him without thinking about it, softly as the dew that just then fell upon them.

When the carriage stopped Daisy awoke. "What's the matter?" she asked, overcome with sleep.

"We have arrived," replied Amadeus and climbed down to help her.

She took his hand and looked at him without recognition. "Oh you, you stuck-up set, you," she said.

She was now quite drunk.

12

SO THAT WAS HOW a woman lived when horror had touched her between the shoulders and she had forgotten about it. She walked as lightly as if she had wings, but below the ground something moved with her.

She did not even know whether she walked lightly. She walked to the small room in the shepherd's hut and on her way there was the sun or the evening glow, the trumpeting of the crane or the sweet song of the woodlark. Things which had been there ever since childhood: the familiar, which was never dangerous, which was as near to her as the walls of her own little room; that which was there, unrelated to its surroundings, not connected with a strange hand, which one day she had struck with an osier switch; not connected with a reed hut above which the stars hung, nor with two juniper bushes in front of which somebody lay in the heather.

She did not know any longer that such a thing had happened, or she only knew it as one knows in a deep dream that someone is standing behind the door. One knows it, but one knows, too, that it is a dream. One will awake, although one does not know how, nor to what kind of a morning one will awake.

She only knows for certain that the bright, the comforting one, he who is almost omnipotent, appears as soon as she stands on the threshold of the hut. The one against whose knee she can lean her head and whose hand she feels on her hair.

And she also knows that the child is there where she is. That is quite certain. She feels it and when she is quite still, she believes she can hear its breath and its heartbeat. That is now nearly all her world. Everything else stands outside it, on a cloudy edge, but her child is her world. Without the child she would not be there; with it she walks lightly as if she has wings, though her feet move heavily by this time.

And what was it that moved along with her beneath the earth? She was conscious of all that happened around her, more clearly perhaps than others believed. For example, that that woman had gone away on New Year's Eve. The story had got about and it had been discussed. She also remembered the woman, her face and her hair. But it fell like a light into a dark water; it just touched the surface and lit up the tops of the water plants. But the plants which were floating as in a soft current reached down into the dark depths, and that was not lit up. What was there was not known. She did not know why the woman had gone, nor whither, nor if she would ever come back. All that was lost in twilight, and in the end it sank down into the depths. These depths were below everything. Below each of her footsteps, below every word that her mother said, even below the eyes of the man whose hand stroked her hair, and of whom she knew that he was a baron and that he was called Amadeus.

It was now as if she must hold his hand more firmly from day to day, lest he too should withdraw into the twilight. He was certain, the only certain thing on this earth. He rose in the morning as the sun rose. He lit up the day, and even in the evening glow his light shone on the things of this world.

Sometimes now the "young mother" took his hand and drew him away with her from the doorstep into the wood, where the birds called and where the resin ran out of the bark, to one of the warm rocks, where they could sit and gaze into the far distance. There the green lizards came out of the moss and one could see how their little bodies breathed in and out. Or the black woodpecker was to be heard, at the sound of whose call one shuddered as if it were full of foreboding – not for the next hour or for the next day, but for the whole future, for all that was still lying in wait and all that was going to happen.

She need not say a word. She only need hold the hand, the other bright hand, and it would hold her, even though the whole world should perish.

The plants breathed, the green lizards and also the child breathed – as quietly as the soft wind that went to and fro among the trees. She was not outside the earth; she was enveloped in its greenness, its comfort, in all that lived and existed.

One day she heard a strange, very low wailing sound. The man listened and then he took her hand. Noiselessly they walked between the bushes, deeper and deeper into the breathing wood. Then they saw what it was that had called: the young of an animal, reddish with white spots, which was lying in the grass with raised head. They heard the doe answer from behind the ferns. A dialogue without words, but as in a fairytale they understood it.

They went softly back, taking care not to touch a branch, until they sat down again by the warm rock. The "young mother" breathed more quickly. She smiled, but her eyes were not as calm as before. Amadeus made no comment; he only smoothed her hair, and now and then it crossed his mind that he was in a completely irrational world. That, behind the silence of the forest, his brothers lived and the people on the moor. That it was day and its hours ought to be used. That he was now sitting here beside a dark fate to which he had voluntarily bound himself. That the wife of his brother Erasmus would smile if she were to see him here, somebody who was waiting for a child that did not belong to him, with a girl who had once hired murderers to kill him. But he remembered that the parson Wittkopp had said that all was good as it was, and that all that had been laid on his shoulders was good. And sometimes he thought so himself and did not doubt it.

He did not know how much of all that had been said and that had happened during the last months had sunk into the "young mother's" distraught mind. But he was frightened when she suddenly gripped his hand more firmly and whispered, "What if it has a mark on its forehead or a harelip?"

"I shall lay my hand on it and there will be no mark," he replied calmly.

"But you are not the Christ Child?" she asked.

He shook his head. "But he has given me power to lay my hand on it in his stead, because he has pity on you."

"Has he pity?" she asked softly, in a faraway voice.

"Since you have had pity."

"When have I had pity?" she whispered.

He hesitated a moment looking down at her. "When you ran across the moor and called, 'Christoph, Christoph, help!' "

"Across the moor?" she said, trying to follow him. "That is how they run in fairytales or in a fever . . . quickly, quite quickly . . . but their feet are heavy . . . Christoph – that's St. Christopher who carried the child – once he held me back, and I tore his white hair . . . but now his hair is beautiful, white hair and the wind blows over it as over yours. . . ."

How does a woman live when horror lurks at the fringe of each hour? Behind the door of her room in her father's house, behind the door of the shepherd's hut, behind each door? Perhaps one can say that she lives as in an eclipse of the sun. Once, as a child, the "young mother" had seen an eclipse of the sun from the threshold of her home. Only the dog had stood at her knee – and the dog trembled and his coat was damp. All the other creatures had hidden: all birds, all lizards, all beetles. Lifeless silence had fallen on all creatures, and a strange half-light permeated from the sky into this silence. The same light that will be there on the day of the resurrection when graves are to open and give up their dead. No lack of light, no veiling of the light, but just a different light. No leaf had stirred on the trees, not even on the aspens, which are always stirring because Judas Iscariot had hanged himself on an aspen tree. A mighty hush had fallen over the earth, and light had become as darkness.

That is how it is under an eclipse of the sun. All is silent but one does not know what is living beyond the fringe. Where moor and twilight merge together, there it may well be that the essence of darkness arises. New, unknown forms and shapes which have risen up under the dying sun, and which wait for the moment when free play shall be given to them. Free play against men and animals, the masters of the earth hitherto, but now they will be its masters no longer. Now darkness will be master, and probably it will be a terrible master.

Now and again something rises on the horizon, something like a figure, and beckons. It beckons with something that looks like a hand. It does not call, because one knows what it wants. Because one remembers – not the figure, but that something was once there on the horizon which now stands behind the doors, behind each door, even behind the smallest. It is what we once were that is now separated from us – with its own face, its own body, its own garment – and this now is lying in wait. It stands quite still. It does not gently scratch at the door like a dog that wants to come in. It stands and waits.

And then comes fear, great, immeasurable fear, with cold drops on the brow and intermittent heartbeat. Not the fear of birth nor of the pains of birth, but the fear of what is gathering in the twilight of the eclipse. As wolves gather in the twilight, or rats gather in a cellar, as men gather before they do murder. Not before they do a single murder, but before the murder of thousands; and when the breath is held, far away on the horizon can be heard the clanking of spades that dig a pit so enormous that the whole moor could be buried in it.

Then she must clutch the dog's coat tightly, so tightly that it begins to whine. Or if he is there, she must rush into Christoph's arms with an impulse that might reach his heart, and his rough hand will gently stroke the quivering shoulder.

Or she must hurry to the hut. She ought not to hurry, and there is a pain, there where the child is on the narrow bridge between day and night. But she must hurry quickly, breathlessly, with wide-open eyes. And there on the threshold or by the hearth is the almighty one, and she can crouch down at his knee and all is well. The shadows recede, they slip back over the pale heather, over the wide expanse of the dead moor to the frontier where life ceases.

"Tell me a story," she whispers, pressing her hands around his knees and holding them fast as she had held the dog. "Tell me a story."

"What am I to tell?" asks Amadeus gently and wipes the cold sweat from her brow.

"Tell a story like Christoph, when the candles were burning."

"About a young woman?"

"Yes, about a young woman who walked across the moor, and a black dog ran in her track, and she was to give birth to a child."

For a moment Amadeus was perplexed and gazed into space – and the girl's wild fear slowly flowed into his own body. But then he laid both hands on the damp hair of the kneeling girl and began to tell: "There was once a young woman," he said calmly and consolingly, "who was to give birth to a child, and the fog witches did not want it to be born. The fog witches were sterile and they did not want a human woman to have children. Out of their fog kingdom they sent a wolf which ran howling into the wood where the woman lived. It sat on its hind legs the whole night long and howled up to the waning moon. But the young woman opened the big Book and sitting in front of the hearth she read in the big Book. She read loudly and happily, that there went out a decree from the Emperor Augustus, and later a decree from King Herod. And that the troopers searched for the children and slew them, but that they did not find this child, because it was already on its way to the land of Egypt."

"Was it a hearth like this hearth?" asked the "young mother," and her deep sigh filled the whole room.

"Just such a hearth," replied Amadeus, gently stroking her head. "The birch logs burned with a beautiful blue flame, and the white bark curled up and gave out a sweet scent. The young woman stretched out her right hand to warm it at the flame. But she went on reading loudly and happily until the wolf stopped howling. For it did not like to hear what she read and it ran back to the fog witches and said that it could do nothing there, for it had no power over the Book."

"No power," whispered the girl, and her hands relaxed around the knees of the man who was telling the story. "No power – neither over the Book nor over the child."

"No! No power," said Amadeus. "Not the least bit of power."

Now it was quite still by the little hearth, and Amadeus put a fresh birch log on the flames. He felt the beating of the young girl's heart at his knees, and he went on stroking her hair, quite gently and quite slowly, as if he would never leave off.

But after a while the night bird called again from the moor and the "young mother" winced.

"Go on with your story," she whispered, "for she has finished with the Book now."

"The Book can never be finished with," said Amadeus gently. "It's like a ring which begins everywhere and ends nowhere. And after the last Amen, it begins at once all over again: In the beginning God created heaven and earth . . ."

"And then the young woman began reading again?"

"Yes, then she read again quite loudly and happily, and when she was in the middle of reading the fog witches sent a dog which was black and it sat on the threshold and scratched at the door."

"It wanted the child," whispered the "young mother," and her hands were clasped more firmly together.

"Yes, it wanted the child," said Amadeus in a carefree voice. "But it listened to what the young woman was reading. Just by pure chance she had opened the Book at the tale of Ruth, and she read what was written there: 'Intreat me not to leave thee, or to return from following after thee: for whither thou goest, I will go; and where thou lodgest, I will lodge: thy people shall be my people, and thy God my God: Where thou diest will I die, and there will I be buried.' And when she had read this loudly and happily, the dog howled, left the threshold and ran across the moor to the fog witches and said that it could do nothing, because nobody had power over the Book."

"Say it once more," begged the "young mother," and her hands were quiet again: " 'Where thou diest. . . .' "

Amadeus repeated it while he caressed her cheek. Then it was quite still again by the little hearth, and when Amadeus turned his head he could see the constellations above the moor, high and silvery in their wonderful silence.

But then an owl hooted in the tall pine trees and the young girl winced again. "Now go on with the story," she whispered, "for sometime the woman must go over the moor after all, because the fog witches called."

"Yes," said Amadeus, "and then she started off just after midnight, and the moon shone brightly on the moor and cast her shadow on the ground behind her. She had nothing but the child that she carried under her heart and the heavy Book which she carried in her hands."

"But did she take it along?" asked the "young mother."

"Yes, of course she took it along. She held it in both her hands and pressed it to her heart where the child lay in the dark. When she had walked for a time and her feet were wet with dew, she turned round and then she saw that the dog was on her track following her, nose to the ground, as dogs follow a scent. Then she cried out and was very much afraid."

"But," whispered the girl, shuddering – "but . . ."

"But there was somebody at her side," said Amadeus in a reassuring tone. "He was the sort of man to whom a woman could say that she did not want him to leave her. He who went at her side bent down and picked a flower, a white wood orchid, one of the kind that grows on the moor and smells so sweet. He picked it and laid it behind them over the track of the young woman. Then they walked on. But when they turned round, they saw that the dog tried to jump over the flower, yet could not do it. It was as if each time a hand seized the dog by the collar and flung it back. Then the dog cringed and howled, and it sounded horrible below the cold moon.

"Then they saw how it began to dig a hole with its forepaws, quickly and hastily, but it took a long time, for the hole always filled with water and the dog had to lap it up with its tongue before it could go on digging. But at last the hole was deep enough and the dog had to find a branch, and with the branch in its mouth, it pushed the flower slowly into the hole, and then scratched back the earth until the hole was closed."

"And all the time the woman could walk on?" asked the girl.

"Yes, all the time she could walk on, and only when the flower was buried, could the dog follow her."

"For the flower had power over the dog," whispered the girl.

"Yes, it had power over the dog. When the dog had come quite near and she could already hear its breathing, the man broke a twig from a fir tree, one of those on which candles burn in winter, and put it over the track. And again the dog had to stay behind until it had buried the fir twig."

"For the twig had power over the dog," said the girl softly.

"Yes, of course, the twig had power over it. And meanwhile the two hurried on. The Book was a heavy burden for the young woman a carry, and the man asked her whether she would not like him to throw it away."

"No," exclaimed the girl, pressing her hands around Amadeus' knees. "Oh no, she did not do that."

"No," said Amadeus. "She did not do that. For it was the Book in which the tale of the manger was told, and of the girl who gleaned in the stubble field and who refused to leave the woman."

"No, the man refused to leave the girl," whispered the "young mother," and then her eyes closed slowly.

"Now you must go to sleep," said Amadeus gently, "and tomorrow we will go on with the story."

"Yes, tomorrow," said the "young mother" dreamily. She let him help her up and fasten the shawl around her shoulders, and then Amadeus led her slowly back through the forest. She kept her eyes half closed, but she smiled. "No power," she whispered when the night bird called, "no power."

Amadeus led her upstairs into her room and lighted the candle at her bedside. "Don't leave me until I have gone to sleep," she begged, and he obeyed.

She undressed like a child, still smiling, and then he sat for a while on the edge of her bed. Her eyes were closed and her face was relaxed and without anxiety. She did not speak anymore.

His hand stroked her hair time and again, quite slowly, until she had fallen asleep. The candlelight cast his huge shadow on the wall of the little room, and outside the window the bluish light of the moon fell on the motionless trees.

Then Amadeus snuffed the wick of the candle and got up. He listened to her quiet breathing for a while, and then he groped his way to the door and down the stairs.

He went slowly back through the wood. The silver light fell in broad beams through the gaps among the trees. He was tired now, almost exhausted, as if he had carried the woman and the child on his shoulders. No wolf was on his track and no black dog, and yet it was a hard way, full of danger and darkness. His hand must not tremble now, not for an instant, and yet he knew so little about mental disturbances.

But he felt that the dead were no longer walking behind him – only the face of the French scholar appeared before his eyes, that beautiful face that was filled with the pictures of the madonnas and the cathedrals. *Ce sont toujours les pauvres,* he heard him say. Always the poor . . .

The following evening the face of the "young mother" was changed, as if her time were close on her. "Light a fire," she begged, "and go on with the story."

When the flame crackled, she crouched down again by his feet. "Are you not afraid?" she asked, looking at him with a distracted expression.

Amadeus smiled. "No, I am not afraid," he replied. "For when they had hurried on for a time and the young woman's feet were tired and she was stumbling, and the dog's breathing could be heard, a cock suddenly crowed behind the moor. The first cock in the wide circle of darkness, and a distant, quite distant clock struck the first hour of the morning.

"With the crowing of the cock and the striking of the hour the whole earth was changed. The dog howled once – and then it was no longer there. The mist floated once more around the reeds, and then it was no longer there. The morning star stood quietly above the moor and it seemed to smile, so safely and beautifully did it stand in the sky.

"Then the young woman sank down to her knees, and where she knelt the soil was dry and firm, juniper bushes stood round about, and there was a little roof with a manger below, such as the foresters build in winter for the deer. There the young woman gave birth to her child and put it into the manger, and as she had no pillow, she laid the great Book under the child's head.

"Then dawn came.

"The young woman raised her head so that she might see the child's eyes. The dawn seemed to shine into its open eyes, but the face was not calm yet, because light and shadow were still passing over it."

"And it was not blind?" asked the "young mother."

Amadeus smiled and shook his head. "Why should it be blind?" he asked quietly. "Did you not hear that the crimson dawn fell into its open eyes?"

"And there was no mark on its forehead?" asked the "young mother" again.

"Why should it have a mark?" asked Amadeus. "The breath of the dog had not even touched it."

"And it did not have a harelip?" asked the "young mother" again.

"Why should it have such a lip," asked Amadeus, "as it had heard in its sleep nothing but the words of the great Book?"

"And the man?" asked the "young mother" after a long silence.

"The man stood at the manger," said Amadeus, "with his hands on the low roof. He stood there like a watchman, and sometimes the young woman fancied that he was wearing silvery armor. She was deeply humble when the man bent down and washed her sore feet with the morning dew. 'Why do you do that?' she asked quite bewildered. 'Because your feet are sore,' said the man, 'and they are sore because they went over the stubble field while you were gleaning the wheat. We ought to have given you the wheat from the barn and not from the stubble field.' "

The "young mother" meditated for a long time, and Amadeus saw that it cost her an effort. Then with her right hand she pulled the hem of her skirt up from her naked feet and looked at them. "But they are not sore," she whispered.

"No, for they are already washed," replied Amadeus.

"Who has washed them?" she asked in a low voice.

"Those who had pity on you," replied Amadeus gently.

"Tomorrow at this time it will be born," said the "young mother" suddenly. "Without mark or blemish, as you have promised."

"Quite so," he replied, while his hands rested on her head.

Next morning she did not get up, and the forester fetched the midwife from the castle and two women from the cottages on the moor. She did not want to see Amadeus, but she wanted him to stay on the doorstep of the house, and there he sat from morning until twilight began to fall. Only the dog was with him, and now and again Christoph sat at his side for a while. "Be comforted now, sir," he said, "now comes the good time for us. Now the earth has worn out its anger."

But Amadeus did not know whether a good time would come. If once the gentle power of fairytales broke, dark forces would arise again. And he did not know how far their power would reach.

He did not hear a sound from the girl's room throughout the whole day. He felt so exhausted that his hands began to tremble every now and then. "What have I been prevailed upon to do?" he thought at one time. "Why do I sit here like a fool and wait for a strange child?"

But then he was ashamed of the thought, stroked the head of the dog, and looked up to the tops of the trees, which slowly began to take on a pinkish hue. Until the forester's wife came to fetch him. "It's a girl," she said, "a beautiful child. Now Barbara wants to see you."

Amadeus had to lean against the doorpost and close his eyes for a moment before he went upstairs. For the others it was good now, all was good, but for him it was not good yet. For him it was only the beginning. He did not know what was awaiting him. It might be anything between heaven and earth. Nothing need have changed and he might go on being the man who in silvery armor stood by the manger before he washed her feet. But on the other hand everything might have changed, the whole foundation of the earth, the world on which her life rested, and together with the child she might plunge into the bottomless pit.

Twilight already filled the room. The window was wide open, and later, much later he remembered that the song of the woodlark had come in through the window, and that he had taken it as a promise of what Christoph called "the good time."

But then it happened that the "young mother" tried to sit up by supporting herself with her hands on the wood of the bedstead. And as she was too weak to manage this she raised her hands again with fingers opened wide, as only horror can open them, and while her big eyes, still disturbed with pains, looked deep into his face, she cried out once. A long, high-pitched wailing cry filled with horror, as only animals cry out in death agony, and then her head and hands dropped back in unconsciousness, and Amadeus had time to perceive that with the last breath of consciousness she had tried to turn her face to the wall.

"Please, go out of the room," he said in a low voice, "all of you – and take the child with you."

They obeyed with perturbed faces, and Amadeus sat on the side of her bed as he had done two evenings before, and with his left hand he stroked back the damp hair from her brow. The glow of the sunset now filled the window opposite with its ever-deepening colors, and the birds sang once more with all the sweet might of their little throats, before night fell on the wood.

The face beneath his hand was as white as that of a dead woman. But there was an incessant quivering and trembling around the closed eyes, as if a candle were being held above her face.

Amadeus did not know how long this lasted. He only knew that the square of the window was no longer red, but was filled with a silvery light, and that he heard the call of the night birds from a great distance. He lit the small oil lamp, in which a wick swam on dark liquid.

He saw how the "young mother's" eyes opened. First they were directed to the silver square of the window; then quite slowly they wandered around the room, and then she looked into his face. After that they closed again, and with his left hand that lay on her damp hair he felt that her whole body quivered. Yes, he believed that he felt each hair quiver under his hand.

He had not considered nor thought out anything. On the spur of the moment he simply went on stroking her hair and speaking as he had spoken the previous evening, as if nothing had happened in between, nothing except the sleep of a young mother who had been afraid and had to be comforted. It was no longer a fairytale that had to be told; now he had to build a bridge from the fairytale into reality. Not that one should say: yesterday it was a fairytale, but today it is reality. But that one must say: yesterday we were restless and afraid and saw only the half of it, but today we are not afraid and want to see the whole.

Amadeus went on telling his story in a low and calm voice, as if he had only stopped a minute ago: "When the young woman saw that her feet were washed and no longer sore, because someone had had pity on her, she looked around for the first time, as if she wanted to remember something. The morning star was fading, and in the East the first red streaks of dawn stood solemnly above the wood. The child lay in the manger and slept and its cheek lay on the big Book which the woman had not thrown away. The child smiled in its sleep, and now in the rising daylight they could see that it was without blemish. 'I must have been here before, long, long ago,' said the young woman, and a small wrinkle appeared between her eyebrows, as if it cost her an effort to remember.

" 'Certainly you were here before,' replied the man, and made a pile of dry twigs so that he could light a fire. 'You were here at a time when a hut stood here, and when you conceived the child that sleeps in the manger now. But it's long, long ago, so long that it is all only like a dream.' "

The young mother had moved her head gently under his hand, so that her eyes could look at him now – large, wide-open eyes that were no longer filled with fear but with a frightful despair.

The spell of the fairytale from which so much comfort had flowed into her during the past days was surely still on her, for she slowly moved her lips, and when Amadeus bent over her, he could understand what she said: "The child is not a dream," she said, "the child is there. I have seen it."

"We have all seen it," said Amadeus, drawing himself up again. "A beautiful child without blemish, but you have given it to me. All know that you have given it to me. One day the Christ Child must have come, perhaps on the Christmas Eve when Christoph told the story, and with his hands he put it into my arms. The Christ Child wished that it should be my child, that it should be our child. He need only raise his hand, and everything happens as he wishes."

She still looked at him immovably with clear eyes that could not be deceived. "Why did I forget?" she asked.

"Probably the Christ Child wished it," replied Amadeus. "Sometimes he wants us to forget. He also wished that I should forget the concentration camp; that's why he has put a child into my arms. Without the child I would not have been able to forget."

"But then they caught the man," said the young mother and gazed at him, as if deep down at the bottom of his eyes the trap was to be seen in which they had caught him.

"Yes, they caught him," said Amadeus calmly. "They caught him because he too had come from the fog witches, just like the wolf and the dog. And he too wanted to get the child. But he could not get it because he had no power over it."

"No power," whispered the girl, as she had done the evening before.

"No! No power. And so that there might be no power, not even in those who had caught him, I had to lie between the juniper bushes in the same place, in exactly the same place. And from that time there was no more power. It was blotted out, and only then could the child within you grow without blemish."

"But I wanted to have you killed there – by violence."

"You wanted it, but then you had pity on me. Do you still remember how you had pity on me? You were sitting in the heather and wanted to look on while I was dying. But you did not see at that time that I lay there to blot out the picture of the other one. And if I had died, the man would not have been there, the man who went with you over the moor and who laid the flower and the fir twig across your track. Do you now recognize what beautiful order there is in everything?"

"Then people thought that you were the father?" she asked, and for the first time a faint blush mounted in her cheeks.

"Yes, they thought so, and they may go on thinking so. But it was far more important that you should believe it, for only with this belief were you able to overcome your illness. You were very ill."

"I struck you," she said in a low voice. "I struck you time and again."

"You struck me," he replied with a smile, "because you wanted to be as I am, and at that time it was not yet possible."

"It will never be possible," she said.

"Oh no, that is not so," he replied. "That day on the moor, when you ran to fetch Christoph, you were so. At that time you had pity; it is difficult to have pity. Two years ago I did not know that I would ever have pity on anybody."

"Take your hand from my hair," she said after a pause. "I am so full of shame that each hair is bathed in it."

But he did not desist, and gently lifted a damp strand from her forehead. "Listen," he said, "you must now understand that everything is changed. There is no longer any shame if one has had pity. Nor is there any shame because they beat me when I tried to escape. There was nothing but suffering and violence in it. But now there is neither suffering nor violence. It is well that you should know that you have done a great deal of good."

"How did I do good?" she asked moodily.

"With your suffering you awoke all the good within us; do you understand that? Without you we would still have been morose and gloomy. And now we have grown bright, as bright as your child's forehead."

"Do not go away yet," she pleaded after a while.

"No, I'm not going away. Do you hear the night birds? Today you are not afraid any longer."

"No, I'm not afraid – will you tell them now that you are not the father?"

"Why should I tell them, since I am. For all these months I have been the father."

"But now I must go away from you," she said. "Go away once and for all."

"Why should you want us to part?" he asked. "When the dog scratched at the door to get the child, don't you remember what you read then? You read: Where thou lodgest, I will lodge. I shall always stay here now by the hearth in the shepherd's hut. I won't go away anymore, and every evening you will come and sit with me by the fire."

"There will be no blemish on the child?" she asked after a pause.

"Never," he replied.

"Not even one which only you will see?"

"Not even such a blemish."

Her eyelids slowly drooped. But when her eyes were shut, she reached out for his right hand, the hand she had struck when she was a child. Her fingers felt for the scar which was still there, and she laid both her hands over it. The owl began to hoot in the tall oak trees, but she no longer trembled.

"Now fetch mother," she whispered. "She must bring the child with her. And you must have a long sleep."

He kissed her forehead and went softly out of the room.

He did not know what time it was. The moon was already low in the heavens, and there was a little stir in the trees as if morning was not far off. The cuckoo was calling, and he remembered that when it called so early, rain would be coming. Now it was good that it was going to rain. It was so lovely that it was going to rain. At first single, big drops would fall, heavy and each for itself. Then they would slowly swell and draw together into a whole, as in a great orchestra, when the instruments come in one after another. The great Pastoral Symphony in which not even the call of the cuckoo was forgotten. Rain would fall plentifully on the wood, on the moor, on the thatched roof of the hut, on the threshold of the house where the young mother lay with her child. On the dark tracks of the wolf and the dog, on the tracks of the year, of the many years in which violence had prevailed, in which hatred, blood and horror had ruled.

But now they would be extinguished. The grass would rise up again, the roots would be watered in the earth, in the cleansed earth which had worn out its anger. Because the people had worn out their anger.

Not all people, but those who had turned aside to find the evening, and with the evening the lost time, the long-lost primitive time when people read in the big Book while the fairytale animals lay on their doorstep; long past years in which a breath of the old wisdom, kindness, and justice whispered through the grasses, the breath of fairytales in which people sought to understand the ultimate; in which they sought to understand it not with contrivances and formulas but with shapes that they themselves created, with the fog witches and the wolves, with the first crow of the cock at dawn, and with the flower that was laid across a track so that wicked feet could no longer follow its course.

It was quite unimportant what they would actually do now, whether the young mother would stay or would go away to earn a living for herself and her child by the work of her hands. Whether the wife of Donelaitis was now letting the sand of the Curonian Spit run through her fingers or whether the sand lay heaped up in her stiffened hands. Whether Erasmus, his brother, would have a child in place of all those dead children who called to him from the highroad, or whether the child that was born yesterday was born to fill the place of those children who were so longed for on the moor – by his brother and by the homesick young wife, and by others too, perhaps, of whom he knew nothing.

Here was the great mystery – that light had risen from darkness, that they had been shown how little enmity there need be between good and evil, that good had very little cause to look down upon evil, because deep, quite deep down they both sprang from the same source. That the great harmony enclosed them both, enclosed all of them, if only they were humble and obedient, and if they were without violence.

Yes, on all this rain would fall, a marvelous rain under which eyes would close in sleep after so much watching and worry. And even as long years before he had awaked, infinitely long years before, so he would awake again, and an old man would be kneeling in front of the hearth lighting the fire, and time that had been broken to pieces would reunite childhood with eventide, and once more they would "dance though sad," because sadness too had become different. Because it was only like the pause between heartbeats, and without these pauses there would be no heartbeats.

Everything was so simple that the sophisticated would smile, as they used to smile at the three brothers, or at Christoph's blue coat, or at the baron who had been willing to be a father so that a woman and her child might step out of darkness into light, so that traps would no longer be set to catch men and beasts, so that gallows would no longer be erected whose shadows fell over the lullabies sung to unborn children.

Was the way so long that the baron had to go to reach the hut, or was the time so long through which he had to go, that it seemed as if that way would never end? Or was he so tired that each step was like an eternity? Between the trees he saw the dawn rising above the earth, a glowing, red dawn which foretold rain. For many years he had seen it rising above the watchtowers, crimsoning the gray barrels of the machine guns that were trained on human beings. He had seen how it colored with its glow the faces of men – faces in ruins, and wrecked faces, and faces turned toward death. He had forgotten that dawn had been created to illuminate the earth and to measure time, because time was nonexistent there.

But now the dawn had reappeared and no violence had been able to destroy it. It had reappeared as if the evening and the morning were the first day, and so it would remain forever. They had not fallen out of the order of time; they had only forgotten it for a while, and now it would never be forgotten again. In this lost corner of the world they would hold fast once more to what was so quickly lost in the great world.

In spite of smiles and jeers they would hold it fast. They would not move the world nor the policy of states, nor change the doings of mankind. But they would have a doorstep to sit on, even if there were no other resting place on earth. Even if it were only a child that would come to sit there. A child that they had saved out of the night of its conception and growth. A dark child which they had made bright. With it they had created the world anew, the whole meaning of the world: that from dark roots golden wheat sprouted, wheat from which bread would be made, bread which would give the next day its strength – the next day and the following days of which time would be composed, time which would stretch into eternity.

Scarcely had Amadeus stretched himself out on his bed when he fell asleep. He woke up for a short time when the first heavy drops fell on the thatched roof. He woke up only sufficiently to realize that it was raining. Not where he was, nor what time it was, and only with some difficulty could he remember who he was. He only realized that it was rain, that it was rain that fell slowly, swelling like a symphony, and that the call of the cuckoo was not lacking in it. And when all the drops had assembled, a gentle comforting murmur which seemed to be infinite was around the hut, around the hearth on which no fire was burning, around the bed on which he was resting. The murmur of the rain in which the faded grasses would rise again, in which his brother's wheat would grow, in which the child lay at the young mother's breast to drink in all the sweetness and bitterness of life. But there was no frontier between sweetness and bitterness, as there was no frontier between sleeping and waking, and probably none between life and death.

It was the sense of life that became perceptible in the pouring rain, and that reached down to one's roots, as it reached down to the roots of grass and wheat.

When Amadeus awoke, Christoph was kneeling before the fire, which was already burning; but Christoph remained on his knees, his hands pressed on the floor, lost in thought as he watched the growing flames. The rain had stopped but the day must have passed, too, for a star was to be seen in the square of the window and the night birds were calling. The raindrops from the old trees could still be heard falling on the roof of the hut.

Amadeus remembered everything that had happened but it was like something that the rain had already obliterated. What was left was only the great peace that enveloped everything: the house, the hearth, the old man and himself, such marvelous peace that he breathed lightly so that nothing should be out of harmony.

But Christoph had heard even this faint sound. He did not turn his head. He only pushed the kettle a little to one side, for the water had begun to boil. "It is good now, dear sir," he said speaking into the fire. "It is as good as it can be among people."

"Were you there, Christoph?"

"Yes, I was there, and I sat at her bedside. She asked me to forgive her, as she asks everybody to forgive her, and I think there is only one thing she is afraid of now, dear sir, that you may want to marry her. If you wanted that, she said, she would feel obliged to go away as far as the other woman had gone."

"She will not have to go away, Christoph."

"I told her so and she believed it. Herr Erasmus has married to have a child and he will never have one. You will never marry, dear sir, and you have got a child even without it. You have gone so far that all this has been left behind you. You have had a greater love than one needs for marrying."

"Do you think I have gone far, Christoph?"

Now the old man turned his face around and looked at Amadeus. "When you came here, dear sir," he said, "you were like a wolf, and I was grieved for you. And now you know that it is the wolves of this earth that are poor and not the sheep. No one needs to know more than that, sir."

"I could not have learned it without you," said Amadeus softly.

Christoph got up and shook the coffee into the boiling water. "It's a good time, dear sir," he replied kindly, "when the nobleman believes that he can learn something from his coachman. But it's a still better time when white hair can learn from gray hair. Sit up now, sir, so that I may bring you your coffee."

13

IF HERE AND THERE people smiled at what had happened, the young wife Daisy was not one to refuse to join in. All the same she was the only one who wept about it at night, and not even Erasmus knew that. He saw more of his wife than others saw, and in many ways he knew more about her than others knew.

But when he brought breakfast to her, as she lay in bed in the morning, she looked at him, her arms crossed under her head; and when – the sun being higher in the sky each day – it seemed to him almost unprincipled to start the day so late, he was still not able to discern from the distant, almost critical expression in her eyes what it was that those eyes had dwelt on during the night.

For when the gaming had come to an end, or the revelry, or the dancing in which, as well as the two young "heroes," American officers now took part, then things did not go as he supposed, that his wife – tired after the gaiety and happy in her own way – fell asleep at once. Not very happy, perhaps, that she had married him, but happy that she was now a baroness, lifted up out of the misery of a haphazard life and taken into the secure circle of a family that had lost everything but had not lost their name.

Even about that the young wife was not so happy as in the beginning. When she lay there with open eyes and the multifarious life of the castle had at length sunk into sleep, the chain of fate linking the vicissitudes of her life began slowly to unwind before her mind's eye. Every night, whether she wished it or not. And she lay there and watched it objectively, sometimes even impassively, with only a cool curiosity, and sometimes with hands that clasped and unclasped themselves as if in prayer or in deep anguish. Those were the hours when she could weep over the two children, bitter, despairing tears, and sometimes tears full of hatred.

Christoph was right that she would be childless, but in his idea of the cause of this he had not been right. And in many other things he was not right either.

Perhaps he knew that a body ruined by a licentious life could not bear children, because nature wills it so. But he did not know that even a heart laid waste may still yearn for children, yes, yearn passionately as for a token of nature's forgiveness and of the relaxing of fate. He did not know that she suffered under the sentence nature had passed on her and suffered so much the deeper because what had been denied to her had been given even to one with a troubled mind.

The door to the second room stood open, and she heard the gentle breathing of the baron, the husband whom she had gained and with him name and title, for whom she had striven shrewdly and passionately, so that a drifting life might once more be anchored to security and comfort. But after the first triumph all satisfaction had rapidly disappeared. The ghosts of the past were still there and were not to be shaken off; they re-emerged everywhere and followed her, as the two young men followed her. It was not guilt that might have been tried in a court of law, nor was it the man called Knolle, who was not at rest under a tombstone, nor had been thrown up again into the light of day by a bursting bomb, but who probably played an obscure but lucrative part in one of the black markets, although he had never in his life owned a factory. But that she had struggled once more – albeit with deceit and guilt – to get solid ground beneath her feet, and that this, too, was sliding away into the dark whirlpool beneath her; that she had tried once more to realize the dream of a hard and humiliated childhood, and where she had succeeded she could not rejoice in her success, because there had been so much somber, naked reality in her life that not even a dream could be kept undefiled in it.

The one thing that might have regenerated her, as a magic fountain could have done, was a child. And this was denied her, the child the others, even the derided and deranged woman, had been allowed to conceive and bear, but which she with her ruined and prostituted body would never bear.

Her name had never been Daisy, but Emilie, which she thought dreadful and hated; really she had devoted her life to overcoming this name, and with it, its origin. She had spent a frightful childhood with a drunken, brutal father and a profligate mother, and in her earliest youth there had hardly been anything that she had not seen and experienced. But she had never thrown herself into it, she had never let herself fall lower than was necessary to add another stroke to the picture of life as she envisaged it.

She had begun her career as a chambermaid in a small, ill-kept hotel in the east of the metropolis. From the East End she had worked slowly up through the center to the West End, until she had gained a firm footing as an attendant in a small nightclub of dubious reputation. The nightclub belonged to Mr. Knolle, whom she married in as cool and calculating a way as she had added up the bills.

It had been a rung of her ladder, a breathing space in the dark, consuming years, after all the abasement and humiliation of her body and soul. There were no illusions about Mr. Knolle. He was a short, stout citizen with the heart of a pimp, and he wanted to get on in life, or at any rate to be successful in the way he pictured success.

It did not mean the same to both of them, but they both had gained a firm footing, and the footing grew steadily more secure, until war and air raids destroyed it like all other foundations. And after the prostitution of her youth and of half her life, after the prostitution of body and soul, once more Daisy was confronted by nothingness.

Not only the nothingness of existence, but also the nothingness of that which even in her depravity had stood before her eyes: the quiet, unseen but longed-for haven, where there would be no husband but only a child. The calm island of a shipwrecked woman, where she would be granted that which she really felt entitled to: the calm existence of a woman worn to death, who holds a child to her heart regardless of who was the father of the child.

In one of the nights when sheets of fire fell from the sky they had separated without regret and without any agreement for the future, as if they had never known each other. What they had dug out with their hands and had dragged along to some safe place, had been broken to pieces, and now nothing was left that they might have carried away. They proceeded again to the marketplace of life – he to the one which, with his wonted shrewdness, he saw rising from the ruins, she to the one where she could deal in the only thing she possessed – her body – and where she could use the skill she had mastered in these years, that which Baron Erasmus with his childlike heart called demimondaine.

On this childlike heart she had fixed her eyes, and she had conquered and won it without the least compunction. However, among her plans and deceits there had still been something else, and that she had not won. It had not been granted to her that a baron, or even one who was not a baron, should bow down to her for no other reason than to lift her up out of the scum of her life. Somebody had bowed down to her to get a child, and he had not cared who gave it to him.

Thus it could not be said that she had conquered and won like an impostor; she had rather been like a drowning woman who had stretched out her hand. His name had not been the final thing she had coveted, although it lured her as cards lured her. In her family there had also been generations who had lived according to the old commandments, before these old commandments had been broken by their children and their children's children. In this woman who was sunk so deep a faint echo of these old commandments still persisted – as an almost blind craving to return to the tranquility of things forgotten, and to pick the thread up again where it touched the most primitive need of human nature – the need to give devotion to a husband and to a child.

And when it became evident that the thread could not be picked up anymore because it had been rotted and decayed by a wild life, nothing remained for her but to take refuge in intoxication. The intoxication of men, of gambling, or of heavy drinking which enshrouded with a kindly mist her dreams which would never become real.

How could Baron Erasmus have known what looked at him out of his wife's eyes when he brought breakfast to her in bed, and with the toe of his shoe pushed aside the cigarette butts which lay on the floor after a long, sleepless night?

Nor did he betray anything of what he thought while he sat in the shabby easy chair at her bedside watching how she put the sugar into her coffee. He stepped further and further back toward the outer fringe of her life. He did not gamble, he did not drink, he did not dance. He only considered it to be his duty to be there when all this was done, as a polite host has to be there. First the guests regarded him with polite shyness, then with slight mockery, and then they did not notice that he was there. For most of them his personality was something completely incredible, but they had to accustom themselves to it, because the evidence of their eyes showed that he really was there. As if he were left over from a fairytale. The fairytales had sunk into oblivion long ago, but the fairies had forgotten to take this one along into the depths. They had let him slip from their hands and had left him up here. He was not to be put aside. They either had to go around him or step over him.

But when at midnight the baron stood in the doorway between the two rooms, his hands folded behind his back and his back leaning against the framework of the door, and contemplated with his calm, sad eyes this picture which was the picture of a new life – the picture of an untidy table covered with cigarette ash, glasses, cards, and money; the cold, greedy, or exhausted faces, the hands which were stretched out or were drawn back again; this manifestation of an altogether unfamiliar, wild, and vulgar life which had once more sprung up so that the mortal peril of the last years might be forgotten in heady frivolity – then he began to realize, and only he, what the meaning of all this was for him, the only meaning that could enable him to go on standing there, looking on: that this was meted out to him as a penance.

Not as a penance for his terrible mistake. Nor as a penance for that night on the snowbound road, from which the voices of the children now rose ever more clearly and were not hushed in silence, since they, too, in the snow-veiled distance had recognized that the baron had not married for their sake, that he might silence their voices with love; but that he had married because he did not wish to hear their voices any longer; that he wanted a child of his own so that he could forget them; that he had wanted a new life that he might forget their dying.

No, this was not a penance for that night when he had deserted the dying people, but a penance for the day when he had claimed a happiness of his own; when he no longer had pity on the children but on himself; and when he had married this woman, not because he had pity on her, but because she had been a complaisant instrument willing perhaps to give him a child, and with it, forgetfulness.

So Baron Erasmus had not done penance. He had not undertaken all this as a penance, but as the means of gaining the happiness he was longing for. He had not undertaken such a task as his brother Amadeus was now carrying quietly on his shoulders, although Amadeus had nothing to do penance for. He had not even undertaken what his brother Aegidius, in the beginning, had been obliged to undertake. He was the eldest and his burden had always been the lightest, the most comfortable, not the heaviest as would have been befitting.

But he had to carry this now so quietly that not even his brothers would realize that it was a burden. He had contracted a marriage with this woman, and he now had to hold his shield over her as over the poorest laborer's child who trusted in the protection of her master.

What oppressed him so much in this new life was not the evil he had to stand by and watch, not that which was no longer part of any moral order, not even the mean and vulgar which were not part of any recognized form, nor the ugly that was no longer ashamed of its ugliness, nor the shamelessness which no longer veiled itself. Nor did it befit him to imagine that he alone carried on his hands and shoes the dirt which the others stirred up without noticing it. But that he was not able to shoulder this burden with kindness. That he was not able to humble himself and to have pity – not even on the woman from whom he had expected a child, to say nothing of the others to whom he was attached by her way of life. That he remained Baron Erasmus who had made a mistake, and who was not able to do anything more than stand quietly by the door and watch what was happening, without letting them read in his face what he thought.

He had been humiliated in his sheltered life. He had not been bound nor beaten as Amadeus had been. He had been as protected as if he had grown up in a shell, and this shell had lain for a lifetime at the bottom of a deep, calm sea.

Now he was not able to humble himself out of love. He did not even understand that nothing humbled a man that was done out of love or pity. He never tried to stop or divert the course of this frightful wheel to which he was now bound. He never uttered a word of reproach to his wife. His manner remained the same as before. But that was all he could do. And he could do it without much effort, because birth and education made it imperative for him.

He did not know and could not know that the gleam of hatred which now and again appeared in his wife's eyes had its origin in just this fact. Perhaps she would have loved him – to the degree that she was still capable of love – if she had seen that he felt compassion for her. When she saw that he did not and would never feel compassion for her, she might have loved him still, if she had succeeded in dragging him down into the twilight in which she lived and breathed, so that she should not have to live and breathe there alone.

But she did not succeed and she knew that she would never succeed, that he possessed what could not be acquired with effort or with diligence or with patience: the unapproachable standing of birth and education; she knew that he was a nobleman who had given her his name as one gives a frock to a poor girl, and who now looked on without moving a feature to see how she put on the frock, smoothed it down, and tried to pretend that it fitted her.

But it would never fit her and he would never give her another dress.

He showed neither anger nor contempt, not even impatience. His eyes looked through all that was happening before them, they looked through the winners and the losers, those who were drunk and those who were sober; it was as if he had been bound and dragged into a second-rate theater and forced to look on at a miserable performance. It did not affect him anymore, because he only had to look on at his own bad performance. Had he been sentenced to a period of penal servitude and had had to glue paper bags he would not have looked differently. She did not realize that he was not ashamed of the performance nor of the penal servitude, but of himself. She had gradually forgotten what it meant to be ashamed of herself.

And yet she had pity for him, not often, but certainly sometimes, always when she had pity for herself. Then she longed to confess that she had cheated him, that she had been just as much mistaken as he. She did not know that this was no longer important to him, that before his guilt all other guilt faded away.

Then she had grown too tired to confess. Neither was there any time left for her. Evenings and nights were filled with noise and intoxication and there was no future, for she would not have a child.

The only one who saw something of the life of Baron Erasmus was Christoph. But he only saw it with the eyes of a faithful servant. Probably he could not look differently at his master's white hair. Sometimes when his master had shyly glanced at him, Christoph remained there during the evening, helped with the preparations, and stood in one of the deep window niches, unseen and unnoticed, looking with his bright eyes at the world that opened before them. Sometimes he looked at his master, who was leaning against the door opposite, and thought that one of his own forefathers would have stood just so, his whip in his left hand, waiting for the time to grasp his master's belt and lead him slowly downstairs to the sleigh with the four horses.

Then times and years, voices and faces flowed together imperceptibly, and the forms of his forefathers, too, flowed together and united with his own, as if the limits of time were dissolving imperceptibly, as if the whole were an uninterrupted, single stream of gray, cloudy water, on whose shore they all stood – all of them – faithful servants of their masters, standing there until they could drive them home, where the baroness or the children waited, the fields and the cattle, or our Heavenly Father of whom the master only need be reminded and then he would turn his back on all this.

When everything had come to an end, the gambling or drinking or dancing, when he had nodded to his master and had taken the glasses into the little kitchen, when he had tidied up and had closed the windows again, he walked slowly and rather laboriously up the narrow path to the moor, sometimes so deep in thought as to be quite lost in it, and stretched out his right hand to grasp his master's belt – but the master was not there. Only the warm air was there, and the constellations and the calls of the night birds. And the slight chilliness of age that he bore along with him, and the consciousness that there was still some anger in the earth to be worn out; that he had felt secure too soon, too hastily and too carelessly, and that the knots of fate were not so easy to undo as the knots in the lash of a whip.

But one thing Christoph was not conscious of in spite of his white hair and his bright eyes. He was not conscious of it because nothing else was granted to him but to put his arm around the shoulders of his master when that master was in danger and need. But it was not granted to him to put his arm around those who, according to his opinion, had brought his master into that danger and need. A life of service had made him faithful, but now and again his faithfulness had made him blind. He did not see how much was suffered here; he only saw that his master suffered.

He spoke as little as Baron Erasmus spoke. If there was much he did not know, yet he thought he would know when it would be time not to wait and look on any longer but to speak.

Nor was it necessary for him to speak. Since there was no longer any need for Baron Amadeus to watch over every step of the young mother with care and apprehension, since the day of the great rains, Amadeus' eyes were open again to all that happened around him. When his brother Erasmus sat with him sometimes in the evening on the alder trunk outside the door – and he never came before twilight – it was always light enough for Amadeus to cast a sidelong glance at his face that wore a mask of cheerfulness, a mask which grew more and more rigid, and beneath this mask to discover that which was sinking into ever deeper sadness.

Erasmus spoke now almost exclusively of their childhood and youth, and it was as if this time lay in an unreal, exaggerated brightness before his melancholy eyes. He talked of this time cheerfully, without a trace of nostalgia but with a deep, almost pious absorption, and sometimes he tried to follow the threads which had been spun at that time and to pursue them into the present. Not only the threads of his own life, but also those of his brothers, as if by doing so he could gain a discernment which would throw light on all that happened, yes, even on the things which were going to happen.

Then Amadeus had compassion on his uncomplaining brother, who seemed to be carrying with silent dignity the burden of a grave error, but he also realized that all this was more than merely the disillusion of a moment, that the root of this disillusionment lay in something deeper than the mere seduction by a human face, that at the root lay the sum of a whole life, a life that had been too protected, too confiding. A romantic life in which decisions and steps were taken as if the lives of others, yes, of the whole world, were still reposing in the principles of an epoch which had long sunk into oblivion, of a life which had never been quite real but which the romantics of the race had believed to be quite real, not only for themselves but for everyone else as well.

This pathetic belief of a child who imagined that even a sophisticated woman need only be taken by the hand to be guided without an effort over the threshold beyond which the realm of the Liljecronas began, or at least the realm of Erasmus von Liljecrona, where kindness, consideration, helping and healing, and last but not least, the gentle silence of the unobtrusive reigned, was as much a matter of course as the breathing of the lungs.

But now this romantic life had been shocked wide awake, as a child is awakened in the night when something dark and terrible is enacted before his eyes: an attack, a deed of violence, a conflagration, or an earthquake. No deeds of violence, neither by man nor by nature, were enacted before the eyes of Baron Erasmus. Nor was it the much more terrible fact that he was bound to another human being and to her companions who transformed themselves before his very eyes in an unimaginable and terrifying way, as in a dream men change into ghosts. Or that his own hand was fettered to those hands that lifted the covering from what should have remained eternally hidden – from the wicked, the ugly, the noisy, the vulgar. As if the covering were lifted from the faces of the maimed and the murdered.

If Amadeus had recognized only this, he would not have recognized more than Christoph had, who without being able to give it a name had recognized his master's need, just as Amadeus had recognized his brother's need. But Amadeus could also see behind this need that deeper and irremediable lack: that his brother was unable to offer himself up. Yes, it had not been given to Amadeus himself in the beginning to have pity on this woman, Daisy, as he had had pity on the forester's daughter, even though he could remember the years when he himself had been bound and beaten, whereas his brother had nothing of the kind that he could remember. Erasmus had not wanted to remember but to forget. He had not known that only he can forget who has drunk the dregs of remembrance to the last drop. He had refilled the cup before he had drunk the dregs. He had thought that he would not taste the dregs through the new wine.

Sometimes it came into Amadeus' mind to sit down at his brother's side as he had sat near Barbara, and to speak to him gently, confidently, and happily as he had spoken to the distraught heart of the girl. "Once a long time ago, a man sat by the fire who held a big, old Book on his knees and read of the times when the Christ Child still walked upon the earth. And while he was reading, he heard on the moor . . ."

But then he realized that he could not speak to his brother as he had spoken to a girl who lived in a dark fairytale. For his brother would not be able to master the last heavy fairytale, in which one lays one's heart bare before the knife.

So nothing was left but to sit quietly by his side and to listen while he talked of his childhood and youth, and to let him feel that the threads were by no means broken, that neither the wintry road with the calls of the children, nor the camp behind the barbed wire, nor the world of the shipwrecked in the small rooms of the castle had the power to break such threads; that there might be error and disillusionment in each life, but nothing was lost as long as hands from the past were still ready to grasp the sinking hand.

Amadeus did not say this in so many words. Actually he did not say it at all. A gesture was enough, or a comforting smile. It was enough in itself to go with the brother who had said goodbye at the beginning of the footpath, an arm about his shoulder, and to remind him of what Christoph had said about the good time, and that the earth had now worn out its anger.

Only once in his many visits did Erasmus refrain from speaking of his radiant and long-ago childhood, in which he used to take refuge. "I have gone the wrong way," he said, staring into the fire on the hearth. "Nobody knows it, not even Christoph, who knows so much. But I know it. I have always aimed at my own ends, and I have not striven for others. I have not made up for what happened on the road. I have made it still worse. I know I shall never be able to make up for it, because it is not granted to me. I ought to have realized it when I was at the head of my squadron, and each time later on when it was a question of facing the last thing. I have always been able to face only the last but one. I am the eldest but I am also the least."

"He who knows that of himself, or thinks he knows it, is never the least; the least is only he who thinks that he is generous when he bends down to the lesser. And you do not do that."

"No longer," said Erasmus. "Not anymore. But I am sure I have done it. And that's why I forsook the children a second time. Besides, I cannot love the inferior; I would like to, but I cannot. And I am too old to change."

"Why do you not go away?" asked Amadeus after a time.

"That I cannot do, brother. I cannot get out when somebody else is in the boat and we hear the rapids. That much nobility is still in me, even though no love is within me. I have stepped over the threshold and the door has closed. It does not matter that it was the wrong threshold."

"But this you ought to know by now," said Amadeus, laying his hand on his brother's shoulder, "that nothing is lost. As long as one passes sentence on others only, much is lost. But if one passes sentence on oneself, nothing is lost. You are not the least, you are only the one who suffers most. Still bear that quietly for a time – quite quietly, do you see?"

"You're now the only one who is at his side," said Amadeus to Christoph the next morning. "You will know when it is time to take hold of his belt, Christoph, won't you?"

Christoph believed that he would know. He did not promise but he felt, as he put it, that God had only spared him so that he might once again do what his forefathers did years ago.

The people in the cottages on the moor and in the forester's house heard nothing of these things. There it was as if the earth had really worn out its anger. The spades in the peat bog sparkled as always in the summer sunshine, and the blow of an ax would echo from the depths of the forest out across the quiet world. The children played or sang or knelt by the flower beds which Baron Amadeus had arranged for them. When the man Donelaitis stood at twilight at the edge of the moor, motionless, and gazed into the distance where perhaps he might see the form of a young woman, bundle in hand, or might perhaps see how she already lay at rest stretched out, with sand and earth on her closed eyes, then the others looked at him from the benches where they sat in front of their cottages, but they never talked about it. Someone had gone away to search for the lost homeland, one who had no child that might have held her back, nor a husband who might have bound her, either by the wrists or by her heartstrings. She had gone away and they could do nothing but fold their hands in the evening glow and say a prayer for her.

Only Baron Amadeus looked at the man in a different way, and once when he met him unexpectedly at such a time and the man looked calmly at him with eyes still filled with the sunset, he knew that it had been right to look at him in a different way from the people in the cottages.

For this man's eyes had changed since that New Year's Eve before the little fire. They were not without sadness, the dull sadness of a child who has been left alone. But they were not filled with this sadness; something like a quiet confidence, a serene calm, had come into them. Not because his wife might by now have reached the shores of the river to let the white sand run through her hand, but because this was not the final thing he had to think about. There was something different that the man saw here in the evening when he looked at the path where her footprints had been. In their place something new began to appear before his eyes, because the evening sky was still crimson, whether he stood alone here or whether they were together; because the trees grew and the peat grew and would not have disappeared in another hundred years. Because Laima, the goddess of destiny, neglected his sorrow as she had the footprints of his wife, and because the sands of the dunes which the wind drove into the lagoon would still be driven there whether or not his wife's hand could reach out to grasp them.

Perhaps the baron was mistaken. Perhaps he saw only his own thoughts in the eyes of this man. And yet he felt as if something passed from these eyes into himself, something that made him quiet and secure, something that must lie there, unnoticed by others, which this man had won for himself and for nobody else.

At this time the forester's daughter also began to come to Amadeus' hut again, not every evening, but so often that it always seemed as if she had only been there the night before. Sometimes she brought the child with her and sometimes she came alone. She was shier now than she had been before, like the deer that only steps out of the forest after sunset. She did not lean her cheek against the knee of the baron anymore when she sat at his side on the doorstep. She clasped her hands around her knee and leaned her head against the door behind her, and then they both gazed into the slowly fading evening glow, where they could now and again discern the shape of a lonely man.

"Sometimes I feel," she once said in a low voice, "as if I ought to go away as she did, carrying the child in a shawl on my back and barefoot, as one ought to walk when there is a long way to go. But where shall I go? She had something to go to – a river or a dune. Nothing bowed her shoulders as she walked; she was guiltless."

Then Amadeus laid his hand again on her head or on her shoulder and smiled as he had smiled when he told her a fairytale. "I have fought for you," he said, "as I have never in my life fought for a human being. You know that. Will you take out of my hand what I have brought up from the bottom of a deep well, when you know how deep the well was and what was lurking at the bottom?"

Then she bent down quickly and kissed his other hand, so quickly that he could not prevent it, and asked his pardon. "Perhaps it is only because I cannot imagine that this hand has done it. I would like to imagine it but I cannot. It's too great a miracle."

"It's always a miracle when one heart troubles about another heart," he replied. "To me it seems as if no other life here has been so fulfilled as yours, fulfilled by a child that we saved when the dog and the wolf were pursuing it. By a bright child that one day will also have children in these dark times. With such a child you ought not to be homesick."

"Your eyes do not yet see a blemish in it?" she asked after a while.

"It will never have a blemish," he answered, "for its cheek lay on the big Book, which the woman had not thrown away when she was hurrying across the moor."

He felt that a slight shiver passed through her body, as if memory touched her with a cold hand, and he went on stroking her hair. "Don't forget," he said consolingly, "that nothing has power over you anymore since you have had pity – nothing and nobody. She who has had pity has atoned for everything. Neither fear nor danger exists anymore for her who has had pity – never again in all her life."

She stayed until the first stars appeared and then she got up. She did not kiss him again. She only laid her cheek against his shoulder and stood so for a time with eyes closed, knowing that he would not turn her away if she had her eyes shut.

Nor did he do so.

For Baron Amadeus, too, there were hours when he lay sleepless on his bed listening to the voices which he could hear outside above the nocturnal earth, hours in which his life did not appear to him as calm, clear, and without any doubts. His book was being printed now, and he looked with cool curiosity at the narrow proof sheets which he held in his hand, and in which he could note on the margin the errors the compositor had made. It seemed to him an almost presumptuous simplicity to hold his life – or at any rate a few years of his life – in his hands and to mark the errors in it with a pencil, as if they were not the errors of the compositor but the errors in this life itself, and as if it were just as presumptuous to let this corrected life go out over his threshold into the wide world.

He felt that there was a certain shamelessness in withdrawing a curtain from something that was fit only for one's own eyes, with the threadbare argument or excuse that it was divested of all that was "personal," so much so that everyone could see himself in it, because behind the individual the universal appeared – fate, or whatever one chooses to call it.

But he was not happy about it, just as he could not have been happy at a fair, where he would have to praise his goods in order to sell them. He had not yet realized that the pains which visited a writer were less than those which visited him when he surrendered what he had written into other hands. It was as if one sold a child and then went home with the price in one's pocket.

Perhaps he thought that the meaning of his life now lay in slowly stripping himself bare, as the saying goes. To have a child that did not belong to him, to write a book that no longer existed for him, or at any rate not for him alone. To sit on the doorstep at the side of a girl who had given herself to another. To sow flowers which blossomed around other people's houses. The whole of this strange life which slowly detached itself from him so that others might take possession of it for a time, those who needed comfort or those who needed support. Perhaps it was the only way to grow old honorably, without bitterness, without the greed and fear of the miser. To give oneself away because one had gathered so much that it would have been wrong to keep it to oneself.

But had he gathered so much, and did he really give it away without an effort? Did not a very low voice call in these hours of the night, warning or enticing him to keep something back? As low as the children's voices called to his brother Erasmus? Was his hair already so gray that no tribute could be paid him save the devotion of a kiss on the hand?

If he had got as far as this in his thoughts then it might very well be that the deep melancholy of the man who stands alone would fall on him, the deep melancholy of those who live for an idea, of those who were in need of "the patience of the saints," who had to gain anew each night the confidence that was attributed to them so that the others should not feel insecure when they stood in the morning on the doorstep to find confidence for their day's work.

Then he walked again across the moor as he had done at first, sat for a time by the two juniper bushes where the "dark one" had lain and later he himself, and slowly he regained his insight, the power to see the mesh of the web into which he himself was woven, the understanding that everything was good as it had been, and that men should beware of wanting to make it better – even a man with gray hair, yes, he perhaps most of all.

Then he could sit again quietly on one of the peat stacks and look at the parson Wittkopp as he leaned on his spade, and together with him he could await the evening.

The parson had been offered a congregation in a large town where the parsonage was still intact. But he had declined the offer. "I don't want to go away from here," he said, searching in his pocket for the bits of tobacco for his pipe. "The women don't smile now when they see me, and the children don't call out cheeky rhymes after me. They have brought so many of their troubles to me that they do not smile, or they would be smiling at themselves. We have no church, no pulpit, and no altar, and I feel that in spite of it the Lord has come a little nearer to us. As if he does not feel quite at home anymore in big churches where everything still goes on as it always has gone on, according to a standard program, as it were, as if nothing special had happened. But something has happened, indeed a great deal has happened. Perhaps it is not sufficient to call it a visitation and to behave as if one had come, to some extent, safely through that visitation. For many have not come through it, neither in the pulpit nor below the pulpit. And perhaps it was even more than a visitation."

"What else can it have been?" asked Amadeus.

"I don't know," replied Wittkopp. He sat now on another peat stack opposite Amadeus, his elbows propped on his knees, and his eyes followed the blue smoke from his pipe. "I don't know, Herr Baron. I feel that we ought to draw a little nearer to the Lord, nearer to the hem of his garment, and as if in a church one can only do that with an effort. Perhaps one could do it there in days of old when 'the congregation of the faithful' was the word. But no longer in these days when there is 'a congregation of the unfaithful,' a great congregation which is as frightened as children are frightened when they see their father smash a looking glass.

"Sometimes I fancy that formerly people had no destiny, no private destiny that belonged only to each alone. There was only the common destiny – of the congregation or of the state – and one could address it from a pulpit in general words because it held good for all.

"But now all people have a destiny, each a destiny of his own. Death, fire, the hangman, violence touched them all, and with each of them it has been different, altogether different. Now we can no longer speak in a general way or say anything that is understandable and binding for everybody. Each individual stands alone before God again; do you understand? As in the old tales Abraham was alone, or Jacob or King Saul. For in those years God spoke to each of them alone and acted as if each of them had been chosen by him. He no longer speaks inside churches; they are not sufficient for him. Perhaps it will not be sufficient for him if the parsons go up into the pulpit again. Perhaps it appears to him too easy, with all the good will that most of them have. I cannot imagine that he sent the demons only that things might remain as they were before. I am sure he had a plan, a purpose, and I am meditating what it may have been."

"And until you have satisfied yourself about it you will not stand in a pulpit?" asked Amadeus.

"No, not until I have satisfied myself. I know that he will give me time. He is more patient than the consistories. I think he will be quite content that I should still cut peat here for a time and sit at the side of a patient's bed in the evenings, or listen when the young baroness in the castle asks me questions."

"Does she ask questions sometimes?" asked Amadeus.

"Yes, she does. She makes out that it is all quite trifling, but that is not how it is. Time has touched her, too, even though she paints her lips. Nor has she grown rich because she can now embroider her handkerchiefs with coronets. She has only grown poor, much poorer than she was. She asks why Sarah with white hair bore a child."

"And you don't know?"

"No, I don't know; generally speaking, I know so terribly little. When I stretch out my hand in the dark from my bed in the castle I always feel that God takes and holds this hand of mine. But if he were to ask me something, I would know nothing – absolutely nothing, like a child that has not learned its homework. He does not want me to know anything. He is quite content that I stretch out my hand. But when I go to the consistory or to the bishop they always want me to show them what God has put into this hand of mine. An empty hand is empty for them. They cannot see the slight shimmer that God has put into it by holding my hand even for a moment, as he puts it into every hand that is stretched out toward him in the night. Just as they cannot see a church where there is no pulpit, no liturgy, and none of the old ecclesiastical regulations."

"But is it not possible that they may suspend you if you refuse to accept a congregation?" asked Amadeus.

"That may very well be," replied Wittkopp. "Obedience is necessary. There can be no organization without obedience, and a church is just like a state on a small scale. That is the terrible thing about it, that it has become like that, and probably had to become like that. The word has remained as it was two thousand years ago, or at least they think that it has remained so. But the interpretation of the word belongs, as it were, to today. Not all of them can jump over a space of two thousand years. For my part I cannot. Now if they suspend me, I shall be glad to remain with the original word and not with the word as they interpret it today. The word is more reliable than all the regulations because regulations are the work of man and the word is not."

"But you are not a heretic, parson?"

Wittkopp smiled in a beautiful, childlike way. "Oh no, Herr Baron," he said, "that I'm not. The heretics were the great sons of God, and I am not great. They loved so much that they could hate, and the church did not burn them because they hated but because they loved so much. The church is never willing that anybody should love God more than what is customary and is ordained. That seems to her dangerous. That is the mark of the church's poverty, that she thinks of danger. He who is safe does not think of danger. Just as the state has killed for twelve long years because it did not feel secure. From fear! More blood is shed from fear than from hatred."

"And you believe that there is no room for you in the church as it is today?"

"Oh no, I certainly don't think that. We never ought to think of ourselves as if a special church is needed for us which is not yet built. When we consider ourselves as something special, we begin to found a sect or even a new religion. We must not think of ourselves as something special, but just as children who stretch out their hands in the dark. And most parsons are not exactly like children. They are so terribly grown-up, for only the grownups always know what they have to say and to do and what is right. It does not strike them that in reality all grownups do and say and think the same. But the children always think differently. They are still at the beginning of thinking and doing. Just as I am, as far as the Bible is concerned. I don't think of what the great teachers of the church said or thought about the Bible. I don't think of any dogma, and not that each church has its own dogma. I still read the Bible as it was in the beginning, do you understand me? As a great fairytale, each page of which is wonderful. For instance that story of Joseph and his brothers, or that of the star of Bethlehem. It is as plain before my eyes as the moor here, as if I only need stretch out my hand to grasp it and keep it forever.

"That's why I do not fit into any church, Herr Baron. It is not suitable for children to go to church. As I am, I am a child of faith, while most of them are masters of faith, and the bishop is the firmest in the saddle.

"That's exactly why I am in my right place here. Those who live in the castle are all like children, bewildered children who have seen something terrible. All of them, in spite of their pretense of security, even the young baroness – all of them felt the earth tremble and saw fire falling from heaven, from the same heaven where according to their childish faith our Heavenly Father dwells. Only children can be as bewildered as they are. For them not only the earth collapsed, but also heaven.

"What have they to do with a church now, Herr Baron, where the high-ups and the grownups congregate again and say what they said twelve years ago or twelve hundred years ago? That all has become safe and firm and orderly again. But in a hundred awful nights they experienced that nothing was orderly or safe or firm. For them, all that falls from heaven falls from God, not from wicked men as they have now been told. And other parsons have prayed for these men, too, that they might come back safe and sound from their fiery flights.

"I think it is quieter for them with me than in a church. What I say does not resound as it does from the stony walls of a church. I don't say it so confidently as they say it there. They can read in my eyes that I, too, am still confused. They know about my wife and my children. I do not wear vestments either, only this coat in which I cut peat. At first they jeered at this coat, but now they don't laugh at it anymore. They understand that God has taken off my vestments for a time, and that makes it easier for them when I talk to them. The others have not taken them off, and some of them have even put on two layers, one on top of the other."

Amadeus listened and he, too, felt enveloped by the great peace which radiated from the parson's face. The peace of one who begins afresh right from the beginning, like children whose card house has tumbled down. "When I sit with you," he said, "all that I have done in these past years seems to have been right."

"Yes, why should it not have been right?" asked Wittkopp. "The brilliant fireworks are over by now, and only the small lights are left which burn calmly by themselves. And the wonderful thing about them is that they don't burn for themselves but for many others who have no longer any light of their own. I am sure the others will begin again with their fireworks, very shortly, probably, and look with contempt on the small lights which do not lead the world forward, as they say – the romantic lights. But we will quietly leave it to them to lead the world forward. By now we have had a few thousand years of experience of where such leadership will take us. The people here don't want to see fireworks anymore. They prefer to see the small lights which burn quietly in the evening, in the shepherd's hut for example. Then they will say: Herr Baron is still awake! It's beautiful for them that they can say so, and when their hearts are oppressed they can just go and knock at your door. Theirs are simple lives, Herr Baron, and we must not try to think of a way to make them less simple."

The two men got up together and walked back across the moor. The summer flowers were in full bloom around the cottages, and children were kneeling around the draw well in the heather and singing. "For them the earth is firm and safe again," said

Wittkopp. "One ought to come here every evening and listen to them for a while."

When they were saying farewell to each other, Amadeus hesitated a little and then he asked in a low voice what the parson thought about Erasmus. "I do not think anything about him," replied Wittkopp quietly. "I only look on. Christoph and I, we look on together. He went into a dark wood like a child, and we two stand each behind a tree, and when it is time, we shall call, 'Here!' At first he felt very confident and he did not need us. He had his bow and his arrows as children have them. But by now his arrows are not worth much and he knows that. Don't worry, Herr Baron."

But Amadeus could not help worrying.

A few evenings later it happened that Christoph was standing in his window niche and the baron was leaning, as usual, in the doorway which led to the adjoining room. The windows were open, because the air was sultry and oppressive, and now and again the bluish shimmer of summer lightning flamed up above the candlelight; the trees in the park could be heard rustling and tossing about and then they sank back into a heavy silence. The voices in the little room were louder and more excitable than usual, and more drink was drunk, in greater haste than ever before. The American officers had stayed away and new guests from the castle had appeared, people who got their money nobody knew how and whose names and titles would probably not outlast the next shower of rain.

Christoph saw that at the top of the table the young "air force hero" kept the bank. He had pulled off his sweater and his hairy hands dealt the cards and distributed the banknotes quickly and noiselessly. On his lips was a fixed smile like the smile on a mask, and only when a distant thunder rumbled far away over the park did he raise his eyebrows as at a childish interference with serious business which the adults had to settle among themselves.

He won almost every game, and the more gloomy the faces of the losers became, the more kindly was the smile on the lips of the mask. Apart from him only Daisy smiled, although she, too, was a loser, but her smile was only like a reflection of his, as if according to a secret agreement they smiled together and only they knew why.

Now a large mirror in an old-fashioned gilt frame hung on the wall to the right of the air force lieutenant, and Christoph's eyes were suddenly riveted on this mirror. The candles flickered in the wind and their light was uncertain and deceptive, but even in this uncertain light Christoph noticed that something strange was happening there in the mirror. And if it happened in the mirror, it must also be happening in real life, from which the mirror received the reflection.

With his bright eyes he looked for a time into the rather dulled glass, and then he looked at Erasmus. But the baron stared at the candle flames as if they shed their light on a coffin instead of on a gaming table, and as if he had to stand guard over this coffin on which the first flashes of lightning began to play more and more brilliantly. The heavy thunder rumbled, echoing for a long time above the nocturnal world, and the dusty glass prisms of the old chandelier which hung over the table jingled softly as if somebody were walking in the rooms above.

Christoph gave a deep sigh, as if he had been summoned to some hard task, and went across the room toward Erasmus. But as he passed behind the chair of the "air force hero" he stopped suddenly and with both hands gripped the left wrist of the man, pulled it from under the tablecloth, and before the man – completely taken by surprise – could prevent it, Christoph drew a card from the gambler's shirt sleeve. He turned it around slowly enough for all the players to see what it was; then he let it fall at the same time as he dropped the arm he had gripped, and was already at the side of Baron Erasmus when the next thunderclap pealed through the window like a load of brass deadening the wild uproar which arose round the table.

A cold wind in which the coming rain could already be smelled extinguished all the candles except one, and Christoph closed the door on this ghostlike scene and laid his arm around his master's shoulders. "Come now, dear sir," he said.

In the flashes of the lightning the baron opened a drawer and took out some papers, but all the time Christoph's arm was around his shoulders.

Between the walls of the passage Erasmus stood still once more and listened. "We ought not to forsake her, Christoph," he said. "She is my wife. You are not doing well by me, Christoph."

But Christoph led him slowly to the narrow stone staircase. "Let it be, sir," he said. "It was not only his hands that I saw under the table."

But Baron Erasmus did not move. He trembled, but Christoph did not know that he was trembling with fear. "I once ran away, Christoph," he said, "when they cried out. And now they are crying again. Even though they cry in anger and not in fear. You are not doing well by me, Christoph; this once I ought to stay when they cry."

"A baron does not stay where they cheat at cards, dear sir," said Christoph, and led Erasmus downstairs.

When they entered the great hall on the ground floor the rain began to pour down, a heavy rain pouring down like a torrent. The storm tore the great door out of Christoph's hands, and for a moment it seemed as if the baron were about to shrink back from the tempestuous night into the safety of the protecting walls.

But Christoph led him down the steps. "Let it rain now, dear sir," he said. "Nobody will be on the road except we two."

The air was cool, as if newly born after the stifling heat of the day, and they tasted the freshness of the rain on their lips. It penetrated through their clothes to their skin and enveloped them in the great flood that was pouring down from the inky sky.

Under the archway with the broken coat of arms the baron stood still and turned around once more. Some of the windows were lit by a feeble candlelight, as if behind them mothers were praying beside their children. Each flash of the lightning lifted the great, massive building out of an abyss, plunged it in a white, spectral light and then let it fall back again into a bottomless pit. Each of the jagged streaks of fire seemed to strike right into the high roofs. In the park they could see the treetops bowed down by the storm.

"I shall never see that again," thought Erasmus. "Never." It was as if a ship were sinking behind him with broken masts and torn sails.

But it did not sink noiselessly. He heard the cries of the drowning, and he covered his ears with his hands so that he should not hear them.

By the time they were halfway up the mountain the storm had receded into the lowland. The rain had nearly stopped, and above the moor the first stars appeared. The wood smelled beautifully pure and each gust of wind showered a flood of raindrops on their bare heads.

The baron stood still, because his heart gave him trouble when he climbed. "Do you realize that we both have white hair, Christoph?" he asked suddenly.

"I know that very well, sir," replied Christoph, "and now we shall be glad of it."

"Do you think so, Christoph?" asked Erasmus. "Yes, later on you will be able to tell a new story – not only that of your forefather who led his master by the belt. But I do not know whether it will be a true story."

"I shall not tell many more stories, sir," answered Christoph quietly, "and I have no grandchild who will be able to tell stories about me."

"Nor have I, Christoph, and yet I had thought . . ."

"Two children have been born this year, dear sir," said Christoph and began slowly climbing up the hill again. "We ought to feel that they were also born for us. We have a share in them, a great share, and more has not been meted out to us. We have not looked often enough into the mirror, dear sir."

"Yes, we two, Christoph," replied Erasmus. "We two."

There was no light in the little window of the hut, but they stood there for a time. The stars were sparkling above the moor, and the night birds called as if the rain had given new strength to their wings. The distant summer lightning slid like searchlights around the horizon.

"Now we are at home here," said Christoph. "It was all a mistake, but now we are home."

In his room in the forester's house Christoph undressed the baron and put him to bed. He covered him up well and drew the curtain over the little window. "I sleep next door," he said. "You only need to call me; I sleep very lightly now."

But he did not go away; he held the candle in his hand and looked down at the floor boards at his feet. "Sometimes it happens, sir," he said, "that people think they ought to be ashamed of themselves. I, too, have been ashamed in my time, and I have learned that it is good to be ashamed. Only when our Heavenly Father is ashamed of us it is not good, sir. Then we must retrace our steps quickly and to good purpose. But until then it is all right. There has been much shame to bear in this house, sir, much shame – good night, sir."

Christoph lay down to sleep on the bare boards in front of the door, but Erasmus did not know this. For a time he looked at the little window which sometimes stood out clear and square when the lightning flashed in it, and he listened to the distant thunder which sank lower and lower behind the horizon. For a while he listened to the echo of Christoph's words: "Then we must retrace our steps quickly and to good purpose."

The house was silent and the earth, too, was settling into silence. The sheets were cool and the air which came through the window and stirred the folds of the curtain was cool. But after a while Erasmus noticed that his cheeks were burning, and again after a time that they were not burning from the rain that the storm had beaten against them but that they were burning with shame. He knew that shame was burning him, but he realized already that Christoph had not done well by him. Even Christoph, old and white-haired, had made a mistake. Christoph had thought that a Baron von Liljecrona was the highest being in this world and that this baron had crossed the wrong threshold into a room where they cheated at cards, in addition to all the other things which went on there. Into a room where even his own wife had cheated – from the very beginning – and Christoph thought that the baron must be taken by the belt and must be led out of his mistake, as his ancestors had been led out of their mistakes.

But only Baron Erasmus knew that Christoph, even Christoph, had made a mistake. Not the "highest in the world" had crossed a wrong threshold, but the "haughtiest in the world." Somebody who had only thought of himself, and who had wanted a child and happiness so that he could forget an old sin. A gambler like all the others who with a new stake wanted to make good an old loss.

And when he had lost his new stake, too, he had run away. Tonight he had run away a second time, just as he had run away on the wintry road. Yes, as he had probably run away all his life when need had called, dire need which had called for the help of bare hands and not for the help of hands in kid gloves. He had not run away because he had feared for his life tonight when the card was dropped on the table, but because he had feared for his hands. He felt that they ought to have been held as a shield before his wife and before the mire in which she had a share. He felt what Christoph had not felt, that he ought to have stayed, and he had not stayed, because to stay was neither inborn in him nor had it been acquired in a long life. The only thing that had stayed was this, that his cheeks were still burning with shame.

He heard the rain dripping from the gutter into an old weatherworn tub which stood under the window. But it was not the rain he heard dripping, it was his shame. The real shame, not the imagined one, in which he had lived till now. Not the shame that he had crossed a wrong threshold, but that he had put on gloves when he saw those who stood behind the threshold; that he had broken open the door again and had run away when to wear gloves had no longer sufficed.

With his heart hammering he sat up in the darkness and saw the faces of all those in the house who should have been asleep but now were awake, raising their heads from their pillows to listen to the shame of the baron which dripped from the roof. Although it was not their own shame, they sat up as the baron was sitting up, propped on their hands, with beating hearts listening to hear whether at last it would stop dripping.

But it would never stop, neither by day nor by night.

There had been many nights for all of them when they had listened as they did now. But at that time they had listened to their own shame – shame for some meanness or for some act of violence. But now it was the shame of him who, they used to think, could never tolerate even a breath of it. The shame of a baron who, white-haired, had run away instead of having pity.

They heard the drops fall, on and on, slowly, monotonously. Their master's shame was dripping from the roof, the bitterest shame that could be conceived, and each drop awakened an echo far and wide – back to the wintry road where once before they had called for him who had hidden himself, as he now hid himself in this room.

Baron Erasmus was terrified; he had never thought that a man could be so terrified; he had not felt like this even when he was pressing his brow into the snow in the wood so that he should not hear the cries.

He got up without making a sound and lit the little candle with trembling hands. There were still some sheets of paper in the drawer of the small table, and he laid them before him and began to write.

"Erasmus von Liljecrona," he began, in his old-fashioned handwriting and with his formal choice of phrase. "Erasmus von Liljecrona, to his beloved brothers Barons Aegidius and Amadeus von Liljecrona . . ." He wrote until the morning dawned, and when fatigue began to overwhelm him he raised his head and listened to the drops falling from the gutter. He knew that this drip, drip would never stop. Never.

When he had finished, he put the few things he had in his pockets at the side of the letter, looked around the room once more and went softly out. When he opened the door he was startled to see Christoph lying there, but he stepped carefully over him, and then he stood still for a moment to look down at the sleeping face. And Erasmus was startled again and even more surprised, when the sleeping man gently raised a hand and clasped his right ankle.

"Let us go together, dear sir," said a voice that was wide awake.

"I must go alone, Christoph," replied the baron and bent down to release his ankle.

Then Christoph sat up. "In my stories there was nobody who went alone," he said. "There was always somebody at hand."

He took Erasmus' arm and went down the stairs with him. On the threshold the baron began to resist and tried to push Christoph back into the dark house.

"Don't mind striking me, dear sir," said Christoph, holding the hand firmly. "I am old enough for you to strike me."

Then the baron went passively with him.

To both of them it seemed as if there had never been such a morning over the moor. As if the earth had been lifted for the first time out of the depths of chaos so that creation might begin. It sparkled with moisture and crystal purity, and even the voices of the woodlarks sounded as if until then no woodlark had sung in this place. Dawn spread over half the vault of heaven. It was so grand and stood so still that it seemed as if it were the dying glow of a great world – the old world, the world that was many centuries old, and as if the new world of this morning had no longer any part in it.

They began to walk around the marshes without any apparent goal, and when the baron stood still, Christoph stood still too. "I should not be surprised," he said quietly, after a long silence, "if the old baron, your father, had come with us. From the roots of the junipers in the homeland to the roots of these junipers – and if I shall not hear him say once again: 'Well, Christoph, how are things going with you?' "

"And what would you answer, Christoph?" asked Erasmus, casting a sidelong glance at him.

"They are going all right, Herr Baron, I would say, they are going all right."

"Perhaps you ought not to say it so confidently," replied Erasmus gently, "not quite so confidently."

They were wet to the hips, but they did not heed it. They saw cranes standing in the dense reeds, and from the depths of the swamps they heard the call of the reed warbler. There was no one about but themselves, and only where a narrow, steep path led from the basalt blocks down to the road did they hear the high-pitched whirr of a car motor, as if it had to make an effort to get up to the summit. Christoph remembered that now and again American officers came up here to hunt scarce game, and he turned aside to walk at the foot of the rocks across the outskirts of the marshes.

Only when they stood again among the reeds and had left the wood behind them did they hear the strange voice. It was not only an alien voice but the language, as well as the tune, was alien to them. The voice was deep and full, as if it were all alone in the world of crimson dawn, yes, as if it did not belong in this world at all and was only being poured forth to feel at home again for a time in the world of its origin. It was a slow, sustained melody, as lonely as if it sounded from the edge of a virgin forest out over a swamp in which the great lizards of primeval times had their abode.

The singer, who wore a flat steel helmet, was sitting at the base of a rock which gleamed red in the morning sun. His rifle lay across his knees and his hands were laid quietly around the butt end and the barrel. It could as well have been a club or a bow that lay across his knees. His skin shone dark in the rising sun. It was a black American serviceman who sat there.

They did not know why he had come up here. Whether he wanted to see the sun and the swamps, or whether he only wanted to sing, far from the loudspeakers and the jokes of his comrades. He might well have seen the two figures among the reeds, but he did not pay attention to them. They were not there for him. Only the earth was there for him, and the sun which rose red-glowing above the sparkling earth, and the song which he sang in his deep, far-sounding voice. It was as if he were standing in one of the wooden chapels in Florida or Alabama, singing into the listening ear of God.

The wind carried the words back into the forest, and Erasmus did not understand much of them.

> Oh nobody knows the trouble I've seen,
> nobody knows my sorrow . . .

And in between, two or three times, in solemn, sustained notes:

> Oh yes, Lord . . .

It seemed to Erasmus as if the man did not sing the whole song, but only the beginning. Perhaps he had forgotten the rest, or perhaps it satisfied him to sing this beginning over and over again. He sat like a magician on alien earth and put a spell on it with his song: on trees, on animals, on the two men who stood there among the glittering reeds and listened. He felt so alone that he would have sung like this even if an army had been standing on the moor – so alone in the deep, dark centuries of a dark part of the earth, where good tidings had now come for sinners and sufferers. And it was of these tidings that he sang.

The voice carried far over the silent moor, a deep, softly vibrating voice, as if it came from a strange, mystic stringed instrument. The morning sun lit up the black face, which shone as if it were oiled, the barrel of the gun, and the motionless hands. It could have been an old idol that suddenly had begun to give forth sound in the soft morning breeze which blew over the wet grasses.

As suddenly as it had begun, it now ceased. It receded into the darkness of the wood and faded away. The high whirr of the motor was again to be heard, and then all was still.

"Do you know what he sang, sir?" asked Christoph.

The baron was still listening, as if this melody had made him forget the whole world. Only when Christoph touched him lightly on the sleeve did he remember where he was.

"I asked whether you know what he sang, dear sir," said Christoph once more.

"Not entirely," replied the baron. "But it's enough . . . *O, niemand kennt das Leid, das ich gesehen habe, niemand kennt meine Trauer* . . . And then he only sang a few times: *O, ja, mein Herr und Gott . . .*"

Christoph had turned his ear and listened attentively. Then they walked on.

Christoph only stopped when they came to the juniper bushes, between which the "dark one" and Baron Amadeus had lain. There they sat down and smoked. The earth was now fully awake. The marshes were steaming from the night's rain.

"Did you want us to sit here?" asked the baron.

"Yes, I wanted it, dear sir. So much has happened here. Everything has happened here. And here I wanted to show you that the earth has worn out its anger. I have been here once already, and I ran the whole way even though I had white hair. Today I walked slowly, but yet my knees are more tired. You ought to remember, dear sir, that I am over eighty."

"I wanted to go alone, Christoph."

"I know, sir; that's why I came with you. My forefather did not let go of the belt either. Do you want to make me less than him, sir?"

The baron did not answer. He looked away over the earth, which rose out of a purple mist and above which he seemed still to hear the song of that strange voice. His face was changed now. It was still tired, but it was as if this face, like the earth, were slowly rising out of the night mist. "Did you hear him?" he asked. Christoph nodded.

"That's what it is like when God is to be found everywhere," the baron went on. "Before this he was in Florida or Carolina, but now, this morning, he was here over the moor. For the man who sang, he was here. He came with that man; he did not stay behind and did not let the man leave home alone."

"But he is always like that, sir."

"No, not always, Christoph. Sometimes he stays behind, far behind, so far that you cannot see him any longer. But then suddenly he is there again, just as if he were singing in the rock. You don't see him, but you hear him. It is a marvelous morning, Christoph."

"If I had a grandchild," said Christoph after a time, and pressed the tobacco firmly into his pipe, "it would have another story to tell now – about a man who went to the swamps in the morning to drown his shame. And how he stood at the pool and bent over it, and suddenly the child was there, or the black man.

"And how they said quite gently: 'Did you want to do that, and did you not know how deep it is?' "

" 'But I have a mark on my forehead,' said the man in a low voice.

" 'A mark?' they asked and smiled, and they each raised a hand – a white hand and a black hand – and stroked his brow. And their fingertips shone when they dropped their hands again.

" 'Did you not have pity?' they asked.

" 'Yes, sometimes I have had pity,' whispered the man in reply.

" 'Did you not know that there is a radiance when you have had pity?' they both asked. No, the man did not know that. He bent his face over the black water and seemed to see a shining flower there in the depths.

" 'Go home now,' they said, 'so that the others have something to look at when it is dark. Only those who have had pity shine in the dark; not the others who lift a lighted candle.'

"That's what the grandchild would tell, sir. But as he is not there and will never be there, you must let me tell it, and just now you are the only one who is listening, dear sir. Nobody else will ever listen."

"Let us now go there where the bright child has been born," Christoph went on, "and I will go with you. We both have white hair now, and here they do not need us so badly anymore. But there they will need us. The woman is often alone, and she will be pleased to have us. She is a quiet woman. Once you thought of raising your hand to smooth other foreheads, dear sir. We did not altogether succeed in doing this. And now she will raise her hand, and all will be well with us. The world was a little too loud and too dangerous for us, dear sir. Now let us go and live where we are welcome in our old age, and let us rejoice in our white hair, dear sir. After this night let us rejoice."

Baron Erasmus listened, his hands clasped between his knees. His expression did not change, but when Christoph had finished, a faint smile seemed to play on his lips. As children will smile when they awake from a dream and notice that the world is different from what it was in the dream.

"I have never told you a story, Christoph," he then said in a low voice. "I was not wise enough for it. But now I will tell you one, yes, I will tell you the same story, only in rather a different way.

"After this night I can tell it in a different way, and after the man by the rock sang his song.

"It is true that a man walked to the swamps in the morning to drown his shame. Thus far your story is true. But what you thought about the shame, Christoph, is not true. For you have thought a little too much of the Liljecronas, Christoph, all your life long. That was good of you, and it will not be forgotten, neither here nor over there.

"But you did not remember that in an old family there are not only haughty and wicked ones, but also weak and weary ones, and those who cannot love as one ought to love. You thought that it was a shame, that I had gone into a trap. You walk unsuspectingly into a trap, but I went to gain happiness and a child. I went to forget that the children were calling. I didn't go from love and I didn't have pity. That you must understand, Christoph, do you hear? I have not had pity, not because I didn't want to, but because I couldn't. I am a greater sinner than the others, Christoph.

"When I saw I could not have pity, I only waited for the opportunity to escape. Yes, quite in secret I waited for it. And last night there was the opportunity for me to escape. From fear, Christoph, do you hear? From fear, just as I fled that other time. That's why I said that you did not lead me well. For you ought to have led me back into the room where the card lay on the table. And at night in the small room I thought that I would not have the courage to go back, because I have not felt love and shall never feel it. And because I shall not have the courage to go without love. That's why I was going into the swamp. Perhaps I might have believed your story if the man had not sung and if the morning had not been so clear. If you are without love and without courage, you believe such stories willingly.

"But now I do not believe them anymore. It wasn't a true story, Christoph, and you, too, have made a mistake here. You made a mistake out of love, and that is beautiful; but you have made a mistake after all.

"For in the true story the child or the black man asked the man whether he had not had pity. But the man did not say that he had had pity sometimes. He hesitated a little, and then he said, 'No, I have never had pity.'

" 'Never?' they both asked.

" 'No, never. Not even when they dragged our brother away. Aegidius did have pity, but I did not. No, I did not.'

"After that the two were silent, but then the child said gently: 'We cannot take the mark away, and for all who have no mark, it will always be a blemish. You are not going to live with those who have no blemish, but with the others. Or would you rather be without a blemish?'

"Then the man was frightened, raised his hands, and said that he would not like that. Perhaps he only wished that the blemish that others had should always appear to them rather less than his own.

"Then the child smiled gently and said that they would see about that, and he ought not to worry now. It was true that a mark could not shine, but it could show that he who had it was a child of God. For only he was a child of God who lived in sin and knew it.

"That's how the child would have spoken. And the man would not have got up to go to a sheltering roof and to live where he was welcome in his old age, and by no means did he wish to rejoice in his white hair.

"But he would have got up to go back to the place he had fled from in fear and confusion – not yet with love and certainly not yet without fear, but without pride, even though without happiness and without a child. As one who knew of himself that he was deeply humble and that he did not succeed in anything, but who also knew that he bore the mark of it, the mark that he no longer wanted to hide under a cloth."

For a time they were silent. Then Christoph got up and said, "He who is old and falls, dear sir, falls hard."

They walked back across the moor. Christoph no longer had his arm around the shoulder of the baron. He walked in his footsteps, and the women and children in the cottages on the moor thought that he had taken a morning walk with his master.

14

WHEN AN HOUR LATER Baron Erasmus entered the castle yard under the broken coat of arms, probably nothing had really changed in the picture that met his eyes. But to him it appeared as if the night's rain – and not the rain alone – had changed this picture, as it had changed the marshes and the fields. It appeared to him as if everything had been washed clean during the night: the dim windows covered with dust and partly broken, the walls from which the plaster crumbled down, the steep roof where here and there a tile was missing. Even the treetops in the park, on which the raindrops sparkled, were like new treetops risen up from the depths, where they had been prepared for this new morning.

He stood still and looked around him as if for the first time. Not at the decay, not at that which recalled a ship thrown up on the shore, but at that which had remained unshattered in the storms of time and had become a sort of home for the shipwrecked.

It was as if he stood here truly for the first time. Not without fear and not without shame, and with the clear perception that he would always be a bad captain for this wrecked ship. And yet he was filled with the gentle cheerfulness that breathed from this clean-washed picture. He had run away but he had come back, and now he would remain.

It did not strike him as anything out of the way that small groups of people were standing about in the courtyard and in the corridors of the castle and were talking to each other in hushed voices. It only struck him that they let him pass willingly and almost with deference, and that the way they nodded to him showed friendly consideration. He thought that perhaps the great rain had washed clean the people's hearts here, as it had washed his own heart.

All this time Christoph walked quietly behind him.

Only before his threshold the baron hesitated for a moment. He looked down at the worn wood, and he realized that the step which he was going to take was a final one. A step toward a decision that could not be undone anymore. But then, with his usual consideration, he knocked gently before he pressed down the latch. There was no answer to his knock.

The first room was as they had left it the previous night, except that there were signs that after they had gone away more had happened. The table was overturned and the carpet was covered with broken wineglasses, scattered cards, and spilled tobacco ash. One of the lofty windows stood open and the storm had swept the rain into the room. The old silk curtains moved gently in the morning breeze.

They stood still for a time and gazed silently at the havoc before them. Then Christoph set the table up again and began to pick up the bits of broken glass. His bowed figure was reflected in the mirror with the gilt frame, and Erasmus saw this double moving silently about its work.

The door to the second room was ajar and at last, after he had knocked again, the baron crossed this threshold too. In this room, also, there was havoc, but of a different kind. The cupboards and the drawers were open; the carpet was strewn with ribbons, bows, and papers; the bed had not been slept in.

The baron hunted about in case some letter addressed to him had been left behind. But there was no letter. There was nothing but the emptiness of a derelict room and the strong scent from an overturned bottle of perfume.

He sat down in the armchair near the door, clasped his hands around his knees, and stared silently in front of him. It overwhelmed him, because he had not expected anything of the kind – this changed picture of the night, and with it the picture of this day. He did not know anything yet, but all this spoke to him in an unmistakable way, even though he could not yet find any sense in it.

Then there was a gentle knock and Wittkopp came in. "They told me that you are here, Herr Baron," he said, and sat down at the open window behind which the sun was drying the wet treetops.

He looked as he usually did, perhaps a little tired, as if a few more wrinkles had come into his face, but quiet and serene as always. And as usual he collected the bits of tobacco in his pocket, filled his short pipe, and began to smoke, after he had asked Erasmus if he had no objection.

For a time all was silent. Only the birds were to be heard, and a child singing far away in the park.

Erasmus leaned his head against the back of the armchair, closed his eyes, and listened. It was now as in a dream when reality dissolves and the strange pictures from the unconscious begin to appear.

"I was called at midnight," the parson began, still gazing out of the window. "There must have been a quarrel, and there on that other bed lay one of the young fellows with a knife wound in his chest. It was evidently a severe stab and I sent immediately for the doctor. No one but the baroness was there. She was packing a traveling bag, and before she went, she came to the doorway. 'He cheated,' she said, looking at the wounded man, 'but I don't know who stabbed him. I am going now, and you need only tell the baron that I am going – nothing else.' Her face was very little different from usual, and even when she looked down at the young man she seemed to take it as a matter of course. Her thoughts were probably already set on the way that she intended to go.

"I asked her whether she had not better stay, at least until this violent crime had been cleared up. But she shook her head. 'The others will clear it up,' she replied. 'This and probably much more. But tell him that I thank him. What he could do wrongly, he did wrongly, but he meant well. It was not his fault that he fell among thieves and did not know the rules of the game. He remained a baron, and that was his mistake. We made other mistakes – I certainly did. Help him a little, as far as he can be helped.' Then she went.

"The doctor considered the stab dangerous but there was no ambulance available. He only told us what had to be done, and also that he was obliged to report the matter.

"I understood that.

"I sat with the wounded man, who awoke from his fever, and when he recognized me he asked me whether I would take a statement which he would then sign. He was convinced that he would not live through the night."

"And did he sign it then?" asked Erasmus.

"Yes, he signed it, and I have no doubt that what he signed was the truth. They were old friends, the woman and he."

"Did you say 'the woman'?" asked Erasmus gently.

"Yes, I did say that, Herr Baron," replied Wittkopp, looking at him. "She was Mrs. Knolle and is so today. The husband is still alive as far as we can tell. Bigamy is punished with prison, and I am told that she went away in the night with the other young fellow. She will not come back. I sent the statement which the wounded man signed to the magistrate by a messenger, so that your marriage may be declared illegal."

"Should you not have waited a little?" asked Erasmus after a pause. "She has not much of a start if the magistrate knows it already."

"She will always have a good start, Herr Baron," replied Wittkopp.

The children were singing again and both men listened. Only when in the adjoining room Christoph had swept up the last bits of glass was Erasmus startled. He was so startled that the parson got up and came over to his armchair. He stood quite still when Erasmus grasped his arm with both hands and looked up at him in painful confusion. "God has made it too easy for me," he said in an anxious undertone. "Why did he make it so easy for me?"

"What did he make easy?" asked Wittkopp stroking the hands of the baron with his other hand.

"I had decided to take the burden upon me," said Erasmus. "I wanted to come back and to stay – without love, it is true, but yet to stay."

"And at first you did not want to come back?" asked Wittkopp gently.

"No, at first I wanted never to come back. Never. I, too, fled last night, before this had happened. And I intended to go so far away that only the toads would have found me."

For a long time the parson looked down upon the white head that lay on his sleeve. "I don't think that he made it easier for you," he said finally. "If it had pleased you, it would not have been good; but it does not please you."

Erasmus shook his head.

"If somebody goes to a law court and finds the law court closed, that can startle and sadden him. It also can cause him to turn around softly and say, 'It was not to be. Why did they close the door so early?'

"But it can also cause him to lay his guilt on the threshold so that it can be found there next morning. Or to stay until they open again. Then it is not made easy for him. Then it is made harder for him, for it is hard to stay on and wait when one can just as well go away."

"Do you interpret it like that?" asked Erasmus and looked at him.

"Yes, that's how I interpret it. The others went away, except this one with the wound in his chest. Without the wound he would have gone away, too. And none of them will ever come back. But you came back, even though the door is locked now, and you will have to stay on the threshold. That's why I say that everything is all right – not too easy and not too hard."

"But I came back without love, parson."

"Probably we can't do anything about that. Love can't be ordered, nor do we know how it is reckoned in the great book if one comes back from a feeling of humility. I think you did come back in humility, Herr Baron, didn't you?"

"Yes, I did," said Erasmus in a low voice. "Or at least I came as one who does not want anything for himself."

"And generally those are the ones who get most," replied Wittkopp. "Not of worldly things, but of those things by which we should really live."

He remained standing there for a time. First his eyes were fixed on the baron's white hair, but then he raised them toward the window where an oriole was singing in a wild cherry tree. "People say," he went on, "that this bird was expelled from paradise, too, and in paradise it sang more beautifully than any other bird. But after the expulsion it is said to have forgotten the song, and now it is trying over and over again to find it. You can hear that each note is a little different from the previous one. The bird is trying so hard. There is no bird's song so touching as this."

"And we?" asked Erasmus.

"It's the same with us, Herr Baron. And so it is with those who went away last night. We remember still, and as long as we remember, all is well. Only when we smile over it and feel as much at home in exile as if there had never been anything different, then all is not well."

The marriage of Baron Erasmus was declared illegal and warrants were taken out against the woman and the young airman. But the two were never found.

Chapter 14

Contrary to all expectation, the wounded man recovered, and one morning he too disappeared. The other guests who had been involved turned again to their affairs and avoided meeting Erasmus. Only the old count did not avoid him when, supporting himself on his stick, he walked through the corridors of the castle to knock at one of the many doors. He stopped when he met the baron, lifted his eyelids with an effort and pronounced the scanty wisdom of his life, that it was *toujours la canaille.* But nobody knew whom he meant.

Slowly the world of the massive, decaying building swung back into place after the uproar and the violence, and through this quieter world Baron Erasmus went kindly, never impatient, trying to judge fairly of the rights that the women with the floor cloths claimed from him. No one had mocked him since "the misfortune," as the women called it, had happened, and when he went into one or another of the many rooms to listen to requests and complaints, the woman would wipe one of the wooden chairs with her apron and invite the Herr Baron to take a seat. He listened kindly and patiently, promised to do what he could, and when he said goodbye he stroked the children's hair. Christoph no longer accompanied him on these visits.

Erasmus once spoke to his sister-in-law about what had happened, and now and again he spoke to Amadeus. He did not talk about it as about a great or even tragic affair, but with a gentle smile, and this smile was serious and without mockery.

He was very fond of his sister-in-law; he was not afraid of the long journey, and came to see her from time to time and to hold the "bright child" on his knees. It still had both its eyes, contrary to the prophecy of the baroness, and none of the laborers' children had been slaughtered since the christening, as she had predicted.

"It's amazing," he said then, "how we can live even when we have done almost everything in life the wrong way. It may be because I always stood in the center of the triptych, and my brothers stood to the right and left to support me. I was the eldest, but I have always done the wrong thing, even at the head of my squadron."

His sister-in-law put down her knitting needles, the ball of wool rolled to the floor, and she looked at him with her warm eyes. "But that's why we love you so much, Erasmus," she said with a smile. "Don't you know that?"

He met her look and his eyes were almost frightened. "Is that the reason?" he asked.

"Yes, that's the reason," she said. "Aegidius may be more capable, and Amadeus is certainly more noble than you two. But you are the most appealing. You are as appealing as a child with white hair. Did you not know that our deepest love is for those who would like to do everything right and nearly always do the wrong thing?"

"But shouldn't I feel a little hurt," he asked after a pause, "to be taken for a child with my white hair?"

She rose to pick up the ball of wool that had rolled out of her lap onto the carpet, and then she stood still at his side and stroked his hair. "A woman never hurts when she looks on a man as a child," she said gently.

With Amadeus he could also speak about the past without any nervousness. For him Amadeus was already beyond the limits set for human beings, and in spite of his brother's gainsaying it, he insisted on it with a quiet stubbornness. "You must let me think so," he said, "because it gives me a sort of equilibrium. The higher your scale rises, the less does it grieve me when mine sinks, or sank as it did a short time ago. I think I am the only one of us who considers us three as an entity. I know that each is different from the others, but it is easier for me to forget this and to see us as a whole. There is so much compensation in it for me. Not that I wanted to evade anything; I realize by now that men in many respects are unalterable. It's splendid that I can now see ourselves as once we appeared to others, as the picture at which they used to smile. It is certainly rare that a picture can be preserved for so long, even until the hair has grown white."

"It's good," replied Amadeus after a pause, "that we know so little about 'the patience of the saints.' Yes, that we know so little about the saints themselves. We only know it from the legends."

"Wittkopp says that the deepest wisdom is lodged in them, the deepest piety and also the deepest love," said Erasmus.

"Wittkopp is quite right," replied Amadeus, still smiling, "but he is also one of the few who know that today is no time for legends. Today the juniper bushes on the moor are more numerous for him than the saints."

Then they talked about Christoph, and they talked about him with some concern. The first thing that struck them both after that night of storm and early dawn was that he seemed to have grown smaller. As if that night and morning had bowed his tall, upright figure, as if old age had brushed him for the first time – as in a fairytale when a cool breath breathed on a man can change him.

And the second thing was that he had grown quite taciturn now. He told no more stories, and even the Bible seemed less familiar to him than before. He did his work as he had always done it, and his bright eyes still watched over the routine of the day.

But his inner security had deserted him, the certainty of all that he said or did; that which rested with deep roots in the past, not only in childhood but much further back in the world of his forefathers, in an age when the Christ Child still climbed into the sleigh. It was as if he had suddenly discovered a wolf trap set by unknown hands for an unknown beast in the familiar and well-protected forest of his life, and now he hesitated at every step and was afraid of setting his foot upon the changed earth.

"It cannot be old age alone," said Erasmus thoughtfully. "There must be something else that he had never expected and that has frightened him now."

Amadeus cast a sidelong glance at his brother and waited to hear whether he was going to say anything more. But Erasmus had nothing more to say.

"You see, brother," said Amadeus, "these old people from our home have looked upon us as their trusted masters for generations. And although among us there has been no lack of those who misused their position, most were indeed true masters. To their dependents they were not just men who had power, but men who stood close to God. That comes from primitive times when the kings were also High Priests. Our people did not understand all we did, but a radiance from a higher world illumined even what they did not understand.

"Our coachmen have always felt that they were kings, little kings, among the people of the estate. They have driven us for a hundred or two hundred years or even longer. Their solemn undertaking was to serve faithfully and never to overturn our carriage or our sleigh. With all their devotion not one of them would ever have thought that one of us could drive better than he.

"While they guided our horses by day and by night, they gradually got the idea that they had to guide our lives gently, too. This idea began when they were leading us carefully into the world of their fairytales and were teaching us their wisdom, while we sat on the oat bin. Some of them were already gray when we were still children.

"And they had the old faith, as they called it, and an older one than ours, because they had risen out of serfdom and had never been touched by learning. Their roots were the roots of old peoples, not the roots of new philosophies. That's how it came about that they gradually felt themselves to be guardians who had to watch over us. Not over our daily work or over our festivals but over our relationship to God. In them there was really still something that had originated in the old legends and fairytales and in the great simplicity of the Old Testament. You will remember that in the stories that Christoph told, this idea of guardianship always played a part. The part of the old people in the fairytales who sit on the doorstep and point out the way to wandering princes.

"That gave them their confidence and dignity. They were not haughty, but they had no doubts. They always had a hand ready to grasp our belt, if, as they expressed it, our Heavenly Father called us and we did not hear. Or when the Christ Child wanted to climb into the sleigh and we would not stop.

"That is what gave them their stature, but it was also a danger to them. Time got ahead of them. A time came in which a man's life was not so simple as it was in times gone by – a time when there were conflicts which they could no longer comprehend or judge. And then there was an instant when a hand was stretched out and it was not the right time, when everyone thought only of his own master when they ought to have thought of the greater good. Then mistakes would be made, and they became aware of these mistakes. And in that instant their inner security fell to pieces. Then they began to have misgivings about those things that they had done rightly all through life. At that instant old age touched them. It was as if for the first time their horses bolted.

"And this, brother, is the moment when we must give them special love, the whole sum of gratitude which we owe them, and also respect, for we owe them respect. They must be sure that, despite all, they have done right in everything, even in their mistakes. It must always seem to them as if they alone could drive us into heaven, because they alone know this last, dark road of which with all our cleverness we know nothing."

Erasmus rested his head in his hands and listened. "How is it, brother," he asked at length, "that everything disentangles itself before your eyes and becomes so simple?"

"Not everything," replied Amadeus, "by no means everything. When she sat here for the first time, nothing got disentangled before my eyes. I was not friendly to her, and I am ashamed of myself."

"And you think you ought to have been friendly?"

"As friendly as to a child that has always been beaten."

Erasmus sighed. "She, too, may have sung like the golden oriole," he said. "She still had her memories, and we have only heard the false notes."

Then he got up, a little troubled and a little consoled. But when on the narrow mountain path the lights of the castle first pierced the darkness, he stood still and a gentle warmth flooded his heart. Now he walked down without fear. Before his mind's eye he saw all the many doors and behind them the many careworn faces. But none of them turned on him in anger or derision as his steps echoed from the stone walls of the corridors.

The master came home and they heard him tread softly so as not to wake the children from their first sleep. He had been visited by misfortune, but he did not make them suffer for it. He held his head high again. He had stayed and had not gone off like the others.

With the first autumn mists the world of the moor was slowly cut off from the rest of the world. The year had turned its furrows, and it had plowed deep. Every year people thought that they had overcome the worst, and then there was still worse to be overcome than in the previous year. But perhaps now the earth had worn out its anger, as Christoph used to say. There had been birth and death, wedding and christening, and the narrow track of a human being had led away from the moor and had disappeared in the distance. Rain and dust had passed over it and people knew as little of it as of the birds that fly south. A man still stood at twilight by the edge of the marshes under the vast, fiery sky, until the glow faded away and mist enshrouded him.

But then the feeble light in the little window of the shepherd's hut was lit, and when someone's heart longed for it, he could go to the dark threshold and knock at the heavy door.

The winter wheat was green in the fields of Baron Aegidius, and the two children who had been born this year were thriving – the one with the old name and the one without a name, and neither of them wanted for love. Misfortune had visited the eldest brother, but he held his head high again. Christoph was smaller and quieter and more bowed, but he was still there, and his blue coat with the silver buttons looked as if age could not touch it.

Once more the wood resounded with the blows of the axes and the plying of the saws, and the parson still stood on the moor leaning on his spade and waiting for the sunset.

There was no peace in the land, and not all had a roof, a coat, bread. The year went quietly on, neither driven nor halted by time, and the people on the moor went with it, because they could not do anything else but go where the year led them, just as their forefathers had done a thousand years ago. The year gave wheat for bread and flax for the spinning wheel. It gave berries and mushrooms, sun and rain. It was the everlasting in the world, even in a destroyed world, as everlasting as God Almighty, who held the year in his hand. He had come with them from their lost home. Neither the conquerors nor the conquered could take the year away, or keep it for themselves, or make it different from what it was. No one was lost as long as he submitted to its will. No one knew what the year would bring, but everyone knew that it would remain there and not go away.

With the autumn mists the two from outside who had come now and again into the world of the moor went away. As if this small piece of the world in which they had taken an interest might now be left to itself. As if it had now proved that it could get on without help, so that from a distance they might quietly remember this small world, which was like an island in the ocean of time.

The first to leave was Kelley, First Lieutenant John Hilary Kelley, who now longed for his wide homeland, and who longed to discard his uniform, which he had worn like a hired fancy dress. His smile was still the same, but his dark eyes and his thin lips were full of melancholy – the melancholy of a man who was homesick, or the melancholy of one who was a stranger in this world: the world of uniforms, of laws, of conquerors, and of masters. Even now, when he was about to return to the great stretches of his homeland, the melancholy was still there, as if he felt that for people like him there was no real home anywhere. There was no real home for those young people who had gone into the war encouraged by fine phrases but had been forced to read the small print below the blatant headlines for many years, till their eyes ached with all they had read. Nor was there a real home anywhere in these glamorous times for those who were out of step with the times, for those who had had to play the game like children dressed up in uniform, so that they should not be cast out and despised.

"They know everything now that they have been here three years," said Kelley, and he made a gesture which seemed to comprise the castle or the landscape or the whole continent. "They sit in front of their loudspeakers or in their jeeps, and they know everything. What a democracy is, or what guilt and atonement are, or what right or wrong is. Who was 'brown' and who was not 'brown,' and what must be done with those who were specially 'brown.' They have few doubts and almost no problems. They cause fire to rain from heaven as in the Old Testament, and it is nothing to them to annihilate in a single second, yes, in the fraction of a second, one hundred and twenty thousand human beings, with a little toy that they drop in a parachute like a child's balloon; most of the dead were innocent people, many women and children among them. They live the safest and grandest life of all nations and they have at their disposal the most effective death that has ever been on this earth."

"But if they had not had it," replied Amadeus, "we two would probably not be sitting here looking into the fire."

"And what would it matter?" asked Kelley. "Are we so sure that we compensate for one hundred and twenty thousand people? Or that we compensate for the destruction of humane feeling?"

"It's not only we two," said Amadeus. "The bullet or the gallows or the ax were not only directed at men like us."

"They were directed at what is perishable," replied Kelley. "The eternal values must not be destroyed in order to save what is perishable."

"And what are the eternal values?"

Kelley gazed at him for a time. "I have seen much and learned much in these years," he said. "But now when I go away, I shall take along in my memory little save all this: this hut and this little fire, the moor and the people, and the conviction that something that I call 'the eternal values' has been set up here. Your hand has had a share in it, Herr von Liljecrona."

Amadeus shook his head. "We have not been able to prevent either misunderstanding or grief, homesickness or death, Kelley."

"We are not supposed to do that, for we do not want to halt life. But here a symbol has been set up, while everywhere else in your country symbols have been cast down.

"I have seen many of the young people of your country, and hardly any one of them asks: 'What are we to do?' Almost all of them ask: 'Whose fault is it?' And almost all of them say: 'The others.' They do not even mean the party or power or evil. They mean the old generation, and many mean the conquerors. They judge, they pass sentence, and they jeer. Many of them have forgotten how large a part they had in the evil, either through doing or leaving undone. 'Look at our suffering,' they say; but they do not say, 'Remember the suffering of others.'

"But here before this fire a symbol has been raised. Nobody said, 'Look at our suffering!' Here suffering was concealed so that the others should believe there was no more suffering – for a time, at least. The old man on Christmas Eve, when he told his stories – and all the other things which happened here, all the other things – we can take it with us, Herr von Liljecrona; even if we don't believe it, we can take it with us."

"What will you do when you get home again?" asked Amadeus.

Kelley got up and straightened his uniform. He held his cap in his hand, and now he really did look like a dressed-up child.

"I don't know," he said. "Only men with a dogma always know what they are going to do. Especially when they are young and already have a dogma – a so-called weltanschauung. But I don't have one. Perhaps I will write a book – on how they play the game in different parts of the world. Books don't hurt. Books are neither laws nor judgments. They can be withdrawn if one sees that one has been mistaken. But one must declare that one has made a mistake. Then a man has always got a profession at his fingertips. The writing of books is still a profession, and sometimes it is lucrative. Perhaps it is so lucrative that the writer can one day cease to lay down the law or to pass judgment or to expel or to commit some other folly. So lucrative that he can care for orphans or cultivate a garden. Don't you think that a man who has only a spade in his hand will be kindly received at the gate of heaven – a spade and nothing more?"

Amadeus did not know, but he thought so.

"Goodbye, sir," said Kelley, and put on his cap. He would have liked to say something more, but he was too shy. He only added: "It is splendid when the example of the defeated helps to make the victors better."

Amadeus' eyes followed him as the evening mist swallowed him up. As he went along he ran his hand along the branches of the young pine seedlings. He was not bent nor crooked like Jakob, and yet he reminded Amadeus of him. They had not burned his wife and children, and yet he reminded him of Jakob – as all homeless people resemble each other. Where was a homeland for those who did not say, "Look at our suffering"? Who had conquered and did not want the fruits of victory? Where was a home for young, perplexed hearts, no matter whether victory or defeat had perplexed them, who were too young to be able to erect a symbol within their hearts, but who looked around to see whether a symbol had been raised somewhere else? For the unbelievers among them, yes, even those who believed in nothing, secretly longed for a symbol. Nothingness was a symbol, too, just as wholeness was a symbol. But their hair was not yet gray. They still thought they would blossom one day, even the most despairing among them.

They did not yet know how much has to be accomplished before one can have gray hair in peace.

They still troubled about the world – about its progress, its happiness, and its righteousness. They did not yet trouble to make themselves better. They still asked, "Where are you, oh Lord?" They did not ask, "Where am I?" And none of them realized that a man always is where his God is.

Then Jakob went away, and the unexpected thing was that he did not go to Palestine, though he could have done so, but that he – with a few others – went back to his homeland. "What does Holy Land mean, Herr Baron?" he said, warming his hands at the fire. "There they kill as the soldiers of Herod killed. There they will build a state, as others have built states. There they will make treaties and alliances, and their young men will wear steel helmets. And when the Holy One, blessed be he, walks through the ancient places and sanctuaries, they will ask him for his passport and hold their bayonets before his naked feet."

"And in the place to which you want to return, Jakob?"

"There it will be as it is everywhere on this earth, Herr Barron. They were beaten and now they rise again to strike back. They will also strike us."

"But why do you go back then, Jakob? Nobody strikes you here."

Jakob looked at him and smiled, and then his eyes wandered back to the little fire. "Don't you know yet, Herr Baron, that the Holy One, blessed be he, is where people are beaten? Not where the gift parcels arrive and music comes out of the loudspeakers?"

"But he can also be where people are not beaten, Jakob."

"Yes, Herr Baron, but only there where beating is already at an end. The house will be burned," he said after a pause. "The village will be burned. But I shall be able to see where it had been. I shall be able to see it by the chimneys and by the little cemetery. They have taken everything, but they could not carry away the chimneys nor the gravestones.

"And there, Herr Baron, where the little stones with the Hebrew inscriptions stand, there will be the real Holy Land. They have no stone yet, my wife and my children. They were burned to ashes, but the ashes will not rest there. The tombstone will rest so that the Holy One, blessed be he, knows where to blow the ashes when he gathers them in his hand. He also has pity on the ashes, if nothing is left of people but their ashes."

"It can happen, Jakob, that one day they will overturn the tombstones once more even there."

Jakob smiled. "If the Holy One, blessed be he, has once laid his hand on a stone, Herr Baron, it will not matter whether they overturn the stone or not. Because they cannot overturn the hand of the Holy One. I shall not be at peace until I have put up the little stone. Others go back to trade or to get rich; there must be such people, too. But I do not want to get rich. You will also remain poor. But when I have arrived beyond the great river, I shall see still the little fire on this hearth. I shall stretch out my hands and they will be warm, as they are warm now from the little fire. I wish to thank you, Herr Baron."

There was dense fog around the hut. The bushes looked like giants who were setting out to walk across the moor. Under the stars peeping between the clouds the wild geese traveled south. From the branches of the pine trees there was a gentle dripping into the moss below.

Jakob bowed, and after a few steps the fog had swallowed him up. For a time his steps were still to be heard, and now and again the sound of his foot knocking against a stone. Then that too faded away, and a deep silence closed in. Only the drops fell gently all around, but they were part of this silence. They fell like grains of sand from a great, dark, invisible hourglass.

Late in the evening the young mother came. She carried a lantern and her shoes were wet through; the mist lay in a thousand drops on her hair.

"I am afraid," she said under her breath. "When mist falls, I always think that somebody is lying at the edge of the marshes and that mist falls into his dying eyes."

Her shoulders were quivering and he led her to the chair by the fire, where Jakob had sat. He put some wood on the glowing embers and took off her shoes. "Warm your feet," he said, "and don't be afraid. There is no fear by this fire."

She wanted to draw her feet back, but he put them on the block of wood in front of the open door of the hearth. "Did you forget," he said, "that the man washed her feet?"

Her tears fell slowly on her dark frock. "I cannot always live in a fairytale," she said gently. "You can't always say: Once upon a time . . ."

Amadeus stood by the hearth and poured the boiling water on the tea. "Here I will always say, 'Once upon a time,'" he said. "Not because we wish to live in a dream, but because we became what we are through what once was. There was much for both of us, more than for others. Let us not forget it. Once you stood on this threshold and looked at me as if I were a marked man. Now you sit here and weep. At that time you could not weep. And everything was 'Once upon a time,' so that you can weep again."

She took the cup and drank. Her hands grew quieter. "No power," she said under her breath. "That's what it is like here – always – and only here. No power."

He looked at her and through her form he seemed to see the bowed man as he went eastward through the fog to put up the little tombstone. "He is the last who will go away," he said, lost in thought. "After this all the others will stay."

Barbara did not understand him and he explained it to her.

"I would like to go too," she said, "sometimes – in the crimson sunset. But I always come here. What stone should I put up while you are alive?"

"And why would you like to go?"

"Because I do not deserve it. I do not deserve anything. I would like to be a servant, nothing but a servant. But they would not take me. 'You already have a master,' they would say. 'It is written in your eyes. Go back to him, because he calls for you.' But he does not call."

"He does not have to call," said Amadeus, "because you are always there. Since we went across the moor together with the dog on our track, you are always there. Once you wanted to rule, and now you want to serve. All that has ceased by this fireside. Nobody rules and nobody serves here. I cannot draw that line anymore between people. They smile at us, but not even their smiles hurt me. Sometimes I think that nothing hurts me any longer, and I am frightened at it. It began when I lay under the bushes and looked up into the stars. It is you who played the biggest part in it. You must not weep any longer. You must be quite happy. That's the great miracle that has happened to us, that once I lay here before this fire, that first night, and it was the darkest night of my life. And that now I am happy, even when I am sad, and that is difficult to understand. And yet it is so. As happy as a flower under the snow. I can't explain what it is like."

She did not take her eyes from his face, which was still marked by deep lines. It was radiant, as if from some inner light, as if he saw something marvelous that was hidden from all others.

"He was not the last who will go away," she then said in a low voice. "For now you will go away further and further. I stretch out my hand, but I don't reach you anymore. And that's why I am afraid, don't you understand?"

He stood by her chair and laid his hand on her hair. It was still damp with the mist, as once it had been damp with fear. "I will never go away from here," he said, "not even in the way you think I would. It is not people I am slowly detaching myself from, but from that in them around which I can clasp my hand as around a fruit. But I shall always be near, so that anyone who thinks that it would console him can lay his hand in mine – you too. You most of all, because you have suffered most. You have been over the border, you alone – not that of death, for that is not the limit, but there where the world falls to pieces, and there alone is horror. I was there with you, and since that time I have not let your hand go."

She listened with closed eyes, as at the time when she had given birth to the child. Then she took his hand from her hair and laid it under the scarf which she wore around her neck, there where her pulse throbbed.

His hand lay quite still, and she felt its warmth flow into her. He did not withdraw it, and she knew that he was looking over her head into the fire. She did not know what he was thinking. She only felt that he had pity on her, and that there was no evil power as long as he stood behind her.

Perhaps it was the happy heart of which he had spoken. Perhaps it was the gentle melancholy over the happy heart – and of that he had also spoken.

The fire went out and she still sat there. The mist drops fell on the thatched roof, and now perhaps it was as she had said when she came: once upon a time. But now it was intertwined with reality. It was no longer something outside herself. It enveloped her and penetrated her, and so she sat as still as a child in the glow of the setting sun.

Then snow fell, and they celebrated their third Christmas. They celebrated it quietly, and probably only Baron Amadeus realized that the year and the times could now do them no more harm. That the earth had worn out its anger, and that they were now on the way to win a happy heart. A perfectly happy heart, or perhaps the happiness of a heart which beams through a gentle sadness. And even this gentle sadness could throw a radiance over heart and life, and perhaps it was this sadness alone which could bestow the final radiance.

That's why the eyes of the women and of the taciturn men were chiefly directed toward Baron Amadeus. All remembered the first Christmas Eve and how he had sat among them as a stranger – one who had been at the gates of hell – and they had not known what memories were still before his eyes. They only knew that he had shaken his head when his brothers had looked at his cello, and that he would not have stopped his sleigh if the Christ Child had stood barefoot in the snow.

And now he sat among them like someone who had found a treasure. Above all the women were touched, because he had put new eyes into the head of the doll Goldie. He had asked Jakob to try and find, on his various errands, two glass eyes from dolls that had been thrown away, and Amadeus had put them in himself, in place of the half-destroyed yellow cloth eyes. He had not wanted to be reminded of a terrible past by the old eyes, and he had believed that all life in the cottages on the moor would be altered with Goldie's new eyesight. "Yes," he said and stroked the hair of the delighted child, "now she has come through everything: homesickness, spotted typhus, and blindness. Now she has won a happy heart, and you can see how the candles are reflected in her eyes. They were not reflected in the other eyes."

This year, too, Baron Erasmus read the Christmas Gospel, and he read it in a clear, steady voice, as if no misfortune had visited him in the course of the year. They all looked at his white hair, how thick and close it lay above his brow, and at his thin lips, from which fear and bitterness had disappeared in this solemn hour.

Then for a time their eyes rested on the lighted candles, and they thought of those who were no longer with them. The man Donelaitis now sat in the shadow of the roof beam where the young mother had once sat, and, of all the eyes, his eyes might be those that looked furthest into space and time.

They did not hear the snow falling outside, but they could see it and all the footprints that it was covering: those of the young woman and those of the old, bent man who had gone east so that he could set up a little gravestone behind the burned-down village; the footprints which led from the castle into darkness and those which led over the wide ocean. So wide was the world beyond the moor, so dark and full of danger, and so small was the space of life in which they were safely settled here. But on the borders of the wide stretches of the world, where the great and heroic things happened and with them those still fraught with evil and disaster, small spaces existed also, which were now being filled with all that their forefathers had already placed in them: with the daily work of humble people and with the enduring patience which only the humble people possessed. The harshness of fate had touched them too – war and death and confusion of heart. But no one had written of it in the newspapers or reported it through loudspeakers. The plow had passed over them, and the mighty of the world who drove the plow had their eyes fixed on the end of the furrows, not on the furrows themselves. The fate of millions rose up in the furrows as the stubble rose up, was illumined by light, turned, and sank down again into the depths. But the fate of those millions was the fate of the humble people, and no one paid any particular attention to it.

Now the movement of the plowshare had left them behind, as they had been left behind after all wars, plagues, and revolutions, in the quiet places where wheat grew and children were born. The eyes of the masters still rested on them. They had not gone the way of glory either, marching behind a flag or behind slogans. They tilled their fields again, or they held the scales in a crumbling castle, or they gave a doll new eyes. Perhaps the world blamed them or smiled at them. But the people on the moor neither blamed nor smiled. They only saw the shield of their masters which was held over them, an ancient shield, and even the dark times had been unable to break it.

Now the two children lay side by side in the little wicker baskets which the young mother had plaited – as if the dark river of the years had cast them up in the rushes by the shore, and they had been picked up and carried onto dry land, as it was told in the Bible. All else that happened to them was as simple as in biblical times: the pillar of fire by night and the sea of death which divided in front of them; and now the little fire on the hearth, the consoling and the imperishable, and the snow which fell silently onto the thatched roof.

The old, eternal times, when great realms had arisen and had been overthrown – and always in their depths humble people who still cut peat and felled trees, and who always began at the beginning, when the masters of the world no longer knew where to begin or where to leave off.

Then the brothers tuned their instruments and raised their bows, as if not forty or fifty years had passed, but as if it were yesterday, and as if "the three maple trees" still stood on "the Memel's farther shore."

But when the women quietly asked Christoph to tell a tale, he shook his head. He sat in the shadow on the edge of the hearth, the short pipe in his trembling hands, and looked at the two children who lay in the little wicker baskets. "A year ago," he said, "I could still tell a tale, because they were not born. They are here without mark or blemish, and now we only have to listen to their breathing."

The candles burned down, and the men heaved up onto their shoulders the heavy parcels which Kelley had sent. The little girl wrapped Goldie in her shawl and they pushed open the door of the hut. In the light of the fire they saw the snow fall, silent and thick. No footprints led to the snow-covered doorstep. The women lit the candles in their lanterns, and the reddish gleam glided along with them down the slope to the moor. The snow-laden boughs of the old trees gleamed white, and when the men brushed against the branches with their heavy parcels, it looked as if little white silver stars were falling down from the sky.

"Stay a little longer," said Amadeus to the young mother, and she sat down again on the floor by the hearth, wrapped herself up tightly in her dark shawl, and held the child closely to her breast.

"I have been wondering, brother," said Aegidius after a time, "whether we ought not to shift this wall farther back into the stable so you can have more room. I always feel as if you can't walk up and down here properly when you want to. And we would bring you a large shelf and books and make it a little more comfortable for you, since you wish to stay here."

But Amadeus shook his head. "Leave it as it is, brother," he said. "I don't walk up and down a great deal now. I prefer to sit by the hearth, and for those who come to me there is always room enough. A man needs no more room than there is in a cell – in a monastery or in a prison. And since I have started to write poetry, I like to fancy that I live in a cell."

"Do you write poetry now?" asked his sister-in-law quietly.

Amadeus smiled, a little shy and embarrassed. "It has come into my mind," he replied, "that I too ought to do something, since so much is done in the world. It was always permissible to write poetry, even in the darkest and most eventful times – just as children are allowed to play."

"I have always known that you will make our name famous one day, brother," said Erasmus.

But now Amadeus looked at him really merrily. "Don't plant laurels in your garden, brother," he said and smiled. "Be satisfied with the potherbs. He who is alone does not write for fame's sake, but because he wants to converse with his heart. He consoles it as one consoles a child, and sometimes the child answers quite softly."

"We live like those who have become submerged," said Wittkopp, "and we did sink down to the bottom. Sometimes I doubt whether we are doing right, but then I am quite calm and confident again. It may be our duty to collect the despised things, and one day in the far future men on their big ships will look down into the depths and see the gleam on the bottom. They will think that it is a treasure, and for them a treasure can only be made of gold. But for us it is not made of gold. For us it is much more, and even poetry contributes to its luster. They will send one of their submarines and one of their divers, but when he clambers on board again, he will open his empty hands and will smile. 'It was nothing but the good, old, religious time,' he will say, 'and seaweed is already growing over it. Wherever you kick it with your foot, it falls to pieces.'

"'But perhaps one ought not to kick it,' one of the passengers might say, 'if it really is that sacred time . . .'

"'We must kick everything that shines,' the diver will say, 'so that we may know whether it is of lasting value. But this treasure is like jellyfish. If you kick them they are nothing but gray pulp.'

"'And if it is the secret of its beauty that must not be touched?' the same voice will ask perhaps.

"Then the diver will smile and take off his huge helmet, and now he will look like an absolutely strange creature. 'It's not my fault, dear friend,' he will say, 'that you have not understood the call of the times.'"

"It's easier for us, dear parson," said Aegidius after a time. "We live and have our being in the unchangeable: in the field or in God's word. We are not measured in comparison with time, nor for the present. But it's different with an old general, and quite different with one who writes poetry."

"As long as a man communes with his own heart, as Herr Amadeus does," replied Wittkopp, "he need have no fear. But when a man communes with time, it is different, because then he is no longer himself, and because those who run faster get ahead of him. But nobody gets ahead of him who writes a psalm or a children's song. They are outside time. Time cannot harm them."

Amadeus smiled and got up and put the sheets of music on the stands. "I would be very glad if we could play "The Ultimate" today." The brothers looked at him, but then they did as they were told. They both remembered what "The Ultimate" meant in their own language. More than ten years had passed since they had played it.

"The Ultimate" was the larghetto of the last piano concerto which Mozart had written. Amadeus had transcribed it for their three instruments. It was only a makeshift, but it had seemed to him as if something immortal remained immortal even when it was played on a linden leaf.

For him it was the ultimate, the highest that a man whom God had inspired could attain, or that a man who tried to commune humbly with his God could reach. Only he could write it who thought that he saw the last sunset through the first shades of darkness, but in such a way that nevertheless the sunset stood above the shadows. Only then had he left time behind him, all earthly time. Only then did he speak again as children speak. With the great simplicity in which word unites with word and sentence fits sentence. With the freedom from fear of a child who feels quite safe, and with the perfect happiness of that child. Without discord and untouched by the fall of man. Where the melody rises like the fragrance from the cup of a flower without effort, even without consciousness, as if it had always been there but only now in the evening of life it rose, as the scent of the dame's violet rises sweetest in the evening.

Between these simple notes there sounded the promise that humankind was blessed after all. It was given not as a religious promise, but because a man had been able to write these notes, just these and no others. Because he might have written them down even in the darkest times – during a pestilence or during a religious war. Because all the powers of the time could not prevent him from writing them down. Because the powers were impotent before him who had heard these notes for the first time. Because it was unimportant what they were called, whether they were called unearthly or celestial notes. For these words only meant that they had left earth and time behind them.

That's why it might be said that humankind was blessed, not only the special being who had conceived this melody, but the whole of humankind, because this lay within its sphere. Not only the curse of war and plague, not only murder and lies or haughtiness and slander, but also this, this quiet, childlike duologue with God – and that's why Amadeus called it "The Ultimate."

When he rested his bow, he looked at the young mother. Invisibly, below the dark shawl, the child was still drinking at her breast. Her eyes had been riveted on his face all the time. From her eyes he thought he could read that she had now stepped over the threshold, the dark, huge threshold which rose between these notes and that lullaby which she had sung in the ravings of fever.

It was as if the child had also drunk these notes together with the milk of her breast. As if the child, too, had now become immune and blessed, raised above its dark origin and the pitfalls of its time. As if he had saved it once more, as he had saved it that time on the edge of the moor, when he had been unwilling that its closed eyes should watch his dying, that dying which the girl had longed to witness.

15

SPRING CARRIES OFF the old people, as its storms uproot the old trees. The frost splits them and stiffens their roots. During the dark winter the old people sit by the fire and yet they are cold. They hold their hands over the flames and look down at the blue veins that stand out under the dull skin. In the dying glow they see the forms of all those who have shaped their life, from their childhood to the present time. The whole web is spread out before them with its dark and its bright threads, but the dark threads are always more numerous. Some look down on the web with regret and some with anxiety. But some can look at it as on a field on whose green wheat snow falls. They see how it falls, too, on the dark and on the empty places. They are tired, as children grow tired at the window when they look for a long time at the falling snowflakes, but they smile, just as tired children smile.

During the long evening hours in the castle, in those two small rooms where there were no longer any guests, Christoph had begun to smile again. He sat with Baron Erasmus before the open door of the stove until he left for the forester's house, and the baron talked to him. Erasmus had never talked so much as in this winter, but at the end of the dark days he had at last succeeded in making Christoph smile again. "You have never known what it is to be in error," he said, "or you have known it but rarely. And you have known nothing of the blessings of being in error. At that time you might have said to me, 'Stay where you are, sir.' But it would not have been good for me. For I was not ready to stay. You would have lost me that night in the forester's house when I heard the drops dripping from the gutter, and you would have lost me that dawn when we heard the black man singing. You would have debarred me from the knowledge of humbleness, Christoph, and the satisfaction of homecoming. If you had not taken me by the belt, there would have been no homecoming for me. You were in error, but God was waiting for this error. Without this error he would not have been able to 'deceive' me."

Christoph realized that. He also realized the warning that lay in it for him. "He who is in charge of horses easily gets proud, sir," he said. "They are always obedient when you treat them in the right way, and it is not good for us, because we begin to think that men too ought always to obey us – especially the people on foot that we look down on from the coachman's box. Only when the horses bolt one day do we get a little uncertain and a little more modest. And I have grown modest now, sir."

When the snow had melted and the woodlark began to sing again, Christoph gave up his service in the castle. He was always tired now, and it cost him a great effort to climb up the hill to the forester's house.

But before he left Baron Erasmus alone, he spent a few days in going through the occupied rooms of the castle, where he would sit for a little while by a fire or on a chair by a window. The women were no longer frightened of his bright eyes, and they no longer spoke of the rights they were entitled to. They let their work fall from their hands for a time and listened to him talking to the children. He did not tell any more stories, but he told them how when he was a boy they used to catch young cranes or sit in the tops of lofty pine trees and rock to and fro in the wind singing the old songs.

And before he left, he stopped at the door of each of the rooms, bowed, and said gently: "Forgive me for Christ's sake."

He said the same in the room of the old count, and he had already closed the door before the count was able to lift his eyelids and stare at the empty threshold, without having understood anything.

He also sat with the people in the wooden cottages on the moor in the evening when the men had come home from work, and there too he bowed and said the same words. But while the women in the castle had been bewildered and had not always understood what he meant, the people on the moor understood him very well, and their eyes followed him for a long time as he walked slowly up to the shepherd's hut with the evening breeze playing in his white hair.

He went to see Amadeus every day, but for the most part he sat in an old armchair by the fire in the forester's house or, if the sun was shining, just outside the door. The little wicker basket with the baby in it stood near him on the ground, and the dog laid its head on his knee so that he could quietly stroke its soft coat. The young mother came out of the house now and again, and sometimes she sat on the doorstep behind his chair and nursed the child. He did not have to ask her to forgive him, because he knew she had done so. She had not forgiven him for a long time after that morning when he had carried her upstairs and she had struck him. That was the time he had taken her by the belt, and that was the time he had not been in error.

"Everything is all right now, sir," he said one evening when Amadeus was sitting with him. "You might have driven again through the world with four or with six horses, and they would have thrown their doors wide open to you, for not all respect for suffering has disappeared from the world, especially when suffering has been concealed, as it has been with you. But now it is certainly better that you did not go away, because it is better to give Goldie two new eyes than to try to give them to the world. The world does not want new eyes from such as you. Listen to the song of the woodlarks, sir, and to those who come to you in the hut. Don't say that you are wasting your life; there will be plenty of others to say that. Look at this child, sir, and at its mother, whom you have lifted out of the swamp. Not many among those who blame you have done a thing like that. It was your fate to be a father to the fatherless. Stick to it, sir, even though they smile."

And one evening when the young mother came to pick up her child, Christoph sat in his chair, and she saw that he had gone to sleep, so gently that not even the dog had noticed it. It still had its head on his knees, which were slowly growing cold.

She held her breath before she lightly touched his hand. Then she stood for a time, the child at her breast, and listened to the song of the thrush in the pine trees. The evening glow lingered behind the moor, and the soft breeze which blew before night fell moved the white hair on which she looked down.

A strip of paper was found in Christoph's Bible, on which he had written in his big childish writing that he wished to be buried near the moor and that his whip should be laid in his coffin with him – nothing else. And this they did.

Amadeus and Wittkopp chose the place, not far from the cottages, where there was a wide view over the moor. A soft, warm rain fell from the light-blue sky, and they could hear the cranes trumpeting above the thin layer of clouds. It seemed as if the whole castle were assembled, and behind the poorly dressed women stood the old count in his greenish, shiny dress jacket, and the medals on his chest sparkled like the evening star, which showed through a gap in the clouds as it pursued its heavenly way.

Baron Erasmus, as the eldest of the brothers, said a few words, but only those who stood nearest to him could understand them.

Then Parson Wittkopp gave the funeral sermon. He spoke of the old man who, with a rod like Moses, had smitten the rock and water had gushed out of it, and of Mount Nebo from where he had seen the Promised Land. They did not know, he said, where the Promised Land had been for this old man – whether in the distant past or in the distant future. They only knew that it had always been where the old man had been, because there had been the land of kindness – and probably they could not imagine a Promised Land that was not a land of kindness.

They did not know where Christoph was now. With all their wisdom and faith they did not know. But to him, the parson, it seemed as if far, far away in the evening glow beyond the moor he could see the carriage which Christoph was driving once more, and how he stopped the horses because a barefoot child stood by the road. And how he made room at his side for the child, and the child smiled and showed him the way between the dark moors and the world of death.

Somehow they were not sad when the earth fell on the coffin, neither the women nor the children nor the brothers. Because they all felt that he had "finished" before he had been called. Of all the precious things, he had been the most precious that they had brought from their homeland, and with him the bright radiance of a past time faded away. But they felt that he had left an afterglow, as the afterglow of the setting sun spreads a golden radiance over sky and moorland.

They thought it was splendid that this honor was now paid to one of their own kind. One who had only held the reins and the whip throughout a whole long life, but who, when it was time, had been able to reach out his hand and to grasp hold of those who were perplexed or were sinking in despair: a baron, or a young mother with a distraught mind, or a child for whom he had found a father.

When they slowly dispersed, each going his own way, and the people from the castle descended the narrow path, they remembered the many stories Christoph had told: "Once when my great-grandfather drove the master . . ." It was to them as if this old man were outside time, and where there is no time one does not pass away but remains with the living, and the years cannot be numbered.

* * *

Yes, that was how a man sat on his threshold when life and death had lost for him that which is called fear. When the treasure that one ought not to touch lay shining at the bottom of the depths, and when the diver had taken off his helmet so that he could hear better what he termed "the call of the times." When the birds pecked the wheat from the hand and the children sat in the heather to listen to the spinning wheel of life as it slowly turned. When the young mother with her child in her arms laid a hand on the back of the chair, and the man felt that he still had to hold and guide her gently until one day life would open another door for her. Not the door of resignation, for resignation is natural only when the hair turns gray and when the hand no longer catches at life to have and to hold, but when it opens for the birds that come for their grain. When the verses that had to be written down came to him, and it was always as if they fell out of the tops of the great trees, on which they had fallen from the stars. They were not formed as clay is formed that is picked up. They were formed, no doubt, but the miracle was not that they had been formed, but that they had been conceived, and no one knew whose gift they were.

Thus he sat when the evening came in its solemn, crimson glow, when he heard the last voices on the moor – children's voices and birds' voices – and then all the stars, which he had not yet counted, came out. When the young mother said farewell and leaned her head against his shoulder, and a soft sadness fell over his heart, and only beneath this sadness beamed the happy heart, as it was called. When each evening out of the darkness of memory and of those dreadful times that sweet joy in living flowed again through his veins, a sweetness such as can only arise out of bitter suffering, after that bitter suffering has been overcome.

Thus a man sat when more and more white strands appeared in his gray hair, as if it were going to bloom once more. But it was snow that from a distance looked like blossom, and if a hand were stretched out to touch it, the aging man had to utter a warning – that it was snow, so that the hand might not be startled. His smile must be such that it, too, did not startle, and he must never forget that to the eyes of young people all things in this world seemed different: trees, birds, children and even the smile and the gray hair. Not inferior, or cooler, or more foreign, but just different, and that not much wisdom or discernment was necessary to see them as he saw them now, simply as the outcome of the years and the sum of all the anguish the dark hours had brought with them.

All the anguish of the dark hours behind the barbed wire, for instance, where, as people said, he had been at the gates of hell; where not only suffering, horror, and death had revealed themselves, but what was more – where man had revealed himself. He who had overcome this – not only death, but also man, who had not lost the image of man and the image of God with it forever – he could now well stand still when the girl's cheek rested on his shoulder. Not unmoved and not with the great inner security that Christoph had had, but quiet and with the patience he had acquired. With the patience that relied on the years, on the healing and consoling power of the years, even though it was by no means yet "the patience of the saints."

He could slowly enlarge the small circle of life, without an effort because it was his lot – his lot that the children from the castle now came more and more frequently to his hut, and that he could bring a little gladness into their needy lives. A magic lantern with the simple pictures of a time long gone, which his brother's wife had routed out from the garret and which shone out in the darkened room of the hut as the treasures in the cavern had shone out beneath Aladdin's magic lamp. Or a puppet show which took Amadeus a whole winter to make, and whose little, phantom-like world moved before the children's wide eyes like an enchantment.

All the wonderful, little things which had lit up the world of his own childhood, and which had been forgotten in a time when only searchlights and great conflagrations had lit up the dark scene, and for which no one outside the shepherd's hut had time because in their free hours they had to go and try to get bread, a coat, or a pair of shoes. Because there was no longer an old woman who in twilight sat by the fire on the hearth with the thread of the spinning wheel between her fingers, telling the old, old fairytales, in which the good and brave get their rewards. Because the merciless age had also been merciless to the children, and many of them would have smiled mockingly when the old woman began: "Once upon a time."

As the diver smiled when someone spoke of the intangible treasure in the depths. Because this "once upon a time" had also got a different meaning for the children, the sense of lost possessions, as it were, not that of lost enchantment; and it would take a long time for the veil of enchantment to be drawn again gently and quite slowly over those bright, critical eyes.

It was Amadeus' opinion that this must be done with all possible zeal if the gleam of the treasure were not to sink right into the depths, so deep that no eye and no ear could ever perceive it hidden under "the call of the times." And that with the shimmering gleam of the treasure the last gleam of a nation would also sink down and down, until its artists and its children would all speak the same language, the terrible language of the diver, who only knocks with his foot against that sunken treasure; a language without enchantment and without mystery, the language of the loudspeakers and the moon rockets.

Spun into the web of this timeless time, Amadeus could write down the verses which came into his mind out of the silence of the universe. For this silence of the universe was still there, even in an era of the demons. Not even the people of this age had succeeded in destroying it; neither the morning wind in the tops of the old trees, nor the evening glow, nor the succession of the seasons, nor their glory in the hearts of the simple people. Even if the commission, with the district administrator at its head, who wanted to acquire the moor and establish a peat industry, shrugged their shoulders when Baron Amadeus refused to consider it and spoke of "the silence of the universe."

He could write down the verses, although they gave no bread, no coat, and no warmth for the poor. Just as Mozart's "ultimate" melody gave none of these things. But he could feel how marvelously his heart was changed when word joined word, and slowly rhyme joined rhyme. When it was as if the sunken treasure in the depths began to shine, even though the poet did not know whether these verses would ever fall on another human ear. Although he did not believe, as Wittkopp believed, or as Christoph had believed, he could think that in writing these verses he was gently communing with God all the time – as it had once happened at the edge of the desert when a disheartened man was kneeling in the sand and suddenly an angel appeared before him with a heavenly smile and brought the good tidings that he had to tell to the man.

Baron Amadeus still thought that, in this world of intellect, a few must be left over who had nothing else to do but "to warm hearts," as he called it, and it made no difference whether they warmed the hearts of some children who lived by a moor, or of the so-called "pick of the nation." Nor did it make any difference whether one warmed these hearts with a fairytale or with a puppet show, with the colored pictures of a magic lantern or with the tale of Joseph and his brethren. It only made a difference whether now and again these children were convinced that a loaf of bread which they shared was better than one which they hid whole and unshared under their coat; and that this was looked upon as better in the end, or proved to be better in the end – even in the last chronicle of the nation to which they belonged.

He did not always know whether he succeeded in convincing anybody of it, but that did not make him uncertain or discouraged. Even if he knew that the Christ Child no longer stood at the side of the road to stop a sleigh, yet he knew that, on the road of life of most of these children, something would stand one day that would remind them of the little room in his hut, of the comforting fire on the hearth, of the man with the gray hair who spun the thread of his tales for them; who, when night drew near, sat down with his strange instrument to call forth with his bow the notes which were like the notes in the fairytales, when in the dark forest those who were disheartened or had gone astray heard in the distance the voice that was to lead them to the golden gate and to free them from all pain.

Thus even the simplest life could still be full of miracles, from dawn that stood crimson above the moor to the late evening hour when the young mother leaned against his shoulder and was able to win a victory over fear.

He knew that he must not strive for the impossible but must lay his hands around that which had been brought within his reach, which nature had given him, and around the little that he had been able to add to it. It was less than others had been given or had acquired, but even a little light could shine far over the moor in the night when someone was in need of a light. And when the light burned without fear, because the hands that lit it were without fear. That was more than the great world had won in general. The nations had not come through the years of enslavement without fear, nor had the leaders of the nations.

But the man in the shepherd's hut had overcome fear, as far as it is granted to a man to overcome it. Even that terrible fear, the fear of man, which had oppressed him in the beginning. Not the fear of death, nor of torture, but the fear of the face of the farmer's wife who had betrayed him that unforgettable night.

For even this fear vanished as soon as he understood that she had betrayed him from fear of being betrayed herself; as soon as he understood that within evil there was so much of misconception and fear that the evil itself almost disappeared.

If only the smallest group of people succeeded in conquering the fear of man, the fear of hunger or violence, the fear of the dreadful emptiness into which the West was now sliding, the fear of the mere fact of a simple existence into which one is thrown as a piece of wood is thrown into a whirlpool – then had been won the most that ever could be won in this world. When in the evening people need no longer ask, "What shall we do until sleep comes at last?" When they need no longer be filled with the terrible desire "to kill time," as the awful saying has it, then the most had been won. For they wished to kill time because they felt that time, which could not be stayed, carried them into nothingness, into the dreadful, endless, deadly silence of nothingness. The more the loudspeakers bawled, the more bright colors there were in the exploding rockets, the faster the airplanes flew and the newspapers were pitched out of the jaws of the machines, the less the world needs to be afraid to pronounce the quintessence in lies, violence, seduction, and shamelessness. The faster the shores, covered with the forms of distorted creatures, slipped by the raging current, shores where should have hovered the mysteries of the Bible or of fairytales, the more the generation that had succeeded in killing millions in the course of a few years would feel – its eyes dilated with fear – that it would never succeed in killing time, which carried them along, indifferent and pitiless, toward that icy shore where the last blow would fall, the very last, silently or in a long resounding thunder of annihilation.

But here, in this little world apart, people did not need to kill time. They only needed to open their hands to receive it, and very often the hands could not hold the abundance that time offered them – neither in their work nor in their hours of leisure. Just as the hands of Baron Amadeus did not suffice to contain the abundance of human destinies, nor the radiance of dawn, nor the "ultimate" melody of Mozart, nor the smile of the child, nor the shy gesture with which the young mother said goodbye in the evening.

Sometimes Parson Wittkopp went away for a week, to bring them news of the outside world – when the bishop sent for him, or when there was a congress of that religious academy which had now been founded, in which clergy and laypeople tried hard to find a new meaning in life, or when the displaced persons met to discuss their future.

He left as the dove which was sent forth out of Noah's Ark, but he did not come back with the olive branch. The waters had not abated yet; the great rains had not yet ceased.

Only after the homecoming did he realize that he had not really gone out to find the olive branch, or a new land that had emerged out of the great Flood, but that he had gone out to find the oldest and simplest thing in life: love. As they set out in a fairytale to find the water of life.

Back from his journey, he told them about it. They gathered in Aegidius' house, where there was the most room and where they could all sit by the fire. Then Wittkopp was like an ambassador who has been sent to the court of a powerful, alien sovereign – without gifts, it is true, but with the faint hope that his long journey would be appreciated and the poverty of his clothing overlooked.

He still collected the bits of tobacco in the pockets of his old coat, and as his pockets were never empty, the bits appeared to them as a symbol of the inexhaustible.

"They are trying hard," he said. "There is no doubt that they are trying hard and that they are of good will. But it always seems to me as if they have forgotten, or unlearned, how to think of the individual, of the simple human heart. It is as if they can only think in classes or in collective groups, as they have been thinking for the last decade and a half, for instance "the church," or "the denomination," or "the faithful," or "the conquered," or "the refugees." It is as if the world has become so huge that individuals no longer exist.

"It does not occur to them to ask whether the church is to remain as she has been for a thousand or two thousand years. Whether the parsons are to remain just the same: the parsons' words, their consoling ministry. Whether the splitting up into denominations is not perhaps a sin; whether the so-called predominance of a church is not perhaps a sin.

"It was quite understandable that the bishop was offended when, meeting me the last evening as I went through the empty rooms, he asked me what I was looking for. I answered, 'For God's footprints.' That was certainly not right, in an assembly in which many a clergyman thought that he carried God's whole heart in his cloak."

"Everything is so much simpler," said Aegidius after a pause, "if we only have to look after children, after grain and cattle, for then everything else comes of itself."

"Yes," answered Wittkopp, "only that very few of us still have either children, or grain, or cattle. And that nearly all the others think that nothing is left to them unless they have these things. They have not recognized, not even after these years, that the things that we can grasp in our hands are always the least important, and that the conception of property spoils us so easily."

"Suppose you had told them about our world," asked Erasmus, "how we have been living here: Christoph, or the young mother, or Jakob, or my brother Amadeus. What would they have said – the bishop or the clergymen or the young people?"

At first Wittkopp smiled, and then he knocked out his short pipe against the mantelpiece. "That's what they would probably have done," he replied, "as one knocks the ashes out of a pipe. No, it's no use talking about that to the outside world. Let us go on doing, as we have done so far, and one day when we have come to the end of what we call life, let us stand at the back of the queue before the last door, like people with a dubious passport, and let us wait to hear what our Heavenly Father will say to us when we appear with our spades, or with Goldie with the new eyes, or with the child that doesn't have a name yet. And we won't be afraid, as we are of the bishop, for instance. No, we won't be at all afraid."

"But if," said Amadeus with a smile, "our Heavenly Father asks whether you have not been a parson, and why you come to him now in a patched coat and with a spade in your hand, what are you going to answer?"

Wittkopp also smiled, as if he understood Amadeus very well. "Then I shall be obliged to say," he replied gaily, "that I wished to dig for a treasure, for the treasure of the primeval times, and that I have been so old-fashioned that I have not dug with words or with thoughts, but with a spade. And perhaps our Heavenly Father will beckon to one of his angels and say: 'Give him a piece of land from the time when the grain of mustard still grew in the field and not in the pulpit.'"

When after such an evening they drove home through the calm summer night, and nothing was to be heard all around but the call of the corn crake in the ripening crops, or the dog which was still barking beyond the moor, they were all silent, and Baron Amadeus no longer tried to count the stars which hung over them in the canopy of heaven. It was enough for him that they were there, as they had been there in "the primeval times," and that they would be there even when time had ceased to exist for this earth and its race of people.

It was enough for them that the earth had worn out its anger, and that on this earth that had now been appeased there was enough for them to do. They had not gone through this time without pain and fear, nor without bitterness or complaint. But now they felt bitter no longer, and some of them were even without fear. They no longer carried their dead on their shoulders but in their hearts, and there they were not oppressed by the weight. They still heard the children call from the distance, but they no longer called in fear. They had left fear far behind them. The dog still barked at one door or another, but it had no longer any power. Now there was always someone who walked across the moor with the forsaken and gently helped these forsaken ones, lest the big Book might be dropped.

The thin mist stood over the meadows, and the trees rose above it like shining towers. Sometimes a cool breeze blew over them, and sometimes the warm, quiet air over the fields smelled of bread. And sometimes a golden shooting star fell silently into the black forests.

"I am sure I know the meaning of it now," said Amadeus in a low voice and lifted his hand as if he had solved a riddle over which he had racked his brain throughout the whole journey.

"What is it you know the meaning of?" asked Wittkopp, without taking his eyes from the seven stars of the Great Bear.

"The song she sang in our childhood," replied Amadeus. "'Dance, my laddie, full of sorrow, dance, I want you to be gay . . .'"

"I think that I have understood it for a long time," said the parson.

Now from this summer onward nothing special happened on the moor and in the little community at its edge, nothing but what happened everywhere and in any age when man submits to life's orders. Time gave them work between dawn and sunset, the first flight of young birds, the first fruits on the trees, the first flowers on Christoph's grave, which had been sown by the children.

Between night and morning it gave them sleep or dreams, or verses to Baron Amadeus, or visions which appeared before the open eyes of the young mother. Time no longer frightened these people. It did not send less illness, nor less disharmony than it sent elsewhere; but if troubles there were, it was as if they were sent with a lighter hand – as if they were more easily healed than elsewhere. As if not only the parson or Baron Amadeus were specially enabled to help them, but as if here the dawn stood so clear above the earth that the darkness of night had no power over it.

It was not that the women in the castle had laid down their floor cloths or set aside their rights in order to sing hymns all day long. They had not begun to sing hymns again after fire had destroyed their homes and they had been driven like cattle into a foreign land. But now they dusted the kitchen chair when Baron Erasmus or Parson Wittkopp came to see them, and it was not so very long ago that they would gladly have put bits of glass on that chair.

It was not that the parson was now successful in leading them back to God, as perhaps the bishop would have wished. Since their burning roofs had fallen in, so many stones had fallen onto their image of God that even the parson's calloused hands would not have been able to clear these stones away. But a good deal had been accomplished, when now and again they could pause before someone else's heap of stones, yes, that they could see the heap at all, when they had such a pile on their own living space. That they could realize that misfortune had visited Baron Erasmus, and that even the half-closed lids of the old count probably covered something at which they ought not to smile.

It was not only that the young mother now went cheerfully through her daily work, and the past lay so deeply buried for her that it was as if the parson had gone to the moor with his spade to bury it.

Nor was it as if all the problems of this life were solved for Baron Amadeus since he had understood the verses of his old nurse.

Even for this small, out-of-the-way world, life remained what it was everywhere: the mysterious face of a sphinx, and no one could ever know with certainty whether the face was about to smile or whether something was happening in the depths of those impenetrable eyes, of which people knew nothing, not even whether it meant a beginning or the end.

But it was now a face into which they could look with some confidence, not without anxiety, yet with a shy trust that a quiet lawfulness was reigning there. With trust, because the age of violence, of fire, of the ax was over, and the age of order would come again.

Perhaps none of them looked with such trust into this face of life as Baron Amadeus when, in the evening, he sat outside his door in an old, shabby armchair. He had lost neither wife nor child, but of them all, it was he who had been nearest to terror and violence, to the ax and to the ruined countenance of man. He had been the most deeply disappointed and the most deeply degraded, and he had perhaps been the most deeply hated.

Yet he felt sometimes as if his trust was not less than the parson's. Probably it was a different kind of trust; it was not so simple and childlike as Wittkopp's, and in the bishop's eyes it would probably count for less. But, as a compensation, he had acquired it more painfully than the others. It had not fallen into his lap; he had dug it out of the glowing ruins with sore hands. He was the only one among them who had killed, and yet trust had come back to him. He was the only one who had come back ready to kill again if necessary, and yet trust had come. And it had come because he believed in people once more, and he did not know how it had begun – whether with his brothers, or with Jakob, or with Christoph, or with the parson when he stood with him on the moor for the first time. His trust had been so great that he had put his revolver into the girl's hand, and the girl had hidden it under her apron and had run across the moor to fetch Christoph. The same revolver whose muzzle had been shifted aside when he had wanted to kill once more.

But there it was, the great confidence, at a time when not even the conquerors had confidence. At a time when the gallows stood as firmly as they had stood for twelve long years, and the barbed wire was drawn around millions of people as lightheartedly as the children on the moor drew white cotton threads around their flower beds. It was there, and it would never disappear, because it was no longer dependent on nations or their leaders, or on the West or on culture, but on the power of the human heart when it is enabled, now and then, to conceive the ultimate melody, or a beautiful lullaby, or to rise again so far above hatred that a sad face might rest against a shoulder and find in sadness the whole happiness of this earth.

"Come now," he said, stretching out his hand to the young mother when she stepped up to his chair. "Come and see how beautiful the earth is – how safe and how near."

She knelt down at his feet in the heather, but after she had gazed for a time at the evening glow, into which the smoke from the chimneys rose slowly and vertically, she turned her eyes again to him. "Why is your face so happy?" she asked gently.

He smiled and went on gazing into the evening. The woodlarks were still singing, and he thought that they had probably known

Mozart's ultimate melody long before that human hand had written it down.

"I have written a song," he said, "that you can sing to the child as she goes to sleep. And I have also thought that we should call her Irene, which means peace."

"And why do you say 'we'?" she asked, and pressed her face against his hand.

"Because it is our child," he replied. "I think you know that by now."

"What is the song like?" she asked after a pause.

"It's one that you can sing," he answered, "and now you must listen to the woodlarks – I would like it to have the same melody." He did not look at her but over her head into the sunset, and into that radiant glow he spoke the verses:

Sleep my child, sleep sweet and still,
Sheepfold stands on windy hill,
Wind comes from the setting sun,
Smells of bread and smells of grain.
Sleep my child, sleep sweet and still.

Sleep my child, sleep sweet and still,
Sheepfold stands on windy hill;
Moon has lit her lamp so bright
Over you and all the night.
Sleep my child, sleep sweet and still.

Sleep my child, sleep sweet and still,
Sheepfold stands on windy hill;
Mother turns the spinning wheel,
Threads of gold for you she spins,
Wind turns wheel at its will,
Spinning wheel at its will,
Sleep my child, sleep sweet and still.

The words fell softly as the dew which was beginning to fall, as if not Baron Amadeus had spoken them but the voice of the evening, which now that the day had faded became softly audible. Amadeus' eyes, which had been fixed on this evening glow, only turned to the face of the young mother when she raised herself up and laid her arms about his knees.

Only then did he bend down to her and look into her eyes. They were now quite clear, and in their depths he saw that which had cost her so many years of her young life, so much pride, so much harshness, so much passion – yes, that for which she had sacrificed body and soul without winning it: the land without fear. It shone peacefully in the depths of her eyes, as if it had always been there, but covered and filled up as a well is filled up, and now the evening glow fell again into their depths.

He put both his hands around her head and looked into her eyes. She answered his gaze without fear, but her face was pale with emotion, and while she embraced his knees more and more closely, she said, sobbing, in a transport of happiness, "I will serve you. I will serve you all my life long."

He bent still lower, looking intently into her eyes – and then he remembered. He remembered how, when he was a child digging in the garden, suddenly beneath his little spade a spring had welled up, a spring of which nobody had known. He saw before him the little pit with the damp sides, and suddenly out of these sides water had seeped slowly and mysteriously, until at the bottom there was a little mirror, and in this mirror he had seen his face.

And just as in that spring of his childhood, the two dark wells before his eyes were filled slowly and mysteriously, until the two mirrors of tears appeared, in which he recognized his own face.

He looked long into them before he drew himself up again, and only then, his hands still around her head, he said: "Don't you know that it is the child whom you must serve all your life long?"

Then he raised her up so that she could look over the moor with him.

Under the crimson sky the lonely man Donelaitis stood, as he stood so often in the evenings, motionless, as if his roots reached down into the dark earth. The brilliance of the sunset enveloped him, as it enveloped bushes and trees. He stood there without moving, and they did not know whether his eyes were closed. But they thought they knew that he beheld something beyond the fiery sky; yes, that he saw beyond the form of a woman with a bundle in her hand, and still farther beyond the distant rivers of the distant homeland, something that revealed itself to him more and more from one evening to the next. Perhaps it might be called: the continuity of life.

And while Amadeus' hand glided over the girl's hair, wet with dew, his eyes were filled to their very depths with the grand sunset, and he thought that he could see what the man at the edge of the moor perhaps saw: the continuity of life.

He did not call it so; his lips formed no name for it. But his heart was so full of confidence and beat so quietly that he might well have called it so.